THE HEATHENS

ACE ATKINS

corsair

CORSAIR

First published in the United States in 2021 by G.P. Putnam's Sons
First published in Great Britain in 2021 by Corsair
This paperback edition published in 2022

13 5 7 9 10 8 6 4 2

A CIP catalogue record for this book
is available from the British Library.

ISBN: 978-1-4721-5672-3

Printed and bound in Great Britain by Clays Ltd, Elcograf S.p.A.

Papers used by Corsair are from well-managed forests
and other responsible sources.

MIX
Paper from
responsible sources
FSC® C104740

Corsair
An imprint of
Little, Brown Book Group
Carmelite House
50 Victoria Embankment
London EC4Y 0DZ

An Hachette UK Company
www.hachette.co.uk

www.littlebrown.co.uk

For Angela
Sweet Child O' Mine

When grown people speak of the innocence of children, they don't really know what they mean. Pressed, they will go a step further and say, Well, ignorance then. The child is neither.

—William Faulkner, *The Reivers*

When we march, we keep moving till dark, so as to give the enemy the least possible chance at us.

—Rogers' Rangers Standing Orders No. 8

THE HEATHENS

ONE

Tanya Jane Byrd, known to her friends as TJ, never gave a damn about being famous. But here she was, four days on the run from Tibbehah County, Mississippi, with that girl Chastity passing along the burner phone to show they now had more than a hundred thousand followers on Instagram. They only had six posts, the newest one from just two hours ago after TJ cut her hair boy short, dyed it black as a raven's wing, and made her ultimatum to that cowardly son of a bitch Chester Pratt. She called him out for not only her mother's murder but the money she and her little brother John Wesley were owed.

On the forty-five-second clip shot outside the Tri-State Motel in Texarkana, she held up her fist on the diving board to an empty pool and said, "Fair is fair," remembering the line from one of her mother's old VHS tapes in the trailer.

"What do you think?" Chastity asked.

"I think I better drop that phone into the nearest creek."

TJ saying *crik* as she had her whole life, never caring about talking proper or right. To hell with how other people said it. At seventeen years old, TJ had no intention of being no different than she'd always been. Famous leader of the Byrd Gang or not. Five feet tall, skin as white as a china plate, and eyes that folks said reminded them of a Siberian husky.

"When we gonna eat?" John Wesley asked. Her nine-year-old brother lying on the other twin bed, kicking his legs back and forth while watching a show about street racers in Memphis. The host some middle-aged douchebag in sunglasses and a tight tank top to show off his big belly and sleeve tattoos.

"We eat when it's safe to go out," TJ said. "Damn, John Wesley. You just downed a pack of them little Krispy Kreme donuts. I swear to Christ, your stomach is gonna get us all kilt."

In the motel room, it was just her, John Wesley, and Chastity. Holly Harkins, TJ's best friend since kindergarten, had decided enough was enough and left them on the side of the road, saying she planned to walk all the way home. Now it was night, they were flat-ass broke, and TJ's boyfriend Ladarius had headed out to steal them another car. They stole the one they had now from a marina parking lot back in Hot Springs after escaping the cops and riding in a boat across Lake Hamilton. TJ was worried as hell about Ladarius after the news of their escape from the law had been broadcast damn near everywhere. GRISLY DISCOVERY. TEENAGE LOVERS ON THE RUN.

It had been more than a week since her mother had gone missing and five days since they'd found her body stuffed in that oil barrel over in Parsham County. The law didn't take long before looking right at TJ, accusing her and Ladarius of things that weren't true, had never been true, trying to make it seem like some kind of race thing, even though her mother had never been too interested in TJ's personal business. Why they decided to up and blame her, she had no idea, but hadn't been about to stick around and find out. Her whole life had been a struggle, trying to break free of folks trying to put her down or use her up. TJ Byrd wasn't standing for that shit anymore.

"Hope Ladarius steals a fast one," John Wesley said.

"Hope he steals a nice one," Chastity said. "Maybe a Lexus. Or a Mercedes like mine."

"Just what are you getting out of all this?" TJ asked.

"Don't you know, TJ?" Chastity asked. "Justice. I want justice for all y'all."

TJ looked over to Chastity, with her ringlets of blonde hair and wide-set blue eyes and that hooked nose that kept her just on the wrong side of being pretty. The makeup and clothes perfect, down to her three-hundred-dollar frayed jeans and little frilly white top. The only frayed jeans that TJ had came from her pants getting worn slap out. All this damn talk about being a social influencer and reaching the world with a message of truth was giving her a headache. The only reason they let Chastity come along with them was on account of her threatening to call the police back at that mansion on the lake. Of course, the girl did have a point, since the house belonged to her rich daddy, and TJ, Ladarius, Holly, and John Wesley had busted in and made themselves at home. Two days at the big house and an endless buffet of stolen steak dinners, smoked almonds, cocktail olives, and mini cans of Coca-Cola had allowed them to rest, catch their damn breath, hole up, and think on where they'd be headed next. *California? Texas? Florida?* Spin the damn bottle, boys.

"I know you're innocent," Chastity said.

"Good," TJ said. "So do I."

"Only your people back home don't want you to be."

"What do you know about back home?"

Chastity gave a reckless little look while she played with the tips of her hair and shrugged her shoulders, a mess of freckles across her chest and a half dozen thin gold chains around her neck. One with a diamond-crusted compass on it saying, DADDY'S LITTLE GIRL IS NEVER LOST.

"You think Holly will go to the police?" Chastity asked.

"Nope."

"How can you be so sure?"

"Because she's Holly Goddamn Harkins," TJ said. "My best friend since we was five, before you showed up and damn well elbowed her to the side."

"I think she got pissed we pretended I'd been kidnapped."

"No shit, Chastity," TJ said. "Why else do you think she gave me the middle finger?"

Chastity didn't say anything but gave a small grin as TJ pushed herself up off the bed and walked over to the curtains. She looked out onto the empty pool and the abandoned storefronts across the road, not a mile over the Texas border from Arkansas, the first time TJ had been in either state. Farthest she'd ever been out of Tibbehah County was a visit up to Memphis to the zoo or Incredible Pizza on John Wesley's birthday. He ate a million pepperoni slices and stuck his whole hand right into that chocolate fountain. He puked all the way back home.

TJ let the curtain drop and headed back into the bathroom, closed the door, and turned on the rusty faucet. She had on a flannel shirt over a red tank top from Walmart and a pair of frayed green camo pants. Her daddy's old .38 was stuck into her waistband with plenty of bullets jangling down in her side pockets. Splashing cool water up into her face, she barely recognized the girl she saw. Her skin pale white, newly black hair up off her head. It had been Chastity's idea to do it. She said it made her look just like some French woman who got burned at the stake.

When she walked back into the room, Chastity had taken her place on the bed, head up on the pillow and scrolling through a new phone they'd bought at Walmart right after leaving Memphis.

"I don't think you should be doing that," TJ said.

"Why?" she said. "It's not registered to you. There's no way to track us. Wow. You should see these hits. We added five hundred more likes in five minutes. I've never seen anything like it."

TJ nodded, her mouth feeling dry and her stomach empty. She nodded to Chastity.

"And what are they saying?" TJ said. "All these people?"

"Lot of boys want to see you naked," she said. "But mostly folks calling you a hero."

"A hero?" TJ said. "For what?"

"For snatching me up to your cause," she said. "For sticking it to that greasy Chester Pratt."

"What the hell do you know about Chester Pratt?"

"Only what you told me," she said. "And that was plenty."

"And you're sure they can't track us?"

"No way," Chastity said, not looking up from the phone. "We're all being too careful."

Deputy U.S. Marshal Lillie Virgil hung up the phone, turned to her partner Charlie Hodge, and said, "They're in Texarkana. The Mc-Cade kid just got caught trying to steal another car."

"Why couldn't these little bastards steal a car back in Memphis down on EP Boulevard?" Hodge said. "I haven't been home in two days. I need a shower and some decent food."

"Kid's in bad shape," Lillie said. "Some dogs got to him."

"Dogs?" Hodge said. "Holy Christ."

For the last twenty-four hours, they'd been working out of the Marshal's office in downtown Hot Springs, an ancient government building up the hill from Bathhouse Row and across from the abandoned veterans' hospital. The big brick fortress with dark windows reminded Lillie of an old-time asylum.

"That'll teach him to throw in with TJ Byrd," Lillie said. "Ladarius should consider himself lucky."

Lillie stood up, reached for Hodge's black slicker, and tossed it to him.

Lillie was nearly six feet tall, with broad shoulders and a walk that some whispered looked a little like John Wayne. She'd been in law enforcement for nearly twenty years, working in Memphis, down in Tibbehah County, and now with the marshals. She was stronger than most men, a better shot than all, and suffered few fools. Lillie reached for her Sig Sauer and Winchester 12-gauge while she waited for Hodge to follow.

"I haven't seen Rose all week," Lillie said. "That doesn't exactly make me mother of the year now, does it?"

"Who's driving?" Hodge said.

"Now you're just trying to be cute," she said. "With you behind the wheel, we'd be lucky to hit the state line by sunup."

Charlie Hodge was in his last years as a marshal, nearly twenty years Lillie's senior. A wiry fellow with flinty blue eyes, gray hair, and a thin gray beard, he'd been both a Marine and an undercover agent in Mississippi, working for years against the Dixie Mafia. They'd spent the day going over the mansion where those kids had hid out for two days on Lake Hamilton and later checking out the marina where they'd parked their boat and stolen a brand-new Kia Sorento.

"What about Quinn?" Hodge said, slipping into his jacket. "You gonna call him?"

"Rather not," Lillie said, already headed to the staircase. "We didn't leave things on the best terms."

"And that Sheriff Lovemaiden in Parsham County?" Hodge said, walking in tandem with Lillie down the steps to the street.

"You trust that bastard?" Lillie asked.

"Nope."

"Me, neither," Lillie said. "He and Chester Pratt have gotten to be thick as thieves and neither one of them have got the sense God gave a squirrel to keep their fucking mouths shut. Gina Byrd was a good friend before she got on drugs and flushed her life down the toilet. Her people had quit on her. But I won't."

Lillie unlocked her Dodge Charger—a special model called the Hellcat confiscated from a drug dealer in Orange Mound—crawled behind the wheel, and pressed the starter. She revved the engine, making it growl and purr as Hodge got in. "Damn, Lil," he said. "Can I at least buckle my belt?"

"Hold on to your nuts and call the locals," she said. "We're southbound and down. These goddamn kids aren't getting away twice."

Sheriff Quinn Colson drove up to Olive Branch, Mississippi, to meet Holly Harkins at a Waffle House off Highway 78. He'd been up for most of the past few days, sleeping little since the body of Gina Byrd had been discovered over in Parsham County. As a retired U.S. Army Ranger and sheriff for nearly a decade, he was used to operating on little to no sleep. In fact, he prided himself on being able to keep moving while living off good cigars and black coffee.

"I'm glad you called," Quinn said.

"You ain't gonna arrest me or nothing?"

"There are warrants," Quinn said. "For you, TJ Byrd, and Ladarius McCade."

"They didn't kill Miss Byrd," Holly said. "You got to believe me, Sheriff. I always liked you. You were always real sharp and stand-up when you came to high school to talk to us about the dangers of drugs and staying away from Fannie Hathcock's place out on the highway. Hadn't been for you, I might've ended up working the pole like my cousin."

"That warms my heart, Holly."

Quinn was a trim, muscular man, now nearly forty, with a face full of sharp angles and dark hair cut high and tight like a man still in the service. That night, and as always, he had on a crisp khaki shirt with a silver star, starched and creased dark jeans, and a shined pair of Lucchese boots. Some folks said he reminded them a little of a young James Garner. He liked that, as he'd admired the man who'd marched with Dr. King and played both Major William Darby and the lead in *Support Your Local Sheriff.*

"I can't go to jail," she said. "I didn't do nothing. I was just trying to help TJ. If we hadn't gotten out of town, she would've ended up in a trash barrel just like her momma."

Quinn knew the investigation wasn't his yet, still officially belonging to Sheriff Bruce Lovemaiden, but there was little doubt that whatever happened to Gina occurred in Tibbehah County. The Byrd family, like the Colsons, had been in Tibbehah since well before the Civil War. Gina Byrd's grandfather was an associate of Quinn's grandfather, running moonshine and evading treasury agents back in the day. She'd been classmates with Quinn and would've graduated with him had she not shacked up with Jerry Jeff Valentine, a man ten years her senior, a part-time house painter and full-time accomplice of the biggest fence in north Mississippi.

"How about you start from the beginning?" Quinn said.

Holly looked behind the counter, all the eggs and bacon and hash browns sizzling on the grill. The air was thick with grease and burnt coffee.

"When's the last time you ate?" Quinn asked.

"That trucker I hitched a ride with gave me some beef jerky."

Quinn handed her a laminated menu slick with oily fingerprints.

"Anything I want?" Holly asked.

Quinn nodded. Holly Harkins sure was a goofy-looking kid, with her mousy brown hair and sad brown eyes. She was tall and gangly with a freckled pug nose, sitting there bland and awkward in a sequined T-shirt of Minnie Mouse reading from the Holy Bible.

"What they're saying about TJ and Ladarius are a bunch of lies," Holly said. "I saw the news. They're trying to turn this damn family tragedy into some kind of redneck Romeo and Juliet. Miss Byrd didn't care at all who TJ was seeing. She was always too stoned or drunk most of the time. Like a damn zombie. She didn't know when TJ was coming and going from the trailer. You know the Byrds. You know their ways."

"Unfortunately."

"TJ's not all bad," Holly said. "She does what she does to take care of John Wesley. If she and him didn't steal shit, they wouldn't have anything to eat. TJ's been keeping the lights on in that house since she was thirteen."

"Her little brother shot at one of my deputies," Quinn said. "Right after they broke into the old Pritchard place back in December."

"Y'all never proved that."

"TJ took everything they stole up to a fence in Ripley," Quinn said. "By the time we got onto it, everything was long gone."

"Those Pritchard boys didn't need it," Holly said. "One of them's dead and the other over in Parchman."

"That doesn't make it free for the taking."

"TJ may be a thief," Holly said. "But she's not a killer."

Quinn nodded. The waitress refilled his cup of coffee as Holly ordered the All-Star Special. Two eggs, grits, toast, bacon, and a waffle on the side. Quinn's phone started to buzz, a call from Lillie that he sent straight to voicemail.

"Holly," Quinn said. "Where the hell are those kids headed?"

"I don't know if I should say."

"You should understand I'm the best chance of getting 'em back safe."

"Oh, yeah?"

"Yes, ma'am," Quinn said. "Some folks are sure TJ did this, especially with the history between her and her momma."

"I don't know."

"You have my word."

"Your word, huh," Holly said. "This is turning into some real Bonnie and Clyde shit out there, Sheriff. Ain't it? That's why I run off like I did. I didn't want to stick around and see how the picture might end."

"You said you knew this girl's mother?" Charlie Hodge asked, he and Lillie halfway to Texarkana by now. The billboards and little roadside towns lit up in the dark night, whizzing past the windows, a little bit of rain tapping at their windshield.

"Yep," Lillie said. "She was a friend until she went and fucked herself up."

"How's that?"

"Mainly by a real piece of shit named Jerry Jeff Valentine who sported a mullet and drove a black Monte Carlo SS. Black with red racing stripes."

"Say no more," Hodge said. "That the kids' daddy?"

"The girl's," Lillie said. "Turned out to be a real hero himself. Drove himself off a bridge and into a creek when that girl was little. Her brother had a different daddy altogether, but don't ask me his name. They're just the Byrds, keeping that same family tradition going from a hundred years back."

"And what's that?"

"Town fuckups," Lillie said. "Gina could've been different. She wasn't like all the rest."

"And her daughter?"

"Meaner than a damn snake," Lillie said. "I can't recall how many times I had to make a call on their trailer after she and her momma got into it. One time, she beat up Gina pretty good, bloodied her momma's nose and left bruises all over that poor woman. TJ fought me, too. Kicking and scratching, while I dragged her out by her damn ear. Something's wrong with that girl. So much meanness. I heard she and that boy Ladarius McCade sure made a pair. He got her into boosting cars and trucks, smash and grabs, and house break-ins. He's been in and out of juvie most of his life. Jesus Christ, poor Gina. Did you see the photos of her body after they poured it from that barrel?"

"Wish I hadn't."

"Those kids ain't gonna go easy," Lillie said.

"You think they have some kind of plan?" Hodge said.

"What do you think?"

"Based on my years as a U.S. Marshal and immense wisdom tracking felons?"

"Yes, sir."

"I'd have to say, I've got no goddamn idea, Lillie," Hodge said. "Kids are like any other felon, making up the song as they go."

"Cowardly her bringing her little brother along."

"You got a real problem with this young girl," Hodge said.

"Gina Byrd deserved better than giving birth to that hellcat," Lillie said. "I can't quit thinking about what those damn kids might've done to her. It's not even human."

"Texarkana will give us four of their units," Hodge said. "We got six marshals from the task force. How do you want to play this?"

"That's not up to us," she said. "Now is it?"

* * *

"I got to go back with you?" Holly Harkins asked, her Waffle House plate completely cleaned. "Don't I?"

"Yes, ma'am," Quinn said.

"What am I being charged with?"

"Well," Quinn said. "That depends. Where do you think they went after leaving Hot Springs?"

"They talked about Texas," Holly said. "Maybe finding a way to get some money and head on to California."

"What's in California?" Quinn said.

"Swimming pools and movie stars," Holly said, offering a sad smile. "All that shit. That wasn't TJ's idea. That was that girl Chastity."

"And who's Chastity?"

"Spoiled little rich girl," Holly said. "Her daddy owns a Chevy dealership up in Fayetteville. She caught us squatting on her lake house. We thought the place was abandoned. Got weeds growing up all over the damn place. Didn't look like anyone had been there for a long while till that girl comes busting in, pulling a gun on Ladarius while he was cooking up some steaks. She's the one who talked TJ into getting on Instagram and telling her story about what happened with Chester Pratt."

"I saw it."

"What'd you think?"

"I think I'd like TJ to drop the act and talk sense to me."

"She ain't gonna do it," Holly said. "She doesn't trust you. She says you're as crooked as everyone else and all you care about is throwing her ass in jail."

"That's not true and she knows it."

"She may take a few things that don't belong to her," Holly said.

"My momma says that girl has sticky fingers. But she has a good heart. I promise you that."

"Where are they headed, Holly?"

"I don't know."

"But if you had to guess?"

"This ain't something I want to guess on," she said. "I'm too worried about what's gonna happen. Now they plan to pretend like TJ kidnapped Chastity. Chastity can convince TJ of damn near anything."

"Why would they do that?"

"More attention," Holly said. "More views. All that stuff."

Holly looked out the Waffle House window and started to cry, wiping the tears away with the back of her hand. Quinn drank some black coffee and waited as someone plugged a quarter into the jukebox and an old Mac Davis song came on. "Baby Don't Get Hooked on Me." Their waitress began to slow dance with a potbellied trucker in all denim and pointed-toe boots.

"This sure is a weird place at night."

"Not much different in the day," Quinn said. "A rest stop for folks wanting to be somewhere else."

"Chastity's dad had this room downstairs," Holly said. "It was a secret room in the basement filled with more guns than I ever seen in my life. Chastity loaded a big bag full of them before we took that boat across the lake."

Quinn dropped his forehead into his right hand. Sleep wouldn't come anytime soon.

"She ain't going quietly," Holly said. "That's for damn sure."

Quinn reached for his phone and called Lillie Virgil's cell.

TWO

Five days ago

Quinn Colson had just fallen asleep beside his wife Maggie and their four-month-old daughter Halley when he first learned Gina Byrd was missing. Maggie was nursing the child in bed, Halley's midnight feeding, as Quinn answered his phone and heard from his second-in-command, Reggie Caruthers, that he'd just left Chester Pratt's house where he'd taken the report.

"Pratt says Miss Byrd hasn't been seen in days and he can't get any answers from her daughter."

"Maybe she got smart and ditched him," Quinn said. "Chester Pratt's old enough to be her daddy."

"Pratt says he went out to the Byrd place this afternoon and saw a mess of blood on some dirty towels out in a burn pile," Reggie said. "He tried to get some answers from Gina Byrd's daughter, and the girl pulled a gun on him."

"Did he say why?"

"The girl said Pratt was trespassing on her land," Reggie said. "The kid's only seventeen."

"Doesn't make her less dangerous," Quinn said. "You know we've had trouble with her before. What kind of car does her momma drive?"

"Oh-seven Nissan Sentra," Reggie said. "Blue. Already got the boys out looking."

"And you want to know if we should wake up the Byrds?"

"Yes, sir."

"Go ahead and make a wellness check," Quinn said. "Let me know what you find out."

"You know me, Sheriff," Reggie said. "I'm not scared of nothing. But those Byrds are a different breed. Don't know how they'll react seeing a black man in uniform rolling up to their trailer in the middle of the night. They still fly the stars and bars out on the county road. Not just the regular one, but the one with Hank Jr.'s face in the center."

"Hank Jr. just kind of solidifies their position on things."

"Sure does."

"Well, shit," Quinn said. "You think I might have better luck?"

Reggie didn't answer. Quinn took a long breath, already knowing the answer, and said he'd call when he got on the road. He crawled out of bed, careful not to disturb Maggie and Halley, Maggie looking up and asking what was going on in a whisper. She had bright green eyes and an upturned nose and a face full of freckles that made her look like a kid when she didn't wear makeup. She was a free spirit who worked as a nurse, devoutly practiced yoga, and had grown things in their family garden Quinn didn't think possible. She and her son Brandon had brought life and color back to their old farm.

Maggie had one of Quinn's old flannel shirts open over her breast. Quinn looked over her half-naked body and smiled.

"Maybe when I get back . . ." Quinn said.

"You've got to be kidding, Ranger."

"Worth a shot."

"The Byrds again?"

"How'd you guess?"

"I heard you say Chester Pratt," Maggie said. "I know he's been dating Gina Byrd for a while."

"Pratt called the sheriff's office and said she was missing," Quinn said. "He's worried something happened to her."

"Like what?"

"No idea," Quinn said. "Sometimes I feel less like a sheriff than a damn babysitter around here. Sounds like some family business between the Byrds and Pratt. He's too old to be catting around with that woman."

"You're older than me."

"Only by a couple years," Quinn said. "Chester Pratt is almost twice her age. And I don't think he has any intention of making an honest woman out of her."

"That would be a tall order."

"Hard," Quinn said. "But true."

"Last time I saw Gina Byrd, I had to stitch up her forehead at the hospital," Maggie said. "She was pretty doped up and we tried to get her to stay. I think she was on the edge of an OD. Someone had cracked a bottle over her head at the Southern Star. Wasn't her first time in the ER."

Quinn leaned down and pulled the sheet up around Maggie and over Halley. The little girl cuddled against her mother and nursed herself back to sleep, bow lips parted and softly snoring. Quinn gave his little girl the lightest kiss and reached for his boots and blue jeans.

A little after one a.m., Chester Pratt drove back to Bluebird Liquors to get his gun. He'd locked up and left without it earlier, clearly not thinking right, and knew he'd have to have some protection back home. Some crazy shit had been happening around Jericho, and he sure didn't want to be caught with his pants around his ankles.

He parked his new black Mercedes, leased with an option to buy, behind the white cinder-block building and looked around to make sure no one had followed.

Pratt was kind of rangy looking, with a sallow face and the deep tan of a man who either owned a boat or cut grass for a living. Pratt had done both. His eyes were blue and clear, hair a light sun-faded blond compliments of Miss Nancy who worked at Shear Envy over on the Jericho Square. Miss Nancy made sure to help Chester get rid of the gray and keep the same shaggy look of the KA pledge he'd been back at Ole Miss in '79. He'd only made it two semesters, but that had been two more than anyone in the Pratt family. Despite his short time in Oxford, he remained a true and steadfast Rebel fan, never missing a home game or a party in the Grove.

Pratt unlocked the back door and went straight for his office, careful not to cut on the overhead lights or that neon bluebird sign outside just in case some thirsty trucker over at the Rebel thought he was open. The last thing he needed was to get in a confrontation with some good ole boy begging him for a pint of Fireball. Pratt opened up his office, turned on his desk lamp, and reached into his middle drawer, looking for his big Smith & Wesson 686 loaded with seven .357 rounds.

The gun was polished silver with walnut grips and as comfortable in his hand as the fellow up at that luxury gun store in Oxford told him it would be. He knew it would take the nuts off a bull elephant at three hundred yards. The problem was he couldn't seem to find the damn thing, reaching up into all the salesmen business cards and pens and a mound of unpaid bills.

"Quit looking," a man said behind him. "Ain't in there."

A flashlight beam shot out from the doorframe and into Pratt's eyes.

"Who are you?" Chester Pratt asked. "What the hell you doing in my business?"

"Figured I'd just let myself in, Mr. Pratt," the man said. "That okay with you?"

"Who sent you?"

"I think we both know the answer to that question."

"I don't want no trouble," he said, squinting into the bright light. "Take what you want. You like Pappy Van Winkle? Hell, I got a bottle of Pappy 23 right behind you. Take it. Take the gun. Just leave me the hell alone."

"I'm more of a beer man myself," the man said. "Mexican food and hard liquor's always tough on my stomach."

"Beer?" Pratt said, standing up. "Hell. I got a cold case in my trunk."

"Sit your skinny ass down and listen up," the man said.

Pratt did as he was told. "What do you want?"

"Mr. Pratt," the man said. "It's high time for a come to Jesus about your current and most precarious financial situation."

Quinn drove up into the hills, well beyond the hamlets of Fate and Carthage, to a one-lane logging road that sliced a diagonal line through the northeast corner of Tibbehah County. Reggie was waiting for him by a gravel drive that ran up to the Byrd trailer, which was lit up like a kerosene lantern. The trailer was an older model, with a homemade wooden porch built out from the front door. A dozen or so broken-down cars were parked alongside and up into the eroded hills that had been logged out a long time ago. The Byrds were one of those families who seemed to thrive in a collection of chaos and filth.

Quinn stepped out of the Big Green Machine, a big-tired F-250 with a roll bar and KC lights, a grille guard with a winch, and a Kawasaki four-wheeler parked in the bed. His cattle dog Hondo stayed put, not being able to hop in and out of the truck like he used to.

"Hope I didn't wake you," Reggie said.

"I was up."

"Halley sleeping much?"

"Every few hours," Quinn said. "I keep asking Maggie if I can help and she keeps saying only if I can grow a set of tits. What kind of answer do you have for that?"

"I got four kids, Sheriff," Reggie said. "Man needs to know when to keep his mouth shut. I promise that will save you a hell of a lot of trouble."

"Appreciate that, Reggie," Quinn said. "You ready to roll?"

"Yes, sir," Reggie said.

They both got back into their vehicles, Quinn taking the lead and driving up the hill to the old trailer. They parked but didn't get two paces when the front door opened and a teenage girl walked out. She was short, barefoot, and in blue jeans and a cutoff T-shirt advertising Elijah Craig overlaid with a flannel shirt. It was the second thing Quinn noticed after the double-barrel shotgun pointed right at them.

"Evening, TJ," Quinn said.

"I was here all night," she said. "Ask anybody. Don't try and blame me for things I ain't never done."

"Wouldn't dream of it," Quinn said, glancing over at Reggie. "You mind lowering that weapon at two law enforcement officers?"

"I know my rights."

Hondo started to bark from inside the truck. The cattle dog wasn't a big fan of guns.

"I'm sure you do," Quinn said. "And I know mine, too. I came to check on your momma. I heard she's missing."

"Who told you that?"

Quinn didn't answer. His hands hung loose at his sides. In his periphery, he could see Reggie had his right hand on the butt of his Glock. But at the moment, they were all taking it cool and in stride. The girl was correct; they had no right to enter her property.

"You mind calling her outside?"

"She ain't here."

"Where is she?"

"Down in Louisiana someplace," TJ said, lowering the shotgun. "Went with some friends to go mud riding down around Colfax. She's been seeing a fella who's got a jacked-up Mule he races in through those bayous and creeks. I didn't ask too much. You know how Momma likes to party."

"I thought she was seeing Chester Pratt," Quinn said.

"Is that who told you to come out here in the middle of the damn night?" TJ asked. "Shit. That bastard's been mooning over Momma for nearly a month now. Can't get it through his head that she's moved on without him. I don't have time for this nonsense. I got to get John Wesley to bed. You do know it's a school night?"

"Heard you dropped out."

"I did," TJ said. "But John Wesley didn't. Can I go inside now? I'm freezing my damn ass off."

Reggie glanced over Quinn. He lifted a chin. "You mind if we just take a look around?" he asked.

"I don't give a damn," she said. "Do as you please."

Reggie nodded over to where smoke was coming from up behind a pile of junked cars and old appliances. The deputy walked off without saying another word, Quinn standing there and smiling at TJ.

"You and your mother been having some more trouble?" Quinn asked.

"Nope," TJ said. "Why are you out roaming the county this late at night, Sheriff? Didn't you get married or something?"

"Yes, ma'am."

"And got a baby?"

Quinn nodded. TJ was backlit from where she stood on the porch, and Quinn couldn't see her face clear enough to know if she was serious or just having some fun with him.

"Maybe that'll calm you down some," TJ said. "Keep you from harassing good and decent people of Tibbehah County in all your spare time."

"Is Ladarius McCade in there with you?"

"That ain't none of your damn business."

"You know he didn't show up for court last week," Quinn said.

"That's what I'm talking about," she said. "That was some real bullshit right there."

"Not to the woman he stole the car from."

"His brother loaned it to him," she said. "Talk to his brother."

"His brother's up in Chicago, TJ."

"Well, I don't know what to tell you," she said. "He ain't here."

"Can I come in and see for myself?"

"Like I said, I got to get John Wesley down for bed," she said. "And I know my damn rights."

Quinn nodded. Reggie reappeared from behind the mound of rusting metal. He motioned with his head for Quinn to follow him back behind the junked cars. Quinn could now smell the smoke, drifting in the cold wind.

"If you hear from your momma, tell her to call us."

"My momma ain't the check-in type," TJ said. "'Night, Sheriff."

TJ walked back into the trailer, slammed the door shut, and turned off the porch lights. Quinn marched through the trash strewn about the dirt lot and joined up with Reggie.

"That girl's got some personality."

"Can't blame her," Quinn said. "She came by it honest. Her mother's a real piece of work."

He kept walking with Reggie over to a pit dug down about four feet into the earth and along the hillside. The dying orange embers of a fire burning in the darkness, a few sparks catching up the cold air and flying into the distance.

"Whatever she wanted to get rid of is long gone now," Reggie said.

Quinn unwrapped a Liga Privada and clipped off the end with his pocketknife. He grabbed a nearby stick and got down on his haunches, poking at what little was left in the firepit. "I guess it's time to hear Chester Pratt's side of things."

Chester Pratt sat a long while in the half-dark, the shadowed figure telling him to stay there and keep quiet. But going on five, ten minutes, Pratt was starting to get restless, hoping the man would go and get on with whatever he was about to do. He wasn't so much scared as he was annoyed.

"We waiting on someone?" Pratt asked.

"Shut your damn mouth."

"You don't like bourbon?"

"I said shut up."

"You can take your pick," Pratt said. "We don't put the top shelf stuff out anymore. Goes too fast. We keep the good stuff for the best customers in the stockroom. Doesn't hurt if you slip me or one of the clerks a twenty or fifty, if you know what I'm saying."

"Anyone tell you that you got a face that needs punching?"

"A few."

Something in the man's voice sounded damn familiar, someone he'd crossed in the store or maybe out in the county. It was rough and guttural, terse and mean. He'd had some words with this fella at some point at time. But only a dumb ass would ask a man with a gun on him, *Say, I know you. Don't I?* That's a good way to get your fool head shot off.

"I know why you're here," Pratt said. "But I don't have the money. I said it was coming and I'm doing all I can to get it. Me and you can sit here in the storeroom until the Second Coming, but it won't make any difference. A few folks owe me, too. When I get paid, then I can make good on what I borrowed. Some folks call that robbing Peter to pay Paul. But no one ever said nothing about Paul giving two shits how business got done."

"And what do you think is fair?"

"What do you mean?"

"Considering you're late and all."

"I think you should explain that I'm working on it," Pratt said. "Hell. You can do what you want to me, but that can't make me get what I'm owed and what y'all are owed any faster. In fact, you do something to me, and that's gonna dry up the whole process."

The man reached over and cut on the lights. The light was white hot after sitting in the dark so long. As Chester's eyes adjusted, he realized he did know the man but just wasn't sure from where. He was a thick, muscular fella with a brushy reddish beard and narrow eyes the color of a swamp. He had on a brown Mossy Oak hoodie and a pair of camo pants with lace-up military boots. He held a big black automatic pistol at his side as he stared right at Chester Pratt, studying on him and appearing to be considering his next course of action. The man was white with reddened cheeks and wore a ball cap over a shaved head. The ball cap had a gold patch with a timber rattler on it, the familiar DON'T TREAD ON ME written below. Only the fella had a more DON'T FUCK WITH ME look about him, spitting some tobacco juice on the floor and walking up to where Pratt sat at his desk. The man stunk of BO and cigarettes, his breath hot and spicy on Chester's face.

"I was told to bring your pecker back on a silver platter."

"I really wish you wouldn't."

"This row back here," the man said. "On the racks? That's all your top shelf hooch?"

"Yes, sir," Pratt said. "Sure is. Help yourself. Some wine boxes over there in the corner, sir."

"My name's Bishop."

"Take what you like, Mr. Bishop."

"Just Bishop," the man said. "Best not to forget it."

Bishop walked over to the floor-to-ceiling metal storage racks and plucked a bottle of Pappy Van Winkle 23. He pulled out the cork, took a sniff, and then shook his head. He dropped it onto the concrete floor, where the glass cracked and the bourbon splattered. That bottle would've gone on the cheap for more than three grand. Bishop did the same thing with four, five, six of his other prestige bottles. Not smiling, not laughing. Just smelling each one and dropping them onto the floor as if they weren't to his liking.

"Ain't a bourbon man, I guess," Pratt said, trying to keep it light. But it sure did hurt seeing nearly ten grand destroyed before his very eyes. Not to mention some of the finest whiskey ever made by man.

"I wouldn't drink this shit 'less I had a Coca-Cola to mix in it," Bishop said. "You agree, don't you, Chester Pratt?"

"Destroying my top shelf items ain't gonna get that money any faster."

"Shut your damn pussy lips."

Pratt wasn't tied up nor had the man pointed the gun on him. But he was afraid just the same. Something in those swampy eyes, narrow and small, made the man seem more animal than human.

"Me and you is gonna be good friends," Bishop said. "I'm coming back here each and every night until we get what we is owed. You decide to bring in the law, and I'll start showing up at your house or over at that country woman's trailer you've been screwing."

"Who's that?"

"You telling me you haven't been knocking boots with that Byrd woman?"

Chester Pratt was quiet. The only sound came from outside, trucks coming and going from the Rebel, and the man's slow, ragged breathing.

"Don't be late, Chester Pratt," Bishop said, knocking Chester in the head with the butt of his pistol. "Last fella tried to fuck me ended up getting cornholed by a cattle prod."

"Good Lord Almighty," Pratt said from the floor, touching the heel of his hand to his bloody temple.

"Yeah," he said. "That fella said the same thing. But I damn sure got his attention."

Quinn couldn't find Chester Pratt at home or working late at the liquor store, so he headed back to the farm for a few hours' sleep. He was back up at five, showered and shaved and cooking breakfast for his adopted son Brandon. The kid was now eight years old, towheaded with bright blue eyes and a near constant smile. Brandon not only didn't complain about having a new sister, he welcomed it, helping his mother decorate Halley's room, and always happy to hold her while Maggie had to make dinner or tend to an errand.

The black skillet hissed and popped as Quinn watched a gaggle of turkeys in his back field, picking around the remnants of their corn.

The landscape barren and shadowed in late February, the stalks brown and broken. Twin pecan trees loomed big and skeletal behind the old farmhouse that had been in Quinn's family since 1895.

"How much longer till turkey season?" Brandon asked, standing beside him and looking out into the same field.

"Three weeks." Quinn flipped the ham. "Since when do you care about turkey hunting?"

"Since I started practicing my call," Brandon said. "Want to hear it?"

"Better hold off," Quinn said. "Your momma's still asleep. She may not appreciate it like I would."

Quinn continued to watch the back field, the turkeys skirting the woods as he cooked up three fried eggs with ham and served Brandon on a bright blue Fiesta plate.

After they both ate, Quinn would drive Brandon to school before heading into the sheriff's office. He'd already called in to Cleotha at dispatch to make sure he wasn't needed earlier. Cleotha, being Cleotha, just said, "Ain't shit going on, Sheriff. Besides a couple peckerwoods in a tussle outside the Dixie gas station last night. Both of them scattered when patrol rolled up on their ass."

Brandon seemed to be deep in thought as Quinn joined him at the kitchen table. The kid now officially a Colson after the adoption last year while Quinn recovered from gunshot wounds from the ambush out on Perfect Circle Road. It had taken months to heal before he could take on Fannie Hathcock and her cronies ruling north Mississippi. Quinn and Brandon had spent many hours walking the woods and doing a little fishing on their private lake. The kid still trying to make sense of his biological father, who was both a decorated Marine and a criminal, guaranteed to spend rest of his life at FCI Yazoo City.

"Where'd you go last night?" Brandon asked.

"Just tending to a little business," Quinn said.

"In the middle of the night?"

"Yes, sir," Quinn said. "No time clocks for the sheriff. I'm on call twenty-four-seven whether I like it or not."

"I bet someone is dead," Brandon said. "You don't usually go out that late unless something real bad happened. Who died?"

"No one died."

"You sure?"

"Well," Quinn said. "I hope not."

The thing about living in a rural county is that one way or another, almost everyone was connected in some way, big or small. Quinn recalled Brandon was in the same grade as the Byrd boy, and they'd come to blows on more than one occasion. "How are things going between you and John Wesley Byrd?"

"Permission to use bad language, sir?"

"Sure," Quinn said. "It's only us."

"That kid's a real asshole."

"How so?"

"He's always messing with me," Brandon said. "Pushing me in line. Saying that you deserved to get shot."

"He really said that?"

"Sure did," Brandon said. "John Wesley's dirty and nasty. I don't think that kid's ever even seen a bar of soap. Smells like a skunk dipped in cow shit."

"The Byrds don't have much money," Quinn said. "You might want to take that into account. Some folks aren't as fortunate as us. He may be angry at you for all you've got."

Brandon shrugged and sliced his biscuit in two, sliding in the egg and ham to make a sandwich. He took a big bite and washed it down with some orange juice. Behind him, through the big picture window, Hondo came hobbling up from the cow pasture, panting hard. Quinn let him into the kitchen, the screen door slamming shut with a creaky *thwap*.

"John Wesley hasn't been in school all week," Brandon said.

"Is he sick?"

"I guess," Brandon said. "I got to say that son of a bitch being gone makes my world a hell of a lot better place."

Behind them, Maggie coughed and Quinn turned to see his wife leaning into the doorway, her eyebrows raised. She had on a white terry-cloth robe, reddish-brown hair pulled up into a bun. Her eyes tired and sleepy as she stifled a yawn with her fist. Hondo snuffled up to her, tail wagging.

Brandon apologized, picked up his biscuit sandwich, and headed past his mom and back to his room to get dressed for school. Quinn rinsed off the plates and slid his stiff uniform shirt over his white tee before kissing Maggie on the cheek.

"I'd prefer Brandon didn't talk like this was Cole Range at Benning," Maggie said.

"We were talking about John Wesley Byrd."

"What about him?" Maggie said, grinning. "Besides the kid being a real son of a bitch."

"Brandon said he hasn't seen the boy all week."

"Did you find his mother?"

"Not yet."

"You think something happened to her?"

Quinn refilled his coffee mug and reached for his Tibbehah County cap. "Chester Pratt was worried," Quinn said. "And now I can't find Chester Pratt."

"Well, you know what happened to Gina Byrd."

"She went off with a new man?"

"Isn't that what she always does?"

"Her daughter says she's just mud riding down in Louisiana."

"While leaving her kids to fend for themselves?"

"Yep," Quinn said. "TJ may be the only momma John Wesley knows."

"A kid raising a kid."

"Wish I could say it was an unusual arrangement in this county."

Quinn kissed Maggie again and headed for the door. Brandon was already outside in the backseat of the Big Green Machine, Hondo sitting up front, ready to ride shotgun.

As he walked around his truck, his cell rang. Quinn answered.

"Howdy, Quinn," a man said. "Bruce Lovemaiden over in Parsham County. Looks like we found a vehicle y'all were looking for? A blue Nissan registered to a Gina Byrd."

"Any sign of her?"

"No, sir," he said. "Appears she crashed the vehicle and just abandoned it. You want to drive over and have a look-see?"

THREE

"You take that dog everywhere?" Sheriff Bruce Lovemaiden asked.

"Only places he wants to go," Quinn said.

Hondo tenderly jumped out onto the roadside, walking up to Lovemaiden. The sheriff patted the old dog's head as Hondo sniffed his hand. "What's his name again?"

"Hondo."

"That's right," he said. "Like that John Wayne picture. The one they shot in 3D."

Lovemaiden was a big man with a sizable belly and a head the size of a bowling ball. Despite him having at least ten years on Quinn, he had the air of an overgrown kid. His dark hair was slicked down and hard-parted like a third grader's.

"Can't say I blame him for wanting to get out of Tibbehah County," Lovemaiden said. "And head on into God's Country."

"Never heard Parsham County called that."

"Says it right there at the county line," Lovemaiden said. That big shit-eating grin plastered on his boyish face. "Welcome to God's Country, please don't drive through it like it's hell."

"Ain't that something," Quinn said.

He shook Lovemaiden's hand and followed him off the sloping highway lined with cedar trees and oaks and onto an unpaved road. Lovemaiden had a funny walk, loping like early man who'd yet to evolve, big hands and long arms swinging at his sides. Twenty meters off the highway and down a gravel road swallowed up by oak branches, Quinn spotted the blue Nissan hanging sideways into a drainage ditch.

"That it?"

Quinn checked out the license plate and nodded.

"I ran the record on that Byrd woman," Lovemaiden said, spitting into the weeds. "She ain't exactly president of the PTA."

Quinn walked up to where the back wheel on the passenger side hung a good foot over the gravel. Lovemaiden pulled on some rubber gloves, opened the driver's door, and hit the trunk release. It popped halfway open and Lovemaiden walked back to open it all the way. The trunk was filled with a flat spare, a cardboard box of assorted junk, and plenty of fast-food wrappers.

"I poked around a bit," Lovemaiden said. "Didn't see nothing of value."

"Can you send some deputies to walk the woods?"

"Walk these woods?" Lovemaiden asked, grinning. "Why didn't I think of that?"

Quinn didn't answer, leaving the question hanging.

"Already have," Lovemaiden said. "Didn't find nothing but an illegal dump over in that ravine. Folks treating this part of my county like a goddamn toilet. You can smell it from here."

"You mind if I have this towed back to Tibbehah?"

Lovemaiden shrugged. "Don't make no difference to me," he said. "One less car in our impound lot. Figured she must've wrecked and called someone to pick her up."

Quinn nodded. Hondo jumped up on his front paws and tried to get at something he was sniffing in the trunk, scratching at the

31

bumper and whimpering. Quinn pushed him back as the dog barked and barked, looking from the trunk up to Quinn.

"Must be smellin' them ole French fries," Lovemaiden said as he reached into the right pocket of his uniform and pulled out a tin of Skoal. He thumped it a few times and opened the lid, pinching a generous piece and plugging it into his lower lip. Quinn was used to dippers. Most Army Rangers he knew chewed tobacco, although he'd always preferred cigars.

Lovemaiden turned his head and spit. "Hell of a thing you went through last year," Lovemaiden said. "First word I got sounded like you were already dead."

"Almost."

"But you sure got 'em," Lovemaiden said. "Yes, sir. You sure did. That woman marshal shooting down Fannie Hathcock. I laughed and laughed when I heard about that. That Lillie Virgil don't take no lip, shot that redheaded bitch down like a dog. No offense to ole Hondo."

"She believed Hathcock was going for her weapon." Quinn scratched Hondo behind the ears, the dog still wanting to get closer to the car.

"Which one?" Lovemaiden said. "A gun or a damn hammer? Yes, sir. I heard all the stories about Fannie Hathcock. Last few years, our little ole county hadn't been nothing but a cut through up to that titty bar. Horny kids from State not being able slow down on account of those wild women."

"That's all over," Quinn said.

"For now."

"For good," Quinn said. "Place shut down last year. County supervisors outlawed nude dancing in Tibbehah. State took over that old airstrip she'd been running. We just want that mess behind us."

"Glad to hear it," Lovemaiden said, slamming the trunk and removing his rubber gloves. He tossed them into a ditch and then turned his head and spit again. "Guess y'all got tired of being the punch line about all that's bad down south."

"Come again?"

"Apologies, Sheriff," Lovemaiden said as they began to walk back to the highway, his arms again slinging to and fro like an ape. The light flickered through the overhead oak branches, buds just forming on the trees. "I know it weren't easy sliding into your uncle's boots. I knew Hamp Beckett well and he was a hell of a lawman."

"He also made a lot of mistakes," Quinn said. "And one or two moral failings."

"Sheriff Beckett said sometimes you got to go along to get along. How about that?"

"I heard that a time or two," Quinn said. "Not exactly original."

Lovemaiden hitched up his gun belt and nodded, his lower lip poking out. "Maybe," he said. "But that old man had been around a long time. That age and wisdom ain't something you can buy. No, sir. That's something those old boys earned. Your uncle kept that county business contained. That's for damn sure. You might study on that sometime."

Lovemaiden winked. Quinn stared back.

"I'll be sending a truck," Quinn said.

He walked off and helped Hondo back up into the Big Green Machine. The dog could get out fine, but the getting in had started to be a problem. Quinn started the engine and U-turned on the back road, a cold breeze blowing through the truck as he looked in his rearview. Sheriff Lovemaiden hung by his patrol car and waved him a pleasant goodbye.

"Where the hell you been?" TJ Byrd asked.

Ladarius, being Ladarius, didn't answer. He just walked on into her trailer, opened the refrigerator, and helped himself to a gallon of milk. He drained half of it, wiped off his short mustache, and turned back to her. "Doing shit."

"Doing shit mean you can't answer your damn phone?"

He shrugged and leaned against the kitchen counter, playing with the keys in his hand and refusing to look her in the eye. Ladarius Mc-Cade was a good-looking kid and damn well knew it, having been with TJ off and on now for the better part of the year. They met at the church revival out at The River, both of them coming back to the cross after a few side roads over the years. Like TJ, Ladarius had left school as a sophomore, throwing in with his Uncle Dupuy down in Sugar Ditch, doing things and running games he didn't talk about. Over the summer, he'd tried to cut it flipping burgers over at the Sonic and that had all gone south after a week, the manager calling Ladarius no-good and lazy after catching him listening to Yo Gotti and smoking a blunt in the bathroom. Ladarius took it all in stride, saying weed made him a better cook. He could feel the right time for the flipping, make sure they were crispy and juicy at the same time. Just like the sign out front promised.

"What's wrong with you?" Ladarius asked.

"What's wrong with me is that the sheriff showed up with one of his deputies last night," TJ said. "They drove up a little past midnight, giving me hell, waking up John Wesley and asking about when I saw my momma last."

Ladarius nodded, stroking his thin wispy goatee. Cool, taking it all in. His hair shaved tight at the sides and the back, the top fade styled big and bleached blond.

"Did you hear what I said?"

"I heard you," Ladarius said. "What'd you tell them?"

"You know," TJ said. "Just like we talked about. I told him she was mud riding and partying down in Colfax, Louisiana. I said she'd gone and met a new man."

"And who might that be?"

"Sheriff didn't ask," TJ said. "But if he would've asked, I'd've said it wasn't none of my damn business. Or his damn business. Folks around here know how my momma is. She ain't happy until she's kicking one boyfriend out and hooking up with a new one."

"Ain't it the truth."

"Ladarius?"

"Yeah?"

"What did I say?"

"You said you can talk about your momma but I can't," he said. "It's cool. I get it. I get it."

A door down the hall opened and they both turned to see John Wesley rubbing his eyes and wandering into the bathroom. That boy had stayed up late playing Fortnite and chatting with his friends. He'd been asking a lot about when he was going to go back to school and TJ made up some kind of bullshit answer about not until Momma got home and could get things straight with his teachers. He believed it. He was always causing trouble, fighting and talking back, getting sent to the principal's office. The principal had offered to tan his hide with a big wood paddle. TJ, stepping in for her momma, told the principal that if he even thought about it, she'd break that damn paddle across his skull.

"You okay?" Ladarius asked.

"Yeah," TJ said. "I'm fine. You get me some cigarettes like I asked?"

Ladarius reached into his T-shirt pocket and tossed her a pack of Kool menthols. "You the only white girl I know who smokes Kools."

TJ lit a cigarette and took a seat in front of a small television they had set up on some plywood and four concrete blocks. She closed her eyes and inhaled, trying to get her mind right and make sense of all that had happened in the last forty-eight hours. It hadn't been pretty. Almost like something out of a crazy dream or nightmare. But at least John Wesley hadn't seen what they'd done and didn't know anything about it.

"What in the hell are you watching?" Ladarius said.

"That's Van Halen, dipshit," she said. "We've been over this before."

"That little nerdy kid in the glasses?"

"That little nerdy kid is Waldo," she said. "Those cool kids are actors playing Van Halen. Eddie and Alex. Michael Anthony on bass. That's David Lee Roth right there. He's the lead singer. When he quit, they replaced him with Sammy Hagar. My daddy called that time Van Hagar. He said the music was still pretty good but he didn't like him as much as David Lee. This is classic stuff. The big hair, the spandex, that smoking guitar."

The black-and-white video for "Hot for Teacher" played off an old DVD. She knew every bit of it by heart from the time Waldo's mother sent him on that bus crowded with all those crazy kids until *Playboy* Playmate Lillian Müller showed up in a bikini and wearing that beauty pageant sash.

"God damn," Ladarius said.

"My granny said Daddy had her centerfold in his room," TJ said. "He thought she was the most beautiful woman that ever set foot on God's green earth."

"How old is she now?"

"Now?" TJ said. "Shit. I don't know. Probably a great-grandma by now. This was a long time back. Daddy said back then folks made good music. Before he died, I remember he used to tell me rock 'n' roll was dead and that no one could rock it out like they did back in their day."

"You remember all that?" Ladarius said. "You couldn't've been five or six."

"I remember every damn word that man told me."

TJ blew out a big plume of smoke as the video headed into that epic drum solo by Alex. She still had every cassette tape her daddy owned, playing them in his black Monte Carlo SS they had out in the barn. That thing couldn't run yet but could still play tapes off the new battery. She had 'em all. Van Halen. AC/DC. Poison. Ratt. Lots of GNR. Man, how she loved GNR. While most girls her age were mooning over Kane Brown and that dipshit with the face tattoos, Post Malone, she was steeped in the classics. Damn, she sure missed her daddy. Wish she'd known him more. The cab of that Monte Carlo was still crushed in good where he'd flipped it down in Sarter Creek when she was only five. The local law back then, Sheriff Hamp Beckett, rolling up on him first, seeing her daddy trapped inside and letting him die. Drowning in not a foot of water.

"TJ?"

"Uh-huh."

"What are we gonna do?"

"What needed doing has already been done."

"I mean about Chester Pratt."

"I'm thinking on that," TJ said. "Sheriff didn't say nothing. Only that Pratt said Momma was missing."

"You think he knows all the trouble she caused?"

"Hush," she said. "Don't say another goddamn word."

Ladarius walked over to the couch and pulled a NASCAR blanket up over his shoulders and around his neck like he was Superman or something and came on over next to her. He wrapped her in the blanket and nuzzled his head up into her neck. TJ didn't move an inch, sitting there straight and watching those boys dressed up as Van

Halen rocking the hell out. She wondered what happened to those kids in the video. They couldn't be much younger than Daddy. Probably old and gray now. Or maybe dead, too.

"We did good with those clothes and all that mess," Ladarius said. "Right?"

"Yeah."

"Burning that shit was smart."

"Cleaned up the shower with bleach, too," TJ said. "Scrubbed it till my hands bled."

"I love you, TJ," he said, reaching his hand up under her T-shirt and pulling her close, reaching for the hook on her bra. The toilet flushed and John Wesley wandered out. He had on that FREEZE WARNING T-shirt that they got from Goodwill. That T-shirt not worth a dime to Ole Miss after the big Christian football coach got caught calling up some hookers. The Goodwill must've had a hundred of them new and still in boxes.

"TJ?" John Wesley said. "Why'd the police come over last night?"

"Looking for Ladarius," TJ said, lifting up her chin and blowing out smoke. "They're gonna put his black ass over in Parchman for good."

"That shit's not funny," Ladarius said.

"It's kind of funny," John Wesley said, walking toward the kitchen. TJ knew all they had left was a half box of Cap'n Crunch and whatever milk Ladarius hadn't drunk. "Van Halen. Hell yeah."

"See?" TJ said, removing Ladarius's hand from her stomach. "That kid's getting a damn fine education."

"When's Momma coming home?"

"Won't be long now, John Wesley," TJ said. "Momma called this morning and said how much she loves you."

She took a deep breath, stood up, and held out her hand for Ladarius's keys.

"Where the hell you going?"

"Getting some more milk at the Dollar Store."

"No, you ain't," he said. "You're going for Chester Pratt. After all the shit's that happened, you ain't gonna let it go."

"No way," she said. "No how. Like I always say, fair is fair."

Chester Pratt didn't get back to Tibbehah until dawn, after an unsuccessful trip up to Memphis to borrow money from an Ole Miss frat buddy who sold used cars over in Germantown. He knew he'd wasted his time when his buddy started witnessing to Chester at The Half Shell about getting his life in order and shunning alcohol and drugs. Chester tried to explain to him that he wasn't a drunk, he was only in the liquor business and had gotten behind a few bills. His pal wouldn't hear it, so damn superior sucking on an O'Doul's and handing him some leaflets for a big megachurch run by Pastor Ben Quick. Pratt had known Quick his whole damn life and wasn't in the mood for any light shows and praise music to get him through the night.

He didn't need Jesus. He needed cash.

Pratt didn't even think about heading back to Bluebird Liquors that bright and shiny morning, and instead drove right across the street to the Rebel Truck Stop. It was a busy day at the Rebel, the pumps jammed up with eighteen-wheelers waiting to get filled up with diesel and plenty of pickup trucks and cars pulled tight near the diner to feed on the "Best Chicken Fried Steak in Mississippi." Pratt had eaten the chicken-fried steak. It wasn't anything to write home to Momma about.

He parked and walked through the main shop with aisles filled with beef jerky, soda pop, candy bars, NoDoz, and Red Bull. They sold cowboy boots and samurai swords and had a walk-in cooler with the coldest beer within fifty miles. He was nearly back to the toilets when he saw the big black dude who worked for Johnny Stagg, Midnight Man, coming out of an unmarked back door. He had an apron stretched tight over his denim utility suit, blackened and stained with barbecue sauce and soot. The man must've weighed four hundred pounds.

"Is he in?" Pratt asked.

Midnight Man grunted. He turned around to the door and knocked twice, Midnight Man telling the man inside that someone wanted to see him. *Someone?* Midnight Man knew damn well who he was. Chester Pratt was *Somebody* in Tibbehah County.

"Come in," the familiar gravelly and countrified voice said.

Johnny T. Stagg sat behind his desk, talking on an old tan landline phone and smiling. His hair had grown back into the familiar gray pompadour he'd worn before spending the last five years in a federal facility in Montgomery, Alabama. He was little older, a little craggier, but with the same odd-shaped skeletal head and ruddy cheeks and nose that made his face appear like an old wooden puppet.

He winked at Chester and motioned for him to take a seat.

Stagg's desk was cluttered with paperwork and framed photographs, a silver bowl filled to the brim with peppermint candies.

"Yes, sir, yes, sir," Stagg said into the receiver. "It's gonna be quite a place. I haven't stopped thinking about the Wild West since I was a kid. You know, all that stuff we growed up on. Roy Rogers, Hopalong Cassidy. Dang Lash LaRue. Reason I came to the idea was that one of my grandbabies, Marla's boy, had never even heard of Jesse James or Cole Younger. Even kids growing up behind us had the *Gunsmoke* and *Bonanza* to watch. They got a little bit of our culture and heritage in them shows. This will be a place to display it while offering the young'uns a safe place and some real wholesome family fun. *Yes, sir. Yes, sir.* I sure do appreciate that. *Mmm-hmm.* Well. When you get as old as me, you start looking on things, and figuring out how a man might make a real difference in his community. Yes, sir. *Mmm-hmm.* Sure do appreciate it. Yep. You have a blessed day, too."

Stagg kept on smiling until he put down the phone and turned to Chester Pratt. The smile dropped. "Glad to see you, Mr. Pratt," he said. "You got my goddamn money?"

"Almost," Chester Pratt said.

"*Almost* ain't no answer," Stagg said. "Looks like you got my message."

"Yes, sir," Pratt said, touching his forehead where that man Bishop had pistol-whipped him. "I don't think all that mess was necessary. That crazy-ass monkey destroyed some valuable inventory."

"If this here deal was just between you and me, it wouldn't be of any great concern," Stagg said. "But what you asked for called for some special favors from Jackson and even help from some boys down in New Orleans. You know I don't like to name names. But they're not exactly the patient type. Consider me sending over Mr. Bishop just a friendly reminder of how late you're getting on what's come due."

"Christmas wasn't what we'd hoped for."

"Christmas ain't never what a man hopes for," Stagg said. "Life ain't all candy canes and cute little elves tickling our nutsacks. You came to me as one businessman to another. Besides, you see that lot out back?"

"You mean the Booby Trap?"

"Booby Trap's long gone, son," he said. "I'm gutting that old cathouse that Fannie Hathcock called Vienna's Place. Took me nearly two weeks to fumigate the smell of dead shrimp and sardines from there. What I'm proposing is a world of family fun and adventure. Do you like the Old West, Chester?"

"Sure."

"With a name like Chester I would hope you would," Stagg said.

"Ole Dennis Weaver. Man, he was something. Come on. Let's go take a walk. Time for me to stretch my legs and for us to figure out some kind of payment plan to get you straight with me and my associates."

Pratt didn't answer as Stagg stood up and came around the desk. Stagg wore pleated khakis, a plaid button-down shirt, and a blue Ole Miss sweater-vest, as he was good friends with the new chancellor. Stagg had lobbied hard for the man to get the job even while he was still serving time in federal prison for tax evasion, bribery, drug dealing, prostitution, gunrunning, and several other crimes that Pratt couldn't recall at the moment. Despite his time in jail, some people around here still claimed he'd been set up.

"We're gonna call it Frontier Village," Stagg said, clasping Pratt on his hurt shoulder. "Ain't that something?"

When Quinn returned to the sheriff's office, he found Lillie Virgil back in the jail talking to Kenny about why north Mississippi didn't have a barbecue joint worth a shit. Kenny, a big-bellied, bald-headed jokester, was always happy to discuss country music or southern cuisine.

"Come on up to Memphis and I'll show you around," Lillie said. "Ever been to Payne's?"

"Can't say I have," Kenny said.

"Then you haven't lived," Lillie said, sitting sidesaddle on the long desk at intake. She was flipping through some paperwork for a check forger named Boyd Hunnicutt who was wanted in federal court in Memphis. "Howdy there, Sheriff. How's it going at home? I'd absolutely love to see you feeding that baby and changing diapers. That would truly make my day."

Kenny snickered and then caught himself. Lillie raised her eyebrows.

"Stop by the house anytime, Lil," Quinn said. "I'd be glad to demonstrate."

"And just why do you have one of your best deputies on jail duty?" Lillie said. "Kenny needs to be back on patrol."

Quinn looked to Kenny, whose eyes widened as he quickly shook his head. He in no way wanted Quinn to tell Lillie Virgil, of all people, that he'd been suffering with hemorrhoids for the last two weeks and the thought of crawling into a squad car brought tears to his eyes.

"Just giving him a break is all," Quinn said, handing Kenny the paperwork Lillie had already signed. "All my deputies rotate duties."

"What's that thing on your seat?" Lillie said, nodding to the donut cushion in the office chair. Kenny had stood up when Quinn had walked back into the jail.

"Nothing."

"Say no more, Kenny," Lillie said. "Had a problem with that myself. I would hate to see you try to patrol out on County Road 177. Until the supervisors fix the roads around here instead of spending their kickbacks at Dollywood, you're in for a real hard ride."

Lillie patted Kenny on the shoulder and followed Quinn through the secured door and down a long hallway with linoleum floors and fluorescent lights back to his office. It almost felt like old times, when Lillie had been assistant sheriff, working with Quinn those first few years after he'd come home and taken over after his Uncle Hamp died. She'd been a good friend and solid mentor as he made the transition from the Army into law enforcement.

"I was only messing with you," Lillie said. "Having kids is the best damn thing in the world. I don't know what in the world I'd do without Rose. Can you believe she just turned ten? I would've invited y'all up to Memphis for the party, but Maggie said you'd been short-handed around here. Do you need me to come back and get these sorry bastards back in line? I feel bad for Kenny, but you can't let a man slide off his duties just 'cause he has a sore ass."

"Offer is appreciated," Quinn said. "But we're doing just fine."

"Boyd Hunnicutt," Lillie said. "Son of a damn bitch. These white-collar criminals give me the damn creeps. Give me an honest meth head or moonshiner, house creeper, or car thief anytime. At least they put some sweat into it. A man like Hunnicutt isn't even honest in his thieving. He does almost everything from his desk and behind a computer. I call that being a weak-ass coward."

"It's gonna be a long ride back to Memphis for Mr. Hunnicutt."

"I'll do my best to explain it all to him," Lillie said. "And I'll drive slow."

Quinn walked over to crack his window, the office overlooking a small parking lot and a chain-link fence around the prisoners' exercise yard. His office was simple and utilitarian: an old wooden desk, a rickety swivel chair, and locked rack with shotguns and rifles under a framed American flag. Since he'd come back on the job late last year, he'd barely had time to put everything back in its place. The interim sheriff, a full-time shitbird named Brock Tanner appointed by that criminal Governor Vardaman, had stepped into the job as if it would be a permanent position. After Tanner was arrested, Quinn had tossed everything the man owned into a dumpster out back.

"What's on your mind, Quinn?"

"How'd you know?"

"You got that sullen, kind of quiet way about you today," Lillie said. "Like someone pissed in your morning coffee."

"When's the last time you spoke to Gina Byrd?"

"Oh, hell, I don't know," Lillie said, checking out new rifles in the rack along with the old. She ran her fingers over each one, a true connoisseur of firearms. "Before I left Tibbehah County, I found her walking the wrong way home from town one night and nearly ran over her. I drove back to her trailer and helped her get settled. Why? What'd she do this time?"

"She might be missing."

"Either she's missing or she's not."

"Her daughter says she's down in Louisiana mud riding and raising hell."

"Sounds about Gina's speed."

"Chester Pratt filed a missing person report on her last night," Quinn said. "Earlier today I was over in Parsham County with Sheriff Lovemaiden. They found her car ditched on a back road. Looked like she'd wrecked it and maybe got someone to pick her up. No one seems to know where she's gone."

"I don't like the sound of that."

"Her daughter swears everything is fine and dandy," Quinn said.

"Christ Almighty," Lillie said. "You know the trouble I've had with her daughter. Don't trust a word that girl says."

"Last night Reggie and I found a burn pile out back of their trailer," Quinn said. "Chester Pratt said he'd seen some bloody clothes and sheets in it when he went out there looking for Gina."

"Oh, hell," Lillie said. "That's not good, Quinn. One of the last times I checked on Gina, TJ had beaten the shit out of her momma. There were bruises all over her. Why's Chester Pratt checking on her?"

"They've been seeing each other."

"God help that woman," Lillie said. "He's old enough to be her daddy. I thought he'd moved up to Oxford and opened some kind of luxury steak house."

"He did," Quinn said. "Closed after six months and he stiffed the landlord. Now he's back and he's got a liquor store out by the highway."

"Finally something that even Chester Pratt can't fuck up."

"Give him time."

"So Chester thinks TJ might've hurt her mother."

"That's the insinuation," Quinn said. "We've been looking for his sorry ass all morning. But can't find him."

"This makes me sick as hell," Lillie said, checking her watch and moving toward the old frosted-glass door. "But I'm not surprised. That daughter of hers is an absolute wildcat. I know Gina probably isn't a great mother. And we both know about her daddy. But damn, Quinn. What kind of teenage girl beats the crap out of their own momma? I'd hoped all that had stopped. TJ's been waiting for a trip down to Central Lockup in Pearl since she came kicking and screaming out of her mom's coot."

"I'd never give you advice, Lillie," Quinn said. "But maybe you should clean up your language? Some folks may find a way to twist it and use it against you."

"Fuck 'em all," Lillie said. "And wait and see. You'll see I'm spot-on about TJ Byrd."

"I saw her last night."

"And?"

"Not much of a conversation," Quinn said. "She walked out onto the porch pointing a twelve-gauge at me and Reggie."

"What did I say?"

"Isn't it the boyfriend or husband almost ninety-nine percent of the time when something happens to a woman?"

"That Byrd house is a tinderbox, Quinn Colson," she said. "Trust me. I'm just surprised it hasn't blown up sooner."

FOUR

"Saw that Pratt fella came crying to you," Bishop said.

"Seemed more concerned about those whiskey bottles you broke," Stagg said. "Not the interest he done owed me."

"Can't do much about the man's intelligence," Bishop said.

"Chester Pratt ain't dumb," Stagg said. "Only shiftless. Lazy and crooked as a tomcat's peter."

"Don't think I ever saw a tomcat's privates."

"Damn things look like a bent-up corkscrew."

Johnny Stagg stood with Bishop in the hollowed-out sheet metal shell that used to house Vienna's Place. The only thing he'd kept was an antique bar Fannie Hathcock owned that had once been in a saloon in Kansas City, Missouri, and was shipped to Tibbehah County piece by piece. That's where they'd serve Coca-Cola, fruit punch, pizza slices, cookies, and candy. Little kids getting into all that wholesome family fun with their very own cowboy hat, a mess of them he'd bought special from all the way over in Hangzhou, China.

"On Monday, they start building the town," Stagg said. "We're gonna have a general store and a saloon. The livery stable is gonna be the game room where they can play Pac-Man and Space Invaders.

Whatever the hell kids are into these days. Only thing I was sure about was having some Skee-Ball and maybe a few of them air hockey tables. In the middle will be the Gold Mine, an inflatable set of tunnels and slides where those children can go buck-ass wild."

"Quite an idea, Mr. Stagg."

"Don't patronize me, son," Stagg said. "I know what you got on your mind. Chaos, dissension, and anarchy. But sorry, there's not gonna be no second Civil War. I've known for a long time that ole Zeke Coldfield should've been institutionalized. Man got his first hard-on watching Mary Pickford at a picture show. All he did was rile you boys up that you were gonna be able to turn back the clock, reset things back to the good ole days when colored people worked the fields and y'all could ride around the Square on horseback. Your head held high while toting an AK-47."

"It was a lot more than that," Bishop said. "Hell of a lot more."

Stagg laughed and shook his head. "Come on now," he said. "How about me and you get back to the real world for just a few moments? If folks believe the only way of making a dollar in Tibbehah came from jiggling titties and fifty-dollar pecker pulls, they never imagined the markup on that good ole family fun that's gonna churn out of this place. I see water parks and Ferris wheels and Putt-Putt golf. Enough wholesome entertainment for the whole goddamn Mid-South. Chief Robbie and those Indians sure gonna be pissed when they see I got 'em beat."

"You gonna need me for anything else?" Bishop asked.

"Today?" Stagg said, reaching into his windbreaker and pulling out a comb. He walked over behind the old bar, the only thing left standing in the big metal shed, and began to style his hair, glad to have it grown back long and proper. "No, sir. Stay close, Mr. Bishop. May have something for you a little later. Ever think about going into the likker business?"

"I don't drink likker, Mr. Stagg."

"'Course you don't," Stagg said. "Man like you got too many ideals and convictions to go down that whiskey river. Just how many of your brethren got killed last year?"

"Just the one," Bishop said. "Colonel Silas Pierce. A true American hero. Quinn Colson nearly cut him in half with a twelve-gauge Winchester. Bled out in that truck wash. Then they arrested twenty-two from our militia. They actually believe that done it. That they shut us all down."

"The Watchmen Society?" Stagg said. "Hmmm. Real-life boogeymen. I know y'all's type."

"I heard you knew Brother Gowrie."

"Sure," Stagg said. "I may have heard of him."

"Y'all did business at one time?"

"I may have sold him some supplies," Stagg said. "Once or twice. That's as far as things went."

"He's a true patriot," Bishop said. "His writings are what brought me to Colonel Pierce and the rest of my brothers."

"Ain't that something," Stagg said. "In my few dealings with him, I never knew Gowrie to be a literate man."

Stagg placed his comb back into the jacket pocket. He leaned back onto the bar and studied all the empty space, the possibilities, and how it would soon be filled with clapboard houses, wooden sidewalks, and the booming laughter of children. He looked up and wondered if they couldn't do something about the metal beams and tin roof. Stagg recalled going to visit the Orpheum Theater up in Memphis when he was a kid and how the ceiling had been painted like the night sky, complete with blinking stars and moving clouds. Surely they could figure out something like that for Johnny Stagg's Frontier Village. The possibilities just tickled him to death. And maybe, just maybe, it would be something that his son would find to his liking and take an interest. It was gonna be damn hard for the boy to stay away now.

"I better be getting back," Bishop said. The man had a long beard that came down to his chest and wore dark sunglasses all the damn time.

"See Midnight Man," Stagg said. "He'll get you paid and fill up your tank on your way out."

"Yes, sir."

"And Mr. Bishop?"

Bishop stopped, ramrod straight and serious like the military man he'd never been. A damn redneck playing dress-up.

"How about you lose the bullshit about the South rising again?" Stagg said. "I'm getting too old for all that mess. If you and me get that straight from the git-go, the better we gonna get along."

Bishop didn't answer, turning on his black military boots and heading for the door.

Quinn liked early mornings on the Jericho Square, right as businesses opened and activity started to buzz in the small downtown. When he'd first come home ten years ago, most of the Square was boarded up, maybe one or two places still alive. Any business left had moved out along the highway, the old movie theater turned into a wayward church with a mentally deficient preacher, the drugstore and hardware stores that been open for decades shuttered. One of the worst sights was of old Nat Sherman's menswear shop, windows busted, ceiling and floor caved in, with kudzu and weeds growing through the floor and pressing against broken glass. No one had the sense or pride to condemn or raze the building, letting the store return to nature in an old town that resembled something from a third world country. But a lot had changed for the better since then.

As Quinn drove counterclockwise on Main, turning toward the Western shop, the old PO, and laundromat, he spotted Luther Varner raising the flags by the town gazebo. He was there every morning at nine a.m. to make sure all was clear and orderly by the veterans' memorial. And he was also there at sundown to lower the flags and return them to Lipscomb's Drugstore, where he was rewarded twice a day with a free cup of coffee at their antique soda fountain.

"Rain's headed this way later on," Quinn said, walking down the path toward the memorial.

"A real shitstorm from what I seen on the TV," Mr. Varner said. He and Quinn shook hands and he returned to securing the ropes on the pole.

"You heard from Donnie?"

"Not since last week," Luther said. "You know he quit that job driving a beer truck? Says your daddy got him some work with a film company shooting in Austin. Can you believe that?"

"Your son and my dad working together?" Quinn said. "Yep. Two of a damn kind."

"Yes, sir," Varner said. "God's own truth."

"Caddy seems happy," Quinn said. "Jason likes his new school and he's looking forward to spring football practice. Caddy's already working for some nonprofit in the city."

"Your sister ain't one to keep idle," Varner said.

Quinn and the old man followed one of the paths that spoked from the center of the Square toward the crosswalk to Lipscomb's. The bell jingled as they stepped into the drugstore and emporium. Most of the store now filled with home accents and small gifts, purses and wallets, decorative rugs, fancy bathrobes with matching slippers, and all kinds of gift bags and candies for the Valentine's Day season. Lots of the stuff decked out in glitter and fake jewels with words like FAITH, FAMILY, FOOTBALL.

Varner took a seat on a barstool, gesturing to Miss Vicki for two cups of coffee. Quinn figured he was drinking the dollar coffee on Varner's tab this morning.

Mr. Varner was a tall, lumbering Marine who'd served long and hard in Vietnam. He'd been a sniper, and despite his age, had come out to assist Quinn on more than one occasion. Like Quinn, he kept his hair buzzed high and tight and dressed in crisp, ironed clothes each morning. His boots were spit polished and shined, as were his new black-framed glasses. His face leathery and weathered under the blocky silver crew cut.

Miss Vicki set down two steaming mugs. The men thanked her. Varner's hand shook slightly as he took a sip. His fingers long and yellowed with nicotine.

"What's your momma say about Caddy connecting with your daddy out there in Texas?"

"You know, she hasn't even mentioned it."

"Can you blame her?"

"No, sir," Quinn said.

"Bet she's got more to say about that new baby of y'all's?"

"She's gonna help watch Halley when it's time for Maggie to get back to the hospital," Quinn said. "I'm glad. Hasn't been easy on her, little Jason being gone."

Varner didn't answer. He looked out the window, the backward script of Lipscomb's hand-painted on the plate glass. OPEN SINCE 1911. The Square was already filling up fast that morning. Nearly every storefront was occupied now, including a new coffee shop, a Vietnamese restaurant, and a mixed martial arts studio. The town looked better than Quinn could ever remember. Trees and bushes were trimmed, sidewalks fixed, and store canopies new and mended.

"Ever miss the way it was?" Varner asked.

"Nope," Quinn said.

"Me, either. All y'all can do now is fuck it all up."

"Appreciate the confidence in the younger generation, Luther."

"Heard someone is gonna open up a gourmet grocery over where that old candle shop used to be."

"Is that right?"

"Might cut into the bottom line at the Quick Mart," Varner said. "We don't exactly deal in nothing gourmet. You think folks will ever tire of Vienna sausages and saltines? Or a bag of cracklins with hot sauce for their lunch?"

"Around here?" Quinn said.

Varner nodded.

"Not a damn chance."

Varner smiled a little as he lifted the coffee and took a sip.

Chester Pratt lived out on County Road 357 in a prefab log cabin with a green tin roof and wraparound porch. He didn't have much property to speak of, just three acres, but what he did have was wooded and lush, with wandering turkeys and deer that would come straight up and nearly eat out of your hands. That morning he'd been so damn tired, he'd turned on the outdoor mushroom heaters and wrapped himself with a Mexican blanket, sitting there in a wicker chair and looking out in the deep woods. He sipped Pappy from a broken bottle he'd salvaged last night and drained into a Yeti cup. He nursed the bourbon, thinking on whether to stay and work out a deal with Stagg, or perhaps head down to Central America for a year or two. He'd heard that Costa Rica was a hell of a place for an American on a fixed income.

Chester had grown giddy with the idea when he'd fallen fast asleep, headlong into a wild dream about endless sugar beaches and clear blue waterfalls and brown Mexican women with nipples as big as silver dollars. He dreamed he was king of some kind of tribe, sitting high on a throne, wearing nothing but a sarong and getting attended to until something went crazy and those beautiful brown women smiled to show pointed teeth. Their eyes glowed red and they attacked, chasing him into the palm trees and some kind of rain forest, making crazy-ass sounds, clicking their tongues and scattering up trees as a squirrel or monkey might do. He found himself alone and screaming on a flat boulder in a fast-moving river, those brown women jumping in after him, gathering around the rocks and beginning to feast on his flesh as if he was a turkey supper. Chester Pratt awoke kicking and screaming, breath caught deep down in his chest and choking for air.

He opened his eyes and looked up into the face of TJ Byrd.

"Didn't mean to scare you."

"Hellfire," he said. "Shit. Shit. I'm not scared one damn bit."

"Why'd you scream like a woman?"

"Scream?" Pratt said. "Men don't scream. I didn't scream."

"You sure as hell just screamed," TJ said, kicking his feet off a glass coffee table. His legs knocked over the Yeti of whiskey and he god-damned her as he reached down and uprighted the mess, a good cup of bourbon seeping down through his deck. This just wasn't Chester Pratt's day at all.

"I asked you before and I'll ask you again," TJ said. "Where's my damn money?"

"Where's your momma?"

"Somewhere where you ain't never gonna find her," she said. "Her welfare ain't none of your concern."

"The hell it ain't," he said. "I'm worried sick about that woman. Did y'all get into it again? 'Cause if she's hurt or you hurt her, I need to know. Right here. Right now."

"This is between you and me," TJ said. "You better get me what I'm owed. Or I'll make your life a hell on this earth. I promise you that."

Chester was more than sixty years old and wasn't used to being lectured by some teenybopper. TJ Byrd was ninety-nine pounds of pure redneck muscle and attitude. She couldn't be more than five feet tall, standing there with her hands on her hips, wearing a heavy camo coat up over her jeans and T-shirt cut up above her bare belly. Her skin as pale and smooth as alabaster.

"That wasn't your money," Pratt said. "That's your momma's money. And any type of financial or business arrangement is between consenting adults. Sorry, little girl. Take a seat at the kids' table. This ain't none of your damn business."

"That money was my money," she said. "Left for me by my daddy's momma. My momma didn't have any more right to that insurance check than a man on the moon. And you come by, a goddamn vulture, picking across the bones of a poor sick woman that you didn't even know. Do you even know her name? Or how she died?"

"I don't know about any of that mess, kid," Pratt said, reclining in the rattan chair, his head still fuzzy and thick from that nightmare and those cannibal women. "Your momma and I talked this over. Contracts were signed. Deals were made. Sorry, but that's the way of the world. You got issue with what she done, talk to your momma."

"I can't," she said. "She's gone."

"Whatever y'all cooked up between you two ain't funny no more," he said. "Where's she at, TJ? Is she okay?"

"I'm not my momma's keeper," she said. "Don't you ever go and send Johnny Law on my ass ever again."

"I didn't send no one on your ass, TJ Byrd," Chester Pratt said, wiping the lid of the Yeti cup with his finger. He took a long pull.

"You're not going to find her," TJ said. "She met up with a new man and gone down to Louisiana for a little R&R. Mud riding. Drinking and partying. She's sick and done with your sorry, wrinkled old ass."

"That's bullshit, little girl," he said. "You know what I think?"

"I don't really give a damn, old man."

"I think you're just upset about me and your momma being in love," he said. "I don't think you can handle that your momma found a little bit of happiness in this world. You don't want that. I know all about you and your worship of your dead daddy. Jerry Jeff Fucking Valentine. Shit. I hate to break it to you, kid, but he wasn't no Billy the Kid. He was nothing but a fuckup and loser. And I swear to hell you're just like him."

That's when that little girl reached into her coat and pulled out a pistol.

"He left me his gun," she said. "And if you and me don't get square, I'm gonna shoot those low-hanging nuts right off you."

"Come on now, girly."

"You had a chance, Chester," TJ said. "You stole my momma's money. Money she only had 'cause she'd stolen it off me. You tried to threaten me, sending the police out knocking on my door like I did something wrong."

"Get out of here," he said. "I'll call the sheriff."

"Do it," TJ said. She reached down on the glass table littered with an empty bag of chips, an overflowing ashtray, and the silver insulated cup of booze. She snatched up his cell phone and tossed it right in his lap. "Call 911. I damn well dare you. Call Sheriff Colson and let him know some seventeen-year-old girl is gonna shoot you. Because you'd be right. But then at least we might can get straight on all the trouble you caused me and my family. You're sitting here drinking whiskey and eating Golden Flake chips while my little brother can't even get breakfast."

"I can help y'all out," Pratt said, reaching back for his wallet. "How much you need?"

"All of it," TJ said. "Eighteen thousand, nine hundred and eighty dollars," she said. "Plus interest."

"What's the interest?"

"Still working on that," TJ said, still holding that gun on him. That little girl thumbed back the hammer and placed her finger on the trigger. "What's it gonna be, Chester?"

"I'm not trying to make trouble," he said. "I just want to find your momma and make everything right. I just need some time. Why won't anyone in this world give me some goddamn time?"

"Two days," TJ said. "You better get me my money, Chester, or I'm headed straight to the sheriff. You can lie to yourself all you want, but you're nothing but a con man and a goddamn thief."

"What did you and Ladarius do with her?"

"What the hell are you talking about?" she said. "You're goddamn crazy, old man. She's safe. And she's away from you."

"She was scared of you," he said. "Scared of her own child and just what you might do to her. I know y'all are hiding something, and I won't quit till I find her."

Sheriff Bruce Lovemaiden helped himself to an extra plate of chicken and dumplings, greens, and cornbread for lunch at Momma Jo's Country Cookin' before swinging right back around to get that Nissan Sentra hooked up for transport to Tibbehah County. He figured he could've easily sent one of his three deputies on duty to get the job done, but Lovemaiden was in the mood to take a little ride in the country and finish his fourth cup of sweet tea. Momma Jo had refilled his cup before he left and he liked to sip on it while he tuned into a talk radio station out of Jackson that gave the news straight and uncut to the working man. As he drove on the snaking gravel road, a little rain tapping at his windshield, the boys discussed all these crazy folks wanting to take down monuments to the Confederate dead all across the South.

Hell, they'd already gotten rid of the statue of Nathan Bedford Forrest up in Memphis, leaving the bones of him and his wife in a concrete box, not a hundred feet from a community basketball court. It was a damn disgrace and a laugh riot that these people wanted to erase the history of his ancestors and folks who'd given their lives for what they believed was right. If Lovemaiden had said it once, he'd said it a thousand times. If some of these damn antifa millennials holding signs and singing rap songs wanted to head on into Parsham County and take down the soldier by the old railroad station, they'd have a real fight on their hands.

He shook his head with the thought of it as the radio headed on into a commercial about a big gun and knife show at the Jackson convention center. Two days of family fun with all kinds of guns, knives, and antique weapons. *"Win a survival backpack valued at five hundred dollars, a brand-new Ranger ATV, or a Vietnam commemorative M16. Special appearance by YouTube sensation and catfish noodler Mary Beth Brown. And boys, don't forget, women are always welcome."*

Lovemaiden wouldn't mind riding down to the capital to see that Mary Beth Brown. One of his deputies had passed around pictures from the internet of her catching the big boys in nothing but a pink string bikini. *Lord.* The thought of them puppies swinging around in that little top nearly made him drive off the dang road. Instead, he belched into his hand while he turned onto the dirt road and parked, checking his watch for the time and phone for a message from Quinn Colson. He figured that tow truck would be here any minute.

The rain fell soft as he got out and stretched, turning his bad back this way and that, and stepped over a narrow drainage ditch to take a leak into a kudzu-filled ravine. He looked down to where folks had come to toss out old TVs, refrigerators, car engines, and buckets of motor oil. This was one of the main unofficial county dumps in Parsham and illegal as hell. Lovemaiden wasn't into hugging damn trees, but he sure as hell didn't like his county to look like a postcard from Tijuana.

As he zipped up his fly, he noticed the buzzards circling the ravine high above him, those big-winged, floating creatures zeroing in on something down in that old gully. Lovemaiden sniffed at the air but didn't catch a whiff of nothin'. Although this was the kind of place where folks gutted a deer shot off-season and tossed the head, legs, and the guts. Or maybe some dog got hit on the road and made it down that hill to die. That ravine sure seemed like a good place to die, as nasty and godforsaken as any in his county.

The buzzards, six, seven of them, continued to circle. Lovemaiden reached into his patrol car for his slicker and slid into it before he carefully walked onto the worn path down into the mess. There were whole rusted-out cars and trucks, even a bass boat and a pile of steel barrels. As he high-stepped through the dead kudzu, the wilted brown leaves crunched underfoot. He walked careful, trying not to get any mud or deer entrails on his new boots.

From up the ravine and on the road, he heard the sound of a rambling truck engine and then the crunching of tires on gravel slowing to a stop. Lovemaiden looked up and squinted at all those circling buzzards. Just what the hell were they all excited about? He got close to a rusted deep freezer, and with a little hesitation, opened up the lid, looking inside. Nothing but some stagnant water. But as he closed the top and turned, he lost his footing and tumbled downhill, sliding deeper into the ass crack of this shithole and rolling into the far side of the hill, where he came face-to-face with the side of an overturned blue oil barrel. *Son of a damn bitch.*

Lovemaiden used the side of the plastic drum to stand, knowing he'd twisted the holy shit out of his ankle. The contents of the barrel had spilled loose down into the weedy patch of ground, and at first Lovemaiden didn't make sense of exactly what he was seeing. Something in his mind seemed to have been jimmied loose. What he saw looked for all the dang world like a human jigsaw puzzle, parts of a storefront mannequin spread out to be snapped back together again. The first thing that hit his brain was that he was looking at one of those Japanese sex dolls perverts buy on the internet for hundreds of dollars.

He hobbled closer, knocking the dirt and leaves off his uniform, unable to take his eyes off a clump of flesh set down near a upside-down vinyl recliner. Lovemaiden toed at it with the pointy tip of his Tony Lamas until he flipped the damn thing and saw he was looking at the severed leg of a human being, as clean and white as a slab of marble.

Lovemaiden felt his lunch rise up in his throat while he hopped on one foot away from the body parts, not being able to make it five feet before he fell onto his ass, crawled, and started to vomit. The vomiting wouldn't stop until he'd purged himself of every damn morsel Momma Jo had fed him. All the greens and cornbread and chicken dumplins he could stand. Damn that woman to hell.

He hobbled and ran until he got to the hill, making his way up the way he came, dragging his hurt foot behind him. He heard a man above calling down to him, but didn't stop, hell, he couldn't stop. He clawed at the kudzu, reaching for loose roots to hold him up as he got back to the road. He'd nearly made it when he saw some huge black fella looking down at him.

"You all right?" the man said in a deep voice.

The man looked like a damn giant, wearing gray coveralls and a baseball cap. He reached down a big hand to Lovemaiden, only it weren't no hand, it was a silver hook.

Lovemaiden screamed, a sound he'd never heard in his life, let go of the roots, and slid back down the hill. The black man, still lording over him, called out something that the sheriff couldn't quite understand. Lovemaiden reached for his gun and fired a single shot into the sky.

"Git!" he said. "Get the hell out of here. Leave me the hell alone."

There was a long silence. Lovemaiden looked up into the dark sky, the falling rain, and the crazy carousel of black birds. His mouth felt dry as a damn bone. The pistol shot rang in his ears.

"Sheriff Lovemaiden?" the black man said. "My name's Boom Kimbrough. Came over to take that Nissan back to Tibbehah County. You sure you're okay down there?"

FIVE

Quinn waited outside Bluebird Liquors for a half hour before Chester Pratt wheeled into the parking lot in his shiny black Mercedes. Pratt crawled out, looking bedraggled and disheveled, and headed straight for the front door as if he hadn't seen the Ford F-250 painted Army green with a silver Tibbehah County Sheriff star. Quinn pressed off the tailgate where he'd been texting with dispatch and called out to the man's back, "Hold up there, Chester."

"Sorry, Sheriff," Pratt said. "Was just about to get up with you. Been a whale of a day."

"Getting a little concerned about Gina Byrd," Quinn said. "Hope you might throw a little light on the situation."

"Oh, I don't know," Pratt said. "Her daughter says she took off with some new fella. That's starting to sound about right. You know Gina. She's a hot-blooded woman who sure likes to party."

"You said you saw bloody clothes in a burn pile out back?"

"I don't really know what I saw," Pratt said. "Sorry to trouble you."

"I was over in Parsham County this morning," Quinn said. "The sheriff over there found Miss Byrd's Nissan left abandoned on a back road. You know anything about that?"

"No, sir," Pratt said. "But it sure as hell sounds like Gina is drinking again. *Lord.* She promised me a thousand times she was through with all that mess. I'm sure you know how low things got for Gina at one point in her life. Said if wasn't for Jesus Christ Himself on the mainline, she wouldn't be here today."

"You told Deputy Caruthers that you thought she might be hurt," Quinn said. "And you believed she'd been in some kind of fight with her daughter?"

"I don't know about all that," Pratt said. "Sorry to have worried y'all, but I need to get back to work. We're two days late taking inventory on the merlots. Damn Christmastime about cleaned me out. Wonder how y'all did without a decent liquor store here in Tibbehah County all these years."

Quinn studied Chester Pratt's face. The man had been sweating, eyes bloodshot. His breath smelled like bourbon and breath mints. Pratt kept his hands on his waist and continued to nod, buzzing with the high energy of someone who wanted to break free of a situation or was in a bad way to get to a bathroom. Quinn scratched at his cheek and smiled. "Just a few more questions, Mr. Pratt."

"Okay, then," he said, rubbing his unshaven jaw. "Yes, sir. Whatever y'all need. However I can help."

"When's the last time you saw Gina?" Quinn asked.

"Oh, I don't know," he said. "Maybe four, five days ago."

"And where was that, sir?"

"She came over to my house for supper," Pratt said. "I cooked two T-bones and made some twice-baked potatoes. We sat around and watched one of those movies she liked. Something about these two old geezers holed up in a nursing home telling stories to each other. You had to go through a bunch of shit and flashbacks just to learn that those two very people were husband and wife but were too far gone to know they were talking about themselves. It sure made Gina cry. But I didn't care for it at all. I prefer a little more action and adventure in my stories."

"Have y'all been having any trouble?"

"You mean fighting?" Pratt said. "No, sir. That's not my style. My ex-wives may not like me anymore but they can never say I wasn't any fun. Kind of hard to yell at each other during one of those weepy-ass movies. Just so you know and not for public consumption, but Miss Byrd stayed the night and we did have intimate relations."

"Good for you," Quinn said. "And did you speak to her after that?"

"Once or twice," Pratt said. "Didn't think too much of it. She'd gone over to some craft store in Tupelo. You know she's been working over at that flower shop in town? DG's Creations. She's been making these fancy painted door hangings for Miss Donna Grace. I got one right there on my front door. See that wood and glitter thing that says Hotty Toddy? That woman sure had more than one talent."

Pratt patted a little rhythm on his thighs, jangling at the keys in his pocket, and rocking up and down on his front toes. "I hope I'm not in any trouble," he said. "When I called, I may have been drinking just a little. Sampling my own product. Maybe I was a little hurt she might've run off with a new man after we shared that romantic dinner at my house."

"Watching sad movies and eating those T-bones?"

"Yes, sir," Pratt said, grinning. "Sure was a special date. Set out candles by the hot tub and everything. I guess I'm just a romantic old fool."

"Any idea who this mysterious other man might be?"

"You're gonna have to ask Gina Byrd that question," Pratt said. "Or maybe one of her girlfriends."

"You have some names to check with?"

"Oh, hell," Pratt said. "I don't know. Miss Donna Grace. Diane Tull at the feed and seed. I think she kept in touch with Lillie Virgil. Did you know she's now a damn U.S. Marshal?"

"Yeah," Quinn said. "Might've heard something about that."

"Now that's a nasty woman right there," Pratt said. "She once pulled me over for speeding and gave me a talking-to with words I never heard coming out of a white woman's mouth. She actually called me a rich, spoiled son of a bitch and to slow down or she'd put me in hot pants and send me along Highway 49 to pick up trash. I figure she was trying to tell me that truckers might get a real kick out of it."

Quinn stood there and waited, not saying another word, letting Pratt fill in the silences and maybe offer a better explanation of why he had been so worried about Gina Byrd. Quinn didn't know much, but he was pretty sure there wasn't any mysterious boyfriend who took her away from the fast-paced life in Tibbehah County to race tricked-out Mules down in Louisiana.

"Don't know what to tell you, Sheriff," Pratt said. "I guess I'd figured Gina had gotten herself straight. That she'd gotten too old to put on a bikini and race around the mud. Damn if I don't feel stupid as hell. I've been married three times and had more women than I can count to cheat on me. I've always been the trusting type. I figure when relations happen between a man and a woman that they got some kind of special bond. You know what I'm saying, Sheriff?"

"Have you tried calling her?" Quinn said.

"So many times my fingers're nearly worn out," he said. "Want to see my cell phone?"

Pratt reached into his pocket without being asked, thumbed through the Samsung and showed a screen with forty-nine calls to the same number and name. GINA. Quinn looked at it and nodded, his own phone buzzing on his hip and showing a familiar number. He held up a hand to Pratt, stepped back toward his truck, and took the call.

"Some bad shit's going down in Parsham County," Boom Kimbrough said. "I came down to get Gina Byrd's Nissan and had to help that sheriff out of some booger woods junkyard after he fired a shot at me. I don't know what's going on. Nobody will tell me nothing. But the county coroner showed up, along with three more deputies and a news van out of Tupelo."

"Roger that," Quinn said. "Headed your way."

Quinn turned to Chester Pratt and said they'd have to continue the conversation later.

"Everything okay out there, Sheriff?" Pratt asked.

Quinn nodded and climbed into the Big Green Machine, heading back to Parsham County.

"Something's a-matter," Holly Harkins said.

"Nope," TJ said. "Everything's just fine and dandy."

"Bull W. Shit," Holly said. "Friends don't lie to friends. If something's bothering you, you better damn well spill it."

TJ drove Holly's mom's beat-up Dodge minivan along Jericho Road headed toward Choctaw Lake, where Holly worked two nights a week at the Captain's Table fish camp. She'd serve up fried catfish and hush puppies until ten o'clock when she'd come out of that cinderblock restaurant smelling like grease and nicotine. The poor girl had to wash her hair twice with Suave rosemary and mint shampoo to remove the stink.

"Why do you think something's a-matter?" TJ asked.

"Hell," Holly said, popping her bubble gum and watching the winter landscape roll by. Nothing but bare branches, dead weeds, and gray skies. "I don't know. Maybe because I've been your best friend since third grade."

"I thought you'd been my best friend since kindergarten."

"We met in kindergarten," Holly said. "But I didn't really trust you until third grade. That's when you stuck up for me with that Harris boy that kept on looking under my skirt on the monkey bars. I still can't believe you put a dog turd in his lunch box."

"Power Rangers," TJ said, grinning. "The look on his damn face. It was worth it. Wasn't it?"

"You are a damn trip, TJ Byrd," Holly said.

TJ took the old minivan up to seventy, after passing a sheriff's deputy headed back the opposite way into town. TJ popped an AC/DC CD into the stereo, blasting "Highway to Hell" through the one speaker working up front. She planned to kick around the lake a little after she dropped off Holly, Ladarius saying he might join her to smoke a joint, maybe shoot some rats that gathered behind the dumpsters. She was down for whatever he wanted after he'd come up with the two hundred dollars she needed bad. That would be enough to keep the lights on at their trailer and pick up some groceries at the Dollar General for her and John Wesley.

"You're quiet," Holly said, brown hair scattering across her chubby, freckled face. She had on her sky blue Captain's Table tee with Matthew 4:18 printed on it. "When you're quiet, it means you're thinking hard about something."

"I'm just zoning out," TJ said. "I ain't thinking about nothing."

"If you can't talk about it with me, who can you talk with?" Holly said. "Ladarius? You really think you can trust that boy? Because I'm not so sure, TJ. I've been hearing some stories about him and that Rhonda Price. Something about those Sonic waitresses on roller skates just makes boys crazy."

"Ladarius doesn't give a damn about Rhonda Price or her fuckin' roller skates."

"Well, I'd watch my back if I were you," Holly said. "You know that character Hot Stuff? That cute little devil that wears a diaper and carries a pitchfork? I heard that Rhonda Price got a tattoo of Hot

Stuff right inside her left leg. I'll let you study on the meaning of that."

"I said I don't give a damn about Rhonda Price," TJ said. "Or if Ladarius hooked up with her. Or about some trashy devil tattoo near her cooter. I got lots bigger problems. Sheriff's giving me hell. Momma's gone missing. And I got to get to the Dollar General to get John Wesley's fucking Cap'n Crunch."

"You shouldn't feed John Wesley that shit."

"Holly."

"Yeah?"

"You asked me what's the matter," TJ said. "And now I'm damn well trying to tell you."

"Why's the sheriff giving you trouble?"

"Why do you think?" TJ said. "Fucking Chester Pratt thinks I know where Momma has gone. But I know he's just trying to make trouble for me because he doesn't want to pay what I'm owed."

"Where is your momma?" Holly said. "She's not really down in Louisiana mud riding with some new man."

"Do you really want to know?" TJ said. "'Cause if I tell you, that means you're in it. You are damn well involved."

"What happened, TJ?"

"You promise not to tell?" TJ said, slowing down in the final stretch of Jericho Road, the hills softening and the flat shimmer of Choctaw Lake coming up into view. It was late afternoon but had already grown dark this far out in the country, shadowed by tall pines and leafless trees, little cypress stumps poking up from around the shore. TJ drove to the crushed gravel lot around the Captain's Table and parked far off from the other cars. She let down a side window, cold air rushing in, and fished out the pack of Kools. Say what you will about Ladarius McCade, but that boy comes in like a Marvel superhero in a pinch. What he did the other night, helping her clean up that mess and make things right. *Damn*. That's a man in TJ Byrd's book.

"Something bad happened, Holly," TJ said.

"How bad?"

"Real bad," TJ said. "So much blood that it took me almost an hour to clean up the mess."

Quinn rolled up on the scene in Parsham County at 1700 hours. It was getting darker and colder fast, a light rain hitting the windshield as he reached for his shiny green sheriff's office jacket with the Sherpa collar. Boom was hanging by his tow truck, the flashing lights of six cruisers and two ambulances flickering across the narrow dirt road. Quinn plugged a cigar into his mouth and surveyed the scene, glad whatever was happening wasn't in Tibbehah County.

"Weren't we supposed to have dinner with your momma?" Boom asked.

"We were."

"Did Miss Jean tell you what she was making?"

"Salmon croquettes, mashed potatoes, and English peas."

"Gravy?"

"You know it."

"Damn," Boom said. "Now we're freezing our nuts off over in Parsham County. How you like that?"

"I got some coffee," Quinn said.

"And I see you brought Hondo."

Quinn looked back to his truck, Hondo sitting up tall in the passenger seat, tongue hanging loose, calm and cool with all the activity going on around him. Quinn walked back to the truck, patted the dog's head, grabbed his thermos, and poured coffee into the silver cup.

"What are you hearing?"

"Dead body down in that ditch," Boom said. "That fat sheriff nearly shit his pants after seeing whatever he seen. Fired a shot when I first drove up. I think my prosthetic must've scared him."

"Lovemaiden has had murders before," Quinn said. "Need I remind you we are in Parsham County?"

"Yeah," Boom said. "I got the feeling that Sheriff Lovemaiden doesn't have many people of color working for him."

"Maybe they're on a different shift."

"Yeah, right," Boom said. "That must be it."

Boom stood tall in gray coveralls and work boots with an old blue Carhartt hoodie up over a CAT trucker's cap. He was a big man, six-foot-five and more than two-fifty. The right side of his face still showed the scars, across his cheek and down into his brushy black beard, from when his Hummer had hit an IED outside Fallujah, sending him and two other Guardsmen flying into the air. Boom lost his right arm while his buddies lost their lives. He seldom talked about it, making his way with a shiny silver hook and sometimes with a modern prosthetic that could be outfitted with a variety of screwdrivers and ratchets for his work as a mechanic.

Since they both returned from the service, Quinn and Boom had faced white supremacists, the Dixie Mafia, and even a damn tornado as they tried to clean up their own backyard in Tibbehah. They shared the same sense of justice to help make their home a better place. Not a vision of what had been but what could be. Quinn only wished Boom could be working as one of his deputies instead of fixing engines at the County Barn. It was more about his police record than his disability. Boom had more than a few run-ins with the law after his discharge. *Assault. Drunk and disorderly. Vandalism of public property.* Boom went through what he called a "period of readjustment."

"They won't let me take the car," Boom said. "Not now."

"I figured," Quinn said. "Where's Lovemaiden?"

Boom lifted his chin down the road where several deputies had gathered in a semicircle. Quinn couldn't quite make out Lovemaiden but started walking up the gravel road in that direction. A few of the deputies looked his way and sussed him out. Quinn knew a hundred white men just like them, lean-faced and dark-eyed, slow with a greeting, only a flicker of acknowledgment as he got closer. Too tough or too stupid to acknowledge him. Soon the circle broke up and Lovemaiden was there, hands on his hips, stomach hanging loose, and looking straight down at Quinn. The man didn't look good, his face drained of color and eyes bloodshot.

"What did you hear?" Lovemaiden said.

"Heard you might've found something."

"Goddamn right," Lovemaiden said. "I ain't never in my life seen something like it. What's down in that ditch wasn't never meant to be found. Doesn't even look human."

"Gina Byrd?"

"If you say so," Lovemaiden said. "Not a lot left of whatever it was. You're welcome to take a look."

"Want to come with me?" Quinn said.

Lovemaiden just stared at Quinn, lifting the Styrofoam cup to his lips and spitting. He didn't nod or answer in any way but followed Quinn toward the hillside. Crime scene tape had been strung up on the ridge overlooking a narrow ditch filled with garbage and rusting metal. Quinn lifted the tape and walked down into the gully lit by bright work lamps like you'd find around a construction site, powered by a generator that hummed down in the ditch. Two deputies waited in the crevice, sitting on top of a junked pickup truck. One of them got up when he saw Lovemaiden and helped lift up another stretch of tape, Lovemaiden making great effort to bend under it and walk toward a group of blue plastic barrels.

"If it hadn't been for the buzzards, I wouldn't have seen it."

A silver tarp had been spread over whatever it was that Love-maiden wanted him to see.

"Sure you ready for this?" Lovemaiden said. "This shit's on me now. Ain't no medals for keeping this in your head, Ranger."

Quinn nodded. He knew he'd seen lots worse, having once used a trowel and his hands to rescue the bodies of American soldiers hastily buried behind a hospital in Nasiriya. That had been almost twenty years ago, but the smell of it and the way those bodies had come apart in his hands was something that would never leave him.

Lovemaiden just stared at him, a most unpleasant look on his face. He spit into the cup again and grunted as he reached down and pulled up the tarp. Quinn turned on his Maglite and shined it onto the trash and weeds, seeing something that he couldn't quite describe spilled out of a blue plastic barrel. The smell of it was almost as bad as those bodies he'd helped uncover years ago, only mixed in with the very strong odor of bleach.

"Whoever done this didn't want it found," Lovemaiden said. "Fig-ured that bleach would eat everything down to the damn bone."

"How long has it been down here?"

"You know the damn deal, Quinn," Lovemaiden said and let go of the tarp. "Ain't no such thing as no goddamn *CSI North Mississippi*. I got state folks rolling over from Batesville to see if they can put this jigsaw puzzle back together. But sure. I hear you. Don't take much to note the proximity of that blue Nissan of your missing woman and this goddamn mess. How long has your woman been gone?"

"Three days."

"Hmm," Lovemaiden said. "Someone went to a hell of a lot of trouble to slice and dice and fill up this barrel with all that bleach. Why the hell leave the vic's car on the roadside like some kind of flashing goddamn sign?"

"Maybe they lured her out here and then planned to move the car?"

"What's her people saying?"

"They say she's down in Louisiana raising hell with a new man."

"You believe that?"

"No, sir," Quinn said. "I sure don't."

"Know anyone who might want to do this woman harm?"

Quinn nodded. "I'm making a list."

"See you share it with me, Sheriff Colson," Lovemaiden said, closing his eyes and letting out a long breath. "I have a feeling me and you gonna be burning up the phone lines between here and Jericho for a while."

Dusty and Flem Nix were often confused as brothers, although Flem was more than fifteen years older and was Dusty's daddy. Dusty was thirty-four now, Flem about to hit that big five-oh. Them boys thick as damn thieves. Dusty was closer to his daddy than most sons, although old Daddy Flem sure could get on a man's nerves. Whistling songs ain't nobody heard of. Grunting instead of making words. They'd been working as roofers for as long as Dusty could hold a hammer. There wasn't a roof pitched steep enough that he and Daddy couldn't climb, repair, or cover in Kool Seal. Summer or winter. He and Daddy had fixed metal roofs so hot they'd scald the damn skin off your hands. And some so damn cold that you couldn't stop your teeth from chattering loose. The Nixes took the hard jobs no one wanted, not even Mexicans, fair money for their hard work, taking what they earned and supporting the rest of the family compound on their ten acres over in Yellow Leaf right behind the Free Will Baptist church. Momma Lennie, who ruled the damn roost in their world, made sure Dusty's twin sister and various cousins and uncles got tended to while Dusty and Flem took on most of the responsibility and the work.

Both men were coal-eyed, midget short, and dark complected, although Flem had grown a little more white-headed these last few years. His whole life, Dusty had to deal with people making jokes about him being born under the damn rainbow, calling him names like "squirt" and fucking "peewee." The only way to get through it, as Daddy told him, Flem being only an inch taller than his son, was to get down and dirty with anyone who gave you some lip.

They spent most of the summers fishing and winters shooting deer, in and out of season. They Nix boys also owned their own processing shop out on their spread in Yellow Leaf. There wasn't an animal they couldn't bleed out and turn into the finest sausage you ever ate. Ain't nobody in north Mississippi could make a jalapeño venison bologna like the Nix family. You killed it, the Nix boys could butcher it.

It had been a hard week, and after finishing up at sunset, Dusty and Flem headed down to Shooter's pool hall to drink some beer and run a few tables before Momma came looking for them. Dusty knew Daddy would do his best to get good and drunk before Momma Lennie came to town and dragged that old man out by his damn ear. Right now, Flem Nix sat propped up in a corner chair, taking hits of a pint of Fireball from inside his paint-splattered Army coat. A cigarette hung loose out his lean face that reminded Dusty of a Halloween skeleton.

"Daddy," Dusty said. "Get up."

"Huh?"

"Get up," Dusty said. "It's your shot."

Flem Nix grunted and got to his feet with much effort, catching the eye of a big, potbellied man in a gray sweatshirt cut off at the shoulders to show off his hairy arms and some bullshit tattoo of the Realtree deer colored in with the Confederate flag. The man's gut hung far and wide over his work pants, lots of fat spilling from under his chin. The fat boy looked at Daddy and then back at Dusty and shook his head before leaning into the table and knocking two balls into a corner pocket.

"What you looking at?" Daddy Nix asked.

"Oh, hell," Dusty said.

"Y'all brothers or something?"

"Who the fuck wants to know?" Daddy asked.

"Don't get all pissy, little man," the fat boy said, reaching up his fist to burp into it. "I just ain't never seen folks built so low to the ground."

"Do you know who the fuck I am?" Flem Nix said.

"Give me a minute," Fat Boy said, rubbing the whiskers on his chin. "You kinda look to me like that little fella used to be on that show with Johnny Knoxville, always getting shot out of a cannon or having his nuts knocked with a sledgehammer."

"Keep on talking like that and I'll knock your goddamn nuts with my fist."

Dusty ambled up by his daddy at the pool table and grinned, turning up a cold Budweiser. Thank the damn Lord that folks could drink in Jericho these days. He was already feeling good as hell after taking a couple of those back pills Momma give him and washing it down with some beer and a little cinnamon whiskey.

"Come on now, Daddy," Dusty said. "This blubberbutt ain't worth your trouble."

"What'd he just say?" the fat man said. He turned to a black fella sitting nearby, smoking a long cigarette under a Bud Light neon sign. The black man's eyes bugged out his head, his teeth as brown and crooked as an old rake. Although he didn't speak, the black man blew out a big plume of smoke.

"I wouldn't make my daddy mad," Dusty said. "He may be little, but he's fierce as a motherfucker."

The fat man didn't say a word, only walked around the table to size up another shot. His black buddy sat close to the far wall, leaning back in a chair, front legs off the ground and rocking up and down as if watching a damn reality show in motion. The air was smoky down in the basement pool room.

"Maybe you ought to apologize," Dusty Nix said.

Their own table hadn't been touched, the balls racked slick and still in the center of the scarred-up green felt. Dusty took a hit of the cigarette and waited.

"That'll be the day," the fat man said.

"You don't have to mean it or nothin'," Dusty said. "Just tell my ole daddy you're sorry."

"Y'all are the two weirdest mothers I seen outside the goddamn circus," the fat man said, knocking the holy shit out of the cue ball and sending two direct and hard in the pocket. "Fuckin' freaks. Both of y'all smell like someone shit their damn drawers."

Daddy Flem shook his head as if the fat man was a sorrowful sight. Dusty knew his daddy could whip both of those boys on his own, but as his daddy leaned into the table to take a shot, he winced with pain. That's when Dusty noticed the stitching and bandages had come undone on his daddy's right side, dark blood staining through his work shirt.

"You okay, Daddy?"

Daddy Flem didn't answer as he busted those balls with a tall and mighty crack, scattering all of 'em across the table, a couple solids into two separate pockets. He'd been playing soft and easy all night, but those boys and the pain of his unfortunate injury coming undone had pissed him off. Dusty finished his beer, knowing that hell was about to come if they didn't get out of here and get home. His daddy had a look in his eye like he wanted to tear that fat boy apart like a field-stripped deer.

"Better get you fixed up," Dusty said.

Daddy Flem didn't answer, leaning into the table again and knocking in an orange solid. He chalked up his cue and walked around the table, looking for a good shot, eyes switching from the green felt up to the fat man. The fat man must've seen it, definitely felt it, standing there with his arms crossed over his big gut, a smile on his face saying, "come on and get you some, old man."

"Ain't nothing," Daddy said.

"You're bleeding."

"Just a busted seam."

Fat Boy looked to the bug-eyed black fella and laughed. "The short ones always give you the most trouble," he said. "Short ones always got the most to prove. Like a little runt dog nipping at your heels."

Oh, hell. Dusty stood up, pretty damn sure that Daddy was about to run the damn table, but also knowing that he might break that pool cue against the fat boy's skull. He reached out and touched his daddy's arm. "Come on," he said. "Let's git."

"Bullshit," Daddy Flem said. "I paid my time."

"Let's go home."

"Shit."

"He ain't worth it."

Daddy breathed in a lot of air through his nose and nodded. He leaned into the table, surveying his options and decided on a shot that put his back toward the fat boy. The fat boy drank some beer and looked away, and that was when Daddy reared back the cue hard and fast right between the fat man's legs. Damn, he got that boy good in the nuts. The man made a high-pitched sound, like a hurt dog, throwing him against his pool table and then coming full out on Daddy, Daddy turning the cue into a club and whacking that man hard and fast across his skull. Somewhere out front, the owner of the pool hall started to yell, saying he was gonna call the cops. But it was too late, the black man was out of the chair and on his feet heading toward Daddy with a malt liquor bottle raised over his head. Dusty saw him, too, and jumped up high on the man's back, punching at the back of his head and biting a nice chunk off his ear. Dusty could taste the gristle and blood in his mouth, spitting it onto the floor, Daddy now having that big fat boy down on his knees where he kept on whacking and whacking like that fat man wasn't nothing but the stump of a stubborn oak, the cue just an old mattock that would tear those roots apart.

The spit and blood went flying until that big ole boy finally fell. The black man already loose and free from Dusty. He had his hand on his bleeding ear, screaming that he was gonna kill both those short motherfuckers. The black man walked to the wall, going for the gun that was most surely in his coat.

But the man was too slow. Dusty had a revolver up into the man's sweating neck, whispering into his bloody ear, "You damn blacks taste just like chicken."

There was the fuck yous and all the threats about how they'd find them and kill them. Just a bunch of wind and bullshit. Dusty wasn't in any mood to get down and dirty but that fat man had played it when he'd disrespected Daddy Flem.

The pool room was still and silent. You could hear the men shift on the old buckled wooden planks. The two or three other tables had stopped cold, all eyes on Dusty and Daddy Flem. Daddy having the grace to take the bloody and broken cue and place it neatly and orderly in the rack. The Nix boys slid into their coats, Daddy doing it with a lot of pain, so much blood on his right flank that Dusty knew the whole damn thing had torn loose. Smoke hung around the low-hanging lights. Whatever soul music had been playing on the jukebox was gone. It was like something out of one of those old-time Westerns Daddy watched before falling asleep in his La-Z-Boy.

"Momma will sew you up."

"She always does."

"You okay?"

They passed by all the eyes and the whispers, the black-as-night owner of the pool hall already on the phone with Johnny Law. They made it out back and into the night and the cold. Daddy leaned on the passenger door before Dusty helped him inside. The sky was endless and dark, a million pinpricks of light winking above.

"It wasn't about him," Daddy said. "I'm still mad as hell at that goddamn bitch who stuck me."

"Do you ever get tired of teaching folks a lesson?"

"I reckon I don't," Daddy said. "Some folks just have it comin' and I'm glad to send them on their way."

SIX

Holly Harkins knew the fella at table eight was going to be trouble, slow, steady eyes on her chest and on her backside when she took his order for the fisherman's platter with double fries and extra tartar sauce. When she'd delivered his food, he'd asked her about the freshness of the fish and whether it had been frozen. She'd wanted to say, "Of course it's been goddamn frozen. How many shrimp and clams do you think you could catch out on Choctaw Lake?" But she'd just smiled and said she didn't know, saying they got shipments twice a week from down on the coast. He'd listened to her, eyes taking in her breasts in the tight blue Captain Table's T-shirt, as he reached for a French fry and dabbed it into the tartar sauce. "Mmm," he said. "I just love fresh young things."

The man stuck around to nearly closing time, Holly finding herself looking out the big windows to the parking lot to see if TJ had come back with her momma's minivan. Most nights TJ was there fifteen, twenty minutes early just in case things got slow and the manager let Holly go. But TJ wasn't there, probably making out with Ladarius somewhere, listening to her Cheap Trick or fucking Quiet Riot, telling tall tales about how her daddy had been a folk hero and things might've been different if her momma had stayed with him and made him a better man.

"You mind me asking you something?" the pervy man asked. Holly looked away from the window and back toward him. He had the corner booth, a table that could seat six, situated right under an old fisherman's net seeded with conch shells, starfish, and rubber turtles. The man had his right arm extended over the back of the orange vinyl seat as if putting an arm around a ghost.

"No, sir."

"How'd you get so damn fine?"

Holly shrugged, having about enough, and not being able to help herself. "Genetics?"

The man reached a finger into his mouth to pry loose something in his back teeth. "Sure your momma and daddy didn't have nothing to do with it?"

Holly shook her head, taking in a long deep breath, as the man stood up and patted her on the rear, reaching into his wallet and leaving a twenty. The meal with tax had been nineteen dollars and some change. He winked as he zipped up his hunting coat and tugged on an orange ski cap and headed for the door.

As he walked out, cold air rushed in, past the two other waitresses and Phil Jr., the son of the owner of Captain's Table. The little group was huddled around the register and staring at a small television that they usually only turned on for Ole Miss games. Phil Jr. had the till pulled from the register, the till just sitting there while he stared up at the screen. Some woman from the Tupelo station talking in front of a stretch of yellow tape, the flashing lights of police cars down a dark, dirty road. *Body found in Parsham County.*

"Has everybody quit but me?" Holly asked. "We got two tables need busing."

"You see this?" asked Becky, one of the older waitresses who'd worked at the Captain's Table since Holly was little. Becky was tall and thick, with arms as big as Christmas hams and a soft, wrinkled face with lots of loose skin around her throat. She wore perfumed powder and makeup, her dark hair dyed and teased high in what looked like a football helmet.

"I don't have time."

"Looks like someone got themselves kilt," Phil Jr. said. The truth never lost on Phil Jr., as being number two at the Captain's Table made him the king of useless information. *Make sure you smile if you want a tip. Make sure to wash your hands after you use the commode or you'll make a customer sick. Always clean and dry your official T-shirt before coming to work or you'll look sloppy. Don't use the Lord's name in vain. Ever!*

"How does a person get themselves killed?" Becky said.

"Drugs," Phil Jr. said. "If it happened in Parsham, it's got to be drugs."

Holly shook her head and lifted a pack of wintergreen gum from the counter while Phil Jr. and Becky weren't looking and slid it into her jean pocket. She was about to turn and head back to the dirty tables when she saw the footage of the blue car being loaded onto the back of a wrecker and being driven away. There was no mistaking it for a blue Nissan just like the one Gina Byrd drove. Something in Holly just gave out at the sight of it, her legs feeling like they might buckle, as she reached for the phone in her back pocket and speed-dialed TJ.

The phone rang and rang.

Where was that damn girl?

The black deputy named Caruthers had picked TJ up on the Jericho Square, where she'd been cruising with Ladarius, going round and round, playing her old CDs and waving to friends, after grabbing a strawberry cheesecake shake at the Sonic and riding past the old high school. At first, she thought it had something to do with the business from the other night, but the way the deputy had approached the minivan with such a sad humble face had placed a rock in her stomach. He didn't even need to tell her that something had happened to her momma. But all he said was there had been some trouble and some concerns and that the sheriff needed to talk to her. She'd left Ladarius there with Holly's minivan and rode with the deputy to the sheriff's office, the man not saying two words to her until he walked her inside and told her to take a seat in a big empty conference room with a windowed wall. She must've stayed there for thirty minutes until Quinn Colson walked in with two men who said they were from Parsham County, Sheriff Lovemaiden and his special investigator Bobby Peden. Lovemaiden looked like a big blimp, the special investigator kind of doughy, with brown hair and a short goatee that did a poor job at hiding his weak chin. Both of them wore tan uniforms.

"We found your momma's car, TJ," Lovemaiden said.

"And Momma?"

Lovemaiden looked to Quinn Colson and then back to her, not being able to say whatever was on his mind. He took in a deep breath, closed his eyes, and shook his head.

Quinn Colson walked over to the table and put a hand on TJ's shoulder. "We found a body," he said. "We don't know if it's your mother. But we wanted to let you know what was going on."

TJ did not cry. She felt like she should be crying, but nothing came out. She just sat there, still and quiet in that big empty conference room, hands in her lap. Her ears still ringing with the sounds of Quiet Riot and Cinderella. She wished she was back in the car now, hands on the wheel and the music cranked up as high as it would go.

She would drive anywhere and everywhere, not looking in her rearview for a minute to see what was chasing her.

"We didn't want you hearing any rumors," Lovemaiden said. "From one of those pesky TV reporters."

"Y'all think it's Momma?"

"We don't know," Lovemaiden said. "Not yet."

She didn't look at him. She looked to Quinn Colson and his lean, hard face and flinty eyes. He still had his damn hand on her shoulder and she shook free. "Y'all think it's Momma?"

Quinn looked right at her. And he said, "Yes."

"Lord God."

"Tell me about the last time you saw her," Quinn said. "And everything she said and did."

"I already done told you."

"You said she was going down to Louisiana," he said. "With her new boyfriend. Is that still right?"

"'Still right'?" she said. "You calling me a liar?"

That fat lawman moved around to the head of the long oval table and took a seat beside the doughy investigator with the goatee. Lovemaiden had a Styrofoam dip cup in his hand and lifted it to his lips to spit. Behind him, through the glass, she saw Deputy Caruthers walking out with none other than fucking Chester Pratt. That's what took so long. Quinn Colson and these two men from Parsham County had been sitting down with that goddamn snake.

She and Pratt locked eyes for just a second, and Pratt, being the true coward that he was, looked away and kept on heading out to the front door.

"That's the liar," she said, pointing. "Whatever he told you is bullshit. Is that what all this mess is about? He's the one y'all need to be grilling about my momma. Chester Pratt is a two-bit con man and true and authentic liar."

Lovemaiden spit again. His left cheek twitched a bit and he set down the cup. "You and your momma were having troubles. Is that right?"

The special investigator, Bobby Peden, now had a yellow legal pad in front of him, jotting down some notes. She saw a cell phone had been pushed to the center of the table, recording what was being said.

"No, sir."

"Y'all didn't get into it the other night?" he asked. "Your momma wanting to send you to that Wings of Faith school up in Missouri? I heard Mr. Pratt even offered to pay your way."

"Bullshit," she said. "Mr. Pratt can't even pay his own damn bills."

"Come on now, TJ," Lovemaiden said. His voice smooth and reassuring and annoying the hell out of her. "Help us out a little."

"My friends call me TJ," she said.

"Okay, TJ," he said.

"But you can call me Tanya Jane."

"Okay, Miss Tanya Jane," Lovemaiden said. "Did you and your momma get in an argument about you going up to that Wings of Faith?"

"Wasn't no argument," TJ said. "I told her there was no fucking way I was going up to that school. They got pictures on their site of girls riding horses and playing volleyball. But if you look at the fine print, all they want to do is scrub the makeup off your face, slip you into a flowered dress, and brainwash your ass. The say their mission is to get a young woman to submit. Submit, hell. Submit to who? Would y'all please tell me what the fuck is going on?"

"I'm guessing they want you to submit to Christ," Lovemaiden said. "That's what all young women need to do at some time in their lives."

"And what the hell do you know about being a young woman?"

The question hung there for a few seconds just as TJ caught the mean stares that Sheriff Colson was giving to Bruce Lovemaiden, looking at him across the table like a man telling another man he needed to shut the hell up. But Lovemaiden either didn't get the message or had no intention of taking advice. He leaned back in a big spinning chair and placed his two fat hands behind his head.

"I got two daughters," Lovemaiden said. "One's married with two grandbabies. And for a long while she got herself lost before she finally came to terms with biblical thinking. Woman's got to get with the program. Get right all the harms she's done. I don't have to tell you there's no salvation without coming clean. How about it, TJ. You ready to lay your burdens down?"

TJ looked to Quinn Colson and back to the fat sheriff and his investigator.

"Lay down my burdens?" she asked. "Where is my goddamn mother?"

"We heard sometimes it got real rough with your momma," Lovemaiden said, shaking his head. "Real rough."

"Chester Pratt told you that?" she said. "Chester is a liar. Where's my fucking mother?"

She screamed the last part and that's when Quinn Colson stood up and told Lovemaiden and his special investigator to wait for him back in the office. Lovemaiden groaned, making a big show out of placing two meaty hands on the table, and pulling his fat ass out of the spinning chair.

"Me and you ain't done, missy," Lovemaiden said. "Not by a goshdang long shot."

"Y'all wait in my office," Quinn said. "I need to speak to Miss Byrd in private."

Chester Pratt parked out back of the chain-link fence behind what used to be the Cobb Lumber Mill before old Larry Cobb cornholed himself by keeping payoff records between him and Johnny Stagg and half the damn county supervisors. Cobb was still sitting in federal prison over in Louisiana while Johnny Stagg was probably working on his second piece of pecan pie à la mode at the Rebel right about now. Just didn't seem fair, Pratt thought, watching the steam come off the massive piles of cut timber, bright lights shining into the big expanse of the lumberyard, trucks still coming and going from the front gates even though it was nearly midnight.

Pratt took a sip of some whiskey in his Yeti cup, leaning back into the heated leather seat, wanting to close his eyes for a few minutes. Just what in the hell had he gotten himself into? All he'd wanted to do was get that damn liquor license and set himself up in a business that he could control. That had been the trouble with everything he'd ever tried to do, someone coming along and fucking up the situation. Like that steak house in Oxford. How the hell was he supposed to know two assholes had the same idea in mind and opened up their steak houses not two weeks after him? And what about the time he'd bought into that fine menswear shop in New Albany just in time for a damn recession? Any other time, he'd been outfitting half the town for blue blazers for Sunday service and selling to all those frat boys who came down by the truckload from Ole Miss because that's what their daddy had done before them. He'd been in cattle, timber, food, clothes, and now liquor. Liquor was the thing that he knew was going to make him a success, a respected member of the Jericho community, maybe a slot on the Chamber of Commerce, perhaps even a time that he might run for Board of Aldermen or get on the sugar tit of being a county supervisor.

He'd done everything right. Only to get himself screwed. Again. Like the old blues song said, if it weren't for bad luck, he wouldn't have no luck at all.

Chester took another nip from his cup, watching all that steam rising from the big ole piles of cut timber, the lights as bright as a Friday night football game. He let down his window, his Mercedes parked in shadow, and lit up a cigarette. He could figure this out. He could get Stagg paid and get that bald-headed monkey off his ass. But first, he needed to find out what in the fuck was going on with Gina. That was a special brand of crazy that he sure as hell didn't need now. Every single one of his wives had been batshit crazy. Chester Pratt sure knew how to pick 'em. If that body they found over in Parsham was really Gina, he'd been right smart to go to the police from the get-go when she up and disappeared. Now they were thinking of him as the concerned citizen and worried boyfriend. He told that Sheriff Lovemaiden the exact damn truth he'd been thinking. If any harm had come to Gina, they better be looking right at her daughter. She'd hurt her momma plenty of times before.

Pratt's car soon filled with light and he looked into his rearview to see headlights coming up slow and easy behind him. Pratt tapped his cigarette out the cracked window and watched two men get out of a truck, the one on the passenger's side seeming to have some kind of trouble walking. The driver reached behind the other man, propping him up, and half-carried him over to Pratt's open window. The men were short as hell and wiry. Pratt could detect their scent from ten feet off.

"What's the matter with him?" Pratt asked.

"Just a little corrective activity with a fat boy at the pool hall," said the one called Dusty Nix. "You know he don't take no lip."

"Anybody follow you out?"

"We ain't no mental defects," Dusty said.

"Just try and stay out of trouble," Pratt said. "Can y'all just do that for a few weeks?"

The older man, the one called Flem, who was either Dusty's older brother, uncle, or daddy, didn't look well at all. His face was as white as a sheet and he kept on holding at his side as if he'd been gut-kicked by a mule.

"He's hurt."

"It ain't nothing," the older man said.

"How bad was the fight?" Pratt asked.

"I don't mean no disrespect, Mr. Pratt," Dusty Nix said. "But did you bring us what you done promised?"

Pratt was expecting this, finishing off the cigarette and flicking it into the weeds beyond the Nix boys. He'd already paid them enough for the job with a little extra promised, and he'd offered to find them some more roofing work with some of his rich friends in Tibbehah. It was a fine and friendly arrangement.

"It's coming."

"Coming?" Dusty Nix said. "If it's coming, why'd you call us up in the middle of the dang night? My momma is about to have Daddy's ass for breakfast for us heading out drinking and raising hell. She doesn't take too kind to that, especially as she's been trying to get Daddy into being deacon down the road at the Assembly of God. That ain't an easy task, Mr. Pratt."

Pratt watched as the older man pulled his hand away from his side and flashed a bloody towel that he'd been holding against him. The older man just stared at Chester Pratt with hollow black eyes before pressing the towel back to his side and gritting his teeth.

"What the damn hell?"

"Ain't nothing," the old man said.

"Looks like something to me."

"We need to get paid, Mr. Pratt," he said. "That there's the deal. You may've hired us on a personal matter. But that doesn't make no difference. Roofing or running roughshod, it's all the damn same. We did like we was told."

"You talked to the woman?" Pratt said. "Right?"

"Yes, sir," he said. "Indeed we did."

"What happened then?" Pratt asked. "Where the hell did she go? What did she say?"

"After we told her to shut her goddamn mouth?"

"Yes," Pratt said. "After that."

"Well," Dusty Nix said, grinning a little. "That's a kind of a funny story. You was right about one thing. That woman sure got her an attitude. Me and Daddy didn't care for it one damn bit and caught up with her for her recklessness."

"What do you mean?" Chester said. "Caught up with her?"

Dusty licked his lips. The old man, holding his bloodied side, just grinned.

Chester Pratt watched them both and felt as if ice water had been injected into his veins.

SEVEN

"Can I get you a Coke, TJ?" Quinn asked.

"Don't you think for one second I don't know what y'all are pulling."

"What are we pulling, TJ?"

"I told you to call me Tanya Jane."

"You told Sheriff Lovemaiden to call you Tanya Jane," Quinn said. "I was hoping you and me might be friends."

TJ laughed at that and shook her head. Quinn smiled, trying to make the girl feel comfortable and at ease. He knew there was no use being tough on a teenage girl who'd probably, almost definitely, just lost her mother. She hadn't been charged with a crime, and at that very moment all Quinn had were a bunch of stories that Chester Pratt had told them. He didn't know much. But he sure as hell didn't trust Chester Pratt.

"You got that fat sheriff to come down on me like a ton of bricks," TJ said. "Accusing me of all kinds of bullshit. Then you kick his ass out and wander on in offering me a Coca-Cola like everything is cool. You boys need to practice a little more before trying that act on me. I may be only seventeen, but I ain't stupid."

"Would it matter if I told you I didn't put too much in what Chester Pratt had to say?"

TJ looked over at Quinn, hands tucked into the opposite sleeves of an old blue sweatshirt, a camo cap reading JERICHO FARM & RANCH pulled down in her eyes as she slunk low in the conference room chair. She didn't answer.

"What about that Sheriff Lovemaiden?"

"This isn't about him, either," Quinn said. "You don't live in Parsham. You live in Tibbehah County. If something happened to your mother, I give you my word I'll find out."

"Why should I trust you?" she said. "Wasn't Hamp Beckett your uncle?"

"Yes, ma'am."

"Then you know what he did to my daddy."

"I heard rumors," Quinn said. "But I don't truck in rumors. I was on the other side of the earth when that happened."

"Your uncle killed my daddy."

"My uncle did a lot of bad things," Quinn said. "No doubt something like that might've happened. But right now, let's talk about your mother."

"You said you believe that body you found is her?"

Quinn nodded as he stood against the far wall of the conference room. After Sheriff Lovemaiden marched out into the SO lobby, Quinn had closed the blinds, leaving him and TJ in privacy. He didn't have much time. A social worker was on her way from Tupelo, and a court-appointed attorney wasn't far behind if they tried to keep her.

"Was it true what Chester Pratt said?" Quinn asked. "About your mother wanting to send you to that reform school?"

"Wings of Faith?" TJ asked. "Yes, sir. That's true."

"Doesn't sound that bad."

"I look like the type to wear skirts down to my ankles and sing hymns?"

Quinn reached over and slid the Coca-Cola can in front of her. She popped the top and leaned back into the chair. "What did your mother think about you and Ladarius McCade?"

"She loves him," TJ said. "She thinks Ladarius hung the damn moon. Sometimes I think she loves that boy more than she loves me and John Wesley. *Why?* Let me guess. You're hearing different from Chester Pratt."

Chester Pratt had told Quinn and the boys from Parsham that Gina Byrd wasn't happy at all about her daughter dating a young black man who'd been in and out of the Walter Payton Unit at Henley-Young juvie. Pratt said TJ and Gina Byrd had a long, nasty fight that weekend that ended with TJ pulling a .38 and threatening to shoot her own mother if she said another word about Ladarius or Wings of Faith. Chester Pratt admitted, somewhat tearfully, that Gina Byrd was concerned for her life.

"Are you going to lock me up?"

"For what?"

"For killing my mother."

"We're not for certain that body is your mother," Quinn said. "Not yet."

"But if she's dead, it looks like you and that fat sheriff have decided I'm the one who done it."

"No, ma'am," Quinn said. "I have no idea what happened. But maybe you do?"

"I can tell you one damn thing," TJ said, wiping away the slightest tear from her left eye. Her voice grown husky. "I'd never kill my own momma. And anyone who said Momma was trying to keep me and Ladarius apart is a damn liar. She loved that boy. The Wings of Faith wasn't about anything but a new Jesus kick. She would've forgotten about it by next Sunday."

"Who would want to kill your mother, TJ?"

"I don't know."

"What about that new boyfriend?" Quinn asked. "Was there really another man she was seeing?"

TJ waited a long beat. She cried a little bit more but then straightened up in the chair and wiped her face with the cuffs of her old sweatshirt. She nodded as she seemed to be thinking about exactly what she wanted to say.

"I don't know," TJ said. "There might've been."

"Why'd you lie?"

"Damn it all to hell," TJ said. "I wasn't lying for me. I was lying for her. She came home the other night covered in blood. She was scared to death and said two men had attacked her outside the Southern Star. She got hold of the man's knife and got loose."

"Why didn't she call us?"

"She was scared," she said. "She thinks she killed one of 'em."

"Sounds like self-defense."

"I think she knew both of 'em," TJ said. "You know Momma. You know what kind of taste she's got in men. I didn't want to know and didn't ask questions. I just helped her get packed and get gone."

"Were those the clothes you burned?"

TJ nodded.

"What did those men want?" Quinn said. "Did she say?"

"I shouldn't say no more," TJ said. "I've told you more than enough. And I have the sense to shut my mouth with cops."

"To help you, you gotta help me."

"I got a kid brother at home," TJ said. "John Wesley's alone wondering where his big sister's at."

"Your friend Holly's looking out for him."

"Think you might've told me that from the git-go, Sheriff?" she asked. "Or is keeping me worried sick all part of trying to get me to trip up? Damn you people. You sure are cut from the same cloth as that bastard Hamp Beckett."

"Can't trip you up if you haven't done anything," Quinn said. "Who were those men who came for your mother?"

"I don't know," she said. "I figured she might've been foolin' around with one of them and things got out of hand. Either that or those boys promised her something to snort or smoke."

"She describe them to you?"

TJ shook her head. She slid down deeper into the seat, camo ball cap down in her eyes, jaws clenched and seeming to be fixated on something deep inside her.

"I'll get a deputy to take you home."

"No, thanks," TJ said. "I'd rather call a friend."

TJ didn't look sad or remorseful. The kid didn't look much like she felt anything. Quinn waited, not sure what else to say. He didn't want to worry her any more than he had to at this point. He needed to get an ID on that body before anything more could get done. And to get that moving, he'd have to work with that tub of shit Bruce Lovemaiden.

"Can I see whatever it was y'all found in Parsham?" TJ asked.

"I don't think you want to do that."

"Why?" TJ lifted her eyes to Quinn, her face softening and her mouth hanging open. "How bad was it?"

"Get some rest," Quinn said, standing up and motioning with his head for her to follow him out. "I'll swing by in the morning and give you an update. I'm real sorry, TJ. You're too young to go through a mess like this."

"My life's been a mess since I was born," TJ said. "Don't shed a tear for me, Sheriff."

Chester Pratt was out of the Mercedes and lighting up a new cigarette. "Y'all want to get the grits out of your mouth and speak a little English?"

Dusty didn't say a word, getting a little worried about Daddy and all the blood on that white towel. Momma Lennie sure was gonna have their ass when they got home. Bleeding out on that towel and being late for supper. One was bad enough but two in the same night was gonna mean hell to pay. That old woman would clock Daddy straight in the head with an iron skillet.

"You said that woman was giving you trouble," Dusty said.

"That's right."

"And you told us to get her mind right."

Pratt nodded. "But that was it, right?" Pratt said. "Gave her a rough talking-to and then let her be? Y'all must've scared her so damn bad that she left town."

Dusty could hear Daddy Flem's raspy breathing and without asking permission, grabbed him by the back of the belt and helped him back into the truck. He left the old truck door hanging open while he walked back to where Pratt was standing, smoking and looking like a cocky rich man. The kind of fella who'd never done a hard day's work in his life.

"What did y'all do?"

"Why'd you want us to give her a scare?"

"That's none of your business," Pratt said, sucking on a cigarette, burning it down to a nub and tossing it into the weeds. "Is it?"

"You see that blood coming out of my daddy?"

Pratt nodded. It had grown cold and the breathing and talking between them came out in clouds.

"That woman cut him bad," Dusty said. "Cut his ass down to the bone."

Pratt said he was real sorry about that. But Dusty could tell he didn't care. He's the kind of man who hires Mexican folks to do a job because they'll never sue your ass when they fall off the ladder and break their damn necks.

"If she done that to my daddy," Dusty said. "Just what do you think she'd do to you? I figure we done you a real favor, Mr. Pratt."

Pratt got real still in the low beams of Dusty's truck, squinting at Dusty's face, finally getting around to asking the question that he knew the answer to all along. Pratt walked toward Dusty and punched a finger in the middle of his chest. "What did y'all do?"

Dusty didn't answer. He grinned.

"What did y'all do?"

"Don't you worry none, Mr. Pratt," Dusty Nix said. "That bitch ain't gonna give you no more trouble. Me and Daddy got us a special place way out and far away from Tibbehah County where we toss out things that ain't no use to us anymore."

Dusty watched as Pratt turned around and yelled through his teeth, hammering his fists over and over on the back of that fine black car. The man looked to be plenty upset.

Holly and Ladarius were at the trailer with John Wesley when TJ got home. Holly had waited on the porch, arms open wide, offering her a big hug. It wasn't until then that the private idea of her mom being dead was really true for TJ. She leaned into Holly and cried, careful not to be too loud for John Wesley. Holly rubbed her shoulders and her neck, telling her how sorry she was and that she knew that her momma was in a better place, up in heaven looking at them and all their troubles.

"Troubles," TJ said.

"What did the sheriff say?"

"Wasn't just one sheriff," TJ said, wiping her face with her coat sleeve. "It was two of them. Some ole fat boy from Parsham County who'd been listening to a truckload of crap from Chester Pratt."

"Chester Pratt?" Holly said. "He says something about you, and then you'd tell the world about the money he stole."

"And who's gonna listen to that, Holly?" TJ said. "Shit. Not if they believe I'm the one who's done this. He's an adult in there with those sheriffs saying that Momma and me got rough and into it all the time and that she and Chester had the good and godly intention of sending me to the goddamn Wings of Faith up in Missouri."

"But that's a lie."

"I know it's a lie," TJ said. "But a lie told so damn big and nasty that it seems like the truth to those two sheriffs. I saw it in their faces."

"Why the hell didn't you tell them about Chester?"

"How am I gonna prove it?" she said. "Momma controlled that money until I turn eighteen. I'd have to show what was hers and what was mine and how she handed that over to her boyfriend. And even if they knew she did what she did, what does that mean? It means she was in love with Chester Pratt and bought into his goddamn liquor store. The things he said about me are much, much meaner. Me and her getting into it on account of Ladarius being a criminal? Or that I got mad as hell about being sent over to that Wings of Faith. I mention the money, it'd just give 'em more goddamn fuel. Those are stories those old boys could believe. I don't know. I don't know nothing right now. Only that Chester Pratt has turned on me and I'm about to go to jail."

"No way," Holly said. "No. That can't happen. We can't let them do that."

"Yep," TJ said. "I've seen those TV shows. Soon as they confirm that body they found is Momma they'll be coming for me. Goddamn it, Holly. What the hell can I do?"

"Get a lawyer," she said. "A real smart one like in one of those John Grisham movies. Maybe a good-lookin' one, too. Like Matthew McConaughey or Matt Damon."

"With what money?" TJ said. "Real lawyers like to get paid."

"Or you can just tell the truth," Holly said. "That Sheriff Colson is a stand-up man. Most of the women in town got their panties in a twist when he married that crazy hippie woman."

"Bullshit," TJ said. "His uncle was a crook. He's a crook. Easiest thing to do is make it look like I done it."

TJ closed her eyes and glanced through the window and into the trailer. Ladarius was sitting up with John Wesley, his arm around her little brother while they watched television, trying to keep the kid's mind occupied. Everything felt so normal and nice that she wanted to tear her guts out. Her mother was dead. Momma was dead. And people were still walking around, laughing, and watching television.

"What in the world do I tell John Wesley?"

"Maybe don't tell him a thing," Holly said.

"What?" TJ said. "What are you talking about?"

"We could run," Holly said. "We could run far the hell away from here. And never come back."

"What about your family and all your friends?"

"You're the only family that matters," Holly said. "Rest of 'em can go straight to hell."

"I don't know," TJ said. "My head's so damn fucked up right now."

"Grab what what's important and let's get out of Tibbehah County before first light."

EIGHT

Lillie had been up half the night, burning up the phone lines with Quinn back in Tibbehah County. Gina was dead, there was little to suggest otherwise, and Quinn needed a primer on Gina Byrd 101. Lillie did her best to help, although it had been years since they'd been close. She laid out all the past boyfriends, acquaintances, the druggies and the crooks, the lowlifes and respectable citizens of Tibbehah County that Gina would have, or might have, known. *Happy Hour crew at the Southern Star. Miss Donna Grace at the flower store where Gina worked part time. Maybe some friends from that new church that put on the big revival in the football stadium. Wasn't that preacher Ben Quick back in town?*

But from everything Lillie was hearing, she'd be looking right at her daughter, TJ. Quinn seemed to have doubts, but given Lillie's experience with the kid, she knew that girl had been a rough customer since she spit the pacifier out of her crib. What Quinn was telling her about the girl seeing goddamn Ladarius McCade and her mother wanting to stick her into a holy roller private school sounded like plenty motive to her.

"Sorry to hear about your friend," Florencia, Lillie's housekeeper, said.

Lillie thanked her as the stout Guatemalan woman cooked breakfast, humming to herself as she worked. Florencia had been working for her ever since she and Rose moved to Memphis and into a century-old bungalow in Cooper-Young. The bungalow was big and roomy, needing some work but still holding a lot of that classic Craftsman style with ornate windows and tapered columns. A soft rain fell out on the street and the kitchen smelled like bacon and pancakes.

"Very sad."

"That's okay, Florencia."

"How she die?"

"We don't know."

"Was she sick?"

"In a way," Lillie said. "She led a certain kind of life."

"She like to drink?"

"She liked to do a whole lot of everything."

"My sister in Guatemala like that," Florencia said. "She what we call a *mujer perdedora*."

"That Spanish for tramp?"

"Loose woman," Florencia said. "Very, very loose."

"I liked Gina Byrd a lot," Lillie said. "She was a whole lot of fun. But I swear you put a quarter in her slot and her ass would play Tammy Wynette."

"*Que?*"

"Don't worry about it," Lillie said. "If you can't laugh, you'll end up crying."

If it hadn't been for Florencia, there was no way Lillie could keep up her work with the marshals. She might have found a desk job somewhere, away from being a POD, a plain old deputy. And Lillie knew what it was like to ride the desk. She'd been sidelined for three months after she'd shot Fannie Hathcock in the back at the Golden Cherry Motel. And although that evil bitch, the queenpin of north Mississippi, appeared to have been going for a pistol and most surely deserved it, there had been a lengthy investigation and a whole lot of questions. The Mid-South media had even dubbed Lillie the U.S. Marshals Service's Calamity Jane, a name she liked and hated at the same time.

The last thing she'd wanted was any notoriety for a justified shooting, especially since there was a legion of truckers out there who looked at Fannie Hathcock as the benevolent mother of lap dances and cold beer on Highway 45. There was even some kind of redneck ballad written about the woman, "The Tears of Fannie." What complete horseshit.

"You like breakfast?" Florencia asked.

"No, ma'am," Lillie said, "I'll get a biscuit on the way in."

"Sit," Florencia said. "Eat. Two minutes."

Lillie shook her head but knew it was no use. Florencia didn't accept no as an answer.

Soon Rose bounded down the steps and into the kitchen, Lillie giving her a big hug before she took a seat at the counter. The little girl had come into Lillie's life almost ten years ago, during an investigation into a baby-trafficking operation right in Tibbehah County. Like Florencia, she'd been born in Guatemala and now appreciated both sausage and biscuits and *pupusas*.

"You carrying the Sig today?" Rose asked. The kid knew her guns.

She was brown-skinned with long black hair and bangs, dressed today in the blue polo shirt and khakis that were her school uniform.

"Yep," Lillie said. "Feels better on my hip. I don't care for the Glock they gave me."

"Y'all find that shitbird who set all those fires?"

Florencia turned around and whacked the spatula against the bar. "No, no, no."

Lillie winked at her daughter and said, "I don't know where she gets this stuff."

Rose giggled as Florencia offered a short prayer for both of them before flipping the pancakes and sliding them onto two blue plates.

"Is everything okay?" Rose asked. "I heard you crying last night."

"Must've been the TV," Lillie said.

"You sounded very upset," Rose said.

Lillie shook her head and cut into the pancakes. "Nope," Lillie said. "Florencia. Can I trouble you for a little more butter and syrup?"

She turned back to Rose and smiled. If she did anything as a mother, it was to keep the world she knew out of her damn home. That little girl had known a lifetime of evil before she'd even turned two. No reason for her to be associated with that shit anymore. The house was still and quiet, pleasant with the soft rain falling outside. Their new dog, a pit bull rescue, snored from across the room on a big, fat pillow.

"Pick me up from school today?" Rose said.

"I'll see what I can do."

"Maybe we can go to the zoo?" she said. "Or the Pink Palace?"

"Maybe."

Florencia widened her eyes again, the stout old woman doubtful Lillie would make it. Just as Lillie was set to argue, her phone buzzed with a north Mississippi area code. Even before Lillie answered, she knew what it was about and what they were going to ask her to do.

She'd been steeling herself for it. But damn, she never wanted to see Gina Byrd in that horrible condition.

Down in Tibbehah County, the rain had just rolled in as Quinn stood on the loading dock of the Jericho Farm & Ranch with a woman named Diane Tull. Quinn had known Diane for years, helping her get some closure on a violent crime that had happened back in 1977 involving his dad and a crew of miscreants called the Born Losers. She'd been friends with his sister Caddy, too, volunteering out at The River and always good to donate supplies to the mission, and even played and sang with the house band at the simple Sunday service in an old barn. Some folks said Diane Tull looked and sounded just like Jessi Colter and Quinn couldn't disagree.

"This sucks," Diane said.

"Yes, ma'am."

"You know I was Gina's AA sponsor?"

"That's why I'm here so early."

"Caddy tell you?" she said. "Damn. I sure miss your sister. I thought someone would step up and take over The River when she left. But that's not gonna happen. Breaks my heart to see that old barn and the land around it turn to shit. No one can do what your sister did for all these people."

"Maybe you could," Quinn said.

"With all my extra time running this old seed and feed?" Diane said. "Hell. Glad to help out some. But what Caddy did wasn't a job. It was a calling."

The Jericho Farm & Ranch sold about everything you needed to survive—fishing gear, shotgun shells, work boots, squirrel traps, vegetable seeds, and fence posts. It was still a few months away from planting season, but Diane was ready to go with stacks of topsoil, manure, and fertilizer. Diane was a good twenty years older than Quinn, with dark skin and black hair streaked with white. Watching the rain from the loading dock, Diane lit a cigarette.

"I wish Gina had called me," Diane said. "I might could've helped. If she needed money, I would've given her some. Damn. This is horrible. Just horrible. Have you talked with Chester Pratt? You know they've gotten real close?"

"I spoke with Chester last night."

"And what did he say?" Diane said.

"A lot," Quinn said. "Man likes to talk."

"Did he say anything about Gina backsliding?" Diane said. "I saw her two, three weeks ago and she wasn't doing so great. She'd been clean and sober for six months but looked headed for a fall."

"I got over to the Southern Star last night," Quinn said. "Spoke to some folks who knew her. Said she'd been a real regular since New Year's."

"Lord God."

A white van pulled up and they both watched as the Stinson family, all nine of them, climbed out and headed into Farm & Ranch. The wife and three girls all had long hair down their backs. The four boys all looked pasty and pimply, like they hadn't seen the sun for a long time. The family was part of some kind of Christian sect that only allowed homeschooling and apparently was against birth control. They weren't Amish, but they weren't far from it.

Quinn waved to the man, always forgetting his first name and just referring to him as Brother Stinson. The whole family hustled inside to load up on supplies.

"Did Gina say she was having some trouble with Chester?" Quinn asked.

"None I heard," Diane said. "Hell, you know Chester is about my age. Too damn old for a woman like Gina. But he's not bad looking, got a nice head of hair and good teeth. He seemed to land on his feet after screwing up every business he tried to open up. He was always taking Gina on trips over to Birmingham or down to Gulf Shores. He had a condo. Maybe a boat down there? She was always posting pictures about it."

"But no trouble?" Quinn asked. "Nothing she ever discussed with you?"

"You mean was he ever violent?"

Quinn nodded.

"Damn, Quinn," Diane said. "How long have we been friends? You know I'd tell you if I knew anything at all. I never heard Chester Pratt being rough a day in his life. Have you? What kept me awake all night is how I might've messed this up. I should've kept checking up on her. Because that's it, isn't it? You think she got hooked in with some rough boys? Drugs and all that."

"Her daughter says Gina got into it with two men outside the bar," he said. "This was three nights ago. Have you heard anything about that?"

"Nope," Diane said. "But you and I both know Gina, God love her, would jump into any car with anybody if she thought they were about to take her to party. Damn, Quinn. It's hard to say all this stuff about her. Dragging Gina down doesn't help anybody."

"Knowing what you know sure helps me."

Diane smoked the cigarette a little more and swallowed, looking to be gathering her composure before she said whatever she was about to say. The wind blew across plastic sheeting around the greenhouse and the rain started to fall a little harder.

"That TJ Byrd sure is a piece of work," Diane said.

"Yes, ma'am."

"You call me ma'am again and I'll kick you off my property," she said. "I was still in high school when your stuntman daddy was jumping over cars to impress all the women in town."

"About TJ."

"Gina tried and tried with that one," she said. "The little boy, John Wesley, ain't easy himself. But TJ has been giving Gina a lot of trouble for so many years. You know who her daddy was?"

"Jerry Jeff Valentine," Quinn said. "He's well remembered at the sheriff's office."

"And everything Jerry Jeff Valentine was into?"

"TJ believes my uncle found him passed out in that creek," Quinn said. "And that he let him die."

"Maybe," Diane said. "Can't say I blame Sheriff Beckett. That man had a mean streak on him a mile wide. And I swear, that girl is exactly like him. You can listen to whoever you like about Gina and drugs and men and trouble. But no one gave that woman more of a heartache than her own daughter. I know for a fact that girl once gave her a black eye."

"What might've happened to Gina is a whole lot worse."

"You mean that she was chopped into little pieces and tossed in a trash barrel?" Diane asked. "Yeah. Half the town knows that already. You need to make a little more progress, Sheriff. This whole county is watching you on this one."

Johnny Stagg watched the morning news out of Tupelo in his back office at the Rebel while Midnight Man swept the floors and bundled up the trash. Stagg remembered a time when old Buddy and Kay Bain would knock out classic country hits on the *Mornin'* show. Now it wasn't nothing but mayhem and murder, maybe a little bit about the weather and prep sports. Stagg turned his chair around to the bank of little TV monitors where he could watch the comings and goings at the truck stop. With a flick of the controller, he could see every face at every pump, every customer eating grits and eggs at the diner, and even the faces and quick hands at the two main registers. Used to be a time when he had his eye on the honey pot out back of the Rebel, a place called the Booby Trap. But the new Johnny Stagg, the reformed Johnny Stagg who'd had a come-to-Jesus moment at the federal lockup in Montgomery, was way past that. His life was now about feeding, fueling, and family fun.

"That man Bishop come looking for you," Midnight Man said. The big black man's voice somewhere between a whisper and a croak.

"What'd he say?"

"Said Chester Pratt was in trouble," Midnight Man said. "His punch was that lady got kilt over in Parsham."

"You kidding me?"

"No, sir," Midnight Man said, lifting out the plastic bag from the trash can and cinching it closed. "That's what he said."

"Well," Stagg said. "Don't that beat all."

Stagg turned from the security cameras back to the main TV and clicked around a little until he found the local news again. He had to sit through some fat Yankee boy telling him that more cold and rain were expected for the week and then some news about a teacher in Aberdeen whipping out his peter in gym class, a tractor trailer jack-knifing over in New Albany, and the State basketball team barely beating those Gamecocks from South Carolina. After some local hi-jinks from Nolan Brothers auto, this one about an old Southern gentleman talking to a man in a gorilla suit, the station cut back over to a live shot of a woman reporter outside the Bundren Funeral Home in Jericho. The woman said the body hadn't been IDed but the Parsham sheriff said foul play was suspected.

"Where'd you hear this woman was friendly with Chester?"

"Everybody," Midnight Man said. "Heard she was a Byrd."

"Which one?"

"Don't know."

"You hear Chester killed her?"

"No, sir," Midnight Man said. "Folks just say that was his woman."

"Damn," Stagg said. "I guess he's going to be looking for sympathies and forgiveness for a while?"

Midnight Man grunted and left the office. Stagg turned off the television and stared up at the monitors. He kept his eyes on the new fella working the till at the diner, watching him make time with one of the waitresses, and then zoomed in on his hands while he made change. Stagg knew every way in the world that the help could cornhole you at a restaurant. He wasn't sure how in the hell this place survived without him. He heard that Fannie Hathcock was a pretty slick customer, but her mind seemed to be more on the poontang and pharmaceuticals than the meat and potatoes at the old Rebel.

Stagg reached over to a silver candy dish and reached for a fresh peppermint. He unwrapped it, plucked it into his mouth, and punched up a well-known number on his phone. After a few rings, a familiar voice answered.

"What in the holy goddamn hell is going on over there?"

"Dead girl," the voice said. "Woman named Gina Byrd. You know her?"

"No, sir," Stagg said. "I most certainly do not. But I know her people. This some kind of domestic situation?"

"I ain't real sure," the man said. "Never really seen nothing like it. That woman was cut up in so many pieces, she looked like chum falling out of that barrel."

"She was in a barrel?"

"Oh, yes, sir," the man said. "Someone sliced and diced her ass and tossed her in there with some bleach. We took her over to Tibbehah to get looked at. Maybe get an ID, although we're pretty sure we know what we got."

"Why the hell'd you bring that mess over here?" Stagg said. "Shit, son. This is your goddamn problem. Don't be trackin' dogshit to my doorstep."

"Our coroner's on vacation," the man said. "Took his wife up to Kentucky to take a look at that Noah's Ark they built at the Museum of Creation."

"Christ Almighty."

"Is that a problem?"

Stagg crunched on the candy for a moment and then cleared his throat. "I guess I was hoping to keep a hard, fast line between Tibbehah and Parsham."

"That won't be no trouble," the man said. "You got my word on it, Mr. Stagg."

"Y'all thinking this is the boyfriend?"

"No, sir," the man said. "Unless you want me to. I think it's the woman's daughter. Seems y'all's sheriff ain't buying into it."

"That Quinn Colson is known for his argumentative ways," Stagg said, reaching for another candy. "Didn't have to be like it was between me and him. He got rid of me and you saw what he got, that red-headed crazy-ass bitch who nearly killed him."

"Why'd you ask about the boyfriend?"

Stagg sucked on the new candy and looked up at the ceiling, a dark water stain spreading around two of the ceiling tiles. It hadn't taken long for that woman to turn the best truck stop in Mississippi into a redneck shithole.

"I may have done some business with him," Stagg said. "At one time or another. Hate to see that boy jammed up too bad."

"You want me to keep you posted, Mr. Stagg?"

"You know I sure would appreciate that," Stagg said. "Sheriff Lovemaiden."

"That smell gets you," Ophelia Bundren said. "Doesn't it?"

Quinn had walked out the side portico of the Bundren Funeral Home and back to the tailgate of the truck. He'd set fire to a cigar just as soon as he hit the door, more than glad to inhale the smoke and fresh air. The rain had stopped but the skies were still dark and gray. An ice-cold wind blew across the slick parking lot.

"Pretty rough."

"Yes, ma'am," Quinn said, drawing on the cigar and leaning against his truck. Ophelia watched him, quiet and reassuring, looking a lot different than she had when they'd been together. She seemed happy and calm, healthy and fit, with smiling brown eyes and short brown hair, a gold wedding band now on her finger. Ophelia was beautiful, and one of the smartest and most resourceful women he'd ever known, but he'd made a real mess of things by not being able to stay away from Anna Lee Amsden. The end of it had come months before he'd met Maggie, Ophelia throwing a steak knife at him, sticking in the kitchen wall a foot from Quinn's head.

When Quinn complimented her aim, she said that, actually, she'd missed.

"Not sure a fingerprint will be possible," Ophelia said. "State folks will be here within the hour."

"What do you say?"

"It's a woman," she said. "Seems to be the age of Gina Byrd. But legally, I can't say unless I can perform a full autopsy. Dental records. I figure the person who did this knew how that all works. In a case like this, no one wants to see that locally."

"You do a damn fine job, Ophelia," Quinn said. "We're lucky to have you."

"I'm glad y'all didn't ask her kid to see this," Ophelia said. "That would mess up that girl's mind for life."

"You did your best to make sense of what you had."

"Wasn't easy," Ophelia said. "Hardest jigsaw puzzle I ever worked. And I wasn't authorized to stitch her back together."

"What did Lillie say?"

Ophelia watched him, wandering up to the other side of the tailgate and leaning in. Under a long black coat, she had on the familiar black pantsuit and cream silk top that was the uniform of her business. Even a little name tag on her right lapel. "Lillie didn't say much of anything," Ophelia said. "After you left, she and I stood there for a moment. She looked at everything I showed her. I asked her if she'd seen what she needed, and she just nodded and asked where to find the bathroom. I'm pretty sure she threw up."

"That doesn't sound like Lillie."

Ophelia offered a weak smile from across the tailgate. She shrugged and looked back over her shoulder at the funeral home.

"You doing okay?" Quinn asked.

"I am," she said. "Congrats on Halley. With you and Maggie as parents, she's bound to be a pistol."

"She is," Quinn said. "Quick and observant as hell. Already taking in this whole crazy world."

"Funny how that goes," she said. "Isn't it?"

"What's that?"

"Life," Ophelia said. "People are here and then they're not. And then new people move in. Things change. Time comes and goes. But this town, this county, never seems to go anywhere."

Quinn smiled at her and they locked eyes for a long moment.

"I don't have any regrets," she said.

"Me, either," Quinn said.

Ophelia turned as Lillie walked fast across the parking lot, her black blazer billowing around her to show the silver Sig on her hip, a lit cigarette in hand. Quinn thought Lillie had quit smoking years ago.

"Jesus Fucking God," Lillie said.

"Sorry to get you down here, Lil," Quinn said.

"Wish I hadn't had breakfast," Lillie said. "Goddamn. Who the hell could do something like that?"

Quinn looked across the truck bed to Ophelia. Lillie hung on his tailgate like someone who'd gotten seasick and was trying to find their legs. She sucked on the cigarette and blew out a big plume of smoke. Her eyes were bloodshot and her face had gone pale.

"You sure it's her?" Quinn asked.

"Goddamn right that's Gina Byrd," Lillie said. "I know."

"Then you recognized it?" Ophelia said.

"Recognized what?" Quinn asked.

"Tattoo," Lillie said. "Right hipbone. Gina got it when we were in eleventh grade. A goddamn bluebird. Ain't that something?"

NINE

I know one damn thing," said Ladarius's cousin Domino, hand on
her big hip, frown on her face, loaded with plenty of that Memphis
attitude. "Y'all can't stay here. I got enough legal problems of my own
without y'all tracking bloody footprints into this house."

"I didn't kill my mother," TJ said, trying to remain friendly and
calm since the woman let them crash at her apartment last night.
"Someone's trying to pin this shit on me and I didn't care to stick
around and let them do it."

"Mm-hmm," Domino said. "Is that right? What I heard on TV
was some real fucked-up shit. Folks saying your momma got dismembered. Y'all know what in the hell *dismembered* means? Means
cut up like a motherfucking Tyson chicken. I mean. *Goddamn*."

Domino lived in a run-down apartment complex near the airport
on Winchester, sharing the space with a boyfriend named D'Shawn
who sold weed when he wasn't loading and unloading planes over at
FedEx. The boyfriend was on the late shift and Ladarius promised
they'd all be gone by the time he got back. TJ and Ladarius had slept
on the couch while Holly slept on the floor before turning on the television and watching the morning news. John Wesley, used to chaos

and crazy, was asleep in a big overstuffed green chair by the kitchen, tucked in a fleece blanket decorated with faces of WWE superstars. The poor kid still didn't know his momma was dead.

"Sorry I can't help y'all," Domino said. "But you know. Things are tight."

"We appreciate you taking us in," Holly said, looking up from the television. *Live at 9* with Alex and Marybeth. "I sure didn't want to sleep in my momma's van. Not in Memphis."

"And what's wrong with Memphis?" Domino asked. She had on a black midriff shirt with the word DIVA written in gold glitter, beaded strands doing their best to cover up her big belly.

Ladarius said his cousin worked days at Dixie Belles, a titty bar just down the road. TJ surprised as hell when she'd first opened the door, the woman short and fat with a long weave with red highlights. She looked like the kind of gal that could break a man's pelvis during a lap dance. The apartment was cluttered and dirty, with old yellow carpet and mismatched furniture that seemed to TJ like it had been picked out of the trash. Busted-ass fake leather couch and a cracked glass coffee table with two empty Papa John's boxes left from last night.

"Time to get up," TJ said, touching her little brother's shoulder. "We got to go."

The little boy opened his eyes and then shut them again. "Go where?"

TJ didn't have an answer as she didn't have any plan at all. The only thought she'd had last night was just drive, get the hell out of Tibbehah County, get the hell out of Mississippi, and then maybe some kind of light or roadside inspiration would show them the way. A billboard. A message in the clouds. A song on the radio. Ladarius kept on promising that Domino was going to be a big help, that she was tied in with some real powerful people. Something about a man she knew named Marquis Sledge who ran South Memphis. But when they rolled up on her place at two a.m., TJ knew it was another one of Ladarius's lies, or what he called harmless bullshit.

As soon as Domino left the room, TJ turned to Ladarius and asked if he'd gotten any money.

"Hundred bucks," Ladarius said. "All Domino's got."

"And what about you?" TJ said.

"Ten bucks," he said.

TJ shook her head, feeling for the first time in this whole fucked-up week that she just might cry. Thinking about what her momma looked like right now, chopped into a million pieces, and the hell that TJ might have to pay even though she hadn't done a damn thing. That hadn't made her sad, only angry that her momma had put her in such a tight spot, running with men who wanted to use her up till there was nothing left. Leaving TJ with no one to help them but their worthless aunt and fucking stealing and lying Chester Pratt. John Wesley tugging at her coat, looking up at her and asking which way they were headed.

"I got people in Chicago," Ladarius said.

"I'm not going to fucking Chicago," Holly Harkins said, quickly turning away from the TV. "We'd freeze our asses off. Not to mention, those folks are plain mean and crazy up there."

"Where you want to go then, Holly Harkins?" Ladarius said. "Disney World? Want to ride that Pirates of the Caribbean? Run around Fantasyland? Maybe hop on Dumbo's back for flight up into the clouds? Yeah, we'll just roll on down and see the big mouse and party with all the money we got."

"You know what the hell I'm getting at," Holly said, turning away. Never being one for a fight. "Just not Chicago. It's too damn cold. Okay?"

"Y'all shut your ass up and think," TJ said. "Think. We need gas bad. We ran into Memphis on fumes last night. And maybe something to eat. After that, we'll get as far as we can get and look at where we are then. If we need to, me and Ladarius can get some money."

"Please," Holly said. "I thought you both had a come to Jesus this summer and had given up all the break-ins and thieving."

Ladarius grinned and nodded, agreeing with his girl. TJ knew that if things got real rough, no one was better for a little smash and grab at a house or a fancy car along the way, maybe trading up from that old minivan for something that the police wouldn't recognize. Even though she and Ladarius were as different as different could be, a hard-ass redneck and smooth black kid from down in Sugar Ditch, they were survivors. If they had to steal, the Lord would most certainly understand.

"Come on now, y'all," Domino said, standing by the apartment door. "Y'all need to get your shit and get gone. Sorry, cuz. But please don't make no trouble for me."

TJ helped John Wesley to his feet and told him to use the bathroom before they hit the road. The boy did as he was told as Holly gathered up their stuff. Domino hugged Ladarius as he headed out the door but blocked the way with her big ass as TJ tried to follow.

"You better not be lying to me, girly," she said.

"I don't lie."

"Looks like you already pussy-whipped my favorite cousin," Domino said, hands back on her hips. "You must be laying down some sweet stuff to drive that boy straight into the gates of hell."

"I love him."

"Yeah?" Domino said. "Looks like you already fucked up his mind. Just don't go and fuck up that boy's life. Ladarius is a good kid with a good heart. I don't want to see his ass down in Parchman anytime soon."

"We didn't do it," she said.

"Mm-hmm."

John Wesley walked out and TJ helped her little brother into his coat. Domino cleared the doorway and let them pass out the door and back out into the cold. Rain fell across the parking lot in the grayish morning light.

"Better not be lying," Domino said as TJ turned and headed down the steps. "Cops ain't shit compared to an angry black woman on your narrow ass."

Kenny was parked along the sloped dirt road to the trailer, looking nervous and apologetic as Quinn got out of the Big Green Machine and into the rain. As one of Quinn's oldest deputies, Kenny was well aware he'd screwed up. Quinn didn't have to berate him for letting TJ Byrd sneak out sometime last night, as Kenny was beating himself up plenty. He told Quinn that he hadn't seen a vehicle come or go on the county road where he'd parked. They both knew the girl, her little brother, and two friends must've snuck out and rendezvoused a decent distance away.

"Shit, Quinn," Kenny said. "I don't know what to say."

Kenny was bald and round, with a neatly trimmed mustache and goatee that had recently grown gray. He'd been one of Quinn's first hires after he was elected sheriff ten years ago and cleaned out his uncle's old crew. There might've been better deputies, but few more loyal and steadfast than good ole Kenny. Quinn had personally witnessed the man bury both his parents after the big tornado hit town, change into his uniform, and report back to the work the same day.

"Maybe someone's still up there," Quinn said.

"No, sir," Kenny said. "I checked."

"But given what happened to their momma," Quinn said. "Maybe we need to get that door opened up and check inside. Just to make sure the kids are okay."

Kenny winked at Quinn, getting the idea of what he had in mind. If Quinn had to run back to town and get a warrant, it would eat up a few hours. If TJ did kill her mother, maybe she left something behind. Or at least, maybe they'd find something to show where those kids were headed. Either way, they needed a look inside that trailer and around the property.

He and Kenny walked up to the top of the hill and mounted the cobbled-together two-by-fours and concrete blocks that made up the porch. There were no trees, bushes, or vegetation in the dirt yard, only the trailer on a little patch of land that appeared to have been scraped clean a long while back. Kenny knocked a few times while Quinn checked the windows. The windows were dirty and it was tough to see, but after a minute or two, Quinn found the door unlocked and they both walked inside the trailer.

The room was spare and not too dirty, with an old tan couch pulled out into a bed toward a TV silently playing one of those *Fast and Furious* movies. Vin Diesel racing down a mountain pass to rescue a woman on top of an oil tank trailer.

"Glad they got the whole franchise back on track after the one set in Japan," Kenny said. "Did you see it? About them rice burners sliding all over Tokyo?"

"Must've missed that one," Quinn said.

The small kitchen was bare except for a box of Cap'n Crunch. Quinn checked the refrigerator to find it empty except for a half bottle of Sam's Cola. Someone had cleaned out the sink, wiped off the counters, and put away the mismatched cups and dishes. Whatever had been said about TJ Byrd, she wasn't a slob.

"Well," Kenny said. "You didn't miss much of nothing. I mean you can't have no *Fast and Furious* film without Vin Diesel. Although I did like that Paul Walker. Damn shame what happened to him, his buddy running that Porsche into a light pole."

"Kenny?"

"Yes, sir."

"You mind checking the outbuildings?" Quinn asked. "There's a barn in back and a couple sheds."

Kenny nodded and hustled out the front door as Quinn walked over and flicked off the television, Vin Diesel now driving backward alongside the truck, the truck driver shooting at him.

Quinn found what he believed was TJ's room first, just enough space for a single bed stripped of sheets and bedding and a makeshift desk from sawhorses and a piece of plywood. Every inch of the walls had been covered in a collage of posters from before Quinn's time: Def Leppard, GNR, even Mötley Crüe. He wondered why in the hell a seventeen-year-old girl would care about all that ancient stuff. The whole room like some kind of crazy mosaic of thirty-year-old movies, rock bands, and more recent newspaper clippings. LOCAL MAN DIES IN CAR CRASH. SERVICE HELD FOR VALENTINE.

He checked her desk and under her mattress, knowing it would take some time to comb through the entire trailer. Just as he was about to search Gina Byrd's bedroom, Kenny ran into the trailer out of breath, his face shiny with sweat.

"Got something to show you, Sheriff."

"Can it wait?"

"No, sir," he said. "Sure can't. I was careful not to touch nothing in that old shed."

They headed back out into the light rain, Quinn's boots loud on the wood steps, and quickly rounded behind the rusted trailer. Kenny pointed to the open door of an old service shed like the kind you buy at a Home Depot or Sears to fill with a riding mower and toolboxes. He handed Quinn his Maglite and Quinn stepped forward and shone the beam onto a concrete pad stained with oil. What he spotted about took the breath from him. He stepped back, making sure he didn't make a mess of anything around that shed.

"That's blood, ain't it?" Kenny asked.

"Yes, sir."

"You see the hacksaw, too?"

Quinn didn't answer, scanning with the Maglite around the shed until he saw the hacksaw not far from the bloody clothes and that one pink, high-heeled boot. Sparkly rhinestones all over the shaft.

"Killed her own mother," Kenny said. "That's some cold-blooded shit, Sheriff."

"She burned evidence before," Quinn said. "Why'd she leave this mess?"

"Maybe there wasn't time," Kenny said. "Those kids hightailed it right quick."

"I'll talk to Lovemaiden and let him know what we found," Quinn said. "No reason to fight over this case right now. That can come after we track down those kids."

"You gonna charge that girl?"

"Well, shit," Quinn said. "I don't believe TJ Byrd has left me with much choice."

Holly was driving the minivan, everyone else asleep as she crossed the Mississippi River and into Arkansas. They could've gone east or north or so many directions, but the signs seemed to be leading her the fastest way out of Memphis and onto some new land, some new territory like in those old Western movies she watched with her granddaddy. TJ rode shotgun with her, leaning against the passenger door, using her blue jean jacket as a pillow, as Holly flipped around the radio dial. There were bellowing black preachers, Mexican music, top country hits, and hot rap out of Memphis. She didn't catch anything that sounded like the news except for some man screaming about how the End Times were right around the corner. Right around the corner? Men like that have been peddling that story for two thousand years. She finally shut the damn thing off as she drove through West Memphis, all the gas stations and truck stops jam-packed early that morning.

They'd filled up when they left Ladarius's cousin's apartment, bought chicken biscuits, some Cokes, Red Bulls, and a chocolate milk for John Wesley. The boy had crawled into the far backseats and made himself a nest with all the boxes of assorted shit TJ had tossed into the van. Somewhere along the way, they'd run over their cell phones and tossed the busted parts in a dumpster. They all hated to do it but knew they'd probably been tracked since leaving Tibbehah County.

Holly worried what her parents were going to say and do once she got home. She hadn't hesitated leaving with TJ for a hot second and now would be the one to get sent up to that Wings of Faith in Missouri. First thing they'd do is sit her ass down with one of Pastor Ben Quick's folks to talk about a biblical solution to their girl's wild ways. But doing this, riding out with Ladarius and TJ, didn't feel wild at all. It felt like the only thing she could do. If she couldn't stand tall with her best friend in the whole damn world, what use was she?

The warm air blowing from the heaters scattered TJ's blonde hair across her face. She'd always been the pretty one. Her face reminded Holly of a china doll, so fine and pale, a perfect upturned nose and those intense-as-hell blue eyes. Her lips slightly parted, the raspy sound of her breath.

Holly kept it right at sixty, making sure they didn't go one mile over the limit. Ladarius said the law would be onto them soon, and on the next stop, they'd need to change out the license plates. Maybe even find a new car. That's the only thing that gave Holly a little pause. A new car. Just what would she do with Momma's minivan? Her family had had this damn thing for as long as Holly could remember. The headrests still had tiny TV screens in them where she'd watched her cartoons and Disney movies, feeling so safe in the child's seat, riding up high around Tibbehah and on long trips to her grandmother's over in Lee County, Alabama.

"Where are we?"

She looked into the rearview, the sun glowing a bright white behind them. It was John Wesley.

"We're in Arkansas."

"Where we headed?"

"I don't know."

"Why'd we leave Jericho?" John Wesley said. "My sister won't tell me nothin'."

"Just taking a road trip, kid," Holly said, trying to keep her tone nice and light. "You ever been this far from home?"

"Nope."

"Well, you're gonna see some pretty country out here," she said. "Folks in Arkansas don't cut down every tree they see. They got lakes and forests, beautiful green hills. You're gonna like this a hell of a lot."

That seemed to satisfy the boy for a bit. And Holly peeked a quick glance over at TJ, still fierce as hell in her sleep. A little blonde hair caught in that perfect mouth of hers. Holly reached over and pulled it away, her hand brushing TJ's, feeling a funny pang in her stomach, as she caught the wheel again, driving west with no real plan of what the next day, the next few hours, might hold.

"Momma's gonna be mad," John Wesley said.

The kid wide-ass awake now, sitting up and peering over the bench seats where Ladarius was laid out.

"No, she won't."

"Hell yes, she will," John Wesley said. "Momma said if TJ did anything else bad, she was gonna send her up north to some Bible school. She said TJ got to be a mess because she skipped out on church too many times to fool around with boys."

Holly laughed and shook her head. Although she couldn't argue with what he said.

"It's gonna be just fine," Holly said. "Don't you worry about nothing, John Wesley. You hungry? I got an extra chicken biscuit up here. And half a Coke."

She lifted her eyes to the rearview again and saw the boy give a big enthusiastic nod. She reached for the paper sack on the console and passed it back to him. Just then, she heard a big tumble and clunk under the hood, a hot revving sound coming from the engine. She checked the gauges, just like her daddy taught her, and didn't see anything. The minivan kept on trucking along past another exit and more big billboards for the ole-time country cookin' at the Cracker Barrel and signs for folks who had got themselves hooked on meth.

When she looked back down, the temperature gauge had shot up in the red. Warning lights flashing on her dash. Holly cussed some and slowed down the car, not sure what else she could do. Ladarius was up now, wiping the sleep from his eyes, and looking over Holly's shoulder.

"Goddamn, girl," he said. "You better pull over."

"We can't stop," Holly said. "Not now."

"Holly, this old piece of shit is about to blow its engine," he said. "We don't have no choice."

The McCade family had a forty-acre slice of property down in Sugar Ditch shared by dozens of families but ruled by one woman: Della Mae McCade. The McCade land was two miles south of the Quick

Stop and another three miles down County Road 121. The trailers and houses stood back to back, winding along a curved road that some say was the best in the county. Any supervisor who wanted to turn out the vote in Sugar Ditch had always made sure of it. There was a machine shop and appliance repair on the land, an illegal pool hall, and a meat processor. Miss Della Mae's house sat at the top of the hill, appearing large and almost feudal to Lillie Virgil as she wheeled onto the smooth black asphalt of the McCade compound.

Miss McCade had been running things, taking rent from her people and keeping order since her husband, "Big Jack," died about twenty years ago. Lillie liked the old woman and respected her hard-edged cynicism of the law. When she walked up to the door of the home, a fine brick ranch with black shutters and a concrete porch, Miss Della Mae was already there, standing in front of a glass storm door, hands crossed over her chest and a scowl on her face.

"What is it?" she said, cracking the door slightly.

"Wonder if I can have a minute of your time, Miss McCade."

"I heard you was gone, Lillie Virgil," she said. "Quit the sheriff's office and moved up to Memphis."

"I joined the U.S. Marshals Service," Lillie said, showing her the badge that hung around her neck.

"And what's that have to do with me?" Della Mae said.

"Came to talk to you about your grandson," Lillie said. "Ladarius."

"His momma lives down the hill," Della Mae said, pointing. "That boy ain't none of my concern."

"Maybe I could come in for a moment," Lillie said. "You've always been a big help to me."

The old woman had let the door go from her fingers and stood there behind the glass, staring, studying on things. She finally shrugged, cracked the door, and nodded Lillie into her home. "Well," she said. "Come on, then."

Lillie hadn't been assigned the case yet. But she would be soon. Lillie heard what Quinn had found in that shed after those kids disappeared, knowing it wouldn't be too long before a warrant would be posted on the NCIC. Lillie had already put in a request to her boss, the Old Man up in Memphis, that she had prior knowledge of the Byrd family and the case and would like to be temporarily assigned to the North Mississippi Task Force. She wasn't sure how he'd react but hoped he'd grant her request as soon as the order popped up.

Della Mae led her into her sitting room, taking a seat in a high-backed green chair that looked as if it was made of velvet. She had on an elaborate housecoat of red, blue, and yellow paisley and wore large, dangling gold earrings. Her hair looked fresh from the beauty parlor, stiff and high in black and grays, and her nails bright red, at least an inch long, and sharp as talons.

"Why you looking for the boy?"

"I think he's in trouble."

"That boy's always in trouble," she said. "Ain't his fault. It's the fault of Mr. Dupuy. That man's not welcome here. And he should've known to keep to himself and away from my grandbaby."

"Some folks think his girlfriend killed her mother."

Della Mae McCade nodded, making a little sound with her tongue, and cocked her head.

"Y'all think Ladarius caught up in that mess?"

"I know it," Lillie said. "He left town with the girl."

"That girl running from the law?"

"Yes, ma'am," Lillie said, leaning forward in the chair, hands clasped between her knees with the Sig digging into her hip. "Her name's TJ Byrd."

"Her people that Byrd family?"

Lillie nodded.

"Lord God Almighty," Della Mae said. "Why would a good boy

like Ladarius go and get himself mixed up with a trashy white family like that? He was raised better."

Lillie didn't answer. A younger black woman about Lillie's age poked her head in from the other room. She was dressed in black leggings with a long red top that hit down below her waist. When she saw Lillie, the woman gave a big grin and waved.

"Oh, hey, Lillie," said Devynn McCade. "What you doing back in town?"

"Gina Byrd's dead," Lillie said. "I came down to ID the body."

"Oh, Lillie," Devynn said, the smile gone. "I'm so sorry. I know y'all were close."

Della Mae's eyes hadn't left Lillie, the older woman sitting erect with her long, manicured nails clicking together. The room smelled like French perfume and down-home cooking. Della Mae was known for her family cookouts and homemade tamales as well as for dispensing her own justice on folks who crossed her. Devynn took a seat on a nearby couch, staying as quiet as her mother expected.

"You say Ladarius is in trouble?" Della Mae said.

"Yes, ma'am."

"And that you're the one gonna go look for his dumb ass?"

"Yes, ma'am," Lillie said. "That's my job."

Della Mae looked to Devynn, lifting her chin. Devynn looked at her mother and nodded. Lillie had known Devynn for about as long as she'd known Gina Byrd.

"Can you bring him back unharmed?"

"I can do my best."

"I need more than that, Miss Virgil."

Lillie swallowed and nodded. "All I can offer at the moment, ma'am."

The room grew still. Lillie could hear music coming from the kitchen, a gospel station out of Holly Springs playing a song that kept on repeating, "something about the name." Lillie smiled at Miss Della Mae and then over at Devynn. She kept quiet knowing that the old woman was thinking on what she'd said.

"All right, then, Lillie Virgil," Della Mae McCade said. "You gave me your word. If that boy's headed anywhere, it's Memphis. He's real close with his cousin Domino."

TEN

Chester Pratt saw Johnny Stagg's cherry red Cadillac El Dorado from across the highway, hanging there at the exit to the Rebel Truck Stop like it just might be headed this way. Pratt walked away from the liquor store and out into the rain, hoping to get in his car and out onto the road before Stagg saw him. But damn if Pratt didn't still have the key in the door when that old ElDo crossed the street and headed right for Bluebird Liquors. If he piled in now, Stagg would know he was being avoided. But if he stayed, Stagg might give him more trouble than he could handle at the moment. Pratt waved as the red Cadillac swung into the parking lot, the driver's window sliding down and Stagg offering a big toothy grin.

"Sure got us a cat strangler today," Stagg said.

Pratt stood there in the cold without an umbrella, getting soaked to the damn bone.

"Been trying to reach you, son."

"Yes, sir," Pratt said. "Had some personal matters to tend to."

"How about you hop in for a little ride," Stagg said. "Get on out of the rain. Me and you need to talk."

"It's not a good time, Mr. Stagg," Pratt said.

Stagg seemed to grin even wider, his teeth as big as tombstones.

"Ain't a request, son."

Pratt, knowing he was beat, nodded and reached for the door handle, crawling into the black leather before realizing that the man called Bishop was seated directly behind him. Pratt shook his head at the sheer stupidity of his situation as the windshield wipers ticktocked across the glass. He sure was fucked now.

"You know Mr. Bishop," Stagg said.

Pratt didn't answer, not liking at all the proximity to the man who'd busted up thousands of dollars of Pappy Van Winkle's finest. The hot blowing air smelled like cigarettes and sweat and a little of the cherry air freshener that hung from Stagg's rearview mirror. Stagg let his foot off the brake and they rolled out of the lot and onto Jericho Road, heading away from Highway 45 and moving toward town.

"Where we going?" Pratt said.

"Oh, just a little drive in the country," Stagg said. "Sometimes I take this ole ElDo for a crawl in the afternoon. I appreciate the opportunity to see the miracle of this lovely county we live in. After five years behind prison walls, you start aching for that kind of scenery."

Pratt didn't answer. Stagg's radio was tuned low, and he just made out the sounds of Brenda Lee, "Break It to Me Gently." Pratt kept his hands in his lap as Stagg drove, feeling that man Bishop's breath on his neck. It smelled like the liver and onion platter over at the Rebel.

"I hope you aren't angry about Mr. Bishop's little visit," Stagg said, effortlessly driving the big old car. He steered with one hand, half his face shadowed, tapping his fingers in time with the tinkling piano. "He ain't a drinking man and mighta gone a little too far."

"I've had a lot on my mind."

"I understand," Stagg said as he approached the old rusted water tower looming over Jericho and the town square. "Sure am sorry about what I'm hearing about that Byrd woman. I understand y'all were kind of friendly?"

"She was my girlfriend."

"Don't that beat all."

"She was murdered."

"Whoo-wee," Stagg said. "Now that's a real sucker punch. I sure am sorry to hear that. I know Mr. Bishop was real broke up about it, too. Weren't you, Mr. Bishop?"

Bishop grunted as Pratt wiped at the back of his neck, that hot breath on him like a gosh-dang dog. The windows fogged up so bad that he didn't know how Stagg could see, maybe just driving from memory around the old veterans' monument and then heading north off that spoke, up toward the Blackjack community and beyond.

"You got any idea on what might've happened?" Stagg asked.

"No, sir," Pratt said. "Some folks believe her own daughter may have done it."

"Her own daughter?" Stagg said. "Hellfire. I ain't never even heard of such a thing."

"She's been seeing some black boy from down in the Ditch," Pratt said, swallowing but feeling a little confidence coming back into him. Stagg and his boy asking him questions and letting him talk. "A real thug. Her momma wasn't happy about the situation. I offered to send that girl to a Bible school for girls up in Missouri. Maybe that's what did it. Hell, I don't know."

"Things like that happen," Stagg said, taking the ElDo up to sixty, curving onto the big concrete bridge, over the swirling brown river of the Big Black. "Hormones. All that rap music and hippity hoppity dancing. I can see how it might confuse a young woman."

"Whoever did it cut her up into pieces and tossed her into a trash barrel," Pratt said. "When I first heard about it, I fell down on my knees. I got so sick to my stomach, I couldn't even feel my legs."

"That's true grief," Stagg said. "Sure can come on like a son of a bitch. *Yes, sir. Yes, sir.* Sure am sorry to hear about it. Thoughts and prayers, Chester Pratt."

They drove for a while, maybe two or three minutes, but it felt like damn near half an hour, before anyone said a word. The music switched over from Brenda Lee and now was on an old Perry Como song about going round and round. Pratt felt like he was spinning himself, looping up and around Tibbehah County with Johnny Stagg and his gun monkey in the back of the ElDo ready to blow his goddamn head off. He felt like he might get sick again, knowing something real bad was coming somewhere around the bend.

"Oh, hell," Pratt said, rubbing his hand on his right knee. "Why don't y'all just go ahead and get it over with?"

Stagg chuckled. "Get what over with?"

"Whatever y'all got planned for me," Pratt said. "I haven't slept or ate for three days. I feel like I've been drinking Drano and my nerves is jangled like a live wire. I can't sit here and make small talk while we low ride and listen to fucking Perry Como."

"Planned?" Stagg said. "Ain't no plan, Mr. Pratt. I'm your goddamn fairy godfather coming to you live and in person. I was thinking that you might be needing a good buddy right now. Someone to confide in and maybe ask for a little friendship and help."

"With what?"

"Oh, come on now, Chester," Stagg said. "You really want me to believe that horseshit about that Byrd girl getting jungle fever and cutting up her own momma? From what I heard, you was into that woman for far more than you're into me."

Pratt held on to the dashboard tight, feeling his stomach turn loose. He took in a lot of short quick breaths, everything around him obscured on account of that inner fog of the car. He wiped his hand on the passenger window to see if he was somewhere he could just jump out and run into the woods. He could do it. Maybe even make it before that Bishop fella shot him in the back.

"I loved that crazy redneck woman," Pratt said. "I wouldn't hurt a hair on her head. This whole thing's got me busted up good."

"'Course you wouldn't," Stagg said. "I bet you're as innocent as Shirley Temple's starched white underbritches. But some folks may not recognize how much you deeply loved and cared for her. Won't be long before that Quinn Colson may be hearing the same type of stories about borrowed money and family squabbles and that woman coming to your place of work, five, six times to demand that you make things right. Right? But, hell. You know that's another story."

Pratt didn't say anything, holding his breath as Stagg slowed the car on the soft edge of the curving roadside. A sign ahead pointed the way to the community of Blackjack. Another sign pointed west up to Fate. He could hear Bishop moving up behind him, the breath getting warmer on his neck, hearing the breathing with all that goddamn Perry Como.

Pratt closed his eyes. If he'd been a praying man, he might've started talking to Jesus.

"I invested in you, son," Stagg said. "And if you get yourself fucked five ways from Sunday, I won't see a return on what I gave you."

"I appreciate all you've done, Mr. Stagg," Pratt said. "Believing in me like you did. Making sure I got that liquor license with my past troubles. Yes, sir. I sure do."

"You can stop stroking my ding-dong now," Stagg said, holding the wheel although the car wasn't in motion. "Here's what I'm offering you. I know a surefire way to cornhole those fucking kids and get the law off your ass. But you better decide right here and right fucking now that I'm more than just an investor. I'll be your partner."

Pratt swallowed again. He tried to breathe. Stagg cracked a window and turned on some cool air to clear the windows. Everything was so damn hot and stuffy in that old red car. All he wanted to do was get out and run as far as his skinny legs would carry him.

"I want half of Bluebird Liquors," Stagg said. "Understand? How 'bout we head on back to the Rebel where you can sign the papers and make it all legal."

"Can you give me a few hours to at least change my undershorts?"

"Better do it fast, son," Stagg said. "This here is a limited time offer."

The man looked to have been asleep, taking several minutes to get to the door after Lillie's constant knocking. He cracked it open, Lillie not faulting him given his ZIP code, and stared through the sliver at her. She introduced them as U.S. Marshals Lillie Virgil and Charlie Hodge.

The man didn't seem impressed. He was sleepy-eyed and had a sloped, shovel face. Even from the distance, she could smell the funk on him.

"We're looking for a woman goes by Domino," Lillie said.

"She ain't here."

The man tried to close the door. Lillie, hand subtly on her Sig, stuck her boot into the threshold. "Mind if we come inside?" she said. "Talk things over."

"Y'all got a warrant or some shit?"

"Maybe a little shit like a badge," Lillie said, glancing over at Charlie Hodge. The gray-headed man standing ramrod straight at her side, dressed in his blue jeans, black button-down, and tweed coat. As always, he looked as if the whole situation amused the hell out of him. "She's not in trouble. We want to talk to her about Ladarius. Her cousin."

"He ain't here, either."

"Can we come in?" Lillie said. "We're getting wet."

"Shoulda brought you an umbrella."

The man stepped back and opened the door a bit more. He was shirtless and Lillie noticed he had some kind of tattoo on his neck. A few more tats on his right chest. He was stocky and muscular, wearing blue work pants and old unlaced work boots. He looked nervous, eyes a little bloodshot.

"Nobody's here," he said. "Damn. What time is it?"

Lillie told him. The rain whipped up again, blowing sideways out on the second floor of the apartment building. The man shook his head, pissed at the situation before he waved them inside, Lillie shocked the man put up so little resistance. She never expected to get beyond the front door. But she wasn't one to argue as she passed him on the way in, Lillie being cautious and aware of his hands and every sight and sound in the room.

"You know where we can find Domino?" Hodge asked.

The man shrugged. Lillie kept talking as Hodge walked on past and checked out the little apartment. He saw what she did, a nest of blankets on two couches, stray pillows, and pizza boxes.

"Y'all had some company?" Lillie asked.

"It was like this when I got home."

"Where have you been?" Hodge asked.

"Work," he said. "I work nights. Domino works days. That's how some folks do it."

"And where does Domino work?" Lillie asked.

"Come on, now," the man said. "I tell you and you go over and harass her. She could lose her goddamn job. Just give me your card or some shit. I'll tell her you stopped by."

Hodge rested a hand on a big overstuffed chair, smiling and good-natured. A real friend to everyone he met. That was until someone pushed him, and no one really liked Charlie Hodge when he was pushed. He became an altogether different man. Lillie figured you got to be like that after working some years undercover with the Born Losers motorcycle gang.

"Ladarius is wanted back in Tibbehah County," Lillie said. "He's on the run with his girl."

"Don't know nothing about it."

"Of course you don't," Lillie said. "But it's in the best interest of those kids they get back home. Can't have anything bad happening to them. They're traveling with a young girl named Holly Harkins and a boy that's nine."

"A Holly what?"

"Harkins," Lillie said. "Holly Harkins."

The man stared direct at Lillie, hands in his blue work pants, muscles bunched in his shoulders up to his thick neck. The smell of weed was heavy in the room. The TV was on and showing two healthy folks engaged in some intense barnyard activity. The sound was down low but you could still hear a good amount of yelling and panting.

"You into nature shows?" Lillie asked.

"Man, I'm just chilling out," he said. "Kicking back a little. You know how it is. Watching me some flicks. Y'all got a problem with some natural acts?"

"What's your name?" Hodge asked.

"D'Shawn."

"You tell us where we can find Domino and we'll let you get back to your chilling out, D'Shawn," Hodge said. "I don't want you pulled into this family mess. Aiding and abetting some juvenile fugitives. I promise it's not going to be worth the effort."

"I don't know her people," D'Shawn said. "Only known Domino since Christmas. Met her down at the shake joint putting on a little show. She was dressed up as Missus Claus. Biggest damn titties I ever seen. She had me sit in her lap and asked me what I wanted her to bring me. I told her how 'bout I give her the best damn candy cane in Memphis."

"Beautiful story," Lillie said. "Some real Hallmark movie shit."

"Girl's trying to work," D'Shawn said. "She don't need no trouble."

"How about you?" Hodge asked. "Nobody's looking for you for anything. Right? No old warrants you forgot about?"

D'Shawn didn't answer, standing there dead-eyed. The folks on the TV screen about to enter a crescendo of happiness, a lot of groaning and moaning, direct talk about what the man was doing and how much the woman sure was enjoying it. Lillie knew the whole thing embarrassed the hell out of Charlie Hodge, his face colored a bright pink. At his core, Charlie was a goddamn Puritan.

"Which shake joint, D'Shawn?" Lillie asked.

"What her cousin do?"

"Wasn't him," Lillie said. "His girlfriend might've killed a good friend of mine. Cut her up into little pieces and tossed her into a trash barrel."

"That's some sick shit," D'Shawn said. "Must be a white girl."

"How'd you know?"

"Shit," D'Shawn said. "My momma told me a long time ago not to mess with a white girl. They turn your ass inside out. Fuck up your damn mind."

"Not all of us are bad."

"Maybe so," D'Shawn said. "Cutting up her own mother? Y'all fucking with me?"

"No, sir," Hodge said.

"Which shake joint?" Lillie said again.

"Right back down the road at Dixie Belles," D'Shawn said. "Domino works that lunch shift with the buffet bar. Chicken wings, onion rings, and hot dogs. Horny old men coming right off the airplane and needing some snacks, good loving, and their monkeys jacked. Ain't no shame in it. It's just a job."

"No judgment," Lillie said, offering her palms. "How about you, Charlie?"

"None whatsoever," he said. "Everybody's got to make a living."

"Don't call ahead," Lillie said. "Okay? We'll keep this between us. Maybe Domino will be so grateful we showed up to help that Christmas might come early."

"Y'all better watch your ass," D'Shawn said. "My Domino is a whole lot of woman."

"So am I, D'Shawn," Lillie said, turning back toward the steps. "So am I."

Dusty and Flem had cut work for the day, the rain coming down too long and too strong to stay up on a ladder. They were cold, tired, and soaked, Dusty turning on the heater in their '87 Chevy Silverado as they headed right for Varner's Quick Mart, picking what was left of the daily lunch specials. Some fried chicken, green beans, and mac and cheese. The old man at the counter, none other than Luther Varner himself, held a cigarette that looked about a mile long and stared at them as if they weren't nothing but shit on the bottom of his shoe. Him and Daddy didn't give the old gray-headed fool the satisfaction of meeting his eye and hustled the Styrofoam containers and cold six-pack of Busch on back to the truck where they ate in silence, smacking their food and slurping their beers like Momma Lennie wouldn't allow back home.

"Ain't you glad I was hard on you, boy," Daddy said. "Or else you might've turned out just like that Chester Pratt, soft as warm butter."

"You was hard on me till you wasn't," Dusty said, mawing on a chicken leg. "Me and Darlene took our revenge against you. 'Specially when you was drunk."

"Maybe," Daddy said. "Y'all ran the house like a couple red Indians. Hiding my Jim Beam and car keys. Tying me to that goddamn chair. If it hadn't been for Momma, I mighta killed you both. *Har. Har.* Remember that time I doused you with lighter fluid and opened up that Zippo?"

"I could never be like Chester Pratt," Dusty said, sucking marrow from the bone. "That man was born soft."

"He's damn lucky to know us," Daddy said. "Doing what we always done, cleaning up someone else's goddamn mess. Making sure things done right."

"You tell Momma?"

"Hell no, I didn't tell her," Daddy said. "Your momma and I got ourselves a deal. Long as I make money, she don't ask where it comes from. She does what she does on our land, tending to her people and collecting all them Disney figurines. And me and you head out and do what needs to be done."

"That Byrd woman had no call to stick you," Dusty said. "You might've bled out."

"So you don't blame me?" Daddy said. "For what I done?"

"No, sir," Dusty said. "I helped you. Didn't I? Held her down while you did your cuttin'."

Dusty scraped up the rest of the mac and cheese with a spork and then took to licking the inside of the container. Daddy Flem cracked open his second beer and sucked it down nice and quick, knowing he didn't have much time before Momma Lennie cut him off.

"Momma ask what we was doing in the shed?"

"Processing meat."

"Smart keeping them clothes and that saw around," Dusty said. "I would've thrown 'em down in that ravine."

"Shit, no," Daddy said, wiping off the beer from his grayed goatee. "That was our fucking insurance policy. Them and that cell phone."

"Wonder if the po-lice found that shit yet?" Dusty said. "Leaving that fancy pink boot sure was a nice touch, Daddy. Real nice."

"That's what I taught you," Daddy said. "Wadn't it? I might've knocked you halfway 'cross the room few times. Choked your ass till you passed out. But I made you learn to do a job right. Measure twice and cut once. Choose stable ground for your ladder. Wear you some good boots or you just might break your damn neck."

"And don't take nothing off no one."

"The Nixes ain't big people," Daddy said. "My granddaddy had to stand on three Coca-Cola crates to bury his head in my mawmaw's titties. Now that old boy didn't take no shit, either. Kilt a man once for patting him on the head like he was a child. That Byrd woman, that goddamn whore, shouldn't'a stuck me like she did. She didn't give me no choice."

"And maybe we'll get something else, too?"

"You talking about from that soft-bellied Chester Pratt?" Daddy said, cracking open his third beer, guzzling it straight down, a good quarter of it running down his goatee. "Now you're talking, son."

ELEVEN

A re you sure it's her?" Donna Grace Webb asked. "Maybe it's some kind of mistaken identity? That kind of thing happens more than you know it. I heard it for myself on one of those *Dateline NBC* shows. Some woman's in trouble, folks think she's dead, but she's really drinking margaritas somewhere down in Cancun."

"I'm real sorry," Quinn said, standing by the worktable of DG Creations flower shop. "I know y'all were good friends."

"So you're sure?" she said. "I mean, real sure?"

"Yes, ma'am," Quinn said. "The body we found was Gina Byrd. Lillie IDed Gina herself. I don't mean to be harsh, but I promise you she's not drinking margaritas down in Mexico."

Donna Grace was a big woman, somewhere in her late sixties, with chubby cheeks and red hair pinned up on top of her head. As Quinn offered a few more details, she looked unsteady on her feet, gripping the side of her table covered with bunches of roses and snipped baby's breath. When he'd come out of the rain and into the little white house, she said she was making a bouquet for a big wedding supposed to happen on the Square tomorrow, that is, if this nasty weather would clear up.

The little cottage seemed almost airless, closed up tight and smelling sweet and old at the same time, like a flower pressed between the pages of book. Donna Grace wore an oversized pink blouse over some fancy jeans with designs on the pockets, trying to look composed while she placed a fist to her forehead and mashed it tight. Tears fell down onto the table.

Quinn hated these kinds of visits about worse than anything. But it was all part of the job, calling on loved ones and friends of folks who died quick and without notice. He took the calls when he could, car wrecks to heart attacks, murders and job accidents, often if he knew the people involved, not wanting to parcel out the worst part of the job to his deputies while he kept to his desk. The least he could do is knock on the door himself and let them know what had happened while looking them in the eye.

"Someone killed her?" Donna Grace asked.

"Yes, ma'am."

"The things I'm hearing," she said. "About the body they found. Things done to it."

Quinn didn't answer. But the stories couldn't be any worse than the truth. He just nodded back at Donna Grace while the woman went back to making the bouquet for the big wedding on the Square. She pruned the stems of long white roses and then set about working on a handful of spray roses, Quinn knowing the difference from all the varieties Maggie had planted last year. Maggie had singlehandedly turned their old farm into a botanical showcase.

"Why?" she said.

"That's what I hope to find out."

"Some folks are saying it was little TJ," she said. "Lord God."

"I wouldn't put too much stock in rumors," said Quinn. "I was hoping you might help."

"With who killed Gina?" Donna Grace shook her head and wiped the mascara off her cheeks with a paper towel. She snuffed out a laugh as if the question was just plain nuts. "I have no earthly idea."

Quinn walked over by the front counter, right alongside the glass refrigerator filled with orders ready for pickup. There was an old FTD sign behind the counter, the same one from when Donna Grace's father owned the shop, golden Hermes hauling ass while holding a big fistful of flowers. The whole idea of someone wiring a shop for a flower order seemed like something for the history books.

"I've known Gina for more than twenty years," Donna Grace said, snuffling but still snipping, gathering, wrapping. "I've been with her through her ups and downs, trials and tribulations. Before her momma passed, I promised I'd look out for Gina."

"And how's Gina been doing?"

"Same as always," Donna Grace said. "Sometimes she's my employee of the month. And sometimes I'd have to fire her ass because she came to work stoned or drunk. Have you called on Chester Pratt? They been seeing each other for a while. Seems like Chester only feeds her trouble, giving her money for pills and as much booze as she can drink."

"Yes, ma'am," Quinn said. "And I'll be calling on him again."

"I knew something was wrong when she didn't show on Monday," Donna Grace said. "We had some words last week on account of her not showing last Tuesday. I would've fired her a hundred times if she didn't have a real knack for colors and organization. She made some right smart door hangings. Just made a whole batch for Valentine's Day. Prettiest things you ever saw in your life. Little hearts and pink carnations. God, Quinn. This can't be right. Nothing about this makes sense."

"Was she having trouble with TJ?"

"Some," she said. "Not any more than any other momma with a teenage girl."

"I heard sometimes things got physical," Quinn said.

"Between Gina and TJ?" she said. "I never heard nothing like that."

"Did she ever mention Ladarius McCade?"

"Lord, yes," Donna Grace said. "Sometimes that boy and TJ stopped by the shop. So handsome and funny. That crazy blond hair of his. Just last week he came in and bought a dozen roses for his grandmother Della Mae. Wasn't that nice? I can't believe the things I'm hearing about him now. That can't be true now. Can it?"

Quinn didn't answer, as running down everything Ladarius Mc-Cade had been charged with over the years would've taken some time. He leaned against the counter, watching Donna Grace tie together the bouquet with baby blue ribbon, eyes down on her work, a few tears still falling. "You know I used to date your daddy," she said. "Before your momma got ahold of him. How's he doing anyway?"

"Fine," Quinn said. "I guess."

"Y'all don't talk?"

"When he left town, he saddled me with some problems," Quinn said. "It's been a few years since we spoke."

"I'm sorry to hear that," she said. "Your father was quite a fella. When he'd come home from Hollywood, this whole town would come alive. He'd always have some new car or motorcycle. One time he brought this hippie gal named Bunny with him. She was a real hoot, crazy as a loon and wild as a march hare, but I liked her a lot. Wore bell bottoms and big ole clogs. Wonder what happened to her? So damn long ago."

"Did Gina confide any personal problems with you?" Quinn said. "I heard she might've been having money trouble."

"Gina didn't have much," Donna Grace said. "I'd think she'd gotten herself straight only to find out she'd blown her money for the week down at the Southern Star. Have you checked with her friends down there?"

"A few," Quinn said. "I heard she had some trouble there the other night?"

Donna Grace shrugged and Quinn turned to the see rain tapping on the front windows of the little cottage.

"I hadn't heard a thing about any trouble," Donna Grace said. "Gina was going through a smooth patch lately. She told me that things were looking up for her and her whole family. They got some kind of insurance settlement that would keep them from having to buy groceries with an EBT card."

"Insurance settlement?"

"Yes, sir," Donna Grace said. "Don't tell me you hadn't heard about that? TJ's daddy's momma died at some broke-down facility up in Corinth. Bunch of families got together and sued the pants off those people."

"I may have read something about it."

"Don't ask me how much they got," Donna Grace said. "But Gina had called the money they got a real gift from God."

"Do you know what she did with the payment?" Quinn said.

"I figured they had a bunch of bills to pay," Donna Grace said, swallowing hard and closing her eyes. "I'm so sorry, Quinn. I've tried not to think about this all morning, convincing myself that Gina is gonna be all right. That those horrible stories can't be true. Not here. Not in Jericho."

Quinn nodded. He offered more condolences while Donna Grace picked up a bouquet and twirled it in her hand, smiling softly.

"Seems like yesterday I was stringing flowers for your parents' wedding," she said. "Jason talked the whole town into donating something. We hung Christmas lights in the old oaks on the Square, folks barbecuing and carrying on until sunup. Your daddy sure was crazy about Miss Jean. Makes me sad sometimes when I think they're not together anymore."

"I guess folks grow apart."

Donna Grace tossed Quinn the bouquet. He wasn't expecting it and barely caught it before it hit the floor.

"Give these to Jean for me," she said. "A little private joke between us. Hope it makes her smile."

Lillie identified herself to the bouncer at Dixie Belles, a muscly white boy in an official Grizz jersey, while Charlie Hodge waited outside in case Domino decided to bolt. Both of them had a good look at the woman's booking photo from 201 Poplar: prostitution, possession with intent, and assault on a law enforcement officer.

The bouncer got a girl and the girl then got another man, this one saying he was the day manager and didn't want trouble. This man was copper-colored, bald as a coot with a Fu Manchu and a physique that looked like a former bodybuilder who one day up and said fuck it. "Nope," he said. "No way. Come back when you got some paper."

"Okay," Lillie said. "But with traffic, I'll make it just in time for the dinner show. I saw the billboard outside. Y'all got a real-life porn star coming to town? That's some real class."

"Kiley Ryan," he said. "She once took on a whole football team by herself. It was some kind of record. Maybe you should stick around, lady. Learn a few tricks."

The man laughed at that, turning to the bouncer, who smirked. Lillie's face didn't change and soon the laughing died down.

"That's okay," Lillie said. "Probably better training for a guy like you. You look like you spent a little time inside. Probably need to keep limber to make some new friends."

"I don't need your shit today," he said. "Bring back some paper or quit harassing my people."

"When I come back with more people, it might delay Miss Ryan's one-woman show," she said. "Or you can just go get Domino and we can all go about our day."

"Just who the fuck are you?"

"Lillie Virgil," she said. "U.S. Marshal. You've probably seen me around before. Shitbirds are drawn to this place like the fucking swallows to Capistrano."

"Why you gotta go and be like that?" the manager said. "Speaking to me like I ain't nothin'. Running down my place. This is the number one gentlemen's club in the Mid-South. I picked up the award myself at last year's expo presented at the Criss Angel Theater in Vegas."

"Criss Angel Theater?" Lillie said. "Whoo-wee. Your momma must be real proud."

The bald-headed manager stood there, his back to the white faux-leather doors into the club. Lillie could hear the pumping dance music and smell the fried food. A sign above the door read: NO CONCEALED WEAPONS: GUNS, KNIVES, ETC. ON THIS PROPERTY. Nothing like a down-home Memphis shake joint.

Lillie was about to press harder as a stout woman with a black and red weave busted out from the front doors. Domino had on a red bikini with no shoes, dollar bills crammed into her G-string. Her backside looked like two scoops of melting chocolate ice cream.

"Heard you was looking for me," Domino said. "What the fuck do you want?"

"Looking for your cousin Ladarius."

"Hadn't seen that boy since Christmastime down in the country," she said. "Momma Della Mae made us a big spread. Biscuits, homemade sausage, and gravy. Fried pies. All that shit."

Domino patted the manager's arm and the man kept on staring at Lillie for a moment before turning and walking away. The bouncer stood by the twin doors into the club.

"He was at your apartment last night," Lillie said.

"Who the fuck told you that?"

"D'Shawn," Lillie said, lying. "Y'all had a little pajama party. Drank some beers, ordered some Papa John's."

"Goddamn," she said. "I'm gonna beat that boy's ass when I get home."

"Where they'd go?"

"If I knew, I wouldn't be telling no Jane Law," she said, looking at the badge hanging around Lillie's neck and the Sig on her hip. "Big, sturdy woman like you shouldn't carry no gun. You look strong enough to work that pole real good."

"Appreciate that, Domino," Lillie said. "Maybe if this whole U.S. Marshal gig doesn't work out, I'll come back and pay you a visit. I heard it's all in the thighs."

"Some in the thighs," Domino said. "A little bit more in the butt. You got to know how to work that big ass. Shake it and smack it."

"Right now my big ass is trying to run down that cousin of yours before he gets himself in any more trouble."

"Gave that boy a hundred bucks and sent him on his way," Domino said, shrugging a little. "Can't do much since he's been pussy-whipped by some little white girl. A white girl that might've gone and killed her own damn mother. Shit. What you think about that?"

"I think me and you need to become fast friends," Lillie said. "Ever heard of Bonnie and Clyde?"

"I saw the movie," Domino said. "Sure had a fucked-up ending."

"Doesn't have to be like that."

Domino exhaled a long breath and shook her head. Her breasts enormous and drooping in the small red top. She had some kind of tattoo on her big stomach written in a fancy scrawl. Domino noticed Lillie staring. "It says, 'everything happens for a reason.'"

"You believe that?" Lillie said.

"Yeah, well, maybe."

"Don't let that kid go down in a blaze of glory," Lillie said. "He's only seventeen."

Domino seemed to consider that, hand with long red manicured nails resting on her fatty hip. She had in colorized contacts that gave her eyes a weird, electric blue glow. The woman looked as if she'd just arrived in Memphis on a spaceship.

"They was headed to fill up that busted-ass minivan and then get as far from down here as they could," Domino said. "If I had to say, maybe Florida. Don't even think about trying to track their damn phones. Ladarius too smart for that shit. They probably tossed all that mess into the Mississippi River. That's the last I heard from him. Said don't bother texting or nothing."

"Then they're headed into Arkansas," Lillie said.

"I didn't say that."

"You got people in Arkansas?"

Domino shook her head. She crossed her arms over her huge breasts and looked Lillie up and down. "You think that white girl really killed her own momma?"

"Not my job."

"You don't care?"

"I care very much," Lillie said. "And if I were you or anyone in your family, I'd reach out to Ladarius and make sure he walks away from this whole flaming shitshow."

"Any reward for that?"

"Maybe."

"How much we talking?"

"Depends on what you got, Domino."

Domino nodded. "Let me see what I can do, Marshal Lady."

Lillie handed Domino her card and pulled up the hood of her black slicker, heading out into the flashing neon lights of Dixie Belles and into the cold rain.

* * *

They'd spent all day outside a repair shop in Forrest City, Arkansas, taking turns walking around the Walmart with John Wesley while Ladarius waited on the repairs to the old minivan. He wanted to make sure none of them got screwed as he believed he knew the most about cars. Turned out it was only a busted belt, but the cost of the repairs knocked them down to fourteen dollars and they didn't get back on the highway until nightfall. TJ was driving now, Ladarius up front, with Holly finally falling asleep in the back with John Wesley. They'd bought some Oreos and Tostitos, Little Debbies, and some cracker and cheese combos. TJ wasn't sure where she was headed but decided to continue on Highway 70 to Hot Springs, no other reason than she knew there was a state park up that way, maybe a place they could park and hole up for a day or two. She had in one of her daddy's favorite CDs, Poison, singing along to "Every Rose Has Its Thorn."

"You know folks think you're crazy listening to that old-school shit," Ladarius said.

"Old-school shit to you," TJ said. "Classic to me. You hear that? CC DeVille. The band was never the same after he and Bret Michaels got into that fistfight at the MTV Music Awards in '91. He was the backbone of Poison."

Ladarius nodded, not giving two shits as he sunk lower into the passenger seat, thumbing through a new cell phone.

"You know where we're headed?"

"Nope."

"You know what we're going to do?"

"We better dump this piece of shit and get us a new ride."

"I switched the plates."

"I know you did."

"And bought this burner phone at the Walmart."

"You told me."

"We can't keep going like this," Ladarius said. "Riding around living off cupcakes and Oreos. Moving from town to town. Pretty soon we're gonna run out of gas."

TJ looked down at the fuel gauge, a little less than a quarter of a tank left. She lifted her eyes to the road. Her stomach grumbled as she hadn't had anything to eat since the chicken biscuit in Memphis. She wanted to leave what they had left for John Wesley.

"You got an ATM card?"

"Shit," Ladarius said. "You know what we got to do."

"Holly says a lot of rich folks have houses up on some lakes."

"Holly ain't gonna go for what you have in mind."

"We only take what we need," she said. "Maybe grab a few things we can sell. TVs or jewelry. Holly knows our situation."

"That keeps us going for what?" he said. "Maybe a day or two. Then what? Driving around until the police come for us and take you back home and me back to juvie."

"Maybe then they'll find out what happened," she said. "Maybe then they'll know Chester Pratt is a lying sack of shit."

"Why's he trying to pin this all on you?"

"I told the sheriff what I knew and he wouldn't listen," she said, punching the old CD player to a new track, "Nothin' but a Good Time." "I promised Momma I wouldn't say a word about her stabbing that man outside the Southern Star. But I did anyway. Now no one believes it happened."

"Did she know them?"

"She said she'd never seen them before in her life," TJ said. "There was two of them. She thinks she mighta killed one. You saw the blood on her clothes. She got a knife free from one of them and stabbed him right in the belly."

"You right," Ladarius said. "Can't trust the law. You and me both straight on that."

TJ didn't answer, agreeing with him. She kept on driving, running through the essential Poison, then Cinderella, and on to Bon Jovi. When the CD switched up to "Wanted Dead or Alive," Ladarius looked over at TJ and shook his head. That one cut a little too damn close, so she changed it up to "Livin' on a Prayer."

"Is that better?" she asked.

Ladarius nodded.

They didn't talk for a long while, Ladarius falling asleep somewhere around Benton while TJ's mind turned to messed-up images that kept popping into her thoughts. She imagined her mother cut up, tossed like trash or roadkill in some old gully, and the idea of it damn near hollowed her out. She wiped her cheek with the back of her hand, following that snaking road up into the hills and then down into the outskirts of Hot Springs, the lights bright in the cold dark, a nice welcome from the desolation of the highway from Little Rock. The signs kept on pressing her on toward Lake Hamilton, passing the old horse-racing track and a place called T-Rex Jurassic Golf and Go-carts, the last sending John Wesley bolt upright and pointing, "Whoa. Look at that."

"It's closed."

"No, it ain't," he said. "Folks racing around that little track right now."

"We got to git where we're going."

"Where we going?"

"Big house on the lake that belongs to a friend of Holly's momma."

"Can we get something to eat?"

"There'll be food when we get there."

"All right then."

They passed more billboards for boat rentals, eighteen-hole cham-
pionship golf, fried fish shacks, and souvenir stores. TJ just figuring
the road would lead them to where they needed to go, handing it over
to the Lord for the direction although she hadn't been to a church
service since her momma and Chester Pratt dragged her to the new
Baptist church out by the Rebel Truck Stop. The road curved up onto
a big concrete bridge until she could finally see water, lit up from the
streetlamps with signs to places called Kahuna Bay and Salty Dog
Marina. More cheap hotels and a big old paddle wheeler like they
docked up on the Mississippi River. TJ kept on driving and curving,
feeling like she was headed right, but then she was lost, the lights of
the lake a distant memory until she hit a long stretch of a country
road with old barns and silos, now scared she'd missed the damn
lake. The gas gauge in the red and they didn't have but five dollars
left between them.

"Where are we?" John Wesley said.

TJ couldn't see in the full dark, turning off the main road by a
wide-open pasture, following the white horse fence and hoping
maybe she could just feel her way back to the water and all the promise she hoped they'd find. Soon she spotted a sign to some kind of
new development and she looked in the rearview at her little brother,
his face lit up like it did at the Chuck E. Cheese in Tupelo.

"What's it like?"

"What's that?"

"That nice house."

"Well," TJ said. "I ain't too sure."

"It's a big house," Holly said. "Bigger than you ever been in, kid."

Holly leaned forward, *God bless her*, and pointed to where the road
forked by a big realty sign. PRICE REDUCED. FORECLOSURE. BANK-OWNED
LAKEFRONT LUXURY. They wound up and around the hill until they

saw an entrance with two tall brick pilings. A fancy hand-carved wood sign said FIREFLY.

"You sure?" TJ asked.

"Uh-huh."

TJ turned the wheel and headed up the gravel road, letting down her driver's window so she could see where they were going. Soon they saw the outline of one of the biggest houses she'd ever seen in her life, with a tile roof and stucco walls and plenty of no trespass signs posted on skinny oaks along a fence line. The house was dark, weeds grown up along the drive and knee-deep up to big front steps. She pulled off the drive and into a thicket of little trees and shut off the engine. John Wesley hopped out fast as Ladarius came awake with a start, looking like a man who'd been free-falling in dreamland, snoring and kicking and then turning to TJ to get hold of himself.

"Welcome home."

"You crazy?" he said. "This place got to be wired up out the ass."

"You saying you can't bust in?" TJ asked. "The great Ladarius McCade? Or was that just a bunch of bullshit?"

"Damn, girl," he said. "You know how to turn those screws."

Ladarius shook his head, got out of the minivan, and soon they all headed up the drive and around the back of the property, up to a big-tiled patio with a view out onto the depths of the endless cold lake. Little lights flickered across the water; green and red bulbs shone at the end of a pier down the hill.

Ladarius disappeared, and five minutes later, he came through the house and opened up the back door.

"I was gonna cut the power," he said. "But there ain't no power. I guess rich folks forget to pay their bills, too. Cut the phone line with my pocketknife. Just to make sure."

"Security box?"

"Deader than hell."

"What's it like?"

Ladarius grinned big and held the door open wide. "How about y'all come in and see."

Ladarius turned on his cell phone, shining the light onto the marble floors. While the outside had gone wild, the inside looked as if someone had just stepped out for a moment and planned to be back any minute. It was cold, feeling even colder in the big house than it was outside, and they could see their breaths as they headed deeper into the mansion.

"I can get the power back on," Ladarius said, blowing into his fist. "What do you think?"

TJ looked to Holly, Holly giving a little shrug, not at all comfortable with breaking and entering. John Wesley stood close to TJ, her arm around his shoulder walking him through the big house, looking up at his sister wondering what the hell was going on.

"Alarm will get tripped," TJ said.

"I'll cut that box loose first," Ladarius said. "Shit. Who you talking to? Come on now."

TJ left John Wesley with Holly to go find the kitchen and she headed back outside with Ladarius. He'd found a screwdriver and a set of pliers inside. TJ held the phone for a flashlight while he pried and pulled, snipping the tag from the electric company off the junction box.

"We needed this," TJ said, closing her eyes. "I prayed about it the whole way from Little Rock. I prayed like I hadn't my whole life. I promised God I'd get straight if we could get a little rest. Lord. I'm so tired I can barely keep my eyes open."

"Let's see how you did, TJ Byrd."

Ladarius opened the junction box and flipped up the master switch, the downstairs of the mansion glowing with warm yellow light. They held their breath and waited, listening for an alarm but hearing only the stillness of the lake and pine trees shuddering in the cold wind.

TJ exhaled and smiled.

"Come on, now," Ladarius said. "Let's see what these rich folks got to eat."

TWELVE

nsurance settlement?" Maggie asked.

"There'd been something in the news about it," Quinn said. "Remember last year all those stories about that nursing home in Corinth? Seems that TJ's grandmother, Jerry Jeff Valentine's momma, died in their care. I don't know how much money they got or when, or if, they got it yet."

It was the next morning, cold and rainy, Quinn in the kitchen with Maggie, relaying every step he'd made after leaving Donna Grace's flower shop on the Square. He'd stopped by the Southern Star again and spent an hour speaking with the bartender, Coonie the Cajun, about the last time he'd seen Gina Byrd. It had been about ten days ago, and he'd had to get her into a taxi, one of only three taxis in Tibbehah County. Coonie said Gina had been a regular most nights, although he'd been off for the last week, down on the coast deep-sea fishing for drum and redfish.

"You think maybe she and TJ were fighting over the split?" Maggie said. "Seeing as how it was TJ's grandmother. Not Gina's blood relative."

"It's a possibility," Quinn said. "I didn't have any choice but to join Sheriff Lovemaiden to file those charges. The mess we found in the old shed didn't help her any."

Maggie refilled his coffee mug and joined him at their old pecan wood table, an original piece that had belonged to his Uncle Hamp and before that his grandfather. The damn thing must've weighed six hundred pounds.

"You look tired," Quinn said. "Sure you don't need some help?"

"Your momma is coming over later," Maggie said. "I can sleep then. Halley slept good last night. I'm hoping she'll get easier than Brandon. I promise you this is a lot better than when Brandon was born. Rick was on his third deployment in Afghanistan and we'd just gotten to Camp Pendleton two months before. I barely knew anyone. The other wives helped some. But it wasn't like being at home."

"Well, you're home now," Quinn said. "And I promise you that my mother will give you more assistance than you can ever need. Or might want."

"She misses Little Jason."

"I know."

"And Caddy."

"Just make sure to keep her busy," Quinn said. "If you like."

"I know she drove your sister crazy," Maggie said. "But I appreciate her. My momma wasn't like Jean at all. I have to be honest, my mother was a hell of a lot more like Gina Byrd."

"Don't say that."

"It's true," Maggie said. "I've told you most of it. Why do think I loved spending summers with my grandmother here? It was about the only place me and my sister had some stability. Our house was up and down all the time. A damn powder keg between her and my daddy when my daddy came home off the road."

"Was she unfaithful?"

"Always," Maggie said. "I hated Friday nights. That's when she'd leave me with my sister and head down to the joint on the county line. It always reminded me of the Boars Nest on the *Dukes of Hazzard*, a real redneck love shack. Most time we didn't see her till late Saturday, coming home with a mind-splitting headache, contrite and small, curled up on the couch and trying to gather enough strength for Sunday service."

"Did your daddy know?"

"He had to," Maggie said. "My daddy wasn't a stupid man. But I think he had his own favorite stops to pull in on the road. I always figured they'd come to some kind of agreement for the good of us girls. If I heard that one time in their fights, I heard it a thousand. I wish to God they'd just split up. Nobody should live that way. Sometimes when things got bad, I mean real bad, he'd knock that woman halfway across the room. Part of me got to believing she deserved it. That sounds awful. Doesn't it?"

Quinn drank some coffee. He reached for Maggie's hand.

Maggie looked comfortable and warm in sweatpants, white tank top, and a heavy hand-knitted sweater over her shoulders. She always made him feel warm and loved when he was with her, a real and authentic connection that he'd never had with Anna Lee Amsden. Anna Lee had been all fire and heat, but without any trust or warmth. From the time they'd been kids, Anna Lee had wanted nothing more than to get free from Tibbehah County and find a man who'd be a lot more than a sergeant in the U.S. Army. She'd finally gotten her wish when she married the town doctor and later moved up to Memphis to get away from Quinn for good.

"What are you thinking about?" Maggie said.

"How damn lucky I was to find you."

"Shacking up with the bank robber's ex," Maggie said. "Making an honest woman of her."

"You've always been an honest woman."

"Now you're just trying to get me into bed."

"I wouldn't fight you if you tried."

"Maybe I wouldn't fight you," Maggie said, sliding from her chair, coming around the table and taking a seat in Quinn's lap. She smelled musky and sweet, her skin salty as he kissed her neck and her mouth. It had been a long time.

Maggie moved along the chair, peeling out of her sweater, and wrapping her arms around Quinn's neck. They kissed for a while, the old chair creaking on the hardwood floor, rain tapping along the kitchen windows.

"We can't go upstairs," Maggie said. "We'll wake Halley."

"I'm just fine here."

"In the kitchen?"

"We've done it before," Quinn said. "Plenty of times when you were rehabbing me."

"Is that what you're calling it?"

"It worked," Quinn said. "Didn't it?"

Maggie reached for Quinn's belt buckle and started to open up his blue jeans as they heard a soft knock and the front door start to open.

"Hello?" Jean Colson called from the hallway. Quinn's mother always having a knack for bad timing. "Brought y'all some biscuits and fried pies from town."

Maggie closed her eyes, took a long breath, and crawled out of Quinn's lap. "In here, Miss Jean. I'll turn the oven on."

"You sure you want this?" the Old Man, also known as Chief Deputy Marshal Dalton Ames, asked. "You being friends with this woman makes things a little complicated."

"Yes, sir," Lillie said. "I pulled the pickup on those kids straight off. I wanted it. The girl and those kids headed into Memphis two nights ago."

"Tag reader on the state line?"

"That damn minivan crossed into Arkansas yesterday morning," she said. "I know those kids, their people, and how they think. I used to deal with the girl when I was a deputy in Tibbehah. A hellcat if I ever knew one."

"Is she violent?"

"Mean as a copperhead."

"Crazy?"

"Deep in that Byrd family DNA."

The Old Man leaned back into his padded leather chair, his brushy gray mustache dropping down over his lip. His eyes were hooded and his gray hair slicked back over his broad forehead. Ames had on a navy suit with a white shirt and a black tie, same as he'd worn the day Lillie had first met him. This morning, he didn't seem too pleased to take Lillie off her current case file and approve a short-term transfer to Oxford.

"Sounds like this might turn ugly."

"Yes, sir," Lillie said. "Based on my interactions with the girl. And her boyfriend's prior history. But when it comes right down to it, I also think I can talk some sense to her, make sure she knows she'll get a fair shake back home."

"Even after she killed her own mother?" the Old Man asked. "Your friend."

"Even then," Lillie said.

"Okay, let's cut through the bullshit," the Old Man said. "No matter what they did or how they did it, nobody wants to see some U.S. Marshals gunning down some damn lovey-dovey teenyboppers on the run. I also can't have any of my people shot because they're trying to be fair and compassionate. You get my meaning?"

"Understood," Lillie said. "You're telling me not to fuck this up. I'll do my best to bring them back alive. But if that girl has other plans, well. That's on TJ Byrd and Ladarius McCade."

"A hard take on a delicate situation, Deputy Virgil."

Lillie was dressed in her blue jeans, white button-down overlaid with a black blazer. She'd worn her best pair of boots and even touched up a little makeup for the occasion. She thought about it for a second and nodded.

"TJ Byrd and Ladarius McCade?" he said. "Damn if that doesn't sound like a couple of outlaws."

"Wish it was only them," Lillie said. "Easier to deal with. That little girl, the one who took her momma's minivan, is a mousy little thing. Kind of girl who goes to church twice a week, makes up her bed with tight little corners, and always hits the high school honor roll. How she threw in with these shitbirds, I have no idea."

"And the little brother?"

"Nine years old," Lillie said. "Different father than TJ. The way I understand it, TJ is pretty much the boy's mother. Gina Byrd was never really around for the kid. The girl took over being the parent, making sure he was clothed and fed, went to school until all this shit went down. The kid won't leave his big sister. He goes where she goes."

"Any leads in Arkansas?"

"Not a one," Lillie said. "Last contact was with McCade's cousin, a two-ton stripper named Domino who works the pole at Dixie Belles. She said she gave the kids a hundred bucks and sent them all packing."

"Are they armed?"

"Everyone carries a gun down in Tibbehah," Lillie said. "Old ladies and toddlers alike."

The Old Man twisted his big chair and gave that long, cold stare at Lillie. He'd already made up his mind but he wanted to make sure

Lillie felt the weight of his decision. He didn't blink once, an American flag pin on the lapel of his crisp ironed suit jacket, as he smoothed down the long mustache with his thumb and forefinger. "Okay," he said. "I'll grant the temporary transfer to the North Mississippi Task Force."

"But?"

"No buts, Lillie," he said in his graveled, rough voice. "Just don't make me look like a damn old fool. You do and I'll make sure you and Charlie Hodge get assigned to Parchman pickup duty. You and me both know how that fucking van smells."

"Like shit."

"Don't track this stuff back to the house," he said. *"Comprende?"*

Jean Colson placed the platter of fried pies on the center of the kitchen table and walked over to the coffeepot to help herself. The old place where she'd been born and raised always felt warm and familiar, a lot more now that Maggie had joined the family. When it had just been her aging brother, Hamp, the place was nastier than a rat's nest. And with Quinn it had been so pin neat, it seemed as if no one lived there at all. But now there was color and life, the sound of laughter and grandchildren tromping up and down to the old loft, reminding Jean of what it had been like when she was a kid, all those years ago.

"You smell like smoke," Jean said. "Thought you were cutting out those nasty cigars?"

"I've cut down some," Quinn said. "And I'm running again."

"That's good," Jean said. "Especially for a man who could barely walk this time last year."

"He's a work in progress, Miss Jean," Maggie said. "He's wearing a twenty-pound vest on his runs and even hung a pull-up bar in the barn."

"Yep." Quinn grinned. "Even cut down on the whiskey."

"Good," Jean said. "Are you still finding those old bottles my brother hid around the house?"

"We found two this summer," Maggie said. "Stuck up under the house and wrapped in newspaper from the seventies. Your brother really went to great lengths to hide his drinking."

"Only person he was hiding it from was his wife," Jean said. "To everyone else it was plain as day."

Jean's brother had been eighteen years older, a man she barely knew but knew all too well at the same time. Like Quinn, he'd gone into the Army, fought overseas, and came home to work for the sheriff's office before becoming sheriff himself for decades. He'd been a good man with plenty of failings, the sum of those years ending with him shooting himself in the head out of guilt not five feet from where she was sitting. God. She was so glad for the bright cheery paint and new windows Maggie had added to the house.

"Do you mind picking up Brandon from school?" Maggie asked Jean. "That's during Halley's nap. And Quinn's been hit hard this week."

"I know," Jean said. "Poor Gina Byrd."

"Yes, ma'am," Quinn said. "It's a real mess."

"She and that McCade boy really do it?" Jean asked.

"Maybe," Quinn said. "Maybe not. Not too many kids kill their parents. And Gina Byrd didn't exactly keep the best company in Tibbehah County."

"I heard those kids were charged with murder?"

"Not much else we could do," Quinn said. "Some evidence was discovered at their trailer. And those kids fled town."

"I've known that boy's mother and grandmother for ages," Jean said. "They're a fine family. How did he get mixed up in all this?"

"Well," Quinn said. "Ladarius McCade does break into homes,

smash windows out of trucks, and steals cars. Same as TJ Byrd. They've been in and out of the sheriff's office since they were children. That's why they ran. They don't believe anyone would listen."

"Especially not that nasty sheriff from over in Parsham," Maggie said, joining Jean and Quinn at the table and reaching for a fried pie. Jean glad to see Maggie finally eating something a little unhealthy, that woman always talking organic this and ethically raised that. You had to live a little.

"Lovemaiden?" Jean asked. "Lord. I haven't heard that name in years. He used to come over here and fish with your uncle out on y'all's pond. Did he mention your uncle when you saw him?"

"Constantly," Quinn said. "He said he respected Uncle Hamp because he went along to get along."

"And what's that supposed to mean?"

"I think it means he believes I was too hard on Johnny Stagg when I came home," Quinn said.

Jean decided not to ask any more questions on that subject, as talking about Johnny Stagg always led to unpleasant conversations. That crooked SOB was a stain on the county, an aberration of what kept her tied and close to Tibbehah County, and the thought of him now being out of federal prison turned her stomach. She forked off a small piece of fried pie and took a bite. She smiled, moving on to something else. "How about you, Quinn?" she said. "Aren't you hungry?"

"Apple?" Quinn asked.

"Peach," Jean said. "Maybe some apricot, too. I didn't ask, Miss Graves being so sweet to make us extra."

Maggie smiled from across the table, her daughter-in-law always making her feel welcome and at home, although she believed she may have interrupted something by showing up a little early. She reached out and patted Maggie's hand and smiled back, being so thankful to God that she'd come into her son's life. A full house with two healthy children and a strong family is all she'd ever hoped for Quinn, not just an empty house filled with cigars and whiskey and old memories, like it had been for poor old Hamp.

Maggie had just cut into her pie when they heard Halley's cries from the baby monitor.

"I'll check on her," Jean said.

"No, ma'am," Maggie said. "It's feeding time. But I'll take that help a little later."

Jean and Quinn watched Maggie leave the kitchen and heard her bounding up the steps into the loft. When she turned back to Quinn, she could tell something was on her son's mind and asked him about it.

"Mom, you know Chester Pratt, don't you?" Quinn asked.

"Chester Pratt?" Jean said. "Is he mixed up in all this mess?"

"He was seeing Gina Byrd."

"Good Lord," she said. "That man is nearly my age. What was he doing with a woman that young?"

"What do you think?"

"Hmm." Jean Colson gave Quinn a look and shook her head. "She had to have been drawn to his money, because it sure wasn't his looks. Chester Pratt hit the damn lottery when he got that liquor license out by the highway."

"How's that?"

"Chester was supposed to partner up with his brother," Jean said. "But they had a falling-out. Real nasty from what I heard. Rough words between those two that maybe came to blows. You know his brother, don't you?"

"Ronnie?" Quinn asked. "I thought Ronnie Pratt died."

"He was real sick last year," she said. "But he made it through. I think this whole business with Chester was what gave him the heart attack. I saw him at church two Sundays ago and he said he'd handed all his family troubles to the Lord."

"Lay your burdens down," Quinn said. "Especially one as heavy as Chester."

"Don't even joke about things like that, Quinn Colson," Jean said. "Do you have any earthly idea how many folks prayed for you in this county after what happened?"

Jean still wasn't able to say out loud that her son had been shot four times in the back. She only referred to his injuries as "the events" or "that time" even though she heard Quinn proudly kept the bullets in a mason jar on his desk. He thought of them as some kind of trophies.

"Ronnie Pratt," Quinn said. "You think he's still holding a grudge against Chester?"

"How many times must my brother sin against me and I forgive him?" Jean asked.

"I get the concept of seventy-seven times," Quinn said. "Although it's often a hard thing for me to wrap my head around."

"Still," Jean said, picking up the plate of fried pie. "I can't imagine that Chester cheating him out of that liquor store business sits right with Ronnie. Why are you asking?"

"Just double-checking on some things."

"I don't like that look in your eyes."

"Too many things are trying to force my hand with those kids," Quinn said. "Like deep and clear footprints that lead your ass right into an ambush."

"Must you use that vulgar language?"

"Only when it's fitting," Quinn said, smiling. "Appreciate the information, Momma. Sometimes it helps that everyone in this county knows each other's private business."

"Are you calling me a busybody?"

"No, ma'am," Quinn said. "Just a well-informed woman of the community."

Chester Pratt had a splitting headache, paying for last night when he'd drained half a bottle of Beam and passed out on the kitchen floor. He woke up late, drank two Miller Lites with some Goody's headache powder, and made sure Bluebird Liquors was up and running by ten a.m. By eleven, he'd left the day manager at the register and headed into town to grab some breakfast at the Fillin' Station diner. Chester knew there wasn't a thing that some fried meat, a plate of eggs, and some black coffee couldn't solve.

He sat there in the back corner of the restaurant, right by the partition to the banquet room where kids usually got handed out Little League trophies, and during darker times the Klan used to meet up on Thursday night as plain and regular as if they were the damn Jaycees. Chester's daddy had been there; his uncle, too. Somewhere in storage, Chester had been handed down his uncle's purple robe, never having the time or inclination to toss the damn thing in the dumpster.

"You look like you need a refill, sweetie," said the waitress, a kindly old woman named Miss Mary who'd been waiting tables since Methuselah was in grade school.

"Appreciate that."

"Can I get you something else?" she asked. "You haven't even touched that bacon."

"No, ma'am," Chester said. "Just feeling a little poorly this morning. My stomach ain't right."

"Well," Miss Mary said. "There's been a flu going around. Hope that ain't it."

"Truth be known, ma'am," he said, "I got the kind of sickness you find at the bottom of a bottle. My own damn fault."

She smiled at him and winked, refilling his coffee and bringing him an extra ice water. Chester felt as if he sat there another twenty minutes, he just might be able to make it through the day at the liquor store and be able to come to some kind of plan that would appease ole Johnny Stagg. The last thing in the world he wanted was to split the damn deed with that man. There was no cornholing in the world like getting cornholed by the devil himself.

At that very moment, on cue and on time, those two nasty-ass sonsabitches, the Nixes, walked through the front door of the Fillin' Station, bell jangling over their little heads and stubby little arms while their coal-black eyes wandered over the open restaurant. Miss Mary told them they could take a seat up at the counter, but those old boys weren't here for the country ham and biscuits. They walked straight on over to where Chester Pratt sat wearing sunglasses and in need of some alone time, taking a seat at the booth right next to his and accepting a menu from old Miss Mary.

Neither man, father nor son, said a damn word. Grunting and breathing up behind him. Chester reached for the coffee, not liking the way his hand shook as he lifted it to his lips.

"I heard they done quartered that woman," the young one said, speaking low and conspiratorial. "Left the head on the body but cut off the arms and legs. Cleaned her out like you would a deer."

The old one grunted some more. They both snickered a bit.

"Whoever done that gonna ride the damn needle at Parchman," the young one said. "Guess the law got to decide if it was her kid or not."

"Wadn't no kid," the old man said, croaking out his words. "Kids don't have no ability to strip that body like it got done, have the fortitude to pickle that woman in a concoction of bleach and special chemicals."

"What you thinkin', Daddy?"

"Son," the old man said. "I got me some good information it had to be some old fella got jilted by this dead whore. I figured this man got himself the best pussy he'd had in a coon's age and went crazy."

The Nixes laughed and laughed but quieted down as Miss Mary wandered on up to the table and took their orders. They spoke low and respectful as they asked for the Fillin' Station lunch plate with extra onion rings and two jumbo sweet teas. Chester didn't turn around after Miss Mary left, his eggs untouched, holding his hands around the coffee. Working with these two pieces of dogshit might've been the dumbest thing he'd ever done in his life. They weren't about to just walk away and wait until things shook out to get whatever else they thought was coming.

"You think that woman might've had a cell phone on her?" the young one asked.

"Don't know," the old one said. "If she did, mighta been all kinds of things on it."

"Text messages," the young Nix said. "Secret recordings of them doing the dirty and them coming to blows. *Shoot.* I could see that shit getting loaded up there on the World Wide Web. Being viewed more times than one of those cats playing old-time tunes on the piano."

Chester had enough. He stood up and dropped a twenty on the table. Just as he turned for the door, he caught the eye of the young one, giggling like something sure had tickled him.

"Something funny?" Chester asked.

"Didn't know you was there, Mr. Pratt," Dusty Nix said, smiling bigger than shit. "Sure am sorry to hear about your girlfriend. Me and Daddy want to wish you our thoughts and some of them good prayers."

"Y'all can go straight to hell," Chester said. "Don't come around me again."

Dusty Nix stood up, the top of his head not even reaching Chester Pratt's chin. He had his hands on his hips and his skeletal head hung high. Both of the men stinking to high heaven, like old rotten meat and rancid urine.

"No, sir," Dusty Nix said. "Me and Daddy just getting started."

"What's that mean?"

Nix looked back to the kitchen and across the restaurant to six, seven other folks out of earshot. "Don't you worry, Mr. Pratt," he said, raising his voice. "We'll get you that estimate right quick."

"I don't need y'all's help," he said. "I don't need anybody's goddamn help."

"You sure about that?"

THIRTEEN

The house was endless, a maze of dozens of halls and rooms with all the furnishings coated with a thin layer of dust, black on TJ's fingertips. She and Ladarius had slept up in that big bedroom on the second floor, while Holly and John Wesley slept downstairs by the big rock fireplace where they watched a marathon of Harry Potter DVDs on a screen nearly as large as a movie theater's. As she got up that morning, standing on a second-floor balcony and looking out on the lake, she thought this had to be the most beautiful place she'd ever been in her life. If only she'd known there was a world outside Tibbehah County, she would've left a long time back.

Ladarius had slipped away early but had come back a half hour ago, carrying in a big wine box loaded down with frozen meat, eggs, and sausage. He and Holly cooked up a mess of it while John Wesley wandered from room to room, sometimes coming up to tell TJ all the amazing things he'd found and asking what he could keep. One room, painted pink with lots of lace and frills, had more toys in it than the Tupelo Walmart, he'd said. John Wesley found a couple of remote-control cars and a few Marvel action figures, TJ saying don't steal nothing but play with what you like.

She carried a bedspread over her shoulders, her breath clouding before her while she looked out onto the lake, as she stepped off the balcony and back into the room with the big four-post bed. The bathroom had a shower as large as their trailer and a big jacuzzi under a huge oil painting of a naked white woman. Her breasts as thick and heavy as two bouncy pink water balloons. TJ figured that must be the woman of the house, spread-legged and big-jugged for only the select few to see.

TJ crashed down into the king-size bed, back under the swirl of white blankets and soft white pillows where she'd slept hard, and pulled a sheet over her head. She wished she could stay there forever, not go outside and have everyone look to her for what they were going to do next. *How the hell did she know what they needed to do or where they should go?*

She wished she still had her phone to see what was going on back home but knew Ladarius had been right. They needed to dump everything before they crossed into Arkansas or the law would know where to find them. Right now, every string connecting them back to Tibbehah had been cut.

She felt like she'd been running a long time before this road trip, going back to the first she could remember, about the time her daddy died, and being passed around from house to house until her momma came back and took over, acting like she'd gotten straight and grown up. But that was all a lie. Everything that woman said was a lie. Gina Byrd had never been a good mother or someone TJ or John Wesley could depend on. If TJ hadn't learned to take care of her own damn self, she wouldn't have made it. But a kid could learn how to drink spoiled milk or walk two miles to the scratch and dent with a sock full of change for a can of Vienna sausages and saltines. A shoeless kid could wait outside her trailer in the deep winter cold because her mom had brought home a nice new man and all the moaning and knocking kept her awake at night. A kid could do about anything, including when Gina got pregnant again, another new nice man wanting to be part of the Byrd Family Shitshow for a while.

John Wesley's daddy, a skinny, quiet fella named Carter Havens, showed TJ a lot of love and support and churchgoing until one morning she woke up to Carter standing over her bed and throttling his peter like there was no tomorrow. He'd placed his fingers to his lips and whispered to her to stay still. She'd told her mother. But Gina didn't listen. She never listened. Soon Carter Havens had gone anyway and then the baby came and TJ became an eight-year-old kid with a real-life doll that ate and shit and consumed every hour she was awake and all through the night. John Wesley would start to cry and Gina would bang on TJ's door and scream she needed some help. John Wesley hadn't been maybe six, seven months old when Gina was back at the bars, meeting up with new men for no other reason than to show bony-ass Carter Havens that she didn't give two shits that he'd gone back to his wife and three kids. That time, those early days when John Wesley had been a baby, might have been her best. TJ had some kind of structure and sense to time. She got up, took care of the baby, caught the school bus, and rode back home in the afternoon to take on chores and watch John Wesley while her momma got dolled up for another night out.

It wasn't strange. Hell, it was all TJ knew. She figured everyone took care of the younger kids just the same.

But then Gina went from being fast and loose to just plain stupid when she first brought home old Donald Evans. That man just plain-out smelled evil: cheap aftershave and liquor sweating from his skin. He'd look TJ straight in the eye and tell her that she and the baby needed to head on to the back room, him and her momma were about to get down to business. TJ one time made the mistake of wanting a glass of water and saw her naked momma pinned down on the kitchen table, Donald Evans with his pants around his ankles, red-faced and rutting like a pig. Old Donald smiled at TJ when she froze up, heart pounding, not sure if she could move, while he finished up, snatching her momma by the neck and saying he was hungry. *Why would Gina put up with that? Why'd she bring such trash into their family?*

Donald Evans. Donald Evans. Donald the Fuck. Goddamn, so many bruises, scrapes, and scars from that man. He did oil changes over at the Walmart in town and would come to their trailer in the evening stinking of sweat and grease and high as hell. He'd sit on their couch and watch their TV, pro wrestling and FOX News, flicking around the remote like he owned the place. Her mother so mousy and so damn small, cooking him frozen suppers and laying with her head in the man's lap. Donald the Fuck not having the human decency to wash the grease off his hands, leaving black smears across her momma's cheek. Smacking TJ across her face if she ever gave him any lip.

When that man hit little John Wesley, it had gone too far. She tried to talk some sense to her momma but Momma wouldn't listen. She tried to wrestle the pills and bullshit from her momma's purse and for the first time of many, boy they got into it. They smacked each other back and forth, TJ having to hold her mother by the throat to keep her away. John Wesley cowering in his bedroom, scared of just what might happen next. The law came then. And they came again—next time she tried to keep Donald the Fuck away from her kid brother. Everyone blaming TJ for being a bad kid, a youth out of control, striking her own damn momma.

TJ pulled the covers up tighter, trying not to think about that time and all the bad times Gina Byrd had brought on herself and TJ and John Wesley. Was she looking for a reason Momma was dead? As much as she wanted to be sad, mourn for her, the thought that Gina was gone gave her a little bit of relief and ease to it all. *Carter Havens.*

Donald Evans. And then a man whose name she couldn't even recall. He showed up a couple of years ago, just after she'd found those pit bull puppies down the road at that abandoned trailer. They were hers and John Wesley's, not long after a hard Christmas when Gina had gone and disappeared for two weeks and that woman from the state tried to take them both away and put them into a new home. A good home with decent Christian people. TJ had met the new man with no name late one night because of her momma's screams. He'd gone and pushed Gina through a thin wall and was choking her. TJ did the best she could, finding an old baseball bat they kept for protection and knocking that man down to his knees. He didn't come to for nearly an hour.

The man left. And her momma didn't say a word about what had happened. The bruised outlines of the man's fingers on her neck. When the deputy came, Momma blamed TJ again, although this time TJ didn't have nothin' to do with nothin'.

Two days later, TJ came home to find two of her puppies gone and the three who were left bleeding out their mouths and backsides. Someone, but she knew damn well who, had returned and filled the water bowls with bright yellow antifreeze. She tried to feed them milk and hold them warm and tight. But the puppies died. Little John Wesley didn't speak for nearly a month. Caught up somewhere in his head with sorrow and shame and wondering why the God they loved so much had brought such horrible misfortune on them all.

TJ heard Ladarius again, calling out to her from the bottom of the steps. *"TJ. TJ. Where you at?"* She kicked off the heavy blanket in the mammoth bed and opened her eyes. Ladarius ran up the steps and peeked into the room.

"Steak and eggs?" he said. "I got us some real good shit."

"Oh, yeah?" she said. "I could use some good shit right about now."

"Come and get it, little girl," Ladarius said. "We're all waiting for you."

Quinn found Boom inside the County Barn, up on top of the big engine of a Mack gravel spreader, his false hand filled with ratchets and twisting hard.

"Brought you some fried pies," Quinn said.

"Miss Graves?"

"You know it."

"Apple or peach?"

"Apricot," Quinn said. "I ate the peach."

"That's selfish as hell," Boom said, back turned to Quinn. "You know peach is my favorite."

Quinn waited as Boom finished whatever he was doing and climbed back down the ladder leaning against the truck. The big man headed on over to the workbench running across the far wall and pulled out a ratchet fitted into his artificial hand. He unlatched his forearm and replaced it with his steel hook. The hook reached out and snatched the paper sack away from Quinn. He sniffed the open sack.

"No wonder you scared the shit out of Sheriff Lovemaiden."

"Speaking of," Boom said. "You come to check out that car? That man left me a hell of a nasty message when he found out I didn't deliver it to the state folks in Jackson."

"Easy to get confused," Quinn said. "Seeing that it was originally supposed to come back here."

"Lovemaiden was none too pleased," Boom said. "What do you want with it? Reggie Caruthers already took prints off the door and inside. Ain't nothing in there but a whole bunch of trash. Reggie checked that shit out, too."

"Can't hurt to take another look," Quinn said. "How's the pie? Almost as good?"

Boom didn't answer, chewing one last large bite as a small radio on his workbench played soul classics from a station in Tupelo. Quinn recognized one of the older hits, "Blind, Crippled, and Crazy" by OV Wright. Boom's daddy, Deacon Kimbrough, used to play that stuff all the time when he'd drive them all over north Mississippi for youth football games. Quinn couldn't recall a time that he hadn't been friends with Boom Kimbrough.

"What you think you're gonna find?" Boom said. "Y'all already found a damn hacksaw in that shed."

"Who told you that?"

"Everybody in town knows."

"Kenny?" Quinn asked.

"I love Kenny, but damn, that boy can't keep his mouth shut," Boom said. "Reggie told me those kids hit the road. Folks saying that Gina Byrd didn't care for her little angel shacking up with a black boy from down in the Ditch."

"That's bullshit," Quinn said. "Gina wasn't a racist. Hell, she dated black men herself."

"Never dated me," Boom said. "I was too damn country-ass for her. She liked those boys who rode up to Memphis and hit those clubs. Ones with gold teeth and spinning rims. Not ones who listened to Charley Pride and hung out in the woods."

Quinn refilled his coffee from Boom's pot. He lifted his travel mug to his pal. "Kiss an Angel Good Mornin'."

"Is Anybody Goin' to San Antone."

Boom pointed to the far side of the barn where Quinn spotted the blue Nissan parked all alone and crooked in the corner. They walked over to the car as Quinn reached into his jacket pocket for a pair of rubber gloves, plastic baggies, and small Maglite. The passenger side was open and Quinn began to search through the glove compartment and center console for any papers, personal notes, or bills that might tell him something about Gina Byrd. He'd already found out she had a checking account at Jericho First National and he'd subpoenaed her bank records that morning. He removed anything of interest and placed it into Ziploc bags for testing, hoping maybe the state lab could grab a print if those Reggie took off the door handles and inside the car didn't work out.

"Gina sure loved Sonic," Quinn said, placing receipt after receipt in the bag.

"Meth monkeys love those tots."

"Is that it?"

"What I heard."

"You hear where she got the money?"

"Who you think."

"Chester Pratt," Quinn said. "Her sugar daddy?"

"Old man liked to keep that girl happy," Boom said. "Same ole sad song."

Quinn started to hum a few bars of "All I Have to Offer You Is Me." He had all four doors open now, in the back and reaching under the front seats. A few red straws and some plastic Coke and Sprite bottles. More receipts from the Huddle House, Piggly Wiggly, and the Walmart in town. He read through them all but not finding much. Every receipt, everything in the car, going in the baggies. He'd inventory them all back at the SO and then send them on to Jackson.

"Just heard from Nat Wilkins," Boom said. "She wants me to meet her down in New Orleans sometime. You know she took that transfer?"

"Oh, yeah?"

"Everyone knows her face in north Mississippi after what went down with Fannie Hathcock," Boom said. "What you think? You think I should go?"

"No," Quinn said. "I think your old ass should avoid meeting up with a smart and beautiful woman. As they're so easy to come by."

"Took you long enough," Boom said. "To get what you wanted."

"But it worked out."

"Maggie could've done better."

Quinn was up front now, looking under the driver's seat, roaming the Maglite around the carpet and up under the floor mats. Dirt and trash, a few loose coins. A glint of silver caught his eye, a thin blade caught between the front seat and the console. He reached for it and pulled it out into the overhead light of the County Barn. The blade's tip was jagged and broken.

"What's that?" Boom asked.

"Spent blade off a cutter."

"That's a roofing cutter," Boom said, walking up beside him. "Gina Byrd do much of that work?"

"Nope," Quinn said. "But she probably knew a few roofers, hanging out at the Southern Star."

"Roofers are rough," Boom said. "But sheet rockers are the worst. Breathing in that dust all day makes 'em crazy as hell."

Quinn bagged the small blade and shut the doors. He looked to all the black powder splattered around the windows, locks, and across the steering wheel and shifter. Reggie had done a fine and complete job.

"You heard anything about Chester Pratt having a fallout with his brother?" Quinn asked.

"Ronnie?" Boom said. "Shit, man. Ronnie's dead."

"That's what I thought, too," Quinn said. "But my mom says he's alive and well. Gone back to selling used cars at the Ford dealership.

Apparently, he's been saying Chester screwed him out of that liquor license."

"Need a lot of money and connections to get one of those," Boom said. "Wonder how ole Chester pulled that one off. Being that he's been the town fuckup."

"Don't know," Quinn said. "But I aim to find out."

Holly Harkins started having regrets a little after midnight, the whole weight of their situation dumped on her head like a heavy concrete block. Not only had she run away, but she'd also stolen her momma's minivan to help her friends get free from the law. Now they'd gone on to break into a mansion and rob some neighboring houses. Ladarius found frozen steaks at one place, a six-pack of fancy beer at another. That's where she drew the damn line. They might be outlaws but they damn sure weren't going to start drinking. Holly poured out every bottle and told that boy to get a hold of himself. *Why was she here? What was she doing?*

Her whole dumb life she'd made stupid quick decisions. Never thinking things out like her momma told her. Like that time she jumped off that rope swing out at Choctaw Lake and broke her leg. Or last summer when she bleached her hair blonde to be the same color as TJ's and turned it orange. So many damn stupid things. Agreeing to take pictures in her underwear for that Gibson boy after they only made out once. It didn't take two hours before every boy in her class had seen her nearly naked ass and those ginormous boobs she hated. *Why did she do it?* Hell, she didn't even like that boy, let alone give two shits about wanting to be with him.

She'd been so certain about telling TJ, Ladarius, and poor John Wesley to grab what they could and jump in the minivan two nights ago. They'd all figure it out on the road. Right? That's what she was thinking, that maybe they could just go somewhere for a while until folks figured out that TJ would never hurt her mom and they could head on home with everything like it used to be. But last night, while everyone was asleep, she scrolled through that new phone they'd gotten at the Walmart and saw what big news they'd all become. This wasn't some small personal shit. Everyone, and she meant *every-one*, was talking about them.

TJ and Ladarius had been charged with murder. Holly's name was in the stories, too, talking about her like she'd been an accomplice in whatever happened to Gina Byrd.

How the hell had everyone gotten things so damn wrong? Maybe they should have stayed in Tibbehah to explain everything. Running had made them all look guilty as hell. *Stupid, Holly. So damn stupid, just like always.*

Maybe it had something to do with her being an only child. Her mother always wanted her to be perfect. There had been dance lessons, and when they realized Holly was too clumsy, she went to the violin. When the violin became too much trouble, there had been ice skating all the way up in Olive Branch before she broke her ankle. And then it was her grades. She couldn't just be an A/B student, but all A's, damn well better be on that honor roll. And church. She sang in the youth choir and helped with Sunday school. When she'd been offered a job at the Captain's Table, her mother worried that might interfere with the Wednesday Bible study. She couldn't even imagine that maybe a teenage girl didn't want to sit through a second service in the middle of the week, listening to their two-bit preacher talk as if he'd been intoxicated by his up-close-and-personal relationship with Jesus H. Christ.

Now that she was gone and Tibbehah was in the rearview, Holly wasn't so sure she wanted to go back ever again. Standing there at the edge of the lake, mist rising from the surface, it seemed to be the first time she could breathe in a long while. Soon TJ would get smart and drop Ladarius or Ladarius would head back home. Then maybe she and TJ could find somewhere new to live, try dyeing her hair again, and think about some new names. She and TJ could even raise John Wesley like he was their own. Maybe Florida. Maybe down at the beach somewhere. And that would end all the days and nights at that musty church or with pimply-faced boys with a thousand hands feeling up under her sweater, praying to God that she would feel something stir inside of her. But she never did.

The only time she'd felt like that had been with TJ, two summers ago, out there in the inner tube on Choctaw Lake. They'd reached out and touched hands, held them for a long while as they watched that sunset, and Holly knew there was no other place she'd rather be.

Holly stood at the end of the pier, her breath clouding before her with a thick blanket around her shoulders. Up the hill, she heard John Wesley call her name. She'd never seen that kid so excited in her life. A big pile of trucks and toys by the television, more food than he could ever eat. "Breakfast," he said, yelling. "Ladarius stole us up some steak."

Holly knew it was wrong, but she couldn't stop smiling. She only wished they could all just stay in that big house forever. Still, she knew that wasn't the way things worked out for kids like them. They were nothing but intruders into someone else's world.

"Heard you were looking for me, Sheriff," Ronnie Pratt said, standing at the doorway of Quinn's office. Hands in his pockets, sunglasses up on top of his gray head. He was a chunkier and shorter version of his younger brother, wearing khaki pants and a blue golf shirt with a Ford emblem. Quinn had left him a message at the dealership as he headed back to town.

"I was about to head your way, Ronnie," Quinn said, standing and shaking his hand. "Appreciate you coming in."

"I've been waiting for you to call," Ronnie said. "Chester said you might be checking up on him."

"He did?"

"Yes, sir," Ronnie said, taking a seat across from Quinn's desk. His ass nearly too wide for the arms. "Damn shame what happened to Gina. First woman Chester had ever been seeing that was worth a shit. She was a damn fine-looking gal, too. Makes me sick to my stomach to hear what happened to her. Chopped up into little pieces by her own child. I don't have to tell you that's what happens when we take God out of schools. Replace 'The Star-Spangled Banner' with all that rap music."

"Is that a fact?"

"Yes, sir," Ronnie said. "You grew up here. Is it like it was back in the old days?"

"Tibbehah County has never had the makings of a Cracker Barrel menu, Mr. Pratt," Quinn said. "Time has a funny way of twisting your memory."

Pratt didn't like the answer, resting his hands over his prosperous stomach. He removed the sunglasses off his head, blew on a lens, and began to polish them with his shirtsleeve.

"Y'all caught 'em yet?" Pratt asked.

"No, sir."

"How far can a bunch of kids run?" he said. "I saw that girl hooked up with some nigger boy. I guess that's how it all starts."

"Mr. Pratt, I came to you for assistance," Quinn said. "But I don't care for that kind of talk and if you use that word again, I'll see to it you leave by the window."

Pratt snickered at that. Quinn just stared at him from across the table until he stopped. He placed the glasses into the V on his golf shirt and swallowed. "Shoot," he said. "I guess y'all elected officials got to be all politically correct these days or the media will be coming for your damn nuts."

Quinn didn't dignify him with a response. He'd nearly forgotten how much he disliked the whole Pratt family. They kept a well-worn kind of cockiness, like they were too good for Tibbehah County. The kind of people that would brag that they were the descendants of plantation owners and Confederate generals while everyone knew their granddaddy, like most everyone else, had worked the fields and owed the commissary come harvest time.

"Weren't you and Chester supposed to be partners in that liquor store?"

"Now we're getting somewhere," he said. "You want me to come down here and stab my own brother in the back. Holy damn hell."

"No, sir," Quinn said. "Just need to know why he went at it himself."

Ronnie Pratt rubbed a hand over his jaw, stubbled with little white hairs. Quinn had heard that every time he sold a car, the manager at the dealership would ring a little bell and Ronnie Pratt would take a nip from a flask inside his coat. Quinn kept waiting for the man to pull it out while they talked privately.

"Chester didn't need me no more," he said. "I reckon he got the money somewhere else."

"Like where?"

"I don't know," he said. "I figured when Chester came to me, wanting me to throw into the pot, he'd already gone to every dumb son of a bitch in north Mississippi with his hat in his gosh-dang hands."

"How much money did he need to borrow?"

"That's a private business matter, Sheriff," Ronnie said. "I don't know if I should be saying all this without my attorney present. You do know ole Sonny Stevens?"

"Best lawyer in the county while he's drunk," Quinn said. "Second best when he's sober. Yeah, I know Sonny. He's my lawyer, too."

Ronnie Pratt started to chuckle again. "I guess y'all need lawyers these days with all this anti-police stuff. You sometimes got to get a little rough with prisoners. Make sure their heads hit the bars on the way in. Har. Har."

"Nope," Quinn said. "I shot three men dead, including a former sheriff's deputy, out at the old airfield a few years ago. You might've read something about it."

Pratt's smile dropped. He again pulled out his sunglasses from his shirt and began to study the lenses in the overhead light. Not liking what he saw, Ronnie Pratt blew on them once more and began to polish with the edge of his shirt, flashing his big hairy belly.

"Altogether, Chester said he needed to come up with right around fifty thousand dollars," Ronnie said. "Give or take a nickel."

"And you were prepared to give it to him?"

"Had to loot my savings for my part, about twenty-five thousand, but who wouldn't want to be co-owner of the only liquor store in three counties?" Pratt asked. "Seemed like the kind of thing that even my baby brother couldn't fuck up."

"Did Chester tell you where he got the rest?"

"No, sir," Ronnie said. "He did not. I hadn't spoken to him since our partnership fell through. His call the other night came out of the blue and I was still sore about him screwing me over. But given the tragedy he'd endured, I didn't want to bring up an old grievance."

"Your compassion is overwhelming."

Ronnie Pratt shook his head, sucked a tooth, and stood up on his little fat legs. He looked at his watch. "My lunch break's nearly over, Sheriff," he said. "Got a woman driving down from Oxford wants to see a real special Expedition. One of them big ones with all the trimmings."

"Good luck," Quinn said, nodding to the door.

"You, too," Ronnie Pratt said. "Sure hope those kids go down in a hail of bullets. Now that'd be better than a sweaty ole Fourth of July. Wouldn't it?"

Ladarius McCade did not care what anyone might have heard, he was no damn criminal. He was slick. He was good at what he did. And sure, he may have taken a few things over the last few years. But that wasn't a crook. A crook hurt people, stole from hardworking folks and families. He'd never done that in his life. Rich folks had so much stuff laying around that they barely even missed it. And if he happened to take their vehicle and drive it over to that chop shop in Byhalia, insurance would pay them back. All he was doing was plying the trade that his great-uncle Dupuy taught him.

Ladarius pulled out another steak from the counter, getting softer but still frozen most of the way through. He tossed it into a black skillet, the meat starting to heat and burn, wishing he now had one of those cold beers damn Holly poured out in the yard.

Yeah, this was all right. Maybe they could go home once the law stopped harassing TJ. Until then, TJ needed good people around her, looking after her and little John Wesley, letting her have some time to heal up after what happened to her mother.

Ladarius couldn't stop thinking about what TJ had told him, about her mother coming home from the Southern Star that night, her shirt soaked in some man's blood, telling TJ that she'd killed a man out back of the bar. Gina Byrd said she had no idea why she was attacked, but TJ had too much experience with Gina Byrd's lies and deceit. That woman was out back doing something that she shouldn't been doing. Maybe trading some of that booty for some pills or to smoke a little of that crystal meth. Whatever she did didn't much matter now. TJ should've gone and trusted Sheriff Colson to find out the truth. Wasn't no doubt in any of their minds, Miss Gina was killed in some kind of revenge. At first, she'd said one man. And then there were two. TJ said her momma was so damn fucked up she barely knew her own damn name. Talking nonsense. Slurring her damn words.

Ladarius forked at the steak, still frozen solid but burning a bit on the other side, smoke coming from the skillet. He turned over the meat and hit the fan, the last thing they needed was for the whole damn Hot Springs Fire Department to be rolling up on their asses. This was gonna be one fine place to hole up for a few days, kick back, eat some good food, and watch some TV. Maybe, just maybe, TJ would start feeling a little better and might let Ladarius do what he'd been wanting to do since they started dating. That girl always slapping his damn hand from her pants when things were getting good.

The only thing that worried him was the law coming, finding them when they didn't expect it. From what he was seeing on the news, folks seemed to be blaming him for what TJ never did. Folks weren't looking for them anymore to ask questions, he and TJ had been damn charged with murder. TJ didn't seem to be bothered by the news, but in Ladarius's world, getting charged with a crime wasn't no joke. Shit. He'd been charged with breaking and entering, theft, assault, and possession. The possession charge had been real bullshit as he was only holding some weed for his cousin Ricky. But murder. *Shit.* This was serious-ass business that was drawing a big old target on his black ass. Come knock-knock time, there wasn't gonna be any time to explain jack shit.

Ladarius turned over the steak again and forked into the middle, good ole blood oozing out into the pan. Maybe it hadn't been a good idea to cook them steaks after all. He was glad that he'd grilled TJ's good and well done, nearly burnt.

Man, there had been a time when he thought he'd be known for something better. Athlete, rapper, actor. Some shit like that. When he was a kid, folks at his church used to tell him he looked a lot like Will Smith, and that pleased him to no end as he'd been a big fan of those *Bad Boys* movies. Even thinking maybe he'd go straight and become a policeman, too. Back two, three years ago there was still time. But now? Shit. Wasn't no way he was headed back. They were headed down the road the preacher called that long, dark path.

The steak was burning and smoking from the pan and he turned off the gas. He used a towel to pick up the skillet and set it down on the marble top of a big island.

He'd just found a fork and knife and was about to dig in when a pretty little blonde girl busted into the room and pointed a gun right at him. Damn, this shit was just getting better and better. Big blue eyes with curly blonde hair.

"Who the hell are you and what the hell are you doing in my house?" she asked.

"What's a pretty little thing like you doing with a big gun like that?" Ladarius asked, smiling. Trying to do his best and most charming Will Smith.

"If you don't put up your hands and step away from the T-bone," the blonde girl said, "you sure as hell are gonna find out."

FOURTEEN

Lillie had a rare few hours off and had taken Rose and their new pit bull, Jerry Lee, down to Tom Lee Park along the Mississippi River. She knew at any moment the marshals might get a lead on those kids and anxiously walked the riverside with her phone in her hand. They hadn't been at the park fifteen minutes when Quinn called, Lillie hoping this would finally be it, that someone down in Tibbehah knew where they'd gone over in Arkansas.

"Let me guess," Lillie said. "Those little bastards came down to the SO and turned themselves in?"

"No such luck," Quinn said. "But I am hearing a few things that trouble me."

"Troubling you?" Lillie said. "If you don't know where they've run off to, I don't much give a damn."

"You need to hear this."

"Oh, hell," Lillie said. "You think TJ Byrd may be innocent. Right? May I remind you I don't give two shits. You investigate. I bring 'em in. And it's not up to either of us whether they're guilty or not. Damn. I sure was hoping you were Charlie Hodge. He's been running down no-tell motels in West Memphis while I get a little time with Miss Rose."

"And how is she?"

"More beautiful and perfect than her momma deserves," Lillie said. "She also eats like a horse and cusses like a sailor. Fluently, I might add, in two languages."

"Wonder where she gets it?"

Lillie had on a Redbirds ball cap and a puffy black coat. It was colder than a witch's tit along the Mississippi, but the sun was high and bright, not a cloud in the sky. Rose ran in circles with Jerry Lee, that muscly dog wanting back the rope bone she'd been tossing to him.

"Okay," Lillie said. "I'll bite. Tell me why you called, Sheriff. Won't make a damn difference to me, but I'd be glad to listen while I spend precious family time with my daughter and our dog."

"When did y'all get a dog?"

"Christmas," Lillie said. "From the shelter. You'd like him. Big, brindle-coated pit named Jerry Lee. He'd tear a man's nuts off as quick as I can snap my fingers."

The wind blew hard across the bluffs, scattering dead leaves down around the wide-open grassy spaces and causing static on her phone.

"Listen, Lil," Quinn said. "Ronnie Pratt just left my office. He said a few months back, Chester needed him to partner up on that new liquor store. But then all of the sudden Chester told Ronnie he didn't need his money. Ronnie says he has no idea where his brother came up with that kind of cash."

"How do I ever get by without knowing that good ole cornpone gossip?" Lillie asked. "I wonder if Li'l Abner's still poking Daisy Mae behind the woodshed."

"These kids ran because they're scared," Quinn said. "Not because they're guilty."

"I know ninety-nine damn percent of the time when a woman gets killed it's the boyfriend or the husband or Colonel Mustard in the kitchen with his dick in his hand," Lillie said. "But then there is the unlucky fucking one percent who give birth to an evil little shit like TJ Byrd. Who just happens to want to knock boots with a crook like Ladarius McCade."

"Hear me out, Lil."

"I appreciate you hopping on the due diligence trail," Lillie said. "I really do. But seriously, who cares about Chester Pratt's business? I doubt he'd let Gina Byrd anywhere near his till. A blind man would've made better change."

"What if I told you that the Byrds recently came into a nice insurance settlement," Quinn said. "And might've been flush for the first time in their lives?"

"If Gina Byrd found twenty dollars on the street, it would be up her goddamn nose in ten minutes."

"Not this kind of money," Quinn said. "Ronnie Pratt says he'd planned to go in with Chester for about twenty-five grand. At the last minute, Chester didn't need it."

"Where'd you hear Gina Byrd got that kind of money?"

"Gina had been saying the settlement was big enough to change their lives," Quinn said. "According to Miss Donna Grace at the flower shop yesterday."

"Let me get this shit straight," Lillie said. "Miss Donna Grace, the fucking florist, has the hotline on the junkie who made door hangings out of old rope and rusted tin cans? Well, let me call up my supervisor and let him know that fucking Petticoat Junction PD has solved the case. We can all stand down."

There was a long silence. Lillie thinking maybe she'd pushed Quinn too damn far this time. He could get real sensitive about his investigations and being a relative newcomer to police work after ten years in the Army kicking in doors over in the Jihad Jungle. But she was tired and worn out and just wanted a few hours with Rose and her new dog. Was that too much to ask?

Lillie took a deep breath. Jerry Lee lay panting on his side while Rose cuddled up next to him. Rose had on a little red ski hat with a toggle ball on top. Her cheeks red and flushed from the running and the cold wind. "Did you contact the bank?" Lillie asked.

"Yep."

"And?"

"I'm waiting on the judge to see Gina's records," Quinn said. "I'm also planning on riding out to see Tabitha Threadgill and see what she knows."

"Big Momma?" Lillie asked. "Lucky you. There are parts of Tibbehah County I really miss. Mornings at the Fillin' Station. Getting fried catfish over at Pap's. But making midnight calls on Big Momma for beating the holy fuck out of her girlfriends ain't one of them."

"She's Jerry Jeff Valentine's half-sister."

"I know exactly who she is," Lillie said. "You don't need to go and tell me about Tabitha Threadgill. I was hog wrestling that fat crazy bitch while you were ogling shaggy goats out there in Kandahar."

"Is that what I was doing?"

"What else are a bunch of red-blooded Army Rangers gonna do for fun while on deployment?"

"I'll be sure not to brief you on what I hear."

"Call me when you clear those kids," Lillie said. "In the meantime, you better watch your narrow ass with Miss Threadgill. That woman makes Fannie Hathcock seem like the fuzzy-ass kitty cat."

"Some days I do miss your way with words, Lillie."

"And other days?"

"Other days I've learned to be my own counsel."

"Glad to hear it," Lillie said. "I knew I trained you right."

Lillie looked at her watch and waved for Rose come on back. Lillie walked toward her car and into the wind, looking at the monorail out to Mud Island and at the old Pyramid that been turned into a Bass Pro Shop and fancy redneck motel. The Mississippi moved fast and strong down to New Orleans, branches and stray pieces of trash caught in the flow.

"One more thing," Quinn said.

Lillie waited, her back to the river and the wind.

"Why'd you name your dog Jerry Lee?" Quinn asked.

"Why else, son?" Lillie said. "Because he's a stone-cold killer."

"Baby," Ladarius said. "I know we just met. But do you mind taking that gun out of my face?"

"You got five seconds to explain who you are and what you're doing here or I'm hitting 911."

"Come on now, missy," Ladarius said. "Let's all be cool for a second."

"Walk one more step and I'll show you cool," the girl said. "My father just bought me this Smith & Wesson and I sure as hell know how to use it. Now answer my GD question."

TJ watched all the cool and bullshit drain from Ladarius's face as the boy froze up before TJ walked out in the open, barefoot with her hands up, and said, "Just some kids looking for some shelter," she said. "We thought this place was abandoned."

"Abandoned?" the blonde girl said. "How many freaky deaky empty houses leave a Sub-Zero fridge and eighteen television sets? And Jesus Christ. Just how many of there are you?"

"Four," TJ said. "Me and my little brother. Ladarius here and my friend Holly."

"Y'all just go around and break into houses for kicks?" the girl asked, still holding a big-ass silver gun in her hands. Her hands shook some, but her hair and makeup were perfect, huge blue eyes accentuated with lots of mascara. She had one of those fake leopard coats with the fur-trimmed hood loose around her neck, the coat open and showing off a frilly white shirt and fancy jeans shredded on her thighs.

"We were cold and we were hungry," TJ said. "And we're about out of gas."

"Nothing to eat here but jars of olives and stale crackers," she said. "Where'd y'all get those steaks?"

"Piggly Wiggly," Ladarius said, lying quick. "Two-for-one special. Sit down and I'll grill you up one. How you like it? You look like a medium-rare kinda girl."

"Both of you need to quit talking and sit down until the cops come," the girl said. "I told my father something was wrong with the security system, but he wouldn't listen. He said everything worked just perfect. Perfect, hell. Works great until some trashy-ass redneck kids break into our house."

TJ nodded, knowing damn well what it felt like to be on the good side of the gun, and walked over beside Ladarius. They both took a seat at the big kitchen island. On the stove top, the iron skillet kept on smoking until the girl walked around and turned off the gas.

"Jesus H. Christ," she said again. "Don't you hicks have any sense? I mean really. You want to burn down the whole GD house. Go ahead and call down the rest of you. Let me have a look at the whole sorry bunch."

TJ yelled for Holly and John Wesley, who were back in the great room watching that big-ass television. They'd moved on from Harry

Potter and now were watching those Spy Kids movies from a long time back. She figured they'd been too busy eating steak and eggs to pay attention to this girl busting all up in the place.

When Holly walked into the kitchen, she immediately dropped her plate onto the floor, sending the meat and gristle and bone flying. "Oh, my god. Oh, my god."

John Wesley followed, smiling, not seeming to care a new girl was in the house and holding a huge automatic gun in her hand. "Howdy," he said. "My name's John Wesley. That's a real nice gun. Where you get it?"

"Sit down, kid," the girl said. "Just how old are you?"

"Nine," John Wesley said, beaming. "But I'll be ten come this June. Where you'd get that gun? Looks like a .357 with a walnut grip. My Uncle Wayne has one just like it."

The girl switched the big gun into her other hand and pulled a phone from her back pocket. She sure as hell was punching up some numbers before her eyes widened and her face lit up. "Wait," she said. "Wait a hot damn second. I know you. Or at least two of you."

"I doubt it," TJ said.

"Yes, I do," the girl said. "You're her. Aren't you? And that's your black boyfriend?"

"Yeah," Ladarius said. "You got me. I'm the black one."

"Y'all killed her mother?" the girl said. "Didn't you? Cut her up and dropped her down in some redneck trash dump down in Mississippi."

John Wesley stopped shuffling around and smiling. He turned to TJ while his face broke apart and his whole body shook, convulsing like she'd seen people do at that church they opened up in the old Hollywood Video. The kid started to speak but something caught in his throat. TJ got up and ran over to him, dropping down on her knees and hugging him tight.

"Go on," TJ said, yelling at the girl. "Call the police. Do what you need to."

"Did y'all do it?"

"Hush," TJ said.

"Really?" the girl said. "I hate my damn stepmother so much my teeth ache. That woman must've done something awful for you to do what y'all did."

John Wesley couldn't take it anymore, standing tall and wiggling free of TJ, little fists balled up at his side. "That's a lie! You're a damn liar! My momma's not dead! She went to Louisiana! You're a bullshit liar!"

"We didn't kill anyone," Ladarius said. "Police wanted to put TJ in jail. Me, too. So we ran. Okay? That good with you?"

Holly hadn't said a damn word since breaking her plate, getting down on her hands and knees cleaning up the mess she'd made. Now she was sitting back on her big haunches, looking up to this girl and back to TJ, not sure which one was more in charge. That was Holly, always looking for a damn leader.

"Please don't call the police," TJ said, pulling John Wesley close, who was now silently crying while glaring at the girl. "I can explain some things. And then we'll leave."

The girl slipped the gun inside the pocket of the fancy cheetah-print coat, still holding the phone in her right hand. "Y'all are famous," she said. "You're all over the damn news. Got your lover under your spell and everything. In love and on the run."

"He ain't my lover," TJ said. "He's just a friend."

"Not from what I'm hearing," the girl said. She nodded to the middle of the island where Ladarius had left half a joint at the edge of a saucer. "Wait a second. Y'all have some weed?"

"Help yourself, sweet thing," Ladarius said.

TJ shot him a look. She turned back to the girl, waiting to see what she was doing. Behind her, she could hear Holly Harkins sobbing, hands over her eyes, not wanting to see what happened next.

"Only an insane person would sit down and smoke a joint with a bunch of redneck outlaws like you," the girl said.

Ladarius reached for the joint and handed it to her. She reached out and took it.

"Well," the girl said. "I guess it's your lucky goddamn day. I just got back from rehab last week. My counselor told me to get out and live my own life. You know? All that good shit."

TJ held John Wesley as tight as she could, looking back to Holly. Holly, covered up in a big blue sweatshirt, had her hands still over her face and eyes, turning her head from side to side and mumbling some kind of prayer.

"Okay, then?" TJ asked. "Are we good?"

"Maybe." The girl smiled. "Let me think about it. One of y'all outlaws got a light?"

To call Tabitha Threadgill unattractive might be a little too generous, Quinn thought. She had to weigh well over three hundred pounds with a face like a bulldog and a temperament to match. The woman started most conversations with "What the fuck do you want?" or "That bitch told you what?" So many crazy women out on her land. For as long as Quinn had been sheriff, Tabitha had always had a string of steady girlfriends, most of them partners she'd met online and coerced to come and stay with her down home on her "Mississippi Ranch." Her ranch being sixty acres of logged-out hills and a narrow patch of skinny pine trees where she lived in a one-story house of indeterminate style or shape, mainly held together with duct tape, Visqueen, and spit.

Quinn turned off the main road and headed onto the woman's land, the small, ramshackle house coming into view. As he parked, he noticed a nice collection of new toys around the trailer. A new above-ground swimming pool covered for the winter, a speedboat up on a trailer, and two matching jet skis.

Quinn walked up the wooden steps and knocked on the door. He heard a television inside and soon some shuffling steps before the dead bolt slid back on the door. A skinny girl, late teens or early twenties, opened up. She had bug eyes and stringy red hair, wearing nothing but an oversized T-shirt that came down past her knees. The T-shirt read: BIG BOOBED AND TATTOOED. The young woman didn't appear to be either of those things.

"Miss Threadgill around?"

"You mean Big Momma?"

"That's right."

"She's out hunting with the girls," she said.

"Hunting season ended last week."

"Really?" the girl said, folding her arms over her small chest, shivering a bit. "Maybe they're just out mud riding. Big Momma's been racing them things around ever since they got here Christmas morning."

"And what's your name?"

"Jenny."

"What do you do, Jenny?"

"Nothing," she said. "Just came down for the weekend. A little fun in the country. Cook a hog. Shoot some guns. You want to come on in, good lookin'?"

Quinn shook his head, about to head back to his truck, when he heard the rumbling of a four-wheeler racing down from the hills and zigzagging through the skinny pine trees. He stepped off the porch and down to the dirt path as he spotted Tabitha Threadgill herself behind the wheel of a big four-wheeler, another skinny young girl riding behind her, arms stretched around the big woman's waist. Two more four-wheelers, same make and model, followed with two heavy-set women driving in a straight line behind her.

Tabitha rode up hard and fast to where Quinn stood, kicking up some rocks and dust. She had on a pair of red pajamas with unlaced mud boots and a big green Carhartt coat. A cigarette dangled from the corner of her mouth. "The fuck you doing here, Quinn?"

"Morning, Big Momma," Quinn said. "Y'all out hunting?"

A nice-sized doe lay slumped over the back of one of the other four-wheelers, glassy-eyed and tongue hanging out. The other two women were nearly as big as Tabitha with their backsides drooping off each side of the narrow seats. They couldn't be much older than Quinn but had weathered faces and almost colorless eyes, hair a strawy mix of white and yellow. One of them appeared to have side-burns and the faint tracing of a mustache.

"Found this doe on the road," Tabitha said. "What of it?"

"I'm not a game warden," Quinn said. "I came to talk to you about Gina Byrd."

"I know she's dead," Tabitha said. "I know someone done killed her sorry ass. You want me to go hang my head and cry about it? Shit."

The two other big women stayed put on their four-wheelers. The skinny girl had come out onto the porch, still shivering while watching the action from the stairs, her stringy red hair blowing over her pale white face. The leafless trees around the property swayed in the cold wind.

"Also just heard your mother died recently," Quinn said. "My con-dolences on both."

"Sad about Momma," Tabitha said, sucking down the cigarette to a nub and pitching it at Quinn's feet. "My asshole half-sister stuck her in a real shithole. Wadn't for that, she'd be alive today."

"Was that up in Corinth?"

"Yeah," she said. "Newspapers called that place Motel Hell. You know, like that movie where them folks eat their guests like a pork supper?"

"I may have read something about it."

Big Momma reached for a pack of cigarettes and set fire to the end of one with a small, skinny lighter. "Something on your mind, Sheriff?" she said. "Or did you just come on out to offer your fucking thoughts and prayers? Because I'm about to freeze my big-ass titties off out here while we shoot the breeze."

Quinn scratched at his cheek, looked down at the dust on his square-toed boots and then back at Big Momma. It wasn't easy looking that woman in the eye, but he did his best. Her eyes were so tiny they were almost lost in the expanse of her face, jowls drooping as she sucked in more smoke.

"Appears you've been having a real time around here," Quinn said. "Nice swimming pool. Some new four-wheelers and a big boat. Yep. Y'all are living the life."

"Don't see how that's any of your concern."

"Just wondering how things turned around for you," Quinn said. "Last time I saw you, you were worried about some man from over in New Albany foreclosing on your land."

"Not no more," she said. "That shit's all over."

"Lucky you."

"Ain't no luck about it," she said. "Paid that shit off with the settlement my lawyer got. A little left over for a few toys. No crime in that. Is it?"

"No, ma'am," Quinn said. "That's a nice one, too. What is that, a Kawasaki? The 750?"

"Yep," Big Momma said, turning to each of her gal pals. Giving what might've passed as a smile if her lips could curl in that direction. "They call these things Brute Force. I kind of liked that as that's been my motto. Right behind 'Momma gets shit done.' This here model has a twelve-hundred-pound towing capacity."

"Bet that comes in handy."

"Damn straight," Big Momma said. The skinny girl up behind her peeking out from around the mammoth back of the woman. "Are we done here? Me and my girls need to strip this here deer."

"Guess that settlement paid out to your mother's whole family."

"Yeah," she said. "That's right."

"Gina Byrd, too."

"Gina?" she said. "Gina didn't get jack shit. That bitch wasn't family. Only that runt girl of hers got a cut. And nothing like the family got, neither."

"Just out of curiosity," Quinn said. "How much was it?"

"Don't see how that's any business of yours."

"Might help me figure out some things."

"Like how far them goddamn kids are gonna get on my ole momma's money?"

"Sure," Quinn said. "Something like that."

"Not too far at all," Big Momma said. "That smart attorney up there in Corinth seen to it that little cunt couldn't touch that money till she turned eighteen."

"Who was in charge of it?"

"Don't rightly know," Big Momma said. The ash on her cigarette drooping long before the wind blew and scattered the ashes across her jacket. "I figured Gina. Guess she ain't gonna be spending none of it now, either. *Ha. Ha.* That's why I don't live for tomorrow. That's why me and my gal pals run and gun and party like hell till this big ole shitshow stops spinning."

"Didn't mean to interrupt your weekend, Miss Threadgill," Quinn said. He tapped at the bill on his cap. "Appreciate your time."

"You ain't gonna call the warden on us?" she said, squinting up from the four-wheeler. "Right?"

Quinn looked over at the big woman to her left. That woman shrugged, turned to the ground and spit.

"You wouldn't happen to have the name of that lawyer up in Corinth, would you?"

"Shit." Big Momma nodded, flicking away her second cigarette into the dead weeds. "Is that all you need? Let me go inside and get his card. My poontang's about frozen to this here seat."

"So let me get this straight," the girl said, joint held high in her left hand. "Some man your mother never saw before in her life attacked her outside some bar called the White Star Lounge. With a damn boxcutter?"

TJ and Ladarius sat with the crazy girl at a black metal table and chairs outside on the deck. The girl said she didn't want her father or stepmother to smell any weed in their vacation home or else there would be hell to pay. She also insisted that the FOR SALE signs out by the road were just a big misunderstanding with the bank. And how her daddy, some hot-shit car dealer up in Fayetteville, already had the whole mess sorted out. The girl had the hood of the cheetah coat up on her head, her face shadowed as she burned down the joint to an orange pinprick.

"It's called the Southern Star," TJ said. "And there were two men.

But yeah. That's pretty much it. Momma had had a lot to drink, which ain't too different from most nights, but she managed to get the knife and cut one man before navigating her way home."

"While smashed?"

"Yeah," TJ said. "Momma was pretty shitfaced when she got home. Lots of what she said didn't make a heck of a lot of sense. I did my best to calm her down, make sure she quit her crying. I took her bloody clothes and got her in the shower. When she finally settled down a bit, she was scared she'd killed the man. And that she might go to jail and those folks with the state would take her babies."

"Your mom has babies, too?" the girl said. "Damn."

"No," TJ said, shaking her head. "You ain't listening. We're her babies. Me and John Wesley. That's just what she calls us."

"Y'all are a little old to be called babies," the girl said. "I'm just saying."

Behind the girl's shoulder, back in the mansion, TJ could see Holly peeking out from the curtains. She'd stayed inside trying to console John Wesley, telling the boy that everything was just fine and dandy. When Holly noticed TJ staring back, the curtains dropped and Holly disappeared. TJ turned to the girl and said, "You never told us your name."

"Chastity."

"Chastity?"

"Yeah," she said. "It means a woman who can't have sex. I mean, ever."

"I know what chastity means."

Ladarius smiled, nearly laughed, and had to cover up half his face with his hand. He reached out and the girl, Chastity, handed back what was left of the joint.

"Back in the dark ages, men used to put these things called chastity belts over a girl's privates," Chastity said. "When the men would go off and fight in the wars or crusades or some shit, they'd take the key with them. Isn't that messed up?"

"How'd they pee?" TJ asked.

"I don't know," Chastity said. "Maybe they had a maid or a trusted servant who would unlock it for them. Anyway, I used to get called Chastity Belt all the time. So many times. *How's your belt, Chastity? You still got it locked down tight, Chastity?* Well. I don't want to talk too much. But my parents sure named me wrong. Nobody ever locked up my parts. My parts are mine, wild and free."

Chastity shrugged and pulled her knees up to her chest. She stared out at the lake for a long time. No one saying anything, TJ and Ladarius exchanging a few looks, not sure if everything was cool with them staying for a while or maybe they needed to haul ass and jump in the minivan. Get the hell out of Hot Springs and away from this crazy-ass girl.

"Say," Chastity said. "I have an idea. In exchange for a big favor, I let y'all stay here for as long as you like. I mean within reason. I don't want you here when the weather gets warmer. I plan to pretty much live at the lake then. Did you know we have two boats? I love to ride around, ski a little bit in my bikini. Everybody knows me around here. If I'm not on Lake Hamilton, nobody is gonna have much fun."

"What will you tell Big Daddy?" Ladarius asked.

"I like this one," Chastity said, her eyes sleepy. "I like him a lot. So he's not your boyfriend? Or he is your boyfriend? Just what is the deal here, Miss TJ Byrd?"

"Yeah," TJ said. "I guess he's mine."

"And what about you, Lafonzo?"

"Ladarius," Ladarius said. "My name is Ladarius."

"Anyhoo," she said. "Are you in? Or are you out? You hold the key to TJ's belt? Do you take this woman here to be your forever partner in crime? And in death do your asses part?"

"Damn," Ladarius said. "That's some dark-ass shit."

"You haven't seen what I've seen on the news about y'all," said Chastity. "That's some truly dark-ass shit."

"That favor," Ladarius said. "What do you want us to do?"

"Since y'all are so damn good at killing," she said. "Could you do me a big solid and ride up to Fayetteville and slice and dice up my stepmother? I'll warn you. She does do CrossFit and keeps in shape. Big old thighs and shoulders. But between both of y'all, I think you could take her. Then, kick back and relax on the lake. You saw that sign out front. *Firefly.* That's what my real mother named the place. So many of those damn things here in the summer, buzzing around and lighting up the lake."

TJ couldn't believe what she was hearing. The girl actually asked them, real casual and easy like it wasn't a big deal, to run up to Fayetteville and kill her stepmother. She had to be kidding. After all, she and Ladarius had just met her. And if this girl Chastity actually believed they were killers, why wouldn't they just kill her ass instead of sitting outside in the freezing fucking cold and smoking a goddamn joint?

"We don't kill people," TJ said. "We didn't kill my mother. We've never killed anyone."

"You said your momma killed some man?" Chastity asked. "But you didn't finish the story. Then what happened? He come back to life?"

"I don't know," TJ said, her mind clouding a bit. "I'm not sure. But I think someone he knew came back for her. Maybe they got to her before she could get out of Tibbehah County."

"What the fuck is that?"

"Tibbehah County, Mississippi," TJ said. "You never heard of it?"

"Nope," Chastity said. "Sounds like the ass crack of the Mid-South."

TJ felt the blood rush into her face, the smug little rich girl calling her a liar, then a killer, then flirting with her boyfriend, and now calling her home a real shithole.

"It's beautiful country," she said. "Runs alongside the Natchez Trace and a big national forest. We got all kinds of wildlife. Big lake where we fish in the summertime."

"Well," she said. "That's nice. Are y'all in or are y'all out?"

"To kill your stepmomma?" Ladarius asked.

"Yeah," Chastity said. "I would really appreciate it."

TJ just shook her head some more and stood up, walking over to a rock wall, setting her elbows on the ledge while watching a hawk circle and circle far out on the water. A small boat passed the mansion and a choppy wake rolled wave after wave toward the shore, the floating docks rising and falling.

"I'm sorry," Chastity said. "I believe you."

"Really?"

"Yes, ma'am." Chastity nodded. "But you do realize that you're gonna have to get other folks to believe you, too."

TJ nodded, wind cutting off the lake and blowing her hair off her face. She reached back and pulled it into a ponytail, wishing she had a hair tie.

"Wow."

"What's that?"

"You're kinda pretty without all that shit covering up your face," Chastity said. "You ever wear any makeup?"

"Sometimes."

"You got a real look to you, TJ," she said. "Those blue eyes. Wow. Those are something fierce. You must be out on social media? Right? You're keeping your people posted on this wild-ass road trip?"

"Posted on what?"

"On your run from the law," Chastity said. "You and Ladarius being innocent?"

TJ had no idea what the girl was saying. Chastity tilted her head and studied her face, like the way a contractor might before taking on a big job. "Yeah," Chastity said. "Won't be easy. But I can do it."

"Do what?" TJ said. "What the hell are you talking about?"

"TJ Byrd," Chastity said. "Wrongfully Accused Hero. Teenage Superstar. You know. Fucking damn well all of it, girl."

FIFTEEN

Johnny Stagg watched with great amusement as his boy Bishop walked Chester Pratt into the back office at the Rebel and slammed his head down onto his glass-topped desk. Stagg appreciated the theatrics of the situation, even though it knocked over some fresh prune juice one of his girls had just brought him.

Pratt didn't even try to fight it. His cheek flush to the desk, staring right at Stagg as Stagg wiped off the spilled purple juice near his telephone line. The boy's face was redder than a damn beet, bug-eyed, and swallowing air as Stagg leaned back in his padded leather chair and placed a bony finger to his lips. *What to do? What to do?*

Damn, it was fun to be back in the goddamn saddle.

"We waited and waited, Mr. Pratt," Stagg said. "And you never showed. Seems like you was trying to make a monkey outta me."

"I wasn't trying to make a monkey out of no one," Pratt said. "Please. Can he please let go of my neck? I got back problems and need to use the toilet."

Stagg reached down and patted Chester's cheek, looking up to Bishop and nodding. "Me and you had a done deal," Stagg said. "Don't tell me you're rethinking my kind and most generous offer?"

"No, sir," Pratt said, standing up and rubbing out some kinks from his neck, red marks across his skin where Bishop had grabbed hold of him. "Everything's just gotten kind of complicated. I know you said you could get me out of trouble with the law. But at the moment, that's not my most urgent and pressing concern."

Stagg leaned back into his swivel chair, nodding, waiting for the bullshit to flow from Chester Pratt like creamed corn out of an old goose. "Mm-hmm," Stagg said. "And what would be more urgent and pressing than keeping your ass on good terms with the law?"

"Just how were you figuring on helping?" Pratt asked. "Just for conversation. You got a line on that Quinn Colson? Do you have some kind of photos or something to make him back off? Maybe Sheriff Colson and the girls from over at the old Booby Trap doing the dirty bop?"

"How I work and what I do ain't none of your concern, Mr. Pratt," Stagg said. "I told you the law wouldn't be on you about what happened to that Byrd woman. And you agreed to make me a full partner in your business right across the road there. That seems about as simple as simple can be. Mr. Bishop? You got that agreement with you?"

Bishop hadn't stopped staring at Chester Pratt. He stood wide-legged and jackbooted in camo pants and a camo vest over a gray hoodie, smelling of kerosene and cigarettes. He reached into his vest pocket and pulled out the contract folded long and halfway and placed it nice and gentle on Stagg's desk. Stagg appreciated the man's professionalism.

"I'll even let you use a special pen given to me by the chancellor of Ole Miss this Christmas," Stagg said. "Sent me a handwritten note and everything. Ain't that class?"

Pratt didn't seem to be listening. He just leaned against Stagg's desk and closed his eyes. Mr. Bishop stood not a foot behind him, stroking his brushy beard, looking like he would take a great deal of pleasure in kicking the dogshit out of ole Chester Pratt.

"It ain't that simple."

"It ain't?" Stagg said, finding himself laughing. "Seems simple to me."

"I didn't kill that woman."

"Sure you didn't," Stagg said. "Sure you didn't. Well, then. Best of luck with Quinn Colson and that ole sheriff from over in Parsham bird-dogging your ass. I won't get in the way. No, sir. Johnny T. Stagg will back right off. You're on your own."

"I didn't kill her," Chester Pratt repeated. His eyes a serious deep blue, the finger marks on his throat starting to fade just a bit. "But . . ."

"I'm listening, son." Stagg reached for the prune juice and rattled the ice in the glass. After five years of fried foods and soggy-ass vegetables at the federal lockup, it was gonna take months before he got his gut working right again. He finished the rest of the juice and set the glass aside, waiting for Pratt to go on and tell him what was on his mind.

"I know these ole boys in town," said Chester Pratt. "A couple of roofers called the Nixes, father and son. You know 'em?"

Stagg shook his head, giving a noncommittal shrug, swiveling right to left in his chair, his eyes absently leaving Chester and looking back over at all the monitors at the Rebel. Just yesterday he'd set up cameras outside and inside of the Frontier Village, and right at that very moment the Haunted Gold Mine was being inflated and filling that big space. With any luck, they'd be opened up for Easter. Maybe get Mr. Bishop or Midnight Man to crawl into a bunny costume and hippy hop it all over Dodge City.

Stagg took a breath. "You might've heard I spent the last few years incarcerated over in Montgomery," he said. "Lots of folks have come and gone in Tibbehah during that time. Can't say I've ever had the displeasure to run across the Nix boys."

"They weren't supposed to kill her."

Stagg understood now, lifting his eyes up to Bishop. Knowing they had the son of a bitch now. Without another word, Bishop snatched up Chester Pratt's bony ass from behind, like a man going to cornhole a fella in the shower, and forced him to grab that fancy silver pen from Ole Miss. "Sign it," Bishop said. "Sign it, you leathery ole fuck."

Stagg grinned. "No need in getting personal about it, Bishop," he said. "But I sure would sign that thing, Chester. 'Cause no matter if you drawn and quartered that woman or had it hired out, the law will be coming for your ass quick and hard, boy. If I were in your predicament, I'd sure as hell add us to your team."

"Those boys are crazy," Pratt said. "They want ten grand from me or they're gonna turn over this cell phone they got. They say I may have texted some threats to Miss Byrd the night they came for her at the Southern Star."

"Signs and wonders," Stagg said. "Damn, Chester. Sounds like you're fucked five ways from Sunday."

Bishop placed his big hairy hand over Chester's slim, bony one and forced him to start scrawling out his name.

"If they get me for murder," Pratt said. "I'll tell 'em you forced me to sign this. It won't be worth any more than a dog turd left on your lawn."

Stagg reached up and over Chester's arm for his fancy porcelain candy bowl, the one that had belonged to his dear sweet wife before she'd lost her damn mind and had to be institutionalized. *God bless her.* He unwrapped the candy and started to suck on its minty sweetness.

"You scared of a couple goddamn roofers?" Stagg asked.

Even as he was being held solid and still by Bishop, Pratt was able to offer a simple nod. "Gina somehow cut the old one," he said. "She got loose and they followed her home. They're the ones who chopped her up and drove her out to Parsham."

"Dumped her and her car at the same location," Stagg said. "Seems like those old boys had a plan to shake your ass down from the git-go. You been studying on that?"

Pratt nodded again. Stagg told Bishop to let him loose, Bishop getting so damn frustrated that a man like Chester Pratt wouldn't bend to his will that he walked over to a corner and punched the brick wall.

"This don't change a thing," Stagg said. "Sign the papers and me and Bishop will make sure you're in the clear."

"These men ain't right in the head," Pratt said. "They live, act, and smell like animals."

"Contractors?" Stagg said. "I got contractor problems half my damn life. They act big and tough, trying to force your hand to get paid more than they're worth. Don't you worry about nothing, Mr. Pratt. Me and Mr. Bishop coming into your business is a true gift from the Almighty. Everything happens for a reason. Now, don't it?"

Chester Pratt stepped back, and for a quick moment, Stagg thought he might try and run out the door. But then better sense seemed to prevail and he turned away from Bishop breathing down his neck and looked right at Johnny Stagg. He let out a great deal of air, his bony shoulders sinking, and then started to cry just a bit. Stagg sure could've skipped that last part but waited and let the boy go ahead and get his emotions behind him.

"Come on, now," Stagg said. "We good?"

Pratt reached out his right hand. And Stagg again offered him the Ole Miss chancellor's silver pen.

And quick as two shakes of a lamb's tail, that boy scratched off his name in three places. He didn't even read what it said or nothing. Stagg grinned and reached for more peppermint candy, offering some to both the men in his office.

"Pleasure doing business with you, Chester," Stagg said. "I knowed your brother Ronnie for a long while. And now I know which of you is the smarter one."

"You really gonna do something?"

"We tried explaining it to you nice, son," Stagg said. "But I'll be dog. You just wouldn't listen."

"What the hell was that about?" TJ asked.

"Shut up," Holly said. "Just please shut up."

"Don't you see it?" TJ asked. "Don't you see how you're making a damn fool out of yourself? Chastity was just helping out. Trying to make sure I look right before she sets things up for us. How the hell else are we going to make folks to listen to me? Your ass ain't on the line, Holly Harkins. It's me and Ladarius that folks are blaming for what happened to Momma."

"Why don't you try and look in a mirror," Holly said. "You look ridiculous. I thought you didn't wear makeup. You look like some kind of. Well, I don't know. Some kind of damn harlot."

TJ shook her head, disappointed as hell seeing Holly act like a fool kid in front of Chastity. *Harlot?* Only a Sunday school regular would talk like that. She and Chastity had just been playing around in that big mirrored bathroom, Chastity making jokes about how much she hated her stepmother and how much that painting of the woman and her big fake tatas embarrassed the hell out of her. Holly had walked in, cupping her hand to her mouth like she'd just seen the worst thing in the world, letting out a little cry and running from the room. All TJ had been doing was letting Chastity give her some fresh clothes and paint up her face a bit. What the hell had gotten into Holly anyway?

"It's just not you, is all," Holly said. "And who is this Chastity? We don't know her. We don't know nothing about her."

"She didn't call the cops, did she?"

"Bless her black heart. While you and that girl were playing house, I'm the one who had to explain things to John Wesley," Holly said. "I told him the good Lord up in heaven needed his mother up there real bad and not to be sad, it was a time to rejoice."

"Did he believe it?"

"I don't know," Holly said. "That boy's real good at holding in his emotions but it sure made him quit crying."

"Come on," TJ said, reaching out and grabbing Holly's hands. They stood together, out in the cold of the big stone patio. "Let's both calm down and think. What Chastity said makes some sense. When I told her what happened back in Tibbehah and how me and Ladarius got blamed for it, Chastity's the one who had the idea of taking the truth to the people. She said we're the ones who should be in charge to tell our own story about Momma, about those men who come for her, and how they're probably the ones who killed her."

"You don't know that," Holly said. "You don't even know if those men were real. You said your mom was high as a kite."

"Then who else would it be?"

"You know damn well who."

"Chester Pratt?" TJ said. "Couldn't be Chester. My momma had that old man wrapped around her little finger. Don't get me wrong, I can't stand that son of a bitch. He may be a cheat and a liar, but he's no killer. He's not like the other men she fell in with. I could tell he was worried sick that she was missing. Naw, Momma went on her own with this one."

"You need to think on it, TJ," Holly said. "Open your damn eyes after you get done making up your face and sweetening your mouth for your new rich friend."

"Sweetening my mouth?" TJ asked. "Damn. She's not my friend. Hell, I just met the girl. Give me a goddamn break. You're acting like a jealous kid."

"Well," Holly said. "You look ridiculous. What's that you're wearing?"

TJ looked down at the little blue sweater dress with a hoodie and little pockets out front, some nice new suede booties that fit her just about perfect.

"Just a dress," TJ said. "She has two closets full of 'em. Why? You don't like the way I look?"

Holly wiped the tears off her cheeks and shook her head. "You look beautiful, TJ," she said. "You just don't look like you."

TJ placed her hands in the pockets of the dress, legs bare and cold as she looked up at the big house, a patchwork of light under gray skies. The wind kicked up again with a little rain and flashing light across the lake.

"Maybe that's a good thing," TJ said. "Wouldn't you just love to be someone else? Even for a second? Who in their goddamn mind would want to be living this fucked-up hand I've been dealt?"

The locals in Forrest City, Arkansas, got tipped that the Byrd Gang may have stopped off at a place called Gage Auto early yesterday with a busted belt on their minivan. Lillie Virgil and Charlie Hodge headed that way the next afternoon, meeting up with Bubba Gage himself at his place a half mile off I-40. Bubba excited like hell to meet them, offering up some bitter coffee and a whole load of BS on just how keen his mind had been identifying the crew. They were quick and shifty. The black kid trying to screw him down a whole fifty dollars. But he didn't take their mess.

"How'd they pay?" Lillie asked.

"Cash," Bubba said, scratching at his cheek. "Wouldn't take a credit card if they tried. You know it'd be stolen. What's that boy's name again?"

"Ladarius McCade."

"Yeah," he said. "He done most of the talking. Real cocky like he knowed more about cars than me. Shit. Kid looked barely old enough to drive. Had bleach blond afro and sported a few earrings. Peeled off that cash like he'd earned every dollar himself."

"Maybe he did."

"TV outta Memphis called that boy a felon," he said. "Ain't that right? That's what they are. Right? Crew of thieving-ass kids."

"Sure," Lillie said, looking over at Charlie Hodge. "If it was really them."

Charlie walked up beside Lillie and showed the man Ladarius's last booking photo from his phone and then scrolled through to a few pictures of TJ. Bubba stepped back, cocked his neck to get him a better view, and nodded. He was a tall, thick guy with a lot of black hair and grease on his split knuckles. He might've been half-decent-looking if someone would hose him off.

"Yep," Bubba said. "That's the boy. Not too sure on that white girl, the one who killed her momma. There was two of them. Just like that gang. And a little kid asking a whole bunch of questions, those girls telling him to sit still, be quiet while they watched that *Paternity Court*."

"Did they say anything about where they were headed?" Charlie asked.

"Last I seen them, the two girls and that kid crossed the road to the Walmart," Bubba Gage said, leaning back into a wobbly little office chair. The office portion of Gage Auto was housed in a small metal shed next to the big, open garage. The walls decorated with photos of great moments of the Gage Auto softball team and a few real nuggets of wisdom like WE SHARE PRIDE IN YOUR RIDE, TRUST IS OUR BIGGEST ASSET, and REAL MEN PROVIDE AND REAL WOMEN APPRECIATE IT. "I told that boy he was damn lucky they didn't blow up their damn engine. They shoulda called a wrecker when they throwed that belt."

"Sure they were headed to the Walmart?" Lillie asked.

"Not a hell of a lot else in Forrest City," Bubba said. "I think I heard they were getting some Little Debbies for the kid. That boy kept on cussing about how hungry he was. I tried to give him a damn donut, but he wouldn't take it."

Lillie nodded. Charlie headed out the door, back to the car. When Charlie Hodge was done, he was damn well done and on to the next thing.

"Let me ask you a question," Bubba said. "Is there some kind of reward for them kids? For information leading to their arrest and all that?"

"Probably," Lillie said. "But what do I know? I'm just some woman grateful to have a job. You men do all the work."

"You seen the sign?" he said. "That's just a little joke between me and my boys. Don't make too much of it."

"Sure," Lillie said. "Every great man has a woman behind him, propping his ass up."

"You're a good-lookin' woman, Miss Virgil," Gage said, smiling. "I'm sure your husband appreciates it."

"I'm not married."

"Good-lookin' woman like you?" he said. "Federal goddamn marshal? *Shoot.* How'd you like to join me for an early dinner over at Iguana's Tex-Mex? Have us some cold margaritas and a few of them deep-fried chimichangas. Maybe head on down to Frog's for some karaoke? You look like the kind of woman who sure could belt out a good ole country song. Me and you doin' some ole-school Kenny and Dolly would just about bring the place down."

"Tell you what," Lillie said. "You head on over and I'll meet you there later."

Bubba looked a little skeptical. "You're pulling my chain?" he said. "Aren't you?"

"If I pulled it any harder, Bubba, you'd go cross-eyed."

"Damn," he said. "I like a woman with some spunk. But not one that carries a Sig Sauer on her hip. That's what it is, ain't it?"

"Yep, a .357," Lillie said. "Sure you can't help us out some? I would indeed appreciate it."

"Oh, I don't know," he said. "I mighta heard a word or two about California."

"California?" Lillie asked. "There you go. I knew you had in you. Two-time business-of-the-year award winner like yourself."

"One of those girls mighta mentioned something about driving until there weren't no road left," Bubba said, rubbing his dirty neck. "Wanted to know how far it was to Los Angeles. Truth is, I don't think those kids had much money left after they paid me."

"Anything else?"

Bubba stepped back and opened his arms wide. "All I got, Miss Virgil," he said. "Sure you can't stay a while? 'Islands in the stream. That is what we are.' Or 'We've got tonight. Who needs tomorrow, babe. Why don't you stay?'"

"You're a real sweetheart, Bubba," Lillie said. "A grease-stained romantic."

"Don't tell no one," Bubba said, pressing a finger to his lips. "You'll ruin my repatation."

* * *

Since she didn't have anywhere else better to go or anything else better to do, Chastity figured she might as well hang with the redneck outlaws for a while. The last thing she wanted was to head back to Fayetteville and fetch coffee for her daddy's pervert salesmen at the Chevy dealership. The ones who made sly little comments about her figure and gave her dirty little winks while sending her across the road to Applebee's for fried chicken salads and jalapeño poppers while they closed that big deal on a brand-new Tahoe.

She hadn't been home but two months from rehab when her daddy and Sharon sent her back to a new place, this one south of Little Rock, a rustic campground that ran about a thousand dollars a day where you could walk hiking trails and sit around campfires with the other addicts, admitting to all your greatest adventures when you'd been flying high on pills and booze. Chastity was there a whole three days before talking a groundskeeper into driving her back to Fayetteville, where she got her silver G-Wagen and hightailed it down to the lake house. Her daddy and Sharon never telling her they'd lost the damn thing in bankruptcy on that stupid outlet mall in Branson.

Chastity figured she could stay here until Daddy came for her, getting all emotional and tearful, explaining once again how her addiction came from her mother's side as Uncle Jeff was a goddamn fuckup himself, despite her daddy trying to help him be a success in life.

"You okay?" TJ Byrd asked.

Chastity was working on a little mascara in the master bedroom mirror, big white light bulbs giving her an up-close microscopic view of her pores.

"I was about to ask you the same thing."

"I'm cool," TJ said. "Don't worry about it. It was no big thing."

"It's just makeup and clothes," Chastity said. "That big girl ran from the room like a scared rabbit."

"She's not used to seeing me like this," TJ said. "Just startled her a bit."

"You in a dress?"

"Without jeans," she said. "And shit-kicking boots and old flannel shirts."

"Weird," Chastity said, rolling the stick around her lips and making a pouty kiss in the mirror. "Very weird."

"Have you seen Ladarius and my little brother?"

"I gave them the keys to the boat," she said. "Showed them where my daddy keeps the gas cans."

"It's freezing rain out there," TJ said. "I don't want my little brother on a boat."

"They're fine," she said. "Any idiot can run those things. I told your brother to put on a life jacket. Say, are you hungry? I'm damn well starved. There's a little place around the corner that serves up hot catfish and shrimp plates. I think you'd like it."

TJ shook her head, the girl looking a hell of a lot better after Chastity improved her appearance by a thousand percent. That little country girl could almost pass for an Abercrombie model.

"Still full off that stolen steak?"

"It wasn't stolen."

"Borrowed steak," Chastity said. "Y'all are still full off that borrowed steak?"

"I don't want nothing to eat," TJ said, moving closer in the bathroom and taking a seat up on the sink counter. "I saw something online that's made me ill."

"I told you to steer clear of that crap," Chastity said. "Remember what I said. Control the message. Use your damn voice and your good looks. You're gonna be the one to tell the whole truth about the real killers."

"Things have changed," TJ said. "I don't know what to think."

"About who killed your mom?"

TJ nodded, pulled out her phone, and showed Chastity as Chastity pulled her hair up into a cute little messy bun. The whole idea of getting the boyfriend and the kid onto a boat was to spend a little more time with TJ to coach her on the finer points of being a social media sensation. She'd already registered TJ's new Insta page, her old one depressing as hell with nothing but pictures of old rock stars, rusted cars, and Bible quotations. The new one was called FREEBYRD.

The girl showed her a story off some news station in Memphis, footage of a bony-looking old dude in a fuzzy sweater with sunglasses on top of his head. The bottom of the screen said BOYFRIEND SAYS TEENAGE LOVERS PLOTTED MURDER.

"What in the fuck is this?" Chastity asked.

"Lies," TJ said. "Lies and bullshit. Bullshit and lies."

CHESTER PRATT: *I was worried about Gina's safety after her
    daughter pulled a gun on us a few weeks back. She said if we
    tried to send her away, she'd kill both of us. We prayed and
    prayed on it. Thinking she'd never do something so horrible.
    Good Lord. It didn't have to be like this. I only wish I could've
    been with Gina when the kids came for her.*
REPORTER: *Chester Pratt says TJ Byrd had bragged about
    Ladarius McCade's ability to steal cars and strip them for parts.
    According to Mr. Pratt, TJ said the same thing might happen to
    them if they tried to separate the two teenage lovers.*

"Holly was right," TJ said, taking the phone back and sliding it into the sweater dress pocket. "Chester's behind all this."

"Who's Holly?"

"My friend," TJ said. "The goddamn girl we were just talking about."

"Big freckle face?" Chastity said. "Sorry. If that girl was any more boring, she'd be damn well invisible."

"Don't say that," TJ said. "Don't you ever talk about my best friend."

"Or what?" Chastity said. "You and Ladarius gonna chop me up, too?"

"That's not funny."

"It's kind of funny," Chastity said, smiling. "I wouldn't joke if I thought y'all were guilty."

"Goddamn Chester Pratt."

TJ reached for a towel on the rack and began to wipe the makeup from her face. Chastity shook her head, so much good work gone wasted. The girl was crying a little bit now, too. Softer than she'd thought TJ Byrd would be when she'd first heard about the teenage killers on the run from Mississippi.

"Why aren't you scared of us?" TJ asked. "Seems like everybody else is."

"Maybe because I don't much give a damn either way," she said. Chastity turned over her forearm to show where she liked to cut on herself a little bit, a long trail of neat and even scars, like someone keeping box scores on a baseball game. Or at least that's what her last therapist had told her.

"No one will listen," TJ said.

"We make them listen."

"How's that?" TJ said. "By making me all gussied up and pretty? That sounds like more bullshit to me. And I'm done with that. I'm ready to fight back."

Chastity put her makeup back into a white leather purse and walked from the bathroom, Sharon's gigantic boobies staring at her like a couple of knowing eyes. She headed on into the bedroom with the big four-post bed and grasped hold, twirling back and forth, drunk with thought. And a little carefree after taking a whole Klonopin with her morning Diet Coke.

"Make them listen."

"How do you do that?"

"Grab hold of something to make people take notice."

"We're just some country-ass kids," TJ said. "Nobody gives a damn about us. Chester has money. He's already sweet-talked the sheriffs down there. And now he's putting out his lies on TV. Only reason he's doing that is to scatter the damn truth."

"You got me," Chastity said, breaking free of the post and walking over to TJ. She grasped the girl's small hands and put them onto her shoulders. "Listen. People are already looking for me. People want me. If folks won't listen, I can help you get the truth and get us both money. Money for me to live my own life and money for y'all to get far, far away from here."

"I don't want to run anymore."

"You call driving from north Mississippi to Hot Springs running?" Chastity broke free and touched her index finger on her lips. "Do you really have a gun?"

"'Course I do," the country girl said, reaching into her other pocket, showing her a little pistol.

"Can you hold it on me while you explain your demands?" she said. "Real mean. Convincing. Wave it around like you're crazy as hell."

"I don't have any goddamn demands," TJ said. "Only the truth."

"If you got Chastity Bloodgood, the whole world will listen," Chastity said. "Be in charge, TJ Byrd. Control the conversation. I learned that from my father. When you have something that people really want and desire, they'll do anything in the world to get it."

"I don't see how kidnapping you is going to improve our situation."

"What can I say?" Chastity said. "I'm an attention-grabber. Once folks are listening, you can sell them on any story you want. Say you didn't want to do it. But it was the only way. I don't know. Just some shit like that. You're a good talker. I've seen you do it with your gang. Some real inspirational shit."

"We're not a gang," she said. "That's all made up."

"Well," Chastity said, widening her eyes and smiling. "You are now. *No other choice.* That's what you tell the world. They left you but no other choice than to hold me hostage until this Chester Pratt tells the damn truth."

SIXTEEN

Saw you on television this morning," Quinn said. "That must've been tough. Talking about what happened to Gina?"

"You bet, Sheriff," Chester Pratt said. "Brought up some rough emotions for me. *Whew-wee*. I had a rock in my throat so big I could barely talk."

"Is that a fact?"

"Yes, sir," Pratt said, sitting across from Quinn at the sheriff's office. Looking contrite and small in the hard office chair that creaked as he crossed his legs. "But I figured it was best for the public to know about the youthful menace out there roaming free."

"Funny thing," Quinn said. "I never heard that story before, about how TJ Byrd threatened your life. Why didn't you mention it to me?"

Reggie Caruthers hung loose by the closed door, arms crossed and listening after starting a recording of the meeting. Cigar smoke floated thick in the air, as Quinn hadn't cared to open a window or turn on a fan.

"You hadn't?" Pratt said. "One of the first things I told Sheriff Lovemaiden when he sat down with me. Sometimes I don't know what I told him and what I told you. So many things mixed up in my mind. But she damn sure did. That little girl told Gina that if we tried to stick her up in that Christian girl school that she'd shoot us both and Ladarius McCade would strip our bodies like car parts."

"That doesn't sound like TJ."

"Really," Pratt said. "And just how well do you know that little girl?"

Quinn wasn't sure how hard to push Chester, not sure he was ready to lay out everything he knew. He figured the best way was to take it casual and easy, act like he just had a few innocent questions that maybe Chester could answer for him. Quinn tapped at the cigar ash and took a draw, letting the smoke curl into the ceiling and the silence hang in the air. The cigar was a nice Undercrown, bold and spicy on his lips.

"She was angry," Pratt said. "Unbalanced mentally. Did you know she carried her dead daddy's pistol with her? A little .38 that she wore on her hip up under those sloppy old flannel shirts. Just in case you get to cornering her, I'm warning you that the girl won't go down without a fight. No, sir. Don't let her cute little face and pug nose fool you. That girl is definitely Jerry Jeff Valentine's kid. Meaner than hell."

Quinn wondered exactly how far Chester would fly back on his heels when it got down to his business and personal finances. He drew on the cigar again as the sun started to shine a little through the dark clouds and yellowed the old hardwood floors. He looked to Reggie and Reggie nodded back, the two working together so long they could read their thoughts.

"I heard TJ recently came into some money," Reggie said.

"Oh, yeah?"

"Jerry Jeff's mother died in the care of a nursing home in Corinth," Quinn said. "Some kind of insurance settlement with the family?"

"Gina may have mentioned something about it," Chester said. "I don't think it was much money. Whatever it was."

"We heard it was around twenty-five thousand dollars," Reggie said.

"That a fact?"

Quinn nodded. He'd seen the cashed check from Jericho First National yesterday. The money coming from a law firm in Tupelo that specialized in settlements and payouts on lawsuits and the like. He wasn't exactly sure how Gina got the money out of TJ's trust and into her account, but it appeared the firm had taken a sizable chunk to get it released.

"Maybe that's why they ran off like they did," Pratt said. "Wind at their back, dreams of living wild and free on her mawmaw's death money."

"I don't think TJ ever saw a dime," Quinn said.

Chester nodded, fumbled a bit with the phone in his hand, absently scrolling through messages. He wouldn't keep eye contact with Quinn, acting like meeting with the sheriff was just a momentary inconvenience. Quinn looked over to Reggie and Reggie shook his head slightly, recognizing Chester for being Chester.

"Something important?" Quinn asked.

"Nope," he said. "No, sir. Just hoping to get word on those kids. I spent the morning with Pastor Quick. Half the town is praying they get caught and don't hurt no one else."

"You're that sure they did it?" Quinn said.

"I most certainly am," Pratt said. "Just what are you getting at, Sheriff? I hope you're not trying to make this whole deal into a real whodunit. You done already put out an arrest warrant for those delinquents. I don't know why you're harassing a grieving man just trying to run a small business in this town. Do I need to reach out to my lawyer?"

Reggie pushed off the doorway and walked around Quinn's desk, taking a seat in another office chair not two feet from Chester Pratt.

Pratt looked to the deputy and then across the desk to Quinn. His face shone with a little sweat, the tips of his ears turning pink.

"Why would you need your lawyer?" Reggie asked.

"Shoot," he said. "Sounds like y'all are trying to accuse me of something."

"And what would we be accusing you of?" Quinn asked. "We're just trying to understand a little more about Gina Byrd's affairs."

"What's it matter about her money?" Pratt said. "She's dead. It don't matter if she was a millionaire or a gosh-dang pauper. Those kids sure as hell killed her and now are out running from the law. If I were you, I'd spend more time trying to track them down before they murder someone else, and stop harassing me."

Quinn tapped his cigar. He looked over at Reggie, who just sat sideways by Chester, staring right at his profile, not shifting his eyes a bit. If Quinn had been on the hot seat, Reggie's stare would've made him a little nervous, too.

"Anything else you'd like to tell us?" Quinn asked.

"No, sir," Pratt said.

"You sure?" Quinn asked.

"I'm sure," he said. "I mean, goddamn. I got a fucking funeral to put together. Ophelia Bundren told me the state people are bringing Gina back home tomorrow. After they finish up with whatever it is they're doing."

Quinn didn't speak for a long while. He set down his cigar and picked up his coffee mug. Reggie sat still in the office chair, watching Chester Pratt go back to his phone scrolling and pecking, scrolling and pecking, his right leg jumping up and down like a piston.

"One thing, Chester," Quinn said. "Was Gina your partner in Bluebird Liquors?"

"'Course not," he said. "Where'd you hear something like that? My brother, Ronnie? Don't put too much stock in his lies, Sheriff.

He's a goddamn used car salesman. Me and him been on the outs for a long while. Hell, he'd sell me down shit creek for a nickel."

"Ronnie didn't say that," Quinn said. "I'm saying that. Gina Byrd gave you almost nineteen thousand dollars back in August. Just what was that about?"

The entirety of Chester Pratt's face shifted and contorted, locking into a grimace, like a man who'd just swallowed a plug of tobacco. His leg stopped pumping up and down and he appeared to hold his breath as his eyes roved from Reggie Caruthers to Quinn.

"I don't think that's any of y'all's business," Pratt said. "That's a personal matter."

"Everything in a murder investigation is personal," Quinn said. "Don't you think, Reggie?"

"You bet, Sheriff."

"I'm done here," Chester Pratt said, standing up and pushing the chair hard behind him. "You got any more questions or accusations, how about you call up Sonny Stevens. I came over here during business hours out of respect to you, Sheriff. But seeing you don't have the same for me, I'll be getting back to work."

Chester Pratt headed for the door and Quinn listened as the man's tasseled loafers slapped down the hallway and out to the front door. Reggie switched chairs and pulled up the seat Chester had been in. His tan uniform was stiff and creased that morning, the silver star polished and gleaming.

"Damn, that man sure is guilty," Reggie said.

"Yep," Quinn said.

"'Least now we know the why," Reggie said. "Just not the how."

"Any word back on those prints from Gina's Nissan?"

"Nope," he said. "What about that blade you found under her seat? Want me to send it over to Batesville? Maybe see if they can rush things up."

"A rush at the lab?" Quinn said. "It'll be six months before we see the report."

"Probably," Reggie said. "How 'bout I run down some of Pratt's recent bankruptcy filings? See just how far his ass is in debt?"

Quinn nodded, checked the time, and picked up the phone to call Lillie Virgil.

"I also want a deputy watching the liquor store and Chester's house," Quinn said. "Tell them to use that old GMC we have in impound. He knows we're onto him but let's not make a point of it. Not yet."

Hello. My name's TJ Byrd and it's come to my attention that several falsehoods and downright lies have been spreading about me since my momma got killed. Now to set the record straight, and I don't have longer than a minute, I had absolutely nothing to do with my mother's murder. The real reason me and Ladarius left Mississippi was on account of being harassed by the sheriff and his people who were sure we were guilty from the word go. The only thing I'm guilty of was washing blood from my momma's clothes and helping her bust free of town after two men attacked her outside the Southern Star. And now, just this morning, I saw that dirty, lowlife son of a bitch Chester Pratt, who, by the way, owes me a great deal of money, go on local TV to spread lies about me and Ladarius McCade making threats on him and my momma's life. This all's on account of them wanting to ship me up to the Wings of Faith School in Missouri in an effort to brainwash me and make me wear long skirts and my hair up in a bun. But that damn dirty lie has shown me that Mr. Chester Pratt, owner of Bluebird Liquors in Jericho, Mississippi, is hiding something. Something like the fact that my momma gave him nineteen thousand dollars of my money without telling me. Sure would be convenient for ole Chester if I wound up in some prison. Think about that, y'all. Just think about it.

"Good," Chastity said. "Just perfect."

"Are you sure?" she said. "Want me to do it again?"

"No, ma'am," Chastity said. "That was raw and real and hit the mark. I'm not going to trim one second of it. Good light. Sweet face. You're what my grandma called wholesome."

They shot the whole thing in one of the dozens of guest bedrooms, nothing much more than an unmade bed, a chest of drawers, and a big leather chair. Someone had hung framed pictures of flowers and fish up on the wall. It could have damn well been anywhere.

"And what about the kidnapping part?" TJ asked. "When are we going to do that?"

"Next post," Chastity said. "Figure we'd shoot that shit down in the cellar. That way my daddy can't really tell we're at Firefly. Maybe tomorrow morning. Right when folks are just reaching for their phones."

"I don't know."

"Sure you do," Chastity said. "We already decided. Don't go back on it now."

Chastity left the room, eyes locked on the screen, while TJ sat down on the unmade bed in the harsh overhead lights. Chastity had turned two more lamps on, without shades to brighten things up a little. TJ took a long hard breath, wondering if going on Instagram wasn't one hell of a mistake, when Ladarius walked into the room and took a seat beside her on the bed. He looked as if he knew what she was feeling, maybe even sensing it down in the living room, and had come for her, wrapping his arm around her, drawing her close.

"TJ," he said. "I love you and all. But we better get loose from this crazy bitch or we're all going to jail."

"She wants us to pretend to kidnap her."

"Kidnap her?" he asked. "You shitting me? If we don't have enough problems, you want to add that on the police's list? Two murder suspects kidnapping some rich white girl. It's time to pack up and get gone. We got enough gas to make it to Fort Smith. Like we said, let's just keep going until there ain't no more road."

"That's no plan."

"You got something better?" Ladarius asked. "Besides playing dress-up with Miss Chastity with her fancy-ass clothes and high-dollar underwear? Tying her to a chair for some kicks?"

"How do you know about her underwear?"

"She gave me a little peekaboo in the kitchen earlier, bending down so I could see the goodies down her sweater. Don't get mad. Wasn't no way to look away."

"I got worse things on my mind than you checking out Chastity's goodies," TJ said. "You see Chester Pratt on TV?"

Ladarius nodded, reaching his free hand into TJ's lap and squeezing her fingers. He nuzzled his face into the crook of her neck, breathing in and keeping quiet. She was glad he was there, standing tall with her while she figured out this big shitshow.

"Chester wants us to burn for what happened to Momma," she said. "Only a guilty man would lie like that, wish some harm would come to a bunch of kids. John Wesley's just a boy. It's like Chester wants us to get caught, maybe shot up and killed."

"Man's gonna shit a damn brick when you tell the world about him taking your money."

"He wanted me and Momma out of the way," she said. "I see it now."

"Now you thinking straight," Ladarius said. "I never did like that bastard. Always calling me *boy* and *Brother Ladarius*, like it was olden times and we running 'round the plantation. That man ain't nothing but white trash, his neck so damn red it looks like it's on fire."

"Come on," TJ said, turning to Ladarius and kissing him hard on the mouth. "Let's get gone before Chastity knows what's happening. I'll tell her as we're leaving."

Ladarius nodded, squeezed her hand again, and kissed her on the temple. Just as Ladarius got to his feet, John Wesley ran into the room and pointed to the windows. "The police are outside," he said. "I seen one of them roll by the house and put on their high beams. Holly and Miss Chastity been running around turning off lights and locking doors. What's happening, TJ? Are they gonna shoot us? They won't try and kill us? Will they?"

Johnny Stagg knew every twist and turn of the state highway that ran from Jericho crossways up to New Albany. He used to ride with his daddy, back in the day, to deliver truckloads full of cow shit to the farm supply outside Pontotoc, Daddy Stagg smoking nickel cigars and singing old hymns to himself, lecturing his young boy on the dangers of likker, gambling, and nekkid women. The old man got so riled up about the whole thing that it didn't do nothing but drive Stagg headlong into that world, snatching up plots of land around Tibbehah from old folks until he had enough money to buy the Rebel Truck Stop outright. He couldn't really fault Chester Pratt for his many ambitions, doing all he could to find leverage in north Mississippi, but one thing Stagg's old daddy taught him was ain't nothing gonna grow without seeding your land with some rich and fragrant bullshit. If it hadn't been for the county supervisors, which he later ran, and for some good judges and folks in law enforcement, Stagg could've never stacked the deck on his eventual success.

Stagg played the radio as he rode up and down those small brown hills, passing family farms, trailers, fillin' stations, and pine thickets. He played a real Lonnie Irving classic about a trucker named Pinball from a cassette tape he sold at the Rebel, *Greatest Hits of the Road Vol. 5*. He tapped at the wheel as he drove, well aware of every little hamlet, every godforsaken country community and crossroads that he passed through. He waved to colored children playing by the side of the road and was cautious as animals sometimes crossed his path; a couple mangy dogs and several deer running like hell from a pasture, jumping a barbed-wire fence, and jetting straight ahead in the twilight. *Good Lord Almighty.* This was some wild country, awake and restless before nightfall.

Lonnie Irving switched over to a rocking little number, Kay Adams singing "Little Pink Mac." Stagg recalled seeing her sometime on *Hee Haw,* or maybe it was the old Buck Owens show, the one they said was broadcast from the Buck Owens Ranch, if there ever was such a thing. Stagg figured maybe so much of what he remembered about the old days wasn't real at all, no more than that Old West town he was constructing in the vacant titty bar.

It wasn't too long until he passed into Parsham County, GOD'S COUNTRY. SO PLEASE DON'T DRIVE LIKE HELL THROUGH IT. A nice little advertisement for a true shithole in north Mississippi. Parsham was a landlocked little county without a major highway, a decent body of water, or a town worth a shit. About every tree had been harvested, the few factories they had shut down, and now they'd even closed most of the chicken houses on account of their troubles with immigration last year. If it hadn't been for Stagg busting free of jail and getting back home, Parsham County might've dried up and blowed away.

Kay Adams kept singing about closing up the honkytonks and throwing away the key so that her love might come on back home. A mile or two over the county line, Stagg saw the place he'd been looking for, an old catfish buffet shut down years ago. Weeds grew free and wild in the gravel parking lot and the roof of the one-story building looked to be falling in on itself.

Stagg got out of his El Dorado and shut the big swinging door, feet crunching on the gravel until he got up close to the front door, open wide and full of electric light. Sheriff Bruce Lovemaiden was inside, kicking around the building, looking at the grease stains and busted trays across the old concrete floor. Stagg had bought the place for almost nothing but the back taxes, keeping it in his back pocket like most of his assets over in Parsham, a decent little place to do business now that his investment dollars weren't welcome in his own home county.

"Ever eat frog legs here?" Lovemaiden asked.

"Can't say I did," Stagg said. "Catfish wasn't worth a durn. Greasy and soggy. Folks here might've stayed in business if they'd learned a few lessons from Pap's. That catfish is so crispy, you can chomp on those fish bones."

"Is that a fact?"

"Yes, sir," Stagg said. "How do you feel about a good ole juke joint opening in this spot?"

"We're a dry county," Lovemaiden said.

"That's not what I asked."

"Well," Lovemaiden said. "I'm sure the supervisors can take the matter under consideration for a donation. Or two."

"Sure they would," Stagg said. "Never met a Mississippi county supervisor that wasn't crooked as a tomcat's peter."

This was the first time Stagg had been in the building. He had handed the key over to Lovemaiden some months ago to make sure no one tried to loot what was left to be looted. There was some kitchen equipment in the back, a big stove and a walk-in freezer. He knew a boy over in Abbeville who could fix durn near anything and make it good as new. Best as Stagg saw it, folks over in Parsham liked to get drunk. And he'd be glad to help 'em chill the beer, maybe bring over a few good old country acts from down in Starkville, get the heartache and fistfighting stoked up again.

"Deputies been on patrol regular," he said. "Here and your other properties, Mr. Stagg."

"Glad to hear it," Stagg said.

Lovemaiden shifted in his old boots, hands on his waist, looking Stagg up and down. "That is why you wanted to see me?" he said. "Right?"

Stagg scratched at his neck. "You ever heard of some boys called the Nixes, father and son who do a little larceny now and then? Maybe some rougher stuff."

"What do you mean rougher stuff?"

"Harassment," Stagg said. "Beat folks up for money. Maybe worse."

"You mean ole Flem and his boy?" Lovemaiden asked. "Shoot, yes, I know that sorry bastard. I ran that family out of this county a long time ago. There's something wrong in their heads. Maybe 'cause they're so damn short. I won't say they're retarded or nothing, but they're animalistic in their ways. That old man, who ain't really that old, younger than me, got caught diddling his niece a few years ago. I mean, these people ain't right. Dirt eaters and all that."

"Well, Flem and his boy have been bothering a friend of mine."

"Don't know how I can help you," he said. "They ain't in my jurisdiction. That's all on your buddy Quinn Colson now. *Haw. Haw.*"

"Just wondered what to expect of them," Stagg said. "I been away for a spell. I'd never had dealings with them, and then a woman works for me said she believed they'd come over from Parsham. Some years back."

"They're crafty little shits," Lovemaiden said. "I'll give 'em that. Took me six deputies and some plain and honest threats to kick them and their whole sorry-ass family out of here. But I'll tell you what. Crime in this county fell about fifty percent with the Nix boys gone. I shit you not."

"Maybe they won't be trouble for much longer," Stagg said, checking out the ceiling and the big pools of stagnant water dappling the concrete. "I'm working on a quick and practical solution."

"Glad to hear it," Lovemaiden said. "Say, you haven't heard any more about those kids who broke loose? We had our deputies out looking since they left Tibbehah. I don't know where they're at. But they sure ain't in my county."

Stagg nodded, placing his hands in the pockets of his pleated trousers, and rocking up on the toes of his brand-new penny loafers. "My heart breaks every time I think what she and that black boy did to her momma."

"Hell," Lovemaiden said. "Thank God you didn't have to see it."

"You knowed that colored kid, too," Stagg said. "Caught him a few times busting in windows over here?"

"A time or two," Lovemaiden said. "He's a nice boy with sticky fingers."

"He been in your jail recently?"

Lovemaiden scratched at his cheek, his head with reddened cheeks roughly the size of a damn basketball. His bloated belly extended so far out from his tan trousers that it appeared that the buttons could pop off his shirt.

"A long time back," he said. "Maybe two-three years ago. Stealing cars before he could drive legal."

Lovemaiden held a Styrofoam cup to his lips and spit. He stood there under the weak light of the few fluorescent bulbs that still worked and waited for Stagg to ask him the favor he'd mentioned on the phone. Stagg always liked to draw matters out—going 'round and 'round added a little drama and emphasis.

"I sure would like to see those kids get what's coming to them," he said. "I was thinking earlier today that Ladarius McCade might've made a few friends over here in Parsham."

"Maybe."

"Maybe one or two boys who recall him talking about his little girlfriend?" Stagg asked. "And maybe what they'd been planning to do to her momma?"

Lovemaiden spit again. "Figure someone with that kind of information would get a little compensation."

"Yes, sir," Stagg said. "But it would make me feel a mite better to pass along that money through the law, let them decide just what that upstanding young person would deserve."

"Some of the boys come in and out of my jail would kill their sister for twenty bucks."

"That a fact," Stagg said. "Sounds like y'all need more to do over here in Parsham. How'd you feel about adding some brass poles around this establishment? Sure would give something for the young women to do. Provide jobs and such. And sure would tickle the men around here."

"I thought you were out of that kind of business, Mr. Stagg?" Lovemaiden asked, grinning and spitting again. "Got right with the Lord and turned over a new leaf."

"Yes, sir," Stagg said. "Yes, sir. But I'm also always looking for ways to invest in the infrastructure and small businesses of north Mississippi."

"You want me to find you a jailhouse snitch."

"Yep." Stagg winked at Lovemaiden and grinned. "If it ain't too much trouble."

"They blocked the driveway," Holly said. "Ain't no way we're getting out."

"Maybe we can all pile in your momma's minivan," TJ said. "Bust right through that roadblock and just keep on driving. How about that?"

"How far you think we'd get?" Ladarius asked. "Two, three miles, maybe. This ain't Tibbehah County, TJ. They got police all over the damn place."

They stood huddled together in the dark and the quiet of the mansion, hearing the rain and the wind outside. John Wesley came into the living room, dragging his small suitcase, Holly already trying to explain to him why they had to leave this big, nice mansion in the middle of the night. She told him there was an even better place down the road, a place filled with ice cream and hot dogs and more video games than he could play in a year. TJ walked to the front window and looked down the driveway, seeing the two police parked sideways. Blue lights flashing without a siren.

"Fuck me," she said.

"Don't tell me you're gonna give up," Chastity said. "Walk outside with your hands in the air and put your faith in a higher power to make things right?"

"Don't be so damn stupid," Holly said. "There's nothing else to do."

"Bullshit," Chastity said, turning to Ladarius. "I just hope that you and little John Wesley didn't use up all the gas in the boat this afternoon."

"We didn't go too far," Ladarius said. "So cold out on that water I about froze my nuts off."

"Y'all head on down to the boat," Chastity said. "I'll turn on some lights upstairs to confuse them. Just don't get all stupid. Be quiet walking down there. Those steps can get slick as glass. And nobody—I mean nobody—say a goddamn word."

Holly had her arms wrapped around herself, shivering like she was cold although they'd cranked the heat up plenty in that big old house. She tried not to make eye contact with TJ but when she did, she just closed her eyes and shook her head from side to side.

"You got a better idea, Holly Harkins?" TJ asked.

"I don't want to leave," John Wesley said. "Why can't we stay here, TJ? Why are those policemen here? What's going on? Nobody tells me nothing."

TJ turned to her little brother, losing her temper for just a second, and telling him to shut the hell up and let her think. John Wesley looked to Holly, who grabbed him by the hand, and marched out to the patio where Ladarius and Chastity waited. The glass doors open, wind and rain blowing on into the marble floors. Chastity motioned for them to come on, so she could get to what she wanted to take with them. TJ figured if they were real quick about it, maybe they could get on the boat and out onto the water before Chastity caught up.

"And don't even think about leaving without me," Chastity said with a wink, dangling the boat keys in her hand.

"You gave the keys back?" TJ said to Ladarius as the girl disappeared up the winding marble staircase.

"How'd I know the cops would show up?" he asked. "Hell."

They ran out into the rain, John Wesley and Holly first, bending over and heading down the steps and down toward the dock. TJ got halfway when the flashlight spun on her and she heard a man's voice telling them to stop. Ladarius pushed her on ahead, TJ feeling the water soak up into her fancy suede boots and her hair cling to her head. The man yelled some more and she nearly slipped at the landing, Holly reaching out for her, offering a hand as she crawled on board. The boat open with only a canopy overhead. John Wesley found a seat in the back, clutching his suitcase, looking mad as hell.

"We're fucked," Ladarius said.

"Not yet."

"Sure we are."

"Come on," Holly said. "Come on. Start the damn engine, Ladarius."

"I don't have the damn keys."

"Then do that thing you do with the cars," Holly said. "Right? Do I have to draw you a goddamn map?"

Even with all the yelling and the cold rain out on the water, Holly swearing took TJ back a little. She looked up the hill and saw two large hulking figures on the stone patio, twin flashlight beams flicking across the boat and their eyes.

Ladarius reached up under the dashboard, feeling for wires and controls while TJ watched the flashlight beams bobbling and twisting down the stone steps, those cops getting closer and closer. She grabbed Ladarius's arm and squeezed it, closing her eyes, praying like hell that all the bad deeds that boy had done wouldn't jinx them. They just needed a little kick, a little electric spark on that starter and they could get across the lake and maybe find a new way, find a new path to keep on trucking west.

The motor started.

She opened her eyes and hugged Ladarius. Ladarius laughed but then stumbled back as Chastity told him to move his ass, the blonde princess already seated in the captain's chair, her key cranked in the ignition, pulling the boat back into the cold black water. The men yelling for them to stop, radios in their hands squawking while they raised their hands in the lights on the dock.

Chastity slid the throttle into high and the front of the boat nearly lifted from the water, throwing TJ and Ladarius down to the deck, Holly and John Wesley huddled together in the seats, cold and shivering from the rain.

SEVENTEEN

The bad weather moved in later that night, Quinn back at home, sitting in the parlor with Maggie, a warm glass of Four Roses in hand and Tanya Tucker on the turntable. Maggie loved "What's Your Mama's Name" and "Blood Red and Goin' Down" and took any chance she had to slip the record into rotation with Quinn's Charley Pride and Waylon. Both of them understood that the classic age of country was long gone, along with common sense, moral responsibility, and the good ole family farm. On a rainy night, the farmhouse seemed like a time capsule, with its high ceilings, beaded board walls, and seed glass windows. Sometimes Quinn could still smell his grandfather's old cherry pipe tobacco despite all the new paint.

Maggie believed it was ghosts. Quinn blamed fluctuating temperatures.

"Was this her first album?" Maggie asked.

"Second," Quinn said. "After *Delta Dawn*."

"She's just a baby," she said. "But sounds like a woman."

"Experience can do that to a kid."

Quinn had kicked off his boots at the front door and locked away his gun for the night, although he kept a loaded shotgun hidden and out of reach of the kids. He'd hung up his uniform shirt, radio, and service belt. His phone, as always, remained on and at his side, the idea of having a night off or even a full night's sleep never an option. Maggie motioned to his empty glass.

"That went fast."

"Just the one," Quinn said, looking at his watch. "Headed back in at oh-five-hundred."

Maggie joined him up on the couch, resting her head in his lap and staring up at him. Both Brandon and Halley were asleep. The baby monitor, not unlike Quinn's radio, remained on and connected with the loft upstairs. The parlor soon went quiet, the A side of the record finishing, whooshing in that center space and waiting to get flipped. Both he and Maggie too damn tired to get up.

"You think those kids are still in Arkansas?" Maggie asked.

"Lillie said they were in Forrest City yesterday," Quinn said. "Their minivan threw a belt."

"And now?"

"Lillie heard they're headed west."

"No other plans?"

"I figure TJ wants far out of Tibbehah County until we finally arrest Chester."

"What's Lillie say?" she asked. "About everything you found out?"

"Lillie has a personal history with the Byrd girl," Quinn said. "And her mother. I don't think she's gonna believe anything until I get something solid."

"Like what?" Maggie said. "A full confession?"

"Maybe," Quinn said. "Chester's digging himself in deep. Lying about threats from TJ and about taking money from Gina. The problem is that he was up in Oxford around the time we believe Gina was killed."

"Are you sure?"

"Reggie drove up and checked out his story," Quinn said. "He was there, drinking at the Library bar with a crew of old frat boys."

"Damn."

"Yep."

"So he hired someone?"

"Or two," Quinn said. "If you can believe TJ, two men attacked her momma. I've subpoenaed his bank records, phone records, and security footage from the Bluebird."

"And?"

"That's gonna take a while," Quinn said. "I just wish TJ had trusted me before she ran. I think she knows plenty about Chester and her momma and could've helped us out. I should've tried harder."

"Sounds like she had her mind already made up about you."

Quinn stood up and stretched before flipping over the album. He walked over to the old rolltop desk that had been his grandfather's and reached for the bottle of bourbon. He watched for Maggie's reaction, as Quinn had hit the bottle a little hard after his shooting, but Maggie didn't say a word. She just stretched out on the sofa, hands under her head, enjoying a little rest before Halley's midnight feeding. She knew Quinn was done with the booze and the pills, a momentary lapse in judgment caused by pain.

"If Gina Byrd cut a man so bad she thought he was dead, he would've gone to a doctor."

"Checked the hospital," Quinn said. "Checked the clinics. First thing I did."

"Nothing?"

"Nope," Quinn said, taking a slow sip, sitting back down, Maggie's head falling back into his lap. She had her reddish hair in a bun, freckled face scrubbed of makeup, little mouth pursed while deep in thought. She wore one of his old U.S. Army sweatshirts, loose and well-worn over a pair of faded jeans.

"Think me and you might make some good use of our alone time?" Quinn asked.

"Hold that thought, Ranger," she said. "Did you check the hospital later on?"

"It can account for two, three days after Gina was killed."

"Sometimes folks don't come in until it gets real bad," she said. "Infection setting in. They might put it off because they don't want to call attention to themselves or don't have insurance. I can check with the desk in the morning."

"You also know some folks at the clinics, too," Quinn said. "They may share something with you they wouldn't share with my deputies."

"Roger that," Maggie said.

"You making fun of me?" Quinn asked.

Maggie nodded, and Quinn leaned down to kiss her hard on the lips.

Quinn could barely remember the cold house and the quiet empty rooms before Maggie and Brandon showed up in his life. The bourbon, the rain, and Tanya Tucker only enhanced the feeling. He was sure he'd have to get back on the road in the morning, maybe sooner—Lillie and the marshals were getting close. They had to be by now. How far could four kids with no money get?

"You look like you're a million miles away, Quinn Colson," Maggie said.

"Hopefully only a few hundred."

"Lillie will bring them in safe," Maggie said.

"I'm not worried about Lillie," he said. "I'm worried who else might get there first."

* * *

Bishop had been parked up in the pine thicket since nightfall, where he'd smoked a half pack of Pall Malls and drank two Red Bulls while listening to the *America First* radio hour. *Illegal Immigrants Running Wild. Minorities with Their Hands Out. Hollywood Homos Radicalizing Youth.* So much immorality and recklessness in this country that he wanted to puke. If it weren't for all the mess last year, Governor Vardaman getting caught by the Feds and Colonel Pierce getting killed, the Watchmen would've been much further down the road. He never thought he'd have to take a job working for goddamn Johnny Stagg, enforcing peckerwoods and white trash that caused trouble. But here he was, late at night in his black Tahoe, hiding behind some skinny trees.

He'd killed the lights and only left twice to reconnoiter and take a piss. A quarter mile away was a nice view of the front porch where he'd go hunting, taking out both those Nix boys like Mr. Stagg wanted. Quick, easy, and efficient. He'd be sitting down to a Lumberjack Special at the Rebel before the sun came up.

Before he headed to the Nix place, Bishop had done a little checking with two of his brother Watchmen. One was a sheriff's deputy in a nearby county and the other had been a death house guard over at Parchman. Both of them knew about the Nixes. The father was a damn piece of work, a killer and pervert who'd done time for manslaughter and diddling some little kids at a storefront church over in Parsham. The son wasn't much better, in and out of jail for assault, meth running, and arson, the deputy told him, for a barn burning that had happened five years ago. Some kind of pissing contest with a fella who'd been unfortunate enough to share a border with these two shitbirds. Not that it mattered one damn bit, but punching the ticket of the Nix boys wasn't going to be a great loss for humanity. The law, the politicians all gone too soft in this country, letting people like the Nixes come in and out of jail like a revolving door. His brother in arms, the Parchman gun bull, had told him that trash like that wouldn't commit crimes if things were much rougher inside. Prisoners didn't have to do a goddamn thing but eat good food, sleep, and watch TV. Life ain't all about fried chicken and mashed potatoes, pounding your damn pud while watching *Judge Judy*.

Bishop squashed the cigarette into the empty Red Bull can and crawled out of his truck. He pulled at his brushy beard before reaching in back for his .308 Browning rifle and two automatic pistols. He'd worn all black tonight, from his ball cap down to his Merrill boots. Slinging his rifle over his shoulder, he guessed those boys wouldn't be but a hundred, hundred fifty yards away when he went to hunting.

Bishop cut the barbed wire and passed without interest under a dozen NO TRESPASS signs, one of them hand-painted and boasting that the owners of the land had both a gun and a backhoe. Bishop had to hand it to these little fucking midgets, they sure did have some redneck style. Bishop was serving the public good by thinning the herd a little. The law wouldn't give a damn. How many enemies could those Nixes have out there? The list would be damn endless, Bishop thought, moving careful and quiet in the wind and the rain. No moon tonight. Going dead silent like Colonel Pierce had taught him in maneuvers down in Guntown.

It took him about twenty minutes to get to that old trailer, where he could watch the house. He checked the back porch of the Nixes' busted old place, the lot filled with junk cars and chicken coops, the trappings of feral white folks, and saw he was a good hundred yards away. From that range, Bishop knew the bullet would drop a few inches, and he'd have to aim high on both those boys. Drop them in the light of the porch and head back quick to his Chevy.

All he needed now was a little diversion. Bishop opened up his rucksack and pulled out a quart of fire starter. Using the old junk cars and thick weeds as cover, he worked over to a woodshed, where he squirted the accelerant all up and down the walls. He clicked on his Bic and watched flames zigzag and light up the building as he ran back to his hidey-hole with his .308. Bishop nearly started to giggle at the game he was playing on those two midgets, smoke curling up into the dark sky. He couldn't wait to see them running from that house, yelling and screaming, dumber than a damn box of dildos.

Bishop jumped up into the old trailer, the roof torn away as the light rain fell over him. The blue tarp over the open ceiling buckling loose and flapping around in the wind. He got to his knees and lifted the rangefinder to his eye.

Bishop picked up the rifle, steadied his hand, and took in an even and slow breath. Damn, this was gonna be fun. He sure hoped those Nixes jumped up and yipped like the armadillos he used to shoot with his .22.

He started to giggle again as a tiny hand put a blade to his throat and whispered, "Evening there, stranger."

"Me and Daddy smelled you a mile away," another man said, his face and body nothing but shadows. "Guess you can't read worth a shit."

"Want me to gut him, son?" the old man said.

"Naw," the young one said. "Take 'em down to the processing house. Let's see what this fella knows."

Chester Pratt's phone buzzed a little before midnight. He picked it up, half asleep, answering like he was working the register at Bluebird Liquors. "Uh-huh, yeah, what do you want?"

"Why'd you say all those lies on TV, Chester?"

"Who's this?"

"Who the hell you think?"

"TJ?"

"Goddamn right it's TJ," she said. "Better check online. I responded to your bullshit. And I'm not going to stop talking till folks get smart and realize why you wanted Momma killed."

"Slow down," he said, pulling the phone from his ear, not recognizing the number. "Let's talk through this."

"I'm done talking," TJ said. "I want my fucking money, Chester."

"I don't know what you're talking about."

"Momma gave you my money," she said. "Having her killed don't change a goddamn thing. I won't stop until I get what's mine and your ass is being cornholed in Parchman."

"Good Lord, girl," he said. "Where'd you learn to talk so filthy?"

"Filth deserves filthy talk," she said. "I'll call back tomorrow night with instructions on how I want my money sent."

"I can't get that all in one day," he said. "That's a whole lot of money."

"Ain't my problem, Chester," she said. "Fair is fair."

"Where are you?" he said. "The law is on you. They're coming fast on your heels, little girl. You and that colored boy."

"Make things right," TJ said. "The truth has a way of shaking out."

TJ ended the call at the marina where they'd left Chastity's boat. Ladarius had crossed the road to a Motel 6 to steal them a new car, Chastity now saying they should head south. She told them all about a fishing cabin her daddy barely even knew he owned in a place called Grand Isle. It was raining hard now, and all their clothes were soaked all the way through.

TJ handed the phone back to Chastity.

"Can that kid really steal us a car?" Chastity said.

"That kid can steal anything."

"All my money is gone," she said. "My credit cards canceled. That fucking creep canceled my credit cards."

"Maybe that's for the best," TJ said. "No credit cards. Only burner phones. We keep to ourselves until I get what's coming to me."

"I heard you talking," Chastity said. "He's not going to pay."

"The hell he won't."

"If you can get me to Grand Isle, my father has another boat," she said. "A big one. We can all get free of this. I think we can make it all the way to Mexico."

"That's crazy."

Chastity shrugged, shivering in a pink hoodie, blowing into her fists and shuffling her feet. "God, it's cold," she said. "Come on. Where'd Ladarius go? Did he leave us?"

"He'll be back," TJ said. "Soon."

Holly and John Wesley sat under the darkened awning behind the marina. John Wesley had his head laying on top of his luggage, cold and half asleep. God, what a damn mess. TJ should've never brought him along. She prayed all this would get sorted out soon. A shitbag like Chester Pratt couldn't keep talking out his damn ass forever; whatever he did would come back on him. That much she knew. That kind of thing was in the Bible. Being on the run had made a believer out of her.

"I got something," Chastity said. "Something we can trade for money."

The crazy girl laid down the big black duffel bag she'd dragged down to the dock with her, TJ convinced it was full of high-dollar dresses and shoes, maybe a bottle or two of that good wine in the basement.

She unzipped the bag and pushed aside some jeans and sweaters and a pair of sparkly boots to show TJ a heavy, dark pile of metal.

"Where you get those?" TJ asked.

"My daddy's," she said. Chastity's bag was bulging with a fancy-looking rifle, a few handguns, and boxes of ammo. "Someone will buy 'em. Somewhere."

"You stole your daddy's guns?"

"Sure," Chastity said. "The TV was too big."

Momma Lennie opened the door and stepped into the processing barn just as the damn fun had started. Dusty and Daddy had stripped that old military boy buck-ass nekkid and bound his hands in chains that lifted him onto his tippy toes. He struggled to breathe with duct tape across his mouth, his face turning a bright red. Under the fluorescent lights, the stainless steel they used to butcher deer, hogs, and cattle shone slick and clean as a mirror.

"Just what the hell's happening?" Momma said. She was tall and skinny, nearly twice as big as Daddy, wearing her Disney Princess nightgown. Old Tinker Bell touching her sparkly wand to the sky. *This Grandma Believes in Holiday Magic!* "This the man who tried to burn down my shed?"

"Yes, ma'am," Dusty said. "Caught him red-handed. He'd set up at Uncle Frankie's old trailer with a deer rifle, about to try and blow a hole in me and Daddy."

"What for?" she asked. "What'd y'all go and do now?"

Daddy had taken to cutting a fresh field-stripped deer swinging next to the man, slicing a juicy rump roast with his pocketknife, and dropping the meat on the table. "Only know one fella want us dead," Daddy said, licking the blood from his fingers. "That'd be ole Chester Pratt. Ole Mister Fancy Pants sent you out to the Nix place? Ole Mister Fancy Pants wants you to take out the trash same as we done took out his whore?"

That thick-bearded man tried to yell and scream through that duct tape. Dusty figured it would smart like hell if they ripped it from his mouth. But he yanked it off anyway, kind of curious just what the man had to say about dealing with old Chester.

"I don't work for Chester Pratt," the man said, turning his head to spit. A good bit of his beard pulled out and stuck on the tape in Dusty's hand. "Christ Almighty."

"You shouldn't never have trespassed, son," Daddy said. "Who was it, then?"

"Let me go and I'll tell you," the bearded man said. "All right? This ain't personal. Someone paid me to punch both y'all's tickets."

"Chester Pratt," Dusty Nix said. "Right?"

"Goddamn Chester Pratt couldn't find his own asshole with a gallon of Vaseline and a divining rod," the bearded man said. "I work for Johnny Stagg. Come on. Let me loose. You don't want no more trouble. You kill me and Stagg just gonna send someone else. Probably a whole mess of them."

"What's your name?"

"Call me Bishop," he said.

Momma Lennie snatched up a butcher knife and walked up to where Mister Bishop hung from the ceiling, slid along the rack with that deer ready to butcher. Her hair was gray and stringy, eyes hollow and black since she quit the smoking and drinking. She flicked at his shrunken pecker with the sharp end of the knife.

"Save his ding-dong for the dogs," Momma said. "They got a taste for that ole bully stick."

"Please," Bishop said. "Turn me loose."

"Tried to burn us out," Daddy said. "Then planned to plug us both on our own fucking porch. Shit, boy. Ain't no reversing down that road and waving adios."

"Why's Mr. Johnny T. Fucking Stagg give two shits about the Nix boys?" Dusty asked.

"Help me and I'll tell you."

"Turn off the lights when y'all are done and don't make too much of a mess," Momma Nix said as she walked back out the door. "Y'all stole all my damn bleach last week."

Bishop rattled the chains and started to yell and carry on, while Daddy nibbled the bloody bit of backstrap in his hand. Dusty stood back and stared at that hairy bastard just hanging there, wondering if they might keep him in storage until they figured out what Stagg wanted besides them being dead.

"Sorry, boy," Daddy said, white whiskers covered in blood. "You made the play."

"I want his rifle," Dusty said, looking down at the man's feet. "And them fancy military boots."

"What about the meat?" Daddy said.

"Might make a damn fine gift for Mr. Stagg."

"Haw, haw," Daddy said. "I like your thinkin', son."

Dusty turned on the sausage maker while Daddy went to the cupboard for a jar of pickled jalapeños and some of that good Cajun seasoning they got at the Piggly Wiggly. Daddy licked his lips, setting the plastic bin in front of the grinder.

Dusty walked up on the man, who was rocking and swaying from the chains, and patted his big belly with his free hand, the other holding the .45 auto he'd taken off him. "Hell, we may not need to add that much pork fat," he said. "This fella got enough 'round the middle."

Bishop yanked and pulled, chains jingling like church bells in that metal shed. That fat boy's face purply red, eyes looking like they might just pop from his head.

Dusty pressed the pistol to the man's temple.

Lots of moaning and crying. A big pool of piss spreading across the concrete floor just before Dusty pulled the trigger. *Blam.*

Bishop hung limp and heavy off the chains. Dusty Nix nodded to his daddy to start on the cutting.

"Good thing Momma went on back to the house," Daddy said. "I don't think she'd want to see what's coming next."

EIGHTEEN

The next morning, the day after she'd tracked the kids to Forrest City, Lillie Virgil and Charlie Hodge headed over to Hot Springs, Arkansas. A security camera at a cabin on Lake Hamilton had shown none other than Ladarius McCade breaking in and stealing a freezer full of T-bones. By the time Lillie and Hodge arrived, the PD had sent out patrols to houses around the cabin and connected the kids to another break-in, this time at a big-ass mansion down the road owned by Vince Bloodgood, a fat fella who presented Lillie with his business card straight off. President and CEO of Bloodgood Motors in Fayetteville.

"I think these killers must've taken my baby," Bloodgood said, shaking his head. "She's a beautiful girl, frail and scared, ran off from home two days ago. Me and my wife have been worried sick. That's her car right there. Nice little Mercedes G-Wagen. Gently pre-owned. Bought it for her sixteenth birthday. How are you doing for a vehicle, Miss Virgil?"

"Why do you think your daughter joined up with those kids?" Lillie asked.

"Wait till you see the mess inside my home," Bloodgood said. He wore a dark blue double-breasted suit, a white shirt with a wide red tie, and styled his hair in an exaggerated comb-over. "Police almost finished up doing what they set out to do. House is a real wreck, ma'am. Looks like that Byrd girl had quite the time, sleeping around every bed like she was Little Miss Goldilocks with her pants on fire."

"Is that what you saw?" Lillie said. "Ain't that something."

"Sexual action all over my family home."

"Mm-hmm," Lillie said. "And just why'd your daughter run away again?"

"She never really run off," Bloodgood said. "Chastity got some idiot at the rehab center to drive her to Fayetteville for her vehicle. Don't you worry about that detail. I called up that center and made sure that ole boy was fired. We'd paid up for two more weeks."

"And what was she doing in rehab?"

"Girl drank worse than my ex-wife," Bloodgood said. "Popped prescription pills like they were Tic Tacs. I prayed on it a long time. Wasn't no easy decision to put my baby in a place like that for the fourth time. Not since what she did with that boy at this place in Aspen. But Chastity and my current wife had a little feud going on. A few weeks back, they really got into it while we were watching *Dancing with the Stars*, Chastity telling her stepmomma that sexy gal from *The Bachelorette* wasn't nothing but a ho-bag. Hell, I didn't even know what she meant. A *ho-bag*. But my wife took some double meaning to it, that Chastity was saying that she was cut from the same cloth."

"Has Chastity been in contact since she left?" Lillie asked.

"No, ma'am," Bloodgood said. "We figured she might've run off to one of our many homes. But this was the last place we expected. It's been shut up since the first of the year."

"I saw the FOR SALE signs," Lillie said. "This place is owned by the bank?"

"Just some financial shuffling is all," Bloodgood said. "It's been a tough year to sell a Chevy. Sure I can't interest you in a new vehicle? You find Chastity and we can work something out. Is that your old Charger over there?"

Lillie nodded. "Government owned."

"What's your personal vehicle?"

"A piece of shit Jeep Cherokee."

"You got kids?"

"A daughter."

"How old?"

"Nine."

"A little girl," Bloodgood said. "Oh, hell. I don't have to tell you a thing. You find me my little Chastity baby and I'll cut you a deal that'll make you blush. I'm thinking you'd like the new Trailblazer a whole lot. You mind me asking if there's a Mr. Virgil?"

"Listen, Mr. Bloodgood," Lillie said. "How about we cut the horse-shit for a second and get right down to it. Besides the boat, have you accounted for everything?"

"Everything?" Bloodgood said. "Shoot. That might take a while. House has sixteen bedrooms and ten baths. Haven't seen nothing yet but I'd be most glad to show you around. Already told all I know to that mean-looking fella with the crew cut."

"Deputy Marshal Charlie Hodge is a pussycat," Lillie said. "He'd only shoot you if he respected you."

"How's that?"

Lillie told Vince Bloodgood to hang tight on the mansion tour and walked on over to where Charlie made friendly with the locals. He introduced her to the sergeant on duty and the patrol officer who'd found the kids late last night. The officer, a tall, skinny, redheaded kid with a pockmarked face, said another officer just found the boat tied up at a marina across the lake.

"Then what the fuck are we doing here?" Lillie asked.

"Ma'am?" the officer asked.

"Call us if you find anything inside," Lillie said, motioning to Charlie and heading back to their car. "Also check out all cars reported stolen in the last twenty-four hours."

"These kids do that, too?" he asked.

"These damn kids do everything," Lillie said.

Quinn met Maggie at the Fillin' Station for breakfast after she'd dropped Brandon at school. She was already seated, Halley still in her cozy baby sling, and waved to him from the back booth kept special for him and the Colson family. His Uncle Hamp used to sit in the same spot, coming here for coffee and a biscuit going back before it was a restaurant and one of only two gas stations in town. There were still plenty of pictures of Hamp Beckett on the walls, framed clippings of him shutting down the Colson family moonshine stills and once making the biggest marijuana bust in Mississippi history over at the Pritchard place. He'd been the town hero before he stuck a .44 in his mouth and pulled the trigger out of shame.

"Mornin' there, Sheriff," Miss Mary said.

Quinn winked at Mary, taking off his hat and coat, hanging them on the rack by the front door under the deer heads and framed bass and crappie. A Bible verse on an old piece of barnwood said to TURN YOUR EAR TO WISDOM AND APPLY YOUR HEART TO UNDERSTANDING.

Outside the hand-painted windows, Quinn saw Sheriff Bruce Lovemaiden pull up and make a great effort of crawling out of his patrol car and waddling toward the front door. Quinn headed back to Maggie, kissing her on the cheek and whispering in her ear, "How'd you sleep?"

Her green eyes lit up over the rim of the coffee mug.

"Just fine," she said. "Until her midnight feeding. And again at four. I would've woke you, but you were snoring."

"Sorry about that."

"Don't be sorry."

Quinn told her he had a little business about to enter the front door. Maggie didn't seem pleased but knew that was the course of trying to meet up in a public place on a weekday. One of the many reasons, most of them health-related, she preferred to make their meals at home and stay off the Jericho Square.

Miss Mary handed Quinn a hot cup of coffee before he intercepted Lovemaiden. The bell above jingled as Lovemaiden walked in and scouted the darkened room. The propane units scattered around the restaurant glowed bright orange. The air smelled of bacon and scalded coffee.

"Thought we were meeting up at the sheriff's office?" Quinn asked.

"Got here early," Lovemaiden said.

"I was about to have breakfast with my family."

Lovemaiden again scouted the room and spotted the only woman and baby in the place. He smiled and nodded, turning back to Quinn.

"Pretty little lady," he said. "Sit down. This can't wait, Quinn."

Quinn took a seat at the first table by the front door. Lovemaiden, who had been all in a rush, reached for his reading glasses and the laminated menu. He scoured the daily specials, lips moving as he did so.

"Sheriff?"

Lovemaiden looked over his half-glasses, his face jowly and hang-dog. He had huge blue eyes and broken blood vessels on his cheeks. His hair combed back off his immense forehead. "That McCade boy planned this killing a while back," Lovemaiden said, leaning into the table and whispering the words. "Seems it was his idea after the girl's mother and Pratt made trouble for them."

"Gina Byrd didn't have trouble with Ladarius McCade."

"Bullshit," Lovemaiden said. "What kind of momma would want her little girl shacking up with a thug like that kid? He spent more time in juvie than he had in social studies. If you don't believe me, I got someone you need to talk with."

"Who?"

"A boy did business with McCade," Lovemaiden said. "Thieving. Stealing cars and raising hell. Spent some time with McCade up in Memphis at one time or another. Ladarius told all in a real heart-to-heart one night. Kid coming to tears saying TJ Byrd was a girl like no other. A pussy made of solid gold."

"I don't appreciate that kind of talk," Quinn said. "Especially about a minor. How about you tell me exactly what he said."

"Oh," Lovemaiden said. "Nothing but damn well near everything. It was the kid's idea to chop up Gina Byrd like a goddamn Thanksgiving turkey and stick her parts down in a bleach barrel. Ladarius planned to get the body out of Tibbehah County so he'd never be tied to the crime."

"What's the kid's name?" Quinn asked.

"I left the whole report with your woman Cleotha at the front desk," Lovemaiden said, grinning wide. "I just wanted to relay the good news live and in person. Okay? A courtesy from one sheriff to another. Now, do you mind if I order? I've been up all night working this gosh-dang mess and sure could use a bite."

Quinn stood up and tapped at the menu on the table. "Try the country fried steak with gravy."

"Good as the Rebel?"

"Better," Quinn said. "I'll call after I take a look at the report."

Lovemaiden grunted as Quinn picked up his coffee mug and

turned to the back of the restaurant. Maggie had Halley up in her lap, nursing her under the privacy of a light blue blanket, old people still scandalized at the sight of breastfeeding in the city limits.

"Is that Lovemaiden?"

"Live and in person."

"Did he find something?"

"Nope."

"Why'd he come to see you?"

Quinn turned to look over his shoulder. Lovemaiden was giving his order to Miss Mary and Quinn offered a half-assed wave before turned back to Maggie. "He wants me to come over to Parsham County to meet a snitch."

"And you don't believe him?"

"Nope," Quinn said. "How about after breakfast, we stop off at the hospital and check out any walk-ins with nasty infected cuts?"

"I need to check in anyway," Maggie said. "They want me back to work in three weeks."

"Three weeks?" Quinn said. "That's not what we had talked about."

Maggie didn't answer, shuffling Halley in her lap. The little girl wide awake now, as Maggie wiped her face with a napkin and handed her over to Quinn. He held his daughter tight, the child's eyes wide and unfocused. Halley so small, light in his lap, while she checked out all the smells and sounds of the Fillin' Station diner.

"She sure is curious," Maggie said.

"Skeptical," Quinn said.

"I guess she comes by it naturally."

They pulled over somewhere between Prescott and Hope, John Wesley and Chastity both needing to pee about the same time. John

Wesley nearly had to use a Coke bottle before Ladarius pulled over the white Kia Sorento he'd picked up across from the Salty Dog Marina. Ladarius parked the SUV up on an access road to nowhere, a slice of asphalt that went up into the piney hills and dead-ended at an endless section of electric towers running down a cleared path. The thick power lines buzzed overhead.

Chastity called it as good a place as any, no mile markers or identifying houses nearby. Ladarius shook his head but held the phone anyway, ready to start the recording, just as he got word from Chastity. Holly Harkins leaned against the hood of the SUV, head down, hoodie obscuring her face as she picked at a clump of weeds she'd found on the roadside.

TJ sure didn't like this. But she kept to script, holding Daddy's .38 down against her leg as Chastity kneeled on the ground. The rolling sweep of it, the gigantic electric towers and desolate slice of road added to the drama, although TJ was sure never to point the gun right at the girl. She let the image of them standing there, her standing with Chastity kneeling, say what needed to be said.

There was no damn reason it had to come to this. But the law and Mr. Chester Pratt of Jericho didn't leave me with no other choice. With me now is Chastity Bloodgood of Fayetteville, Arkansas. We've taken her on our journey in an effort to shine the light on our cause of innocence. We may be just no-count trailer trash, or that's what y'all are saying online, but Chastity here is that blue-eyed blonde rich white girl that just might get y'all's attention. We will stop at nothing to make sure we are heard and that Sheriff Quinn Colson of Tibbehah County arrests that lying bastard Chester Pratt for my momma's murder. I'm not saying he killed her all by himself, but we know he sure as hell knows who did. He knows those two men who attacked my momma outside the Southern Star. What he's been saying about

*me, my best friend since kindergarten Holly Harkins, and my
boyfriend Ladarius McCade ain't nothing but a damn dumpster fire
of lies. My momma loved Ladarius, never wanted to see us apart. The
only mistake my momma made was cuddling up to a leathery old con
man like Chester with his tired-ass khaki pants and those fucking Ole
Miss sweater-vests that cost more than our rent. She trusted him.
Trusted that old bastard so much she looted a bank trust set up in my
name, filled with twenty-five thousand dollars from a legal settlement.
I hope the authorities are aware of this knot in the goddamn hose line.
And if not, they better check out his lies. I want me and my kid
brother John Wesley back home along with Ladarius and Holly. As
far as Chastity goes, we're offering her free and safe return once
Chester Pratt is in jail. Until then, she'll remain our prisoner, going
with us wherever the road takes us. We didn't ask for trouble. We don't
want trouble. We just want someone to cut through the thick fog of
bullshit and lies and get those men who killed my momma. She may
have been nothing to y'all. But she was damn sure the world to me
and John Wesley.*

TJ nodded to signal she'd finished and Ladarius stopped the recording, sliding the phone into his back pocket. TJ reached down and
helped Chastity off her knees. Chastity not looking pleased as she
dusted off the knees of her fancy jeans.

"Damn it to hell," Chastity said. "I told you to threaten me. At
least push me around, stick that pistol to my head. My *free and safe
return*? What kind of shit was that? You need to ask for a reward. My
daddy will pay. My daddy will do about anything in the world for
me. Come on now, TJ Byrd. Be bold. Be brave. Show me that stone-
cold criminal that I know you can be."

"She's no criminal," Holly said, shouting as she slid from the hood
of the car. "Are you out of your damn mind, Goldilocks? We don't

want trouble. We want less trouble. How the hell is TJ pointing a gun at your dumb head gonna make things easier for any of us? You just want the drama? The drama is making you excited and crazy. Just why were you in that rehab center, Chastity Bloodgood? I don't think it was just drinking and pills. I think you're a goddamn crazy woman."

Chastity smiled and shook her head, trying to make it look like Holly was the one who'd now gone crazy. The day gray and cold, pine trees making wave-like patterns up into the hills. Cars zoomed up and down the Arkansas highway.

"Post it," TJ said. "Or don't. C'mon. Let's get back on the road."

"What's the use of kidnapping if you don't threaten me?" Chastity said. "Don't be so damn small and dumb. We need some money, girl."

Ladarius walked up between them, placing a hand on TJ's shoulder as he knew this just might go to fist city. No one spoke to TJ like that. Or at least, no one ever did it twice.

Chastity rolled her eyes and headed back to the SUV, opening the back door and slamming herself inside. John Wesley walked from the woods, where he'd had a longer transaction than expected, and asked Ladarius if they had any napkins in that car. TJ had been concentrating so hard on what to say and what to do for Chastity, that she nearly missed Holly turning a hard shoulder and marching down the sloped grassy hill to the highway. TJ shouted down after her. *Where in the hell was that girl going?*

Holly kept on moving down the slope through waist-high weeds, headed down to the road, marching back toward Hot Springs. She was almost to the highway.

"Shit," TJ said.

She yelled to Holly. But Holly broke into a run, charging down the hill toward the shoulder of the road.

Holly stopped just before she crossed the highway and turned back to face them, lifted her right fist, and offered her middle finger to them all.

Stagg hung back from the workers inside Frontier Village that morning, the hammering and the high whine of an electric saw so loud it rattled the metal walls. Inside the empty Diamond Saloon, he watched the boys work on the little stage where they'd have real-life can-can girls putting on a revue for all the daddies, flipping up their skirts and showing a little thigh. It wouldn't be the fifty-dollar pecker pulls Fannie Hathcock offered, but Stagg knew having some pretty girls around wasn't ever bad for business.

He'd just taken out a pen to doodle an idea for some old-timey lighting for the electricians when Midnight Man appeared. He told Stagg two fellas had come to the Rebel wanting to talk.

"What do they want?"

"Won't say," Midnight Man said. "Look like a couple midgets to me. Smell like shit."

"Must be some carnies," Stagg said. "Come over to sew up that busted seam on the bouncy house. Send 'em on over."

Stagg handed the sketch to one of the electricians and headed out the swinging doors, taking pleasure walking on the wooden sidewalk past the open windows that would soon be filled with glass. He looked up at the dark ceiling where they would project the moon and stars, a little slice of American history and wonder right here in Tibbehah County.

Stagg popped a peppermint candy in his mouth and glanced around at the whole world taking shape, hoping they could get that old bouncy house working again. He'd been on the phone for two days with some woman from Florida who'd sold it to him with all the defects, saying she'd never promised perfect condition.

Stagg leaned on the wood railing as the front door opened, filling the darkened space with bright light. Two small figures entered the metal structure, tiny shadows, craning their heads this way and that, checking out all the changes going on inside Fannie's old titty barn.

The older of the two started chatting up one of his carpenters, asking him what in the hell were they building. The younger one didn't seem as distracted, soon taking note of Stagg and walking on over to the village, crossing markings where they'd be laying the mini railroad tracks, coming up in front of Stagg's General Store and removing his dirty baseball hat.

"Mr. Stagg?"

Johnny Stagg nodded.

"I heard you was hiring."

"Yes, sir," he said. "Y'all the ones who know about fixing bouncy houses?"

"Matter of fact we do," the man said. "We know how to fix all kinds of houses. Especially ones with a bad foundation, maybe in need of some additional security and enforcement."

"What you driving at, son?" Stagg said. "Ain't nothing wrong with this foundation. I done poured it myself more than twenty years ago. It's withstood pole dancing, fistfights, and even an old boy plastered out of his mind on Aristocrat vodka. Drove his truck right through the establishment."

"Where's that man Bishop walks behind you?" the little man said. "Tends to your business?"

Stagg didn't like the way he was asking or the fact that he hadn't seen nor heard from Mr. Bishop since late last night. The realization of who these fellas were must've showed on his face because it seemed to give great pleasure to this stocky little guy. He grinned bigger than shit and placed his hands on his hips as if he were a man twice his size.

"You a Nix?" Stagg said.

"I'm Dusty Nix," the man said, nodding. "And over there, that gray-headed fella is my daddy. He goes by Flem."

"That's a mighty old-fashioned name."

"Suits him," Dusty Nix said. "He's a mighty old-fashioned man. We come to talk to you about some work."

"What kind of work?"

"Same as Mr. Bishop done," he said. "Only we do much better."

Stagg laughed and shook his head. He patted his pockets for another piece of peppermint candy but couldn't find none. Dusty Nix reached out his hand, no bigger than an eight-year-old's, and tried to pass him a little yellow butterscotch. Stagg let his hand hang there, not wanting to touch nothing come from that midget's pocket.

"Few men better than Mr. Bishop," Stagg said, suddenly feeling as alone and naked as a fella with his peter out on a rifle range. "He'll be around real soon."

"Is that right?" Nix said, slipping a few pieces of hard candy into Stagg's shirt pocket. He stood close, plucking a Pall Mall into the side of his mouth and flicking on a lighter.

"You got something on your mind, son?"

"I did," he said. "But that's been taken care of. Make sure to give us a call if Mr. Bishop don't show."

Dusty Nix nodded to his daddy, who hobbled over like a man with a wooden leg. He held some kind of package under his arm in a plain brown wrapper. The older man presented it to Stagg as if he'd just trucked the crown jewels into Tibbehah.

"What the hell's this?" Stagg asked.

"Cajun sausage we make special during deer season," the old man said, his lower teeth a wreck of rotten little brown pebbles. "Chop it up and mix it with some eggs. A little spicy, but sure do taste like a little bit of heaven."

Stagg accepted the package, the meat feeling warm and wet in the palm of his hands, as he watched the two odd little men head for the door. Midnight Man was quick up on his shoulder, breathing hard and giving a soft grunt as they disappeared into the parking lot.

"What they want?" Midnight Man asked.

"They wanted us to know Bishop fucked up," Stagg said, handing off the package to Midnight Man. "Throw this shit in the dumpster. I'm headed home to shower."

"Something a-matter, Mr. Stagg?"

Stagg looked down at the wetness on his hands. Blood had soaked through the package.

Of all the dumb things Holly had done in her life, throwing in with TJ and Ladarius had to be the King Turd of them all. Just to run down a short list: aiding and abetting murder suspects, stealing her momma's Dodge Grand Caravan minivan, ducking out on Phil Jr. over at the Captain's Table, and taking the Lord's name in vain at least sixteen times since leaving the Tibbehah County line. Now she was walking into the cold wind right at this very moment, trying to make her way back to Hot Springs, and hopefully on back to Mississippi before she started down a stretch of road that she could never come back from.

"Holly!" someone yelled.

She glanced quick over her shoulder and saw TJ hanging out the passenger window of that white Kia.

"Come on," TJ said, yelling some more. "Get in. We're gonna get busted if you don't check yourself."

Holly lifted her hand and extended her middle finger again, a salute to freedom and sanity, continuing her walk north along Highway 67. She was prepared to walk all the way back to Tibbehah County if necessary and would just as soon hop in a hot rod with the devil himself than climb in that car with TJ and that ridiculous girl who went by the name of Chastity. Wasn't nothing chaste about that girl, running after both TJ and Ladarius at the same time. Holly shoved both hands in her coat and kept on walking ahead, Ladarius riding up behind her now, honking the horn. TJ and Chastity yelling to her now to come on and get inside.

"Leave me alone," Holly said, screaming.

She figured she might run for it. Maybe make a break for the trees and lose them for good. The thought of finally tearing away from TJ left a hard feeling in her heart, like something real bad inside her had got rotten, meat going spoiled. As she walked, she started to cry, and goddamn, she hated to cry. All the feeling of being kids with TJ and playing on the monkey bars or swimming in Choctaw Lake, sitting with TJ as she tried to work on her dead daddy's Monte Carlo, acting like a miracle had been performed when that motor turned over not once, but twice, that old black piece of shit not being worth nothing other than playing those old cassette tapes of Cheap Trick and Bon Jovi. "Livin' on a Prayer." What a shitty lie that had been.

"Get in the fucking car," Ladarius said. "You're gonna get our ass caught."

Holly stopped walking. Ladarius pulled up beside her, both TJ hanging out the front window and Chastity hanging out the back, smiling so big it looked as if her big rosy cheeks might break.

"Not with her," Holly said. "Dump that crazy bitch right here and right now. Or y'all best move on. It's time to make a goddamn stand, TJ. You ain't known that girl but a day."

Ladarius revved the motor, rolling slow and easy beside them. Behind them, Holly facing south while the car faced north, she spotted a highway patrol car running fast and hard down the highway. The patrol car flashed its lights at them but kept on driving, heading on to something bigger and more important on down the road. Her heart had nearly stopped.

But it had been enough. TJ slid on back inside the car, looking straight ahead and telling Ladarius to go ahead and go. *Stand on it.* Chastity poked out her lower lip and gave a fake-ass crying face before Holly pulled her fist back and rushed forward to smack her good in her nose. That glass window went up real fast. Now it was just Holly and TJ.

"I thought you were my friend," TJ said.

"You made your choice."

"We ain't coming back," TJ said. "Not now. Not ever. Hope you got on your good shoes."

"Y'all aren't gonna make it," Holly said. "You know that. Right? That crazy-ass girl is gonna get all y'all killed."

"Go to hell."

"That's where y'all are headed," Holly said, walking more, more determined now than she'd ever been. "But not me. I'm headed home even if I have to walk the whole damn way. Just don't expect flowers and tears on y'all's grave. I'm over it."

NINETEEN

Raven Yancy stood on the running board of the Big Green Machine and leaned in the passenger window to get a better look at Halley. Halley had settled into Maggie's lap as they'd waited for Raven to get a short break at the emergency room, eyes closed and sleeping as the cold wind whipped around the truck. The black woman, long and lithe with prominent cheekbones and large brown eyes, was dressed in her bright green scrubs and held her cap. She shivered and hugged her arms around her waist, saying she didn't have much time.

"Still don't know how this man got you pregnant," Raven said. "When he left the hospital, he could barely walk."

"Maggie inspired me," Quinn said.

"Inspired something," Raven said. "Y'all should've been more careful. You might've busted up a lung. Cracked another rib."

"We were careful," Maggie said. "Although we had to get creative."

"Mm-hmm." Raven held up the flat of her hand and shook her head. "I get it, Mags. Don't need diagrams and in-depth explanations."

Quinn leaned onto the center console, so Raven might hear him better. He asked if she'd heard about or seen any patients in the last week or so that might have stab wounds.

"White males," Quinn said.

"Always causing trouble."

"Some bad folks," Quinn said. "If you do know them, or have contact with them, contact me first."

"What kind of cuts?" Raven said.

"Stab wounds," Maggie said. "Deep-tissue puncture wound or it might just be an infected laceration. They'd come in needing drainage, maybe wound debridement."

"Hmm," Raven said, smiling down at Halley's sleeping face. "Can't think of anything right offhand. Cut folks usually come in around the holidays. Someone getting testy about the turkey. But I'll ask around, maybe call out to some of the rural clinics, too."

"Appreciate that," Quinn said.

"This has something to do with Gina Byrd," Raven asked. "Right?"

"Maybe," Quinn said.

Maggie narrowed her eyes at Quinn and shook her head. "She might as well know everything," she said. "If you can't trust my best friend, who can you trust?"

Quinn nodded, cell phone buzzing next to his coffee tumbler. It was Reggie Caruthers and he pressed mute as he answered Raven. "I think two men attacked Gina Byrd before she was reported missing," Quinn said. "One of them might've been stabbed. It would've been bad enough that Gina got away from them."

"'Least for a while," Raven said.

Maggie swaddled Halley deeper into a soft blue blanket, a beanie with earflaps snug on her head. Maggie had knitted both the blanket and the beanie for her.

"If you find those men attacked Gina," Raven said, "you think those kids might be innocent?"

"That's the idea," Quinn said.

"Ladarius McCade is my second cousin," Raven said. "He's a good kid. Gets in trouble but wouldn't ever hurt no one. You know the type?"

"I used to be the type," Quinn said.

Raven stepped off the running board, arms hugging herself tight as the scrubs fluttered around her. "I'll do all I can," she said.

"Dinner soon?" Maggie asked.

"What y'all cooking?" Raven said.

"Maybe some tofu power bowls," she said. "With brown rice."

"My mother cooks for us, too," Quinn said. "Chicken and dumplings with some peach cobbler for dessert."

"Sorry, Maggie," she said. "But that's what I'm talking about. Count me in."

"I'm hungry," John Wesley said.

"We're all hungry, kid," Chastity said. "But we can't go out. Not till it's dark."

"Why not?" John Wesley asked.

TJ came out of the bathroom, wrapped in a towel and drying off her hair as Ladarius gave her a nice once-over. Four people and two single beds. Not much for privacy here at the Tri-State Motel in Texarkana.

"Lots of people looking for us," TJ said. "We just need to be careful."

"Bad people?" he asked.

"Not bad," TJ said. "But not good for us. We'll get something to eat a little later. Just rest up now."

"I don't want to rest," he said. "This place sucks. Smells like puke and piss in here."

"Hush your mouth."

"Tell me I'm lying, TJ," John Wesley said. "Why can't I just walk out and get some air? There's a swimming pool outside. And some swings."

"It's too cold," TJ said. "And that old pool is empty."

"I'd rather freeze my damn peter off than sit around in this stink," John Wesley said. "TV's busted, too. Can't get nothing but the weather and shows of folks trying to sell you jewelry. You can pay for a movie called *Three Musketeers* but Ladarius won't let me."

"It's a flick," he said. "Ain't fighting with those swords."

TJ reached into her bag for some underwear, jeans, and a fresh clean hoodie. She changed in the steamy bathroom and walked back out to tie her hair up in a bun. Everyone was quiet now. Chastity on her phone, scrolling faster than she thought humanly possible, with John Wesley and Ladarius laying in the bed, cover turned down on account of all the stains. They watched two old ladies selling a wood cutting craft set. TJ knew it had to remind John Wesley of Momma, the way she'd sit for hours outside at her workbench, making door hangings for Miss Donna Grace's flower shop. WORK HARD/PRAY HARD. WELCOME, Y'ALL. SIMPLY BLESSED. And TJ's personal favorite, WELCOME TO THE SHITSHOW. HOPE YOU BROUGHT ALCOHOL. That one really made her momma laugh.

"You all right?" Ladarius asked.

TJ nodded.

"Wanna step outside for a smoke?" he said.

Chastity turned and looked up from her screen. "Okay."

"You stay here," Ladarius said. "Watch John Wesley. We'll be right back. Got something private to discuss with TJ."

Chastity winked at the both of them, like they were going to go back to that stolen car to fool around. Everything they'd been through, being chased out by the cops, running that boat across the cold lake, and having to steal a car, and now Chastity was thinking they're about to get down and dirty. That girl had no limits. No wonder Holly left.

"Here," he said, handing TJ a cigarette.

They didn't go anywhere, just hung by the motel door, TJ taking a seat in an old ratty chair outside the window, watching the traffic roll on by.

"John Wesley's right," Ladarius said. "This place sucks."

"Took all the money we had."

"Chastity's holding back," he said.

"Credit cards," TJ said. "But how dumb would that be?"

"Pretty damn dumb," he said. "I still don't like what y'all did. Posting that shit online. You with a gun, acting like we kidnapped that stupid girl. That ain't gonna get us nowhere but jail."

TJ took a drag of the cigarette and let it out slow. She was bone tired, sinking in the chair, wanting to close her eyes just for a minute. "But she's not wrong."

"About getting money?"

"We got one night here," she said. "Then what?"

"Her daddy would know where we at."

"Ways around that," she said. "Venmo and shit. Only one big thing. We're gonna need another car. Especially by tomorrow when the word's out."

Ladarius smirked and scratched at his neck with the back of his fingers. "Are you asking your boyfriend to use his great and fine talents to get y'all's asses down to Louisiana? Or wherever the fuck we're going."

"Nothing fancy," she said. "Doesn't have to be nice. Just something that'll get the five hundred miles due south."

"Still need food," he said. "Still need gas."

TJ passed him the cigarette and reached for his hand and smiled up at him, while he looked out at the highway, back and forth across the road. Nothing but an empty dirt lot, cracked asphalt, and a used car lot a half mile back.

"Let me handle the money," she said. "You get us a new ride."

"And how are you going to get us more money?" he said. "Rob a damn bank?"

"Chastity wants to cut my hair real short and dye it black."

"And what's that gonna do?"

"She said we need a lot more followers and more views," she said. "She said I need to present an iconic image. Whatever the fuck that means."

"It's about shaking down her ole man," Ladarius said. "And sticking it to Chester Pratt."

"That's the idea."

"Well," Ladarius said, grinning and rubbing his goatee. "Good luck with all that. I don't know how that plan will work out, but I bet that hair's gonna look hot as hell."

Johnny Stagg was at the Rebel, back in his office, trying the best he could to wrap his mind around what he'd just seen and smelled, put warm and wet right in the palm of his hand. He hadn't thought too much about what he'd sent ole Mr. Bishop to do. After all, that was the cost of doing business in his county. But to have tables turned on him, flipped damn well upside down, was unacceptable. Those midgets came to him with their damn hands out, wanting a little something extra for leaving Chester Pratt alone and asking to come into Stagg's fold as trusted employees of his organization. They couldn't be serious. But they damn sure were.

Stagg spun in his chair, checking out the flat-screen monitors, now live and in living color. Two screens brightening up with the noon news out of Memphis and Tupelo, Stagg clicking up the sound to hear if there was anything new about that TJ Byrd and the McCade boy. And damn if wasn't all their lead story, *Mississippi Teens Suspected of Kidnapping Fayetteville Girl*.

A picture of a pretty blue-eyed girl flashed on the screen, looking for all the world like that troublemaking Nellie from *Little House on the Prairie*. Stagg remembering that time Nellie pushed that ole Laura Ingalls right into the dirt, the little punk arguing about playing Uncle John or Ring Around the Rosie. Or that time Nellie sucked on a peppermint stick at her daddy's general store and called those Ingalls girls country trash that didn't have a penny. Nellie was a damn hoot. This little old girl looked cut from the same cloth. Evil-eyed and mischievous.

Stagg grinned, thinking about just what in the damn hell TJ Byrd had gotten herself into. *Murder. Kidnapping. Extortion.* She was turning out right smart. For country trash.

The news showed video of TJ Byrd standing on the roadside somewhere with that girl from Arkansas. From that sly little grin on that blonde-headed girl's face, she was in on the whole dang charade. TJ Byrd stood with a gun in boots and an old flannel shirt saying that if Chester Pratt came forward and confessed his sins they'd let that girl go free and clear.

Stagg flipped around from station to station until he heard an interview with a fat fella named Vincent Bloodgood, Chastity's father. Stagg guessing Chastity was the Nellie lookalike, the images flashing on the screen of the girl at the beach, on some lake, and even up on the billboards with her fat daddy. A DEAL AIN'T NO DEAL LESS IT'S BLOODGOOD.

BLOODGOOD: I'll do whatever it takes to get my daughter back.

Is that a fact?

BLOODGOOD: My girl doesn't want to be a part of this mess.
These gosh-dang kids need to be punished for all they've
done.

That can be arranged.

BLOODGOOD: If you've seen Chastity. Or heard from her. Or
know anything about her, call the hotline we set up. I'm
offering a fifty-thousand-dollar reward for any information.

*Wonder what that fat boy would pay to get Nellie on back to Fayette-
ville?*

Stagg picked up the phone and called the kitchen for Midnight
Man. They'd spent most of the afternoon going over orders for
T-shirts and bumper stickers on both sides of the TJ Byrd debate to
sell at the Rebel. On one side, FREE BYRD or TIBBEHAH COUNTY TOUGH
with HOME OF THE INFAMOUS TJ BYRD AND LADARIUS MCCADE on the
back. On the other, TEARS FOR GINA BYRD and JUSTICE FOR GINA. Right
now, sales were about neck and neck on both sides of the issue. Stagg
figured kidnapping some blonde-headed, blue-eyed Chevy princess
might just kill any support of FREE BYRD sentimentality. TJ Byrd done
cornholed herself with that one.

Midnight Man soon walked in, dressed in his XXL black trousers,
white T-shirt, and a big white apron splattered with smoke and black
grease.

"Yes, sir."

"What'd you do with that sausage?"

"Tossed in the dumpster," he said. "Just like you said."

"You think it was Bishop?"

"Don't know what to think," Midnight Man said. "Seen some hairs in that mess. Make me sick while I was cooking that barbecue today."

"You think you can find those Nix boys?" Stagg said. "Bring them here?"

"What for?"

"Ain't none of your concern, Midnight Man."

"Don't mess with those people, Mr. Stagg," Midnight Man said. "Please. They busted in the head. Smell like damn goats."

"Then have them meet me at the truck wash," Stagg said.

"Those short boys?" Midnight Man said. "Come on, now."

"Get 'em here," he said. "I might have a little errand for them."

Stagg picked up the phone, calling 411 for a listing in Fayetteville, Arkansas.

Quinn dropped Maggie and Halley back at the farm and doubled back to town, Hondo riding shotgun, as Quinn dialed up Sheriff Pollan over in Calhoun County. Pollan had offered Quinn assistance since he'd first become sheriff. A straight shooter and lifelong John Wayne fan, Pollan was always glad to ask about Hondo.

"How's my favorite dog?" Pollan asked.

"Riding shotgun at the moment," Quinn said.

"Damn fine dog."

Quinn gave a quick rundown on Gina Byrd's murder, although Pollan had already heard most of it. He didn't stop Quinn until Quinn asked him about a potential witness who Pollan had locked up in his jail a time or two.

"Leon Doaks?" Pollan asked. "You got to be kidding me. Whatever he's peddling, don't buy it. He'd sell out his own sister for a pack of smokes."

"Professional snitch?"

"He's made a good living out of it," he said. "Is he in your jail?"

"Parsham," Quinn said.

"Hate to put down a brother sheriff, but Bruce Lovemaiden is a real shitbird," Pollan said. "Don't trust him. And damn sure don't trust Leon Doaks. Lovemaiden's used him before. Last time on a double homicide he couldn't solve if his life depended on it. He got Doaks to say the suspect confessed the whole thing over a jailhouse supper. That ole boy is over at Parchman Farm right now ready to ride the hot needle."

"Roger that."

"And Quinn?"

"Yes, sir."

"Watch your damn back," Pollan said. "Lovemaiden's a crook. He's always been a crook. Some folks I know say he's thrown in with Johnny Stagg after Stagg got out of the pen. They think he's running some of his old commerce through Parsham since you came back on the job. It's not as easy of a corridor, but it beats you folks making trouble."

"Things have been slow since Stagg got back," Quinn said. "He's building an Old West village for the kids out back of the Rebel."

"Where Vienna's used to be?"

"Yep."

"Sounds like a sleight of hand," Pollan said. "Have to hand it to Stagg. That old boy couldn't go straight if you shot his crooked ass from a cannon."

TWENTY

Ladarius had seen the used car lot and garage on the way into Texarkana: Gonzalez & Smith Motors, an old gas station surrounded by a ten-foot-tall chain-link fence. Good a place as any to do a little shopping, check out what suited them best, and roll on out the front gate with no one watching. Just in case someone spotted him, he'd borrowed TJ's hoodie overlaid with his leather jacket. He covered half his face with a bandanna and did his damn best to be quiet and smooth, scaling that tall fence out back and dropping down to the gravel lot without a sound. Most places kept the keys up front by the register or sometimes a few late drop-offs had the keys stuck under a front mat or even in the ignition. Wasn't much to stealing most cars but having the balls to do it.

As far as what came next, he wasn't wild about the plan. But it was all they had, drive on down to Louisiana and lay low at Chastity's daddy's cabin on Grand Isle. If things got tight, no one listening to what TJ had to say on social channels, they could gas up that boat and drift on over to Old Mexico. Ladarius never drove a boat in his life before yesterday, but turns out there wasn't much to it.

He couldn't make any sense of that girl, Chastity. Pretty little face like a Barbie doll with plenty of big attitude. He couldn't figure out if the girl wanted to fight him or fuck him. Making sly little jokes that seemed like flirting but always leaving a knife in his back. *You're a lot smarter than you look. Don't know what TJ and I would do without you. How good can you be if all you do is get caught?*

Ladarius's feet crunched on the gravel as he made his way to the back of the repair shop, past the dumpsters and plastic drums filled with dirty oil that had him thinking back on things he'd heard about Gina Byrd. How could anyone think he'd do something so fucked up? Killing a woman and chopping her up. What kind of damn animal would do some shit like that?

He moved quiet and easy to a back service door, testing the knob first but then having to bust it loose with a screwdriver. From dropping into the yard to entry, he couldn't have taken more than fifteen seconds. He walked inside and began to sort through the key chains hung on the wall when he heard that growl. At first, he thought maybe it was himself, because he hadn't had a bite to eat since they left Hot Springs. But when one growl turned into two, maybe three, he was damn sure the space was filled with some wild-ass animals.

He grabbed two sets of keys and ran for the front door, tripping over his own feet before unlocking the door and racing outside. Looking back, he saw it was dogs, a damn pack of mangy mutts, six mean motherfuckers with hair raised across their backs, barking and howling for him, coming right for his ass. He tried to read the writing on the repair tags while he hid behind an old Honda Accord, dogs sniffing and scattering around him. One jumped up on the hood of the Honda, spit dripping from its teeth.

Ladarius held up his hand, trying to talk sense to the animal. "Come on now, puppy," he said. "We good. We straight. Just be cool."

Down the row, like a gift from God, he spotted an old silver Buick

Regal like his granddaddy used to drive. He knew these cars, learned how to steal on these cars. All he needed was to bust open the steering column and use his screwdriver to crank the engine. It was like his granddaddy was sending him a message from up in heaven. *Here's my gift, young man. A busted-ass old Regal to run you home. But after that, you better get your life straight. You hearin' me?*

Ladarius nodded, looking straight up at those dogs, trying to be cool and talk some sweet sense to them. He took a deep breath and ran for the Buick.

He only made it maybe ten yards when one of those dogs got hold of him, yanking his ass back by the leg of his jeans. He fell face-first in the gravel, more dogs on him now while he heard more barking and growling, the whole pack tearing at him. Motherfuckers biting him in the legs as he kicked and punched, blind to it all now, feeling that hot blood run down his legs, knowing what it was like to be eaten alive.

He yelled and screamed, flat on his back, looking up into the streetlights and flapping red flags. LOW MONTHLY PAYMENTS. HOT DEALS. E-Z TERMS.

Nobody heard him. Ain't nobody coming.

"Mr. Bloodgood," Johnny Stagg said. "Sure do appreciate you taking my call. How are you this fine evening?"

"Is this about that Yukon lost its transmission?" Bloodgood asked. "Because that vehicle was sold as-is and was in fine and good condition when it left my lot."

"No, sir," Stagg said. "I'm not calling about a Yukon. I'm calling about your little girl."

There was a good bit of silence then, electric and cold, on the airwaves between Tibbehah County and Fayetteville, Arkansas. No one spoke until Stagg cleared his throat.

"You know where she is?"

"Got some ideas," Stagg said. "Those wild kids, TJ Byrd and Ladarius McCade, come from my neck of the woods down here in Tibbehah County, Mississippi. I know them and their people real well. I want to apologize for the pain and distress they've caused the Bloodgood family."

"What did you say your name was?" he asked. "Again."

"Johnny," he said. "Johnny T. Stagg."

"You ain't kin to that ole boy in the Dixie Mafia, are you?" Bloodgood said, as if the thought really tickled him. "*Ha Ha*. Heard of a fella named Stagg that ran a titty bar for truckers and got himself caught paying off half the politicians in Mississippi."

Stagg didn't answer, letting the long bit of silence hang there and speak for itself.

"Oh," Bloodgood said. "I see."

"I've been the target of much slander and lies over the years," Stagg said. "Got caught up in a political witch hunt by a local boy who thought he was Buford Pusser reincarnated. But that time, that old history, don't have a thing to do with what I'm offering you at the moment. I seen you on the news offering a reward for information about little Miss Chastity. Lord, she is cute as a button."

"Yes, sir," he said. "She's a real pistol. Can you help me?"

Stagg reached for the candy dish on his desk, selecting a butterscotch he'd just been gifted. He leaned back in his office chair, taking his time to unwrap it and pop it into his mouth. "Have you heard a word from your daughter, Mr. Bloodgood?"

"Only what I seen on the internet," Bloodgood said. "Over there on that Instagram TikToking."

"Mm-hmm," Stagg said. "Well, I don't know much about them things. I'm an AT&T man myself. But speaking theoretically, what would you say if I might offer the safe return of Miss Chastity while making sure those kids who took her get what's coming to them?"

"I'd say I'd be mighty grateful, Mr. Stagg."

Stagg sucked on the butterscotch, trying to make the flavor last a bit longer. Liking the feeling of being back in the saddle, turning his chair to and fro, making this work and come to pass.

"You and me are businessmen, Mr. Bloodgood," Stagg said. "You do understand that true heartful gratitude comes with a price tag."

Chester Pratt was tired of being harassed.

Ever since TJ Byrd took to the social media airwaves to convince the world she was innocent and he was the bad guy in this drama, man, how his life had changed. He'd been getting nonstop harassing phone calls at his home and over at the liquor store. *Hello there, Killer. Why'd you do it, Chester? You are a sick, sick man.* Kids, gosh-dang kids, would race by him on the Jericho Square giving him the high sign, and worst of all was seeing those stupid-ass FREE BYRD T-shirts they were selling at the Rebel.

Chester had to squirrel himself away in the stockroom just to get a little break, telling ole Jimbo out front to tell anyone who asked that "No, Mr. Pratt is not around and probably won't be for a long while." Jimbo knowing not to ask much more than that, fine with ringing up the weekend liquor sales and knocking that phone off the hook. Ass-pocket bottles of whiskey and gallon jugs of Aristocrat vodka, boxes of wine for the ladies who wanted to drink themselves numb as there was little else to do in Tibbehah besides Sunday services and Taco Night at the El Dorado.

Chester hoped and prayed, really praying to his Lord that all would be forgotten and forgiven. He meant it. Hell, it wasn't his fault what happened to Gina, all he'd been trying to do was scare her a little bit, make her back off on trying to get a return on her investment so durn quick. He'd told her, just two nights before he'd sent the Nix boys, that you couldn't make your money back in a few months, that wasn't the way of the world. He said he'd be able to come up with half by summertime, right around margarita season, and if she had any problem with that then she could just go and find herself a lawyer. But Gina didn't like that. Didn't like that a bit, 'cause she knew what she'd done, looting her own baby girl's savings, was illegal as hell, and if Chester didn't step up with her money, TJ was going to make a big ole family feud. The way Chester saw it, TJ still was to blame for the mess. She should've had more respect for her momma and her decision-making.

Chester added a little more Beam to his coffee and closed his eyes while he lay back in a big old leather chair patched up in duct tape, breathing deep into his nose, not wanting to turn on the damn TV or check his emails on account of all the hate out there. Why oh why would these stupid-ass kids fall for a hick like TJ Byrd, take her side in what was a most personal and private matter?

Knock, knock.

"I told you, I'm not here," Chester said to the closed door. "Jesus H. Christ, Jimbo."

The Nix boys, Dusty and his daddy, walked into the storeroom, nobody around to even stop them, strolling on down the rows of booze like they owned the place. Flem licking his dry lips, thinking that he must have died and gone to heaven, floating on that old whiskey river. The grizzled old fucker plucking himself a bottle of Blanton's and uncorking it with his teeth.

"You expecting someone else?" Dusty Nix asked.

Chester Pratt didn't answer.

"Mr. Stagg wants to know if you heard from the Byrd girl."

"Mr. Stagg?"

"See?" Flem said, chugging down a quarter of that little round bottle. "You was expecting old Bishop. Military man who'd been giving your ass fits. The military man come to take out the Nix boys on Nix land. Wadn't he a real thorn in your backside?"

"I don't know any such person," Chester said.

"Hell, you don't," Dusty said. "You made a deal with Stagg to shoot us in the back."

"No, sir," Chester said. "Why would I throw in with Johnny Stagg?"

"'Cause a Nix can't be had," Flem said. "A Nix sets out right fast on what needs doin'. Don't worry none, Chester. We ain't here to kill you. Not right yet."

Chester Pratt swallowed, not moving from the overstuffed leather chair. He waited for these two to walk down row after row and knock over bottles, same as Bishop had done a million nights back, back before he'd made the deal with the devil. Mr. Stagg now his legal partner in Bluebird Liquors.

"We're asking again," Dusty said. "Have you heard from the Byrd girl?"

"Once."

"When?" Dusty asked.

"Two nights ago."

"And what did she say?"

"She thinks I killed her momma," Chester said. "You heard it. Everyone's saying it."

Dusty Nix put his hands on his waist, looking like he just might break into a little Irish jig, clodhop his old boots around the storeroom. But he didn't. He stood stock-still, scratching at his stubbled, bulging neck and cutting his eyes over at his daddy for nearly finishing that bottle. "Quit now," he said.

"Sorry," Pratt said. "I can't help you."

"What number'd she call with?" Dusty asked.

"The girl used a burner."

"What number?" Dusty said. "Maybe I'll get lucky. Have her talk dirty to me. I seen her little tatas and that tight little ass on the internets."

"Y'all shouldn't have done what y'all did," Chester said.

Dusty Nix smiled, his teeth brown and broken, before turning his head to spit on the floor. Daddy Nix put down the bottle and walked to a far corner where he started to urinate into a box of champagne bottles.

"You the one who wanted Gina Byrd gone," Dusty said. "You said as much. And she's the one who went ahead and stuck my daddy. Bled like a pig all in my truck. Had to get him to the hospital yesterday on account of him catching the fever, blood and pus spewing out of his insides."

"I'm not going down for this," Chester said.

Flem finished up and turned around to zip up his fly. Dusty walked up close to where Chester sat, Chester smelling his rotten breath at five feet. As Dusty moved into the overhead light, Chester noticed his flannel shirt was unbuttoned and open loose, the man having the damn balls to wear one of those fucking FREE BYRD T-shirts.

"Y'all fucked me," Chester said.

Dusty Nix nodded. "Maybe," he said. "But you got a choice here. When that girl reaches out again, Mr. Stagg wants you to agree to her terms. You hear me?"

"I don't have the damn money."

"Don't you worry your pretty old head about nothing," Dusty Nix said, reaching down for Chester's phone and snatching it right out of his hand, scrolling through his personal calls. "You get the girl to meet you and we'll take care of the rest."

Chester felt his insides turn to cherry Jell-O, heart sinking down into his drawers. Everything had gone way past what he'd wanted. He never wanted Gina dead. He didn't even want to see TJ's little smart ass hurt. And what about poor John Wesley? Shit, how far were these peckerheads prepared to go? They wouldn't leave the job site until everyone who touched that money was dead.

Dusty Nix caught Chester staring at his T-shirt.

"Like it?" Dusty asked.

Chester didn't answer. His mouth too dry to talk.

"Mr. Stagg sells 'em half off for friends and family," Dusty said. "You make contact with the girl and I'll see if I can't hook you up."

Ladarius figured this is how you go out, stealing hundreds of cars and busting into dozens of homes, and nothing much happens until you try to boost an old Buick Regal and six mangy dogs eat your ass. He was on his back, kicking and punching, screaming like a little bitch, the dogs going to town on his legs, when he heard the shotgun blast.

That gave the dogs a little jump. Ladarius felt like he could barely hold his head up, losing blood and his ass pumped good with adrenaline. He scooted on back, feeling the gravel up into his skin, not wanting to look down at his legs and knowing he couldn't see much in the shadow. The shotgun blasted again. *Blam!*

He fell back, trying to catch his breath, not caring if whoever this was wanted to pump some shells into him. Anything was better than six dogs. Anything was better than getting eaten alive down at Gonzalez & Smith Motors, red and green flags flapping in the cold wind. The dogs looked back and trotted away from him.

Ladarius closed his eyes. Opening them again, he saw a squat

Mexican man dressed in a fancy-ass black cowboy shirt, black jeans, and a black cowboy hat.

The man had the shotgun aimed tight on Ladarius.

Ladarius covered his face, waiting for the blast.

"*Ladrón negro,*" the man said, turning his head to spit. "*Por qué viniste aquí?*"

Ladarius didn't get the first word but understood the second.

"I can't feel my legs."

"*Estúpido,*" the man said, shaking his head. He removed his cowboy hat and looked around the car lot. One of the mangy black dogs trotted up and licked at the man's strong brown hand. The mutt had Ladarius's blood across his nose.

"I'm bleeding out," Ladarius said. "Help me. You gotta help me, man. *Por favor, señor.*"

The man pulled a phone from his back pocket. He began to speak in clear, deep English giving the name of the business and address. *Hector Gonzalez. Gonzalez & Smith.*

"The dumb boy is injured," the man said. "My dogs. Yes. They ate him for dinner."

Lillie Virgil had had about as much fun as she could handle that day, spending most of the morning checking out video surveillance at the Salty Dog Marina on Lake Hamilton and later speaking to an old couple from St. Louis who'd had their new Kia Sorento stolen by the notorious Ladarius McCade. The old folks seemed more fascinated than pissed about what happened, wanting to know all about Mc-Cade and TJ Byrd, asking if Lillie thought they'd try to ride it out to the bitter end.

Lillie told them she had no idea but they sure better be checking on getting a new car. Ladarius McCade could be mighty hard on a vehicle.

She and Charlie checked into the Embassy Suites, grabbed dinner, and headed back to the Hot Springs Marshal's Office before calling in to the Old Man back in Memphis and then Florencia at home. Lillie talked to Rose and gave her the PG version of events, Rose not that interested anyway and telling her all about a new trick she'd taught Jerry Lee. The dog would now sit still, not moving a muscle, with a treat balanced on the end of his nose. When Rose said okay, that dog popped a tongue across his nose and swallowed it whole.

"Just like his namesake," Lillie said.

"What's that, Momma?"

"Just a little joke," she said. "Be good. Be good for Florencia."

"When will you be home?"

"Soon."

"You promise?"

"I would, kid," Lillie said. "But I'd be lying. How about I tell you I'm doing my best?"

"Are you going to shoot those kids?"

"I'd never shoot those kids."

"What if they try and shoot you?"

Lillie didn't answer, the question broken up by the sound of Jerry Lee's barking and Florencia coming back on the phone. Lillie told her to go ahead and cash that second check. She also told Florencia she didn't know what she'd do without her. Thanking her for being there for Rose when she couldn't.

Lillie set down her phone.

"Ain't easy," Charlie Hodge said.

"How'd you do it?"

"I lied to my kids and told the truth to my wife," he said. "I never held anything back. Even when I went undercover."

"I don't have a wife."

"Maybe you oughta get one."

"I don't need a wife or a husband," Lillie said. "That's what I pay Florencia for."

Charlie Hodge smiled. He sat across from her at a borrowed desk. The remnants of their fried catfish dinner sat between them, both of them working on daily reports for the Old Man. A marshal couldn't use the damn bathroom without having to log every damn detail.

"Do you date much?"

"Charlie."

"Don't mean to be nosy," he said. "Just hadn't seen you slow down much these last few years. Longest amount of time I've seen you take off is after what happened down in Tibbehah."

"When I shot Fannie Hathcock."

Charlie didn't answer, knowing it was a sore spot for Lillie. She knew she'd done everything right. Reacting a second slower could've gotten her killed. But knowing that she'd shot a woman armed with only a silver-plated cigarette case was something that continued to haunt her. Why couldn't Fannie have just been her damn self and come up with a pistol. She'd been wanting to shoot Lillie since they'd first met.

"She'd nearly beat that Fed to death," he said. "If you hadn't killed her then, she would've sent someone for you."

"I know."

"Maybe hurt your family, too."

"That had crossed my mind."

"Maybe some time off," Charlie said. "After this. Take Rose down to Disney World or something. Go over to Branson and see Donnie and Marie."

"You must be shitting me," Lillie said. "Donnie and Marie?"

"Hell, Tony Orlando then," he said. "Don't tell me you don't like

Tony Orlando. Everybody loves that song 'Tie a Yellow Ribbon Round the Ole Oak Tree.'"

"I'd rather have a lobotomy."

Charlie looked as amused as ever with Lillie, saying maybe they should head back to the Embassy Suites and get some rest. They'd be up again at five a.m. if not sooner, hoping to maybe catch those kids on a tag reader if they crossed state lines. But she had her doubts. She bet Ladarius would've changed those plates straight off, although they couldn't find any that matched back at the motel by the marina.

"Is this all that excitement and adventure you promised me?" Lillie asked, closing her laptop.

"If I'd told you the truth, would you have still wanted to be a marshal?"

"You bet your ass," she said.

As Charlie started to shut down his laptop, Lillie got the call from her supervisor in Memphis. She clicked off and set down the phone and turned to Charlie.

"They're in Texarkana," she said. "The McCade kid just got caught trying to steal another car."

TWENTY-ONE

The same night Ladarius McCade got caught in Texarkana, Quinn got a call from Holly Harkins that she was stuck at a Waffle House in Olive Branch and needed a ride home. He met her up there and they talked a great bit, Quinn driving her back to Jericho at day-break and organizing a tearful reunion with her parents before she was set to go in front of a juvenile judge. He felt for the girl, but she had stolen her parents' van, broken into a mansion in Hot Springs, and assisted two murder suspects in their run from the law. Quinn promised Maggie he'd do all he could to help the girl, but at the moment she just had to stay in custody until it all shook out.

Quinn was back in the office, no sleep that night, reading through the last twenty-four hours of reports. While he'd been gone, some genius had decided to try and pull the ATM out of the Rebel Truck Stop, making a real mess of the glass doors before getting hung up on a brick wall. Reggie noted in the report the two suspects must've been working with low mental acuity since they drove off horizontally from the doors and not in a straight line. The chains dug into the wall and one of the suspects had to get out to free the truck. Quinn read a quick description of the two, dozens of shitbirds he knew crossing his mind.

"More coffee, Sheriff?" Cleotha asked.

Quinn nodded and Cleotha took his cup.

He leaned back in his swivel chair, watching the sun come up over the jail, and reached for a fresh cigar from his humidor. A Liga Privada provided by one of the Rangers in his company who lived in Miami and now worked for a wholesaler. They were expensive sticks and had been used against him on more than one occasion as proof he'd taken kickbacks.

Quinn set fire to the cigar and was deep in the paperwork from the night before when his cell buzzed again. He expected it to be from Maggie, both of them trying to organize a dinner at his mother's house, Jean excited about the prospect of getting Boom and Raven Yancy together. Jean continued to be fixated on the idea that Boom just hadn't met the right woman yet.

Quinn answered.

"Sheriff Colson?"

"Speaking."

No one said anything and after a long pause, Quinn nearly hung up the phone, thinking there was a broken connection. He asked if there was anyone there.

"It's me," the voice said.

It was a young woman. Quinn didn't need to ask.

"Holly Harkins said you wanted to talk to me."

"Hello, TJ."

"I know y'all got Ladarius," TJ said. "I saw it on the news. I just want to know if he's all right."

"Where are you?"

"I asked if he's okay, goddamn it."

"He's going to be fine," Quinn said. "But he's hurt pretty bad.

Could've been killed. How about y'all stop all this crap and come on in? You're making yourself look bad, running from state to state, trying to act like you kidnapped that Bloodgood girl."

"Maybe I did," TJ said.

Quinn didn't answer. Outside his window, he watched the weekly gathering of families coming to visit with prisoners for the morning. Some set out lawn chairs, others just stood on the free side of the fence, keeping their hands away from one another, although he'd caught a few try to slide a Little Debbie or body part or two between the chain link. There were baby mommas and baby daddies, mothers and grandparents. Little children ran loose and wild in the parking lot as their father did time in the drunk tank or waited out time before being transferred to Parchman. There were check forgers and wife beaters. Killers and drug addicts. Men and women paraded out into the open yard if they wanted free time in the cold air and a little check-in with the family.

"Did you see my post about Chester?" TJ asked.

"Yes, ma'am."

"But you don't believe it?"

"I'm still investigating the death of your mother," Quinn said. "I'm looking into everything."

"Then why'd you charge me and Ladarius?"

"Why'd y'all run?"

"I asked you first."

"We found some evidence outside your trailer."

"Whatever shit you found," TJ said, "wasn't ours. How stupid do you think I am? If I'd killed my momma, I'd sure have cleaned up the mess. Chester Pratt has strung you and that fat sheriff from Parsham right along."

"I know."

"What?"

"I said I know," Quinn said. "But need y'all to stop running. Stay where you are and I'll work something out. I'll come for you."

"Bull W. Shit."

"I need you to trust me."

"Like my daddy trusted your asshole uncle?"

"If you haven't noticed," Quinn said, "I'm not my uncle."

"I get blamed for everything," she said. "Even when I didn't do it. Even when it's not my fault. Sometimes you get looked down on so much, you just start acting like what's expected of you. You know? What's the damn point? Might as well be an outlaw. It's what folks want to see."

"I understand."

"No, you don't."

"I ran wild when I was your age," he said. "I stole some cars. Got drunk a lot. Hunted on posted land. Hell, one time me and my best friend stole a fire truck."

"Shit."

"Ask anybody," Quinn said. "I was mad as hell and didn't know why."

"I know what you're doing," TJ said. "And I don't have time for no Dr. Phil bullshit, Sheriff. I just wanted to know if Ladarius is alive."

"He's gonna be fine," said Quinn. "But he's off the field and you're on your own."

"Just to save you the trouble," she said. "He's not like that traitor, Holly. Ladarius won't say nothing. 'Cause he don't know nothing."

"I know about the insurance settlement," Quinn said. "I know your mom took it from you and gave it to Chester."

"Then why don't you get up off your ass and do something?"

"Come on in," Quinn said. "You keep running and I promise you, y'all are gonna get hurt. Ladarius damn near bled out after he got eaten up by some dogs. He was trying to steal y'all a car."

"Oh, God."

"I know you're telling the truth," Quinn said. "But I need time. I need more interviews. More evidence to process. I'm trying to put this whole thing together."

"Bullshit."

"What more can I promise you?"

"Not a goddamn thing," she said. "I don't hear anything but just more lies. More time won't change a damn thing."

The line went dead. Quinn turned back to look into the jail yard. Someone had brought a big blue sheet cake to the Saturday gathering and his deputy Kenny was behind the fence making sure it was shared between all the prisoners. Kenny took a small piece for himself as he led all the men in orange in a fine rendition of "Happy Birthday."

Quinn couldn't help but shake his head. Kenny sang so loud Quinn could hear him from behind the glass.

Lillie didn't say a word, walking into the hospital room and taking a seat at Ladarius McCade's bedside. The kid's eyes were open, plastic tubes coming out of his nose, while he watched one of those fixer-upper shows on television. *Flip or Flop* or maybe *Masters of Flip*. One of those dumbass shows. That was Ladarius. Always looking for new trends in the world of B&E.

"You remember me?" Lillie asked.

He looked her up and down. But didn't seem to have an answer.

"You should," Lillie said. "Cut you a few breaks along the way, kid. Until you broke into Dr. Stevens's old house, pulled the copper wiring from the walls, and tore out those antique light fixtures after he moved up to Memphis."

"What do you want?"

"Got to get you home, Ladarius."

"Sheriff Colson send you?"

Lillie shook her head and reached for the U.S. Marshal badge hanging from her neck.

"Just hookin' and haulin' today," Lillie said. "Congratulations. Doc says you should be good to travel tomorrow. I know your grandmother can't wait to see you. I'm sure she'll have plenty to say."

"Ha."

Lillie leaned forward and pressed the off button on the remote. It was early morning and the room was quiet. A tray of untouched food waited on a nearby table. Rain tapped at the window with gray skies, bare trees across the hospital parking lot. A grand day to be in Texarkana.

"Where are they?" Lillie asked.

Ladarius shook his head. One eye was half-closed and his lip was busted. His lower body had been covered in a sheet, but Lillie knew enough about the damage down there. Those dogs took a good deal of prime USDA right out of his legs.

"I'll make sure they're safe," Lillie said. "Can't say the same for some peckerwood deputy in Shit City, Texas."

"How you know they're headed through Texas?"

"I don't," Lillie said. "But y'all were headed west. Right? That was the general idea I heard. You and TJ planned to keep on driving until there was no more road. Maybe make a death pact while you drive off that pier in Santa Monica."

"I don't know what you're talking about."

The patrol officer watching the door ducked inside right before the nurse entered. She ignored Lillie entirely as she took the kid's vitals and made sure he was nice and comfy. *Did he need to get more rest? Was he thirsty? Why hadn't he touched his food?*

"I'll help," Lillie said, bringing the tray over to his bedside. She pushed the adjustable table over and positioned the tray above his bandaged legs. "Me and Ladarius are old friends. I've known this kid since he was stealing tricycles down in Sugar Ditch. Good times."

The nurse wasn't sure what to do. She looked at the patrol officer, and he held up the flat of his hand and nodded. The nurse left in a huff.

Lillie settled back in the chair as the officer left. She forked some scrambled eggs and held it to Ladarius's face. "Open up," Lillie said. "Here comes the airplane. But I got to warn you, kid. By the time you go to trial, you'll be eighteen. Folks over at Parchman got a whole different program for pretty mouths."

"Hell with you, lady."

"Why'd you run?"

"Shit."

"Did you do it?" Lillie said. "Did y'all stab and cut up TJ's momma and stick her in that pickle barrel over in Parsham County? Sure would love to know."

"Hell no," Ladarius said. His voice hoarse and pleading. "That ain't my style. I never hurt no one."

"Whose idea was it?"

Ladarius shook his head. He dead-eyed the dark television screen, thumping his fingers on the rails of his bed, looking like a man who sure wanted to bolt but knew his legs wouldn't take him far.

"I don't have much time," Lillie said. "Help me out. How can I get in touch with TJ? Maybe we can have a heart-to-heart, real woman-to-woman shit, talk about boys and manicures and running from the law on a homicide beef. You know, all the good pillow fight bullshit."

"We didn't do it."

"I'm beginning to see the light."

"You are?"

"Y'all got a hell of a friend in Sheriff Colson," she said. "Isn't my job one way or another. But I thought you kids were guilty as hell."

Ladarius was quiet. She lifted up a piece of bacon and he shook his head again, making a stink face. With all the marks on his cheeks and lips, it looked like it might hurt the kid to chew gum. Lillie put down the bacon and stood up. She heard a voice in the hall, someone arguing with the plainclothes about access to the patient.

"I can get cleared to take you back tomorrow," Lillie said. "But I'd prefer getting a head start to TJ and that girl y'all kidnapped."

Ladarius snorted and turned his head away from Lillie. Lillie circled the bed and came over to the other side, watching the kid, looking at his sly little smile. Kid ate up that damn canary, feathers all over his mouth.

"Kidnapping isn't funny," Lillie said. "Y'all just upped the goddamn ante five hundred percent for some Barney Fife fucknuts to get an itchy trigger finger."

"Shit," Ladarius said. "That girl Chastity kidnapped her own damn self. She talked TJ into going along, said it would make folks listen up about Chester Pratt."

"Well," Lillie said. "That was dumber than shit, now, wasn't it?"

"Sure seems so."

Lillie placed her hands on her hips up under her black blazer, hearing the nurse coming up behind her and making a lot of racket. She wanted Lillie to turn around, but Lillie didn't move.

"Which way?" Lillie asked.

"Don't know."

"Which state?"

"I don't know."

Lillie shook her head. She stepped back and lifted her chin at the nurse and two other nurses who'd entered the room trying to make a show. Ladarius McCade hadn't been in their care twenty-four hours, but he'd already charmed the damn panties off the hospital staff.

"Long ride back to Tibbehah," Lillie said. "Hope you like country music. I got a new Margo Price record I just can't wait to play the whole way back."

They had made it twenty miles south of Shreveport when TJ knew they were about to run out of gas. She pulled off the highway and into the first truck stop she spotted, hiding among the dozens of eighteen-wheelers. Chastity had to use the bathroom. John Wesley was hungry and wanted to know why they'd left Ladarius. TJ had to explain that she and Ladarius had a system. If he wasn't back before six, something bad had happened and they needed to head on.

"He knows how to find us," Chastity said. "He's just waiting for the right time."

"Right time for what?" John Wesley asked.

Chastity didn't answer and opened the door, running out into the rain and toward the big, sprawling travel center. TJ leaned back into her seat and shut her eyes. She hadn't slept all night. Ever since Ladarius headed out, she'd felt a sickness in her that something wrong was about to happen. Now they were stuck in Louisiana with three dollars and some change, a stolen car with hardly any gas, and no plan on how they were going to keep on heading south to Grand Isle and this great place Chastity kept bragging about.

"Can we eat?" John Wesley said.

"In a little while."

"We need gas."

"I know."

"Why'd Holly and Ladarius both leave us, TJ?" he said. "Are they mad at you?"

"Jesus Christ," she said. "Would you please let me sleep? I just need some quiet. I need to think on some things. Damn, John Wesley. Just let me breathe for a hot damn minute."

She was mad at herself for actually believing that Chester Pratt might stand up and halfway do the right thing. Somewhere she'd made sense of Chastity's plan to call out his crooked ass online, make folks turn their attention on Chester, including Chastity's supposedly rich and powerful daddy. But that was probably what got Ladarius, made him get mad and maybe a little sloppy stealing them a car. After the news of the kidnapping got out, their faces were damn near everywhere.

The rain fell harder as she saw Chastity standing by the side doors to the truck stop, talking to some old man in a ball cap. The old man reached into his back pocket and pulled out his wallet, crushing some bills into Chastity's hand. TJ watched the girl lean over and kiss the man on the cheek before running through the lot, zipping around trucks in the rain, and back to their car. She slammed the door behind her, shaking the rain from her hair.

"Well," she said. "We can eat. Or we can drive."

"How much did you get?"

"Twenty dollars," Chastity said. "I told him I was the leader of a youth choir group and we'd run out of gas."

"Isn't that sweet."

"No man can resist a pretty little girl with a Jesus complex."

"You and John Wesley go ahead," TJ said. "I just want to close my eyes for a minute."

"I could do it again," Chastity said. "You know."

TJ had her seat reclined, eyes closed, trying her best not to worry about Ladarius. At least she knew he was alive and okay, even if he had been caught. Maybe that was all for the best. She shouldn't have gotten him or Holly mixed up with this mess. This was her fight, and she'd keep running and telling the truth until that son of a bitch was in jail.

"You okay?" Chastity asked.

"I'm fine."

"You should've been with me inside," she said. "They got TVs up all over the place and all I saw was you and Ladarius. You two are famous as hell. More famous than I'll ever be. I only saw me one time and no one seemed to even notice. They said he's in stable condition. Did you know some dogs got on him?"

"I know."

"How'd you know?"

"I called the sheriff this morning," she said. "The one back in my home county."

"Rookie mistake, TJ Byrd," she said. "I don't think you need to call anyone until we're watching a mariachi band and drinking tequila somewhere in Cancun."

"Hell of a dream."

"You got something better?" Chastity said, eyeing TJ and reaching out to brush the black bangs from her eyes. "The new hair is a good look. Glad I made the post last night before we had to leave Texarkana. Let your fans know about the new TJ Byrd."

"Maybe some of the cops won't recognize me now."

"That's not why we did it," Chastity said, patting TJ's leg before opening the passenger door. "We did it because it looks cool as hell."

Quinn headed on over to the Rebel to check out the busted glass doors and decimated ATM, hoping not to run into Johnny Stagg as the experience was almost always unpleasant. But there was Stagg himself, standing in the broken doorway strung with yellow tape making small talk with Kenny and Reggie, recounting the scene of the nearly great robbery. He was quick to offer video surveillance burned on DVDs and a few theories on who might be responsible.

"Good morning," Quinn said, standing under the gas pump portico.

"Far from good, Sheriff," Stagg said. "You should've seen the mess a few hours back. Scared the whale out of my woman working the register. She hadn't seen those boys sneaking in and figured we got hit with an earthquake. Woman's still picking glass out of her hair."

"I see."

"I don't understand how a couple fellas roll up to the biggest business in this county and feel comfortable pulling out a money machine at their leisure," he said. "Doesn't seem right."

Quinn removed his sunglasses and scratched at the corner of his eye with his little finger. The front doors hung misshapen and twisted, pebbles of broken glass across the side entrance. A neon sign in the window advertising they were open twenty-four hours and offered HOT FRESH COFFEE, the latter being a damn lie.

"Can you see much on the tape?" Quinn asked.

"Not at all," Stagg said. "One fella was white. Other was black. Both around six feet tall, wearing masks up over their faces with baseball caps. Other than their color, couldn't tell which from which. Either one of them wasn't no brain trust. Tried yanking that machine through the brick wall and not the glass doors."

"I heard," Quinn said. "They take anything else?"

"White fella took a couple Slim Jims," Stagg said. "You can see it on the tape. Slips a mess of 'em into his jacket pocket just as clear as day. They wasn't in the store more than two minutes. White boy is the one who wrapped the chain around the machine, while the black boy goosed up the truck."

"Maybe you shouldn't keep your ATM so close to the door," Quinn said. "This one yours or does it belong to a vendor?"

The reddened skin on his bony cheeks and bulbous nose turned a brighter red. "If y'all were doing your cotton-picking job maybe I wouldn't have to worry where I place my machine," he said. "And it's a vendor. Some fine folks I do business with down in New Orleans."

"That a fact?" Quinn asked. "We've had some complaints about bank card hacks. Thought it might be some card readers out on your pumps. I'll check out the machine, too."

Stagg sucked at his tooth, placed a skeletal hand into his khaki pants, jingling some change. "You do that, Sheriff," he said. "I got me some work to do."

Stagg turned and Quinn followed him in through the busted door. Over the entrance to the diner, Quinn spotted several T-shirts in all sizes and colors pinned up along the wall. A wide yellow banner read GET YOUR TJ BYRD GEAR HERE. SUPPLIES LIMITED.

Stagg stopped halfway, right near the beer cooler. He offered a big grin.

"Homegrown heroes," he said. "Ain't that something?"

"Is that what they are?"

"Ole Machine Gun Kelly was born and raised in Memphis," Stagg said. "His wife Kathryn come from Saltillo. Just part of the landscape around here, son. Guilty or innocent don't make no difference to me."

"Kind of bad taste," Quinn said. "Don't you think? On account of what happened to the Byrd woman."

Stagg shrugged, moving away from Quinn for a moment to shake a few hands. Give a laugh or two about today's homemade pies. Chocolate and pecan. *Yes, sir. Yes, sir. Midnight Man done outdid himself today.* Quinn watched and waited as Johnny Stagg did Johnny Stagg, holding court at the Rebel.

"What were you saying again, Sheriff?"

"I said selling T-shirts and bumper stickers about a homicide is in poor taste."

Stagg grinned. He scratched at his cheek and looked down at his brand-new cordovan loafers.

"Don't you think?"

"Just a little local color," Stagg said. "Don't mean nothing personal by it."

"Gina Byrd's body was found over in Parsham."

"Everybody knows that."

"Heard you've been doing business in Parsham, Johnny," Quinn said. "You and Sheriff Lovemaiden gotten to be real tight."

"What if we had?" he said. "You think I know something about that killing? 'Cause I don't. I never met those kids before in my life."

"But you do know Chester Pratt?"

Stagg didn't say anything. Quinn's cell buzzed in his pocket and he declined the call. He turned to see Kenny working to take prints on the door, Reggie on the ATM itself. A brisk cold wind blowing the tape around the entrance.

"Breaks my heart," Stagg said. "What that man's been through."

Quinn nodded. His cell buzzed again, noticing the same number calling back, but not recognizing it.

"Hold that thought."

"I'll be in my office," Stagg said, winking. "Case you need me."

Quinn walked toward the door and took the call, moving past Kenny and out under the portico and the gas pumps. A young woman's voice said, "I think I got your man."

Quinn put a finger into his left ear to hear the caller better. "Come again?"

"I said I think I got your man," the woman's voice said. "Deep cut. Bad infection. This is Raven, by the way."

"Tell me."

"Man didn't leave a name," she said. "Came into a mobile clinic up toward Blackjack. I have the paperwork right here."

"Any description?"

"Got more than that, Sheriff," Raven said. "A nurse I know took the pointy tip of a blade or a razor or something out of the wound. About as big as thumbnail. That make any sense to you, Quinn?"

TWENTY-TWO

TJ slept for a few hours, barely noticing when Chastity and John Wesley got back from the truck stop. The cold winds that followed the rain buffeted and shook the stolen Kia, the sky a deep red streaked with black clouds. They'd both gotten the cheeseburger special with fries and a Coke, a whole five dollars to spare since Chastity decided not to tip the surly waitress. The woman nosy as hell, asking where they were going and where they had been, wanting to know if they were traveling alone or with Momma and Daddy. Chastity told TJ she'd put that old woman right in her place, saying all she wanted was some ketchup for her fries and to be left the hell alone.

"A whole five dollars," TJ said.

"Five-dollar bill."

"Maybe we should gas up?"

"We can't leave until we got twenty dollars," Chastity said. "That way we'll be sure to make it to New Orleans."

"New Orleans?" TJ said. "You never said anything about New Orleans. That's not on the way."

"Sure it is," Chastity said. "And I have a friend who lives down there. I texted him. Don't you worry. It was private and all. I'd trust this boy with my life. We did three weeks in rehab in Jackson Hole. He's got a nice house over at Audubon Park. I think it's a fine rest stop before heading on to Grand Isle."

"That sounds dumber than hell."

"He knows the situation," Chastity said. "He's cool. He's been following our adventures online. He and his friend think you're cute, too. Which helps. Boys are so damn stupid. They'll do anything in the world for a pretty face and a tight little ass."

"Maybe he's fooling you," TJ said. "Maybe he's already called the police."

"Not this kid," Chastity said. "He's just like you. Doesn't trust the police at all. His family is fucking loaded. Oil money and all that. They had to pay a ton to keep his record clean. Says his whole life was almost ruined after he got busted at the House of Blues with nothing but a fucking dime bag and some pills."

"Sounds like a real winner."

"Trust me," Chastity said. "We can make a few new posts, too. Light's too damn bad right now. I don't want to mess up our next big step. This is the post where you introduce me as your new partner in crime. Once you explained what happened with that asshole Chester Pratt, I joined the TJ Byrd movement. A big push by young folks to get heard and be listened to. That's it? Right? That's what makes you so important. You got framed for killing your own mother but had to run because no one would listen. But all that's about to change. Once you're cleared, you'll be famous. And I'll make sure you stay famous."

"And what if your plan turns to shit?"

"Gas up my daddy's boat and cut over to the Yucatán, baby," Chastity said. "Party city. I know people there, too. I hooked up with a bartender at an all-inclusive last Christmas with my family. I told him I was eighteen. His name is Pablo and he'd do anything in the world for me."

TJ nodded and leaned back into her seat, looking through the windshield splattered with raindrops. "Fine," she said. "But we need more money."

"That's nothing," Chastity said. "Leave that all up to me."

Some rough weather blew into Tibbehah County that night, making Quinn and Boom late for supper at Quinn's mother's house. There had been a nasty accident on the road to Burnt Oak, two kids out joyriding had turned over their truck in a drainage ditch. Both were okay, but one had busted up his leg pretty bad. Boom had been out along Highway 45, pulling a county vehicle from where it had skidded from the road and dove deep into some mud. He and Quinn looked worse for wear when they'd showed up. Quinn took Boom's jacket, splattered in mud, and hung it out in the hallway as Jean fixed them each a warm plate.

Jean sat Boom next to Raven Yancy in the fancy dining room. The two both politely taking the set-up in stride. Maggie had told Quinn that Raven was seeing a cardiologist from Oxford. And Boom was still pining for a hotshit federal agent named Nat Wilkins.

"Not much has changed," Jean said. "You boys always late for supper."

"A sheriff can do a lot," Quinn said. "But damn if I can't fix the weather."

"You might've called."

Quinn bowed his head and said a quick prayer over his plate. He cut his eyes over at Boom, and Boom grinned. Quinn mumbling, "Yes, ma'am."

Maggie looked amused by the situation as she worked on a little salad she'd made, being careful to add a nice helping of the chicken, so as not to offend. She had a big gray cardigan worn over her Lucero T-shirt and blue jeans. Her hair was up in a messy bun and her eyes looked so tired that Quinn didn't dare complain about his day.

"How'd she do?" Quinn asked.

"Finally sleeping in the next room," Maggie said. "Thanks to your mother."

"Maggie needed a little break," Jean said. "I was glad to help. Halley can't help that she's just excited to see everything. Wants to be up every second. Don't blame her a bit."

Brandon had already left the table and moved into the TV room. He watched *Teen Titans Go!* while Quinn updated them a little on his day, asking Raven if she'd heard anything about the boy with the busted leg.

"Leg was broken in four places," Raven said.

"Damn," Boom said.

"Doctor was about to set it as I left," Raven said. "His daddy was mad as hell. He thought the kid had a real future as a kicker for the Wildcats. Broke the good leg, too."

"Those boys out low riding?" Boom said.

Quinn nodded, taking a bite of the chicken and dumplings, his favorite of his mother's meals. She made everything from scratch and used whole pieces of chicken. The perfect meal on a cold, rainy night.

"Glad me and you didn't do nothing like that," Boom said.

Jean nearly spit out her boxed Chablis. She remembered too many times of calling in favors to her brother after Quinn and Boom would get caught doing mischief out in the county. Jean always had to set things straight, smooth things over with the law or someone Quinn and Boom had mistakenly wronged, before Boom's daddy, an old-school fire-and-brimstone preacher, found out. Boom's daddy's answer to everything had been to "jerk a knot in that boy's ass."

"You got a second to talk?" Quinn asked, motioning down to Raven's empty plate.

"Can't this official business wait a second," Jean said. "Did you know Raven hasn't seen a single Elvis movie? Not even *Blue Hawaii*?"

"Damn shame," Boom said.

"He was a good man," Jean said, smiling sweetly, lifting her wineglass halfway. "That Elvis. Remind me to tell you a story of going up to Graceland with Quinn's daddy back in '76. That was a hell of a time."

"Daddy nearly got killed," Quinn said.

"Elvis and his boys saved him."

"Wait," Maggie said, holding up her hand. Looking as if she might've choked on her peach cobbler. "What happened?"

Quinn got up, kissed his wife on her cheek, and motioned for Raven to follow him outside. "You tell her, Momma," he said. "I heard it all before. Raven and I need to talk a little shop."

Quinn slapped Boom on the back, reminding him he needed to hear the big story of Jason Colson '76 once again, and headed outside with Raven. They stood by the back door, the rain blowing sideways across the sloped backyard and up to the old treehouse where Quinn used to play G.I. Joe and Caddy used to sell mud pies. Then it had become Caddy's son Jason's Indian fort and now Brandon's space station, and it wouldn't be long before Halley would take over that little piece of real estate. Jason Colson had built it on one of his rare stretches home from his work in Hollywood.

"Is that really true?" Raven said. "What your mother was saying about Elvis?"

"Some of it."

"And the rest?"

"Like my daddy," Quinn said. "A walking contradiction. Partly truth, partly fiction."

"And you?" she asked.

"What you see is what you get."

Raven smiled, cold wind blowing across the metal furniture and rain dripping down the awning. She reached into her purse and pulled out a plastic baggie filled with a jagged little piece of metal. "Here you go," she said. "Nurse who worked on the man said he was real short."

"How short?"

"Below five feet."

"Damn," Quinn said. "That is short. And how old?"

"Fifties," she said. "Maybe older. White-headed with a white mustache. He was intoxicated, possibly on some painkillers. She said the man kept on begging her to write him a scrip for Oxy. But she couldn't unless he provided some ID. Said another man had brought him in, just as short, and maybe twenty years younger. She figured they were kin."

"No names?"

Raven shook her head and handed him a printout from the clinic. Quinn read through it quick by the light spilling from the kitchen window. He nodded, folding the paper and placing it in the breast pocket of his uniform. This was it. This was their man.

"Heard Ladarius got caught."

Quinn nodded.

"I know he's hurt," she said. "But could've been a lot worse. Think you might help that boy out when he gets home?"

"He's facing a bunch of charges."

"Sounds like someone offered you a hand," she said. "Way back when. You don't have to say anything, Quinn. Just keep an open mind. Kid's got to grow up sometime."

TJ took the last five bucks to grab a burger while Chastity promised to stay put and watch John Wesley. TJ hadn't been gone all of fifteen minutes to use the bathroom and grab the burger when she returned to find Chastity gone.

"Where'd she go?" TJ said.

It was late, full dark except for under the glow of the tall lights over the big semi parking lot. The wind had quieted down a bit, but every few minutes, a big nasty gust of cold would rattle through the trucks.

"Said she was gonna get us some money," he said. "So we can get the hell out of this shithole."

"Which way?" TJ said, tossing her uneaten burger in the passenger seat.

John Wesley pointed into the big maze of trucks. TJ shook her head and grabbed the handle, headed out into the tall semis, the smell of diesel and burnt oil everywhere. Some of the rigs had on their parking lights, glowing hot orange and red, the doors high above the asphalt where she was walking, not being able to see who was inside or where that crazy-ass girl had gone.

Two men stood outside a Peterbilt, leaning against the grille smoking cigarettes, giving her a good look-over as she passed. One of them winked at her. The other asked if she were cold. "Come on and hop up inside my cab," a rangy old redneck said. "I'll warm you up right quick."

TJ didn't answer them, being used to men like that her whole life. She'd met them at the grocery store and church. He looked pretty much the same as the deacon who offered up bubble gum from his pant pockets in exchange for a hug. They were the men who touched her hair and little rump. The ones that used to come home with Momma, and TJ would wake up to them sitting at the kitchen table Saturday morning, crunching their cereal while John Wesley tried to watch cartoons. Checking out her tight little body in her T-shirt down to her knees, wondering if she wouldn't be a better and newer model than old Gina. Damn, TJ thought. Why did Ladarius have to go and get his ass caught?

She turned the corner to see a huge purple Kenworth with tall chrome smokestacks and endless custom purple lights across the grille. PURPLE PEOPLE EATER had been airbrushed across the passenger door. Inside the cab she could hear muffled music playing, that old song her grandmomma liked so much. "Fancy" by Reba McEntire. The song so wild and haunting coming from the other side of that truck cab. The purple and green lights glowing on the puddled ground.

TJ kept on moving, along the trailer, still hearing Reba singing, until she heard that first scream. Something knocked hard against the cab door, the whole cab shaking back and forth.

TJ reached up under her flannel shirt and patted the butt of her daddy's .38. Goddamn it. That stupid girl sure knew how to find trouble. She ran up to the rig, hopped up onto the sideboard, and started banging on the door. "Let her out!" TJ said, yelling. "Goddamn you."

"Mr. Stagg," Chester Pratt said. "No offense. But do you have any idea of the folks you're working with now?"

Stagg stood beside his cherry red El Dorado, the shadow of the metal hull of Frontier Village looming behind them. The trees blocked the view of Highway 45, cars and semis blowing past the bright white light of the grand Tibbehah Cross. Ole Man Skinner's legacy to the wretched of this world before kicking the bucket last year.

"I got to be getting home," Stagg said. "You got something to say, go ahead and say it. Or else just hold on to your peter till the morning."

"The Nixes ain't like people you normally deal with," Chester Pratt said, a little out of breath, his hand shaking while trying to light a cigarette up under his umbrella. "These men don't have any honor. They couldn't spell honor if they tried. They're both more like animals. I got took by 'em. I paid them for a job and then they tried to shake me down. Trust me now. They'll do the same to you."

Stagg stood, car door open, rain tapping down his pompadour. He grinned big and wide at Chester and told him how much he appreciated his concern.

"Why'd you send them?"

"Didn't they ask you nothing?" Stagg said.

"They want me to set up a meeting with TJ Byrd."

"Well, all right, then."

Stagg had on a cowboy slicker bought at a Western wear shop over in Calhoun City, stiff and waxed, water pebbling off the canvas. Chester Pratt looking at him, holding that umbrella, like a child who'd lost his way.

"Don't know what you want me to say," Stagg said.

"You gonna kill her, too?"

"No," he said. "That's not the plan."

"What is the plan, then?" Chester said. Goddamn crying now. "Do you know what those boys did to Gina? Just for trying to fight back? They cut her up like a side of meat, stuck her over in that trash barrel in Parsham. Good Lord, Mr. Stagg. Ain't none of this shit worth it."

"That business ain't none of my concern."

"Thought we were partners."

"This ain't about liquor," Stagg said. "Now is it?"

"And what about your boy Bishop?" he asked. "What became of him? He's deader than hell, ain't he?"

The thought of it brought to mind that bloody sack of sausage the

Nixes delivered. The smell of Cajun spices and jalapeños still hot in Stagg's nose. He looked at Chester, wetter than a duck's dingaling, feet ankle-deep in water with half his sniveling face in shadow.

"Boy, this game ain't for you," Stagg said. "You want to run with the big dogs, run a liquor store? To get things done, you got to deal with some unpleasantness. Hell, I've been dealing with unpleasantness since I opened up the Rebel. Just last night, two old boys tried to steal an ATM from me and nearly tore out my wall. But you move on. You do what needs getting done. And if that means working with some folks like the Nix boys. Well. I guess that's how that old song goes."

"Even if I knew," Chester said. "I wouldn't tell you where those children are at. I guess I just don't have it in me."

Stagg nodded and crawled into the El Dorado. The big car door still wide open, rain pelting the black interior as Chester Pratt walked up to the door.

"Those kids ain't safe out there," Stagg said. "If the law don't get to them, something else will eat them alive. Those boys will bring 'em back. Get things settled the way they should be."

Chester swallowed and nodded. "TJ," he said. "She knows. She knows all about the money I took from her momma. Won't be long till the law will be coming for me, too. You get that. Right?"

Stagg shut his door, cranked the ignition, and let down his window just a crack.

"A damn shame," Stagg said, knocking the ElDo in drive. "You stay dry out there, Chester. You hear?"

TJ banged on the truck cab with the flat of her hand as she heard more yelling from inside. She was about to give up and run for help when the door opened hard and fast, sending her flat on her back. A huge man, one of the biggest goddamn men she'd ever seen, stepped out on the sideboard. He had a shaved head and a handlebar mustache, a large old belly and only one good eye, the other covered in a black patch like some kind of redneck pirate.

TJ scrambled backward. The one-eyed man was shirtless, with reddened skin covered in white hair across his stomach and over his arms and thick neck. Inside, she heard Chastity's voice, begging for help.

"Who the fuck are you?" the man said.

"I came for my friend."

"Your friend's busy," he said. "Her mouth's full."

TJ, halfway soaked from the puddle, pushed herself up in the dark. She reached across her to her left hip and grabbed her daddy's .38 and aimed it square at the man's pecker.

"You don't get down from there and I swear to Christ, mister, I'll geld your fat ass in one shot."

The man's work pants were unbuckled, hanging down below his big belly. The sagginess nearly made him trip as he dropped to the ground. TJ raised the pistol toward his chest now, knowing he wasn't about to stop. She just might have to kill the son of a bitch.

Behind the man's shoulder, Chastity appeared in the open door. She had blood across her face, one eye snapped shut. That frilly little white shirt ripped away, exposing a hot pink bra.

"I'm sorry," Chastity said, sobbing. "God, I'm so sorry."

"Step away, mister," TJ said.

The man buckled his pants, not bothering to zip his fly, moving on toward her with his hand out, grinning. He walked slow and heavy, breathing rough, red smears of blood across his saggy chest. "Give it here, little girl," he said. "And I'll let you suck my peter, too."

"Shoot him!" Chastity said, screaming. "Kill the bastard!"

TJ walked backward, feet splashing in the water glowing purple, gun raised up on the man until he was damn near close enough to touch. He reached back and slapped TJ hard against the face and sent her reeling. The one-eyed man reached out, trying to take her daddy's gun. The slap just like a thousand damn stings from all those last-call dates her momma brought home from the Southern Star. Damn near taking Gina piece by piece until there was barely nothing left. TJ had the horrible thought that maybe whatever Chester Pratt had done was an act of mercy. That her mother had been gone for years.

TJ could taste the blood in her mouth as she pointed the gun at the man's chest and fired twice. One hit him in the mouth, the other tore at his belly, the huge one-eyed sack of shit still reaching out for her as he collapsed down on one knee and then the other until he gagged and fell face-first into a puddle.

"Holy shit," Chastity said. TJ walked over to her and offered her a hand. "Holy shit. You did it. You really did it."

"Are you all right?"

Chastity began to cry some more, trying to hold her frilly shirt together over her little bra in the dim light and cold wind. Her face and hair a mess, the top of her fancy blue jeans ripped, with claw marks all up and down her stomach.

"Did he?"

"I just asked him for a twenty," Chastity said. "A lousy goddamn twenty dollars. He said he wanted a hug. Wanted to talk. He told me I was as pretty as his daughter."

TJ pulled at Chastity's arm as she hovered over the man's body, staring down at him, face-first in the puddle. Chastity kicked hard at him a few times, crying and sobbing, until she stopped cold, reached down, and plucked the man's wallet from his back pocket.

"We need to run," Chastity said, wiping at her face with her tattered shirt. "Right now. And real fast."

TJ pulled at the girl, stashed the gun into her jeans, and headed back to the stolen car and John Wesley. Her feet sloshed through the puddles as the gunshots rang in her ears.

Not much farther. Not much farther and they'd be safe.

TWENTY-THREE

It was a full forty-eight hours later before Lillie saw the footage of TJ Byrd and Chastity Bloodgood at the truck stop. She and Charlie Hodge had concentrated much of their efforts in Texarkana at the lovely Tri-State Motel and multiple visits with Ladarius McCade. But that kid, God love him, would not break. Whether true or not, right or wrong, he would not give up his girl. When she did ID TJ and Chastity from the security video, she and Charlie were off, only eighty miles south to Shreveport, Louisiana, or what Lillie liked to call the armpit of the South.

The witness was most surely dead, a prime specimen of man named Floyd Eugene Hicks. Most of the folks at the truck stop didn't recall the girls, either, besides a woman named Gladys—*why the fuck were waitresses always given names like that?*—who recalled Chastity Bloodgood being a surly little bitch who told her to mind her own damn business and didn't even leave a tip.

"That's a hell of a rig, though," Charlie Hodge said.

The cops hadn't moved the Purple People Eater from the lot, still parked in the same place with crime scene tape marking the unceremonious spot where Floyd Eugene Hicks bled out, facedown in a puddle of rainwater and diesel. The sad end to a glorious working man who dabbled in a little pedophilia and sex trafficking on the side. Six-four and three hundred thirty pounds of whale blubber. Lillie was sure the shitbirds would fly slow and low at half-wing today, crying tears of pain that such a man left the earth.

"Kid did pretty good with a .38," Lillie said. "Someone that young should've missed. Only she looked to get him where it counted."

"Locals think the kids robbed him."

"That sound right to you?"

"Nope," Lillie said. "You saw his priors. This sick fucker probably tried to get them into his cab. Maybe he did."

"Only one way to find out," Charlie said.

Lillie opened up the driver's door. Damn. The smell was something to behold. To describe it wouldn't do the rank scent justice.

"Lord God Almighty," Charlie said.

"Not exactly red roses and French perfume."

The sun filled the front seats of the cab but Lillie had to look for the switches to turn on the lights in the sleeper. It was the kind of scene that would make Martha Stewart shit her pants. A bare mattress on the bunk, a half dozen plastic milk jugs filled with an indeterminate yellow mixture, dirty T-shirts and stained underwear, a tiny little TV with a cigarette lighter plug and dozens of DVDs strewn about the floor.

"Wow," Lillie said, pulling on a pair of latex gloves and shuffling through the DVDs. "Mr. Hicks was a real cinephile. Looks like he was preparing to stick it in damn near anything that had a hole. Didn't know they sold this shit down South. Looks like the kind of material you'd get in a Bangkok flea market."

"Few years back I had to take a course in sex trafficking on the web," Charlie said. "Agent leading the talk said there was something out there for everybody. One of the marshals, being a smartass, said, 'What about rhinos?' Took the agent about two hot seconds to find that very thing."

"Glad to have that in mind next time I take my kid to the zoo."

"Sorry, Lil."

"Sorry for what?" Lillie said. "That sickos live among us? I learned that a long time ago."

Lillie sifted through the man's belongings, knowing the local cops took four guns out of the rig. Two pistols, a shotgun, and an AR-15, just in case Mr. Hicks decided to take the Purple People Eater into a military hot zone.

"I think local investigators missed a few items," Lillie said.

"The duct tape."

"Stun gun and some rope," Lillie said. "Shit. Kind of funny to think that he messed with TJ Byrd. One of those days when you believe there really is such thing as karma."

"Did the cop run down everything on the evidence list?"

"You mean ole Eb back there?"

"Yeah, Eb."

"You know his name really isn't Eb and he didn't get the reference," she said. "But he is the spitting image of old Tom Lester."

"Nobody remembers the classics."

"Damn shame," Lillie said. "What's wrong with America?"

Lillie grinned, toeing at a few sex toys left in the cab, trying her best to not imagine how they worked or that a man like Floyd Eugene Hicks might've been going to happy town while driving eighty thousand pounds down a U.S. interstate.

Something caught her eye stuck under a stack of DVDs. A thin gold chain. She bent down and found part of a broken necklace, a little gold compass dangling at the end. DADDY'S LITTLE GIRL IS NEVER LOST.

She showed it to Charlie. "Ain't that a heartbreaker?"

"Guns, dildos, and DVDs," Charlie said. "What could've gone wrong?"

"Eb did mention they grabbed three phones," Lillie said. "How about we head on over and take a look. I'll pass along this golden compass. Aren't we due a big fat break right about now?"

They'd been sleeping in that nasty old house for two days, not at all what TJ expected, and sure as hell not a good place to bring John Wesley. Folks stopping by at all hours, tattooed and scratchy, as if clocks didn't exist down in New Orleans, money being exchanged before they'd head to the back room where business was transacted. Chastity's friend Graham seemed nice enough when they got there, early twenties with frat boy hair and a shaky little smile, sliding back a door to a little study where he'd set out a couple of air mattresses and showed John Wesley the TV and Xbox. There was a hot shower and a place to sleep, a little food, if not a lot in the way they'd been living.

She thought hard about what had happened south of Shreveport, although once she and Chastity got back into the car, they never said a word about it. TJ wasn't sure if it was out of fear, trying to pretend it didn't happen, or trying to protect John Wesley. Chastity pinned her ripped shirt back together, TJ used the cash in the trucker's wallet to fill up the tank at the next gas station, and they rode in silence all the way into the city.

Once they settled at the house near Audubon Park, TJ got clean and changed her clothes, checking nonstop to see if anyone had connected her and Chastity to that old trucker. She saw not a word about that online, but did see that little video they made at the Tri-State Motel, not all but a minute, had been viewed more than a quarter million times. She had to show it to Chastity twice to make sure she wasn't seeing things that weren't there. The comments were better than great. They were damn well beautiful. WHERE ARE YOU, CHESTER PRATT?, TJ BYRD IS INNOCENT!, FIND THE REAL KILLER, and FLY FREE BYRD FLY. Screenshots were shared, art was drawn, and hashtags were made. So many pictures of TJ up on that diving board, lit by the orange-and-black February twilight, fist held high proclaiming her innocence and why she ran.

It was her. But it wasn't her. It was a new woman with jet black hair, boy short, and attitude to match. It kind of scared her, but she liked it all the same.

Chastity went straight to Graham's bedroom, shutting the door behind them, and she didn't see her much after that. Every so often, Chastity would appear in the kitchen, wearing an oversized Saints T-shirt and sucking down some orange juice straight from the bottle. Her eyes had grown black and electric, a lazy smile on her face as she'd touch TJ's arms and neck as if they were in the same dream. Two times she had to tell the girl to quit it.

The first full day they were in the house, she took John Wesley down to St. Charles Avenue, where they caught a streetcar downtown. The French Quarter jam-packed, TJ just then figuring out they'd come right in the middle of Mardi Gras. For the first time in a while, she felt she could walk among people, a shit ton of them, without anyone giving her so much as a glance. She and John Wesley walked down Royal Street and listened to some black kids playing old-time music with horns, trombones, and tubas. Folks tossed out beads from balconies and she bought two hot dogs from a street vendor with a little of the money that Graham had given them. It was all nice, like some kind of noisy dream, with more light and color and music than her brain could hardly handle. St. Charles Avenue was packed when they got back to Graham's, John Wesley making friends with some kids on the parade route, scrambling up a ladder to catch more beads thrown from the passing floats. The world outside the music and the color felt far away, and she halfway entertained the crazy idea that maybe they could stay awhile. Whatever Graham did in that house was his own damn business; long as they were safe and protected, maybe they'd be okay. A wanted killer—for real a killer now, after the one-eyed trucker—couldn't be too choosy about her associations.

The back door to the house into the kitchen was cracked open when they got there, most of the lights off with only the sound of a radio playing somewhere. John Wesley went straight for the Xbox and she dropped her backpack while heading into the living room, old floors creaking underfoot, hearing some moaning coming from the bedroom. Chastity and Graham probably at it again, rekindling whatever made their blood boil for each other back in rehab.

But this time the sounds didn't come from his bedroom, they were coming from the little study where she and John Wesley had slept and stayed that first day. She moved the sliding door aside and found three different boys, laying crossways on their air mattress and on their sheets. One of them had his shirt off, a goddamn needle and a rubber tie-off on his fucking arm. They looked tired, one boy in an office chair had a cigarette in his lips, nodding off as he stared right into TJ's face.

"Where the fuck is Graham?" TJ asked.

No one answered. She wasn't sure if they were knocked out or dead, snatching John Wesley's blanket out from under one, sending him toppling to the floor. The space smelled of sweat and body funk, maybe someone pissing their damn pants. She could hear John Wesley in the living room hitting the Madden 19, the game just kicking off as she walked from room to room in the two-story house, opening and shutting doors, looking for Graham and Chastity. There were beer cans and bottles of booze everywhere. The kitchen island covered in all types of cocktails and cigarette butts, a mirror that had been pulled off the wall still coated with a fine white dust. She found a nude girl passed out in a shower and a boy sitting on the toilet. Fucking junkies.

She was about to grab John Wesley and head out, go anywhere but here, when Chastity and Graham bungled into the front door. Laughing, nearly falling over their feet. Graham looked even older than TJ first thought, in a long-sleeved button-down shirt and khaki pants. His face skinny as hell, stubbled and pockmarked. Sometime last night Chastity had mentioned he'd gone to Vanderbilt for a while, until he got kicked out.

"Well, hello there," Chastity said. "Superstar."

"This shit ain't funny."

"It's a little funny," Chastity said, squeezing her thumb and forefinger together, giggling like hell. "Don't you think?"

"Where you been?" TJ asked. "Who the hell are them people?"

"*Them* people," Chastity said. "Isn't she hilarious? That little country accent."

"Y'all had some kind of damn party," TJ said. "Fucking junkies strung out all over the place. Some nekkid girl up in the shower with a boy passed out on the commode. Come on, Chastity. Hell. You're better than this."

"Did you see?" Chastity said, using Graham to keep her balance. "Did you see this shit? Fucking three hundred thousand likes?"

"Yeah," TJ said. "And it don't mean shit."

"It means they're listening."

"Yeah," Graham said. "They're listening. That's good. Right?"

"Shut up, Graham," TJ said. "Either clear these junkies out or me and John Wesley are long gone. Y'all hearing me?"

"Fine," Chastity said, pushing past TJ's shoulder. "Just give me back my goddamn phone."

"I don't have your damn phone," TJ said. "I got the one Ladarius gave me."

"Bullshit."

But some thought made Chastity freeze up, standing there cold in the living room, until she ran into Graham's bedroom. TJ followed as she watched the girl tear into her purse and her bag, tossing her clothes and personal shit all over the floor. "Damn it," she said. "Damn it. I must've dropped it."

"Where?"

"You know damn well where," Chastity said.

"What?" Graham said. "What? What's the big deal? Girls. Girls. Chill the fuck out."

"This crazy little bitch shot a trucker," Chastity said, crossing her arms over her chest. "And now the police will blame me. What the hell have you done?"

Quinn waited for Holly Harkins in the meeting room at the sheriff's office. She'd bonded out two days before, after he'd brought her back to Tibbehah County. Her parents cooperating fully, not pressing charges on the stolen van, but she'd still have to answer to the folks in Hot Springs about that big house they broke into. She walked into the room alone and Quinn asked her to take a seat.

"I appreciate you coming over," Quinn said. "I told your folks I talked to the DA over in Hot Springs. I let him know it was your decision to cut loose from TJ and Ladarius. Also let him know you'd been a big help to me. Helped me get in touch with TJ."

"Yes, sir," Holly said.

Quinn joined her at the big oval table where he conducted most of his morning meetings with his deputies. No matter how many times they'd gotten the room straight, it always went back to cluttered storage. Boxes of reports and files stacked against the wall, folded parcels of new uniforms and orange jumpsuits for the prisoners. Quinn hated being in the middle of all that chaos but had cleared a nice spot for him and Holly.

"Did you talk to TJ?" Holly asked.

"I did," Quinn said. "But I need you to do it again. She got into some bad trouble in Shreveport. A man got killed and things have gotten a whole lot worse."

"More serious than killing her mother and kidnapping?" Holly said. "That was bullshit anyway. That's why I left. Little Miss Chastity Bloodgood just couldn't stand that she wasn't the star of the show. What happened? Did Ladarius shoot someone?"

"Nope," Quinn said. "Ladarius got picked up the day before in Texarkana. He was trying to steal a car and some dogs got to him."

"Dogs?"

"Nearly bled out before they got him to the hospital," Quinn said. "Now I'm worried about TJ. And I'm worried about John Wesley. TJ brought a lot of this on herself. But her little brother's only nine years old."

Holly nodded. She nibbled at her cuticles a bit, not meeting Quinn's eye when he asked if she'd like a little coffee. Only muttering, "Yes, sir."

Quinn stood up from the table and walked around to the community coffee pot that Cleotha had stoked a few hours back. Some good strong stuff made from beans they roasted up in Oxford. He poured out two cups and brought some creamer and sugar to the center of the table.

"Who was it got killed?" Holly asked.

"Some old trucker," Quinn said. "There's some video of TJ and Chastity coming and going from the restaurant at the gas station. It put them there right about the same time."

"Why?"

"Local sheriff and the news call it a robbery gone bad."

Holly chewed at her fingernails some more. She reached for the coffee and poured in three packs of sugar and some creamer. "And what do you call it?"

Quinn sat back down and took a sip of coffee. He thought about it a second and decided to level with the girl. "I don't know," he said. "I talked to the sheriff there. Doesn't look good. Man was shot with a .38. Doesn't TJ carry her daddy's .38 on her?"

"Yes, sir," Holly said. "I told you that. But TJ wouldn't just walk up to some man and point a gun. That's crazy. TJ is a lot of things, but I swear she's not crazy, Sheriff. She's scared. I've known her my whole life. Whatever happened, she's got to be scared to death."

"Will you try contacting her?" Quinn asked.

"My folks said to do anything you asked me," she said. "Said that was the only way I might get my life on track. That and meeting up with Pastor Dale later tonight. He wants to have a sit-down with me in his office."

"Sounds like a lot of fun."

"My dad still won't talk to me," Holly said. "Phil Jr. already said I was fired at the Captain's Table. But sent along his thoughts and prayers. How's that for local support?"

"They'll get over it," Quinn said. "I understood y'all were scared. And TJ probably pushed you a bit. She can be persuasive as hell."

"Whatever happened with that trucker, I know it was that Chastity Bloodgood," Holly said, placing her hands around the warm mug but not taking a sip. "That girl is fast as hell. I believe she must have a lightning bolt down between her legs. The kind of girl that finds trouble wherever she goes."

"You think TJ follows her lead?"

Holly thought on it a second. "I sure hope not," Holly said. "I just pray to God that TJ and John Wesley get free of that girl. I know one thing. They sure as hell can't trust her."

Chastity and Graham had taken her daddy's guns to a pawn shop in Mid-City and sold them all for eight hundred bucks. They were worth a hell of a lot more, but eight hundred bucks' cash was a lot for no questions asked. After a stop at Graham's buddy's apartment for a few purchases and for Graham to shoot up, they finally headed back to his house, taking a few bumps of coke off the dashboard of his Land Cruiser to get them up and running for the night. She was feeling pretty damn good, seeing and hearing damn near everything in the city, until TJ Byrd met them at the door, pissed as hell about Graham's friends hanging out in his damn house.

She didn't have time for this. After everything she'd done for this ungrateful little redneck. Her daddy always warned her to only hang out with people that made her a better person. He even gave her a daily devotional with shit like that listed each day. *Your perspective in life will determine your destination. Life is not waiting for the storm to pass but about you dancing in the rain. The struggle you're in today is developing the strength you need tomorrow.* Daddy always had nuggets of that horseshit on him, passing them out like chocolate drops to her and her brother or his salesmen who couldn't close the goddamn deal.

She lay across Graham's bed, forearm across her eyes, Graham passed out next to her, the bed feeling like it was spinning 'round and 'round like a game of chance. Just when she felt like things might get better, that she might get to her feet and walk outside to see the floats, a new wave of nausea would hit and keep her in the bed. God this stuff was so fucking good, and so fucking awful at the same time. Funny how a person walks into rehab as an alcoholic and skips out as a goddamn junkie.

Chastity could hear TJ yelling at Graham's friends in the next room, telling them to get out, leave them the hell alone and not come back. This girl who'd never been in a real house, born and raised in a tin roof trailer, acting like she had a little piece of real estate on Audubon Park. What a goddamn joke. Next thing she'd know, TJ would be taking off her hot pants for Graham, whispering in his ear about all the things she and Ladarius McCade used to do down in Tibbehah County, real country-ass barnyard tricks.

And now the phone. It may not have been TJ's fault she dropped it. But the cops would think she was the one who shot that one-eyed trucker. She wanted some fun and thrills on the road, not to end up in jail.

Chastity had enough and stumbled to her feet, finding her way to Graham's chest of drawers under one of his daddy's old posters for Jazz Fest '89. His goddamn dad who lived in Atlanta but kept a house in New Orleans for his old folks' parties and for his son to kick back and have some personal time to himself. Daddies could be so fucking stupid.

She found Graham's phone where he'd left it. Stashing it away from his so-called friends while he slept. She looked back to see him snoring in the twisted sheets, his scabbed-over arm dangling loose and free off the mattress.

She dialed the number, listening to it ring and ring until she heard the right voice.

"Daddy?" Chastity said. "I'm scared. Will you help me?"

* * *

Johnny Stagg was helping with the midnight countdown at the Rebel when his phone rang with a Fayetteville area code. He nodded to Miss Nadine and Midnight Man to give him a little privacy and picked up the handset, leaning back into his office chair. "Johnny Stagg speaking."

"Mr. Stagg, this is Vince Bloodgood over in Arkansas," he said. "I sure I hope I didn't wake you or your family at this ungodly hour."

"No, sir," Stagg said. "I was just about to drink a warm glass of milk and hit the hay. You caught me just in time."

"I've been thinking."

"Yes, sir."

"About what you and me talked about," Bloodgood said. "Does that offer still stand?"

"My word is gold, Mr. Bloodgood," Stagg said. "Ask anybody."

"I just want Chastity back," he said. "These Federal folks keep on dicking 'round. Now they're saying Chastity might've been involved in a killing down in Shreveport. My little baby? Some marshal woman called me up earlier and I swear to you she talked as direct and dirty as a goddamn man. How you like that?"

"If it's the same marshal I'm thinking on, she's a real nasty woman."

"Yes, sir."

"Well," Stagg said, leaning back into his highbacked chair, holding the handset, the spiral cord stretched across his old metal desk. "What can I do you for?"

"My baby," Bloodgood said. "My sweet little Chastity is being held by that country trash and some junkies down in New Orleans. Can you please help me?"

"You don't want to work with them Federal folks?"

"I only want justice done," Bloodgood said.

Stagg didn't say a word, the office windowless and quiet, a hum of warm air coming in from the ceiling. He let Bloodgood's words just hang in there for a moment, giving them meaning and weight.

"You understand, Mr. Stagg?"

"Yes, sir," Stagg said. "I most surely do. I'll get my best men right on it. Sharpest two fellas I've ever met. Now what's that address down in the Big Easy?"

TWENTY-FOUR

Reggie Caruthers walked into Quinn's office and shut the door behind him. It was past six now, dark and cold outside, and Reggie still had on his slick green sheriff's coat with the Sherpa collar. Quinn had been waiting for him, Reggie coming on to take over the night shift even though he'd been working through the day. Time didn't much matter now anyway, and Quinn had already warned Maggie not to expect him for supper.

"How'd it go?" Quinn asked.

"You were right."

"Tell me all about it."

Reggie took a seat in an old wooden chair before Quinn's desk and pulled out his notebook. He was as direct and driven as they came, and Quinn was damn lucky to have him as his chief deputy. His uniform immaculate, boots shined, with mustache and short afro cut to precision. Reggie was a man of details.

"Looks like Chester Pratt had some roof work done at his home and during the renovation of the liquor store building," Reggie said. "I spoke to his neighbors and stopped by Bluebird this afternoon. His manager didn't seem to like the folks on the job but admitted they did good work. Nix & Nix Roofing and Remodeling."

"Brothers?" Quinn asked.

"Father and son," Reggie said, reading over a few more details he hadn't shared yet. "I need to ask. How'd you get your eye on these two?"

Quinn opened up the right-hand drawer of his desk and pulled out two Ziploc baggies. One contained the broken blade he found in Gina Byrd's car and the other was the blade tip Raven Yancy had gotten from the nurse.

"Shingle cutter," Quinn said. "Made by Rigid. I never did think of Chester as a do-it-yourself-er."

Quinn shook the pieces out onto the table, prints already taken off both, and showed how the tip fit right on with the blade. Reggie didn't move, staring down at the exact match and then looking back up at Quinn. "These boys are no joke," Reggie said. "Flem Nix, the daddy, did time in Parchman for manslaughter and arson. The boy, Dusty, has more than a dozen assault charges. He was the main suspect in a killing over in Calhoun County a few years ago. Only one problem."

"They couldn't find the body."

"Yep."

Reggie tossed the two printouts of Nix and Nix on Quinn's desk. Quinn checked out their descriptions, noticing both didn't stand much more than five feet tall. He tapped at the height and weight. "This right?"

"Apparently so," Reggie said. "Either makes them easier to find or harder to spot."

"I need you to take these photos to a nurse that works at a clinic up in Yellow Leaf," Quinn said. "They'd be closed now and you'll have to find her at home."

Reggie stood up and picked up the photos. Just as he was about to leave, Cleotha came barreling in the door with a stack of pink message slips. "Didn't want to bother you when you were with that girl, Sheriff," she said. "You got a mess of calls on the tip line. Five of them from that Chester Pratt man. I don't want to say nothing bad about nobody, but that man sounded drunk as hell."

Quinn looked to Reggie, and Reggie raised his eyebrows before moving past Cleotha and back into the hallway.

"Man said he knows TJ Byrd is about to get killed," she said. "He was messed up and babbling on. But sure did sound like he was blaming himself."

Quinn grabbed his cap and his jacket and headed for the door.

Dusty and Daddy got to New Orleans that night, worn the hell out from the road and hungry as a goddamn horse, trying to get over to the address Mr. Stagg had given them. But the roads were closed with some kind of street parade and they had to double back to the main drag downtown. There wasn't a fucking parking spot anywhere, folks trying to charge them twenty dollars just to pull in a dang lot. They ended up leaving their truck over on Rampart Street by an old cemetery and walked back to the center of town. They didn't get two blocks before some raggedy man offered to show them his peter for a buck right before they saw a whole group of men walking down the sidewalk dressed up like goddamn Barbie dolls. Big blonde wigs and bikini tops. Dusty recalled his preacher telling them that New Orleans was a modern-day Sodom and Gomorrah, and now he was sure the pastor was right. This was the kind of place folks went after strange flesh, needing a little housecleaning by way of fire and brimstone. Everything stunk like a sewer ditch, the air heavy with cigarettes and liquor breath. His head spun with all the neon and glitter, people drunk and their necks heavy with all kinds of baubles and beads. Some man walked up to Daddy and placed a giant cup of beer in his hands before walking over to the street corner to throw up.

Daddy didn't do nothing but take a big ole sip and kept walking. The old man's eyes were as big as silver dollars.

"Don't tell Momma nothin'," Daddy said.

Dusty nodded. They watched as a crew of women walked down the street, flapping their shirts up and down in the cool breeze, giving everyone a chance to check out their titties. The cold air feeling good on his face as they'd been stuck in that truck for eight hours driving south. Stagg had given them five hundred dollars each with orders of calling him on a burner phone if they needed any more.

All they had to do was get that pretty little girl and treat her nice. If anyone made trouble for them, Mr. Stagg didn't have any problem with him or Daddy gutting them like they did Gina Byrd. Only thing Stagg said was not to mess with that Bloodgood girl. Dusty got it but had to explain that to Daddy, who damn near creamed his shorts when he got on that girl's Instagrams. Pictures of her in her swimsuit or walking a dog in her tight exercise pants and little bra.

Daddy finished the beer right quick and they headed on into a big Popeye's on Canal Street. They ordered a couple chicken boxes with extra biscuits and found a hard table by the window to eat and watch out for the crazy people walking past them. Daddy's eyes lit up at one point, a chicken leg stuck in his teeth, while he saw some woman going to town on some boy with his pants 'round his ankles. Right there on the fucking street. Folks passed them by, not giving them a glance, like that woman was playing "Yankee Doodle Dandy" on some kind of magical flute.

"Ain't never seen nothing like it," Dusty said.

Daddy chewed his food, unable to talk, taking in all the neon, sex, and the smell of chicken grease. All of the sin being just too much for one man to take.

"Woman at the counter said it's the Mardi Gras," Dusty said.

Daddy didn't answer, setting to work on his little Styrofoam cup of red beans and rice.

"This thing's going on all weekend long," Dusty said. "They say streets should clear out later on."

Daddy scraped into the tub and forked up the beans and rice, chewing with his mouth open. His black eyes flicking outside the window, better than anything that old man ever seen on TV. More jiggling boobies and flesh than he saw in a lifetime of watching *The Dukes of Hazzard*. Daddy was right, that Daisy Duke was something else, but never, not one time in those old tapes, did she lift up her shirt and flash those titties. His old man hadn't been in New Orleans but twenty minutes and already seen more titties than he had in his whole life. The old man going into some kind of wide-eyed state, not unlike when the spirit came over him down at the Assembly of God and he started speaking in tongues.

"Daddy?" Dusty said. "You okay?"

"Can't figure if what I'm seeing is a woman," he said. "Or a man."

"Judging from that big bulge in those slick gold pants," Dusty said. "I'd say that's a buck."

"Huh," Daddy said. "But that fella done—"

"Where you want to stick that Bloodgood girl?" Dusty said. "When we get her?"

"Truck bed," Daddy said. "I fit a big fat doe in that toolbox last week. Gag her up and she'll ride high and nice."

"You gonna eat that biscuit?" Dusty asked.

"Get any closer, son," Daddy said, grinning, rice and beans all in his white beard. "And you're gonna lose a finger right quick. Put you in your place faster than we did that Chester Pratt."

* * *

Quinn parked the Big Green Machine in front of a tall metal building next to Chester Pratt's new log cabin. Hondo was with him and he told the dog to stay, getting out of the big truck to find another dog, an aging chocolate lab coming up to sniff at his leg.

He patted the dog and headed up onto the big wraparound porch. All the lights were off, his breath clouding before him, as he knocked on the front door.

Quinn had tried Chester on his phone several times and over at Bluebird Liquors without luck. It gave him a fair amount of concern that all the lights were off in the house and it didn't appear that Chester was around. Maybe his Mercedes was parked inside that big metal building.

He knocked on the door again, knowing he had every right to enter the house based on those crazy messages. A wellness check was most certainly in order for a man in that mindset. Fortunately, the side kitchen door was open, and Quinn walked on inside, turning on the kitchen and porch lights and allowing the lab to follow and get warm.

Nothing looked out of place. The kitchen was clean. The big open living room with a rock fireplace was empty. There had been a fire recently and the smell of woodsmoke was strong.

Quinn called out to Chester and walked deeper into the house. He heard a shower running and the bathroom door slightly open. He knocked at the door and again called out to Chester. Nothing.

He headed on in the small bathroom and pulled back the curtain. The tub was empty and the water ran cold.

He turned off the water and moved back into the hall where the dog had waited for him. Quinn patted the old dog on the head. "Where's Chester, old boy?" he asked. "Chester. Where's Chester?"

The dog wagged its tail, not showing much interest, but trotted down a long hall to the last door at the end and nosed open the door. Quinn followed the dog into a big bedroom, barely lit by a table light by the bed. Underneath a large woven blanket, he spotted the top of a man's face.

Quinn moved closer. He was snoring. The breath reeked of bourbon and cigarettes.

"Chester?" Quinn said, shaking the hump in the bed. "You hear me?"

The hump moved and Quinn pulled back the sheet to see Chester Pratt curled up in a ball wearing only his tighty whiteys.

"Oh, Lord," Chester said. "What's going on? What's happening?"

Quinn stepped back and opened up the curtains, the porch lights shining through the windows onto the heart pine floors and the walls decorated with framed prints of men in duck blinds with labs running loose. He turned on the nightstand light, nearly knocking over a bottle of pills and a half-drained bottle of tequila.

"I thought you were dead," Quinn said.

"Why would you think that?"

"Can you stand up?"

Chester blinked at the harsh light and pushed himself up to a seated position.

"You ran out of hot water," Quinn said. "I'll put some coffee on."

Quinn walked to the kitchen, let the lab back outside, and filled up the coffee machine. A good twenty minutes later, Chester came out in a black silk robe, showing off way too much of his stick-thin white legs. He had on one sock and his normally perfect hair looked a lot thinner, with a large bald patch in the back. Funny. Quinn had never spotted the toupee before.

"Why are you here?"

"Worried about you, Chester."

"No, you weren't," Chester said. "Nobody worries about me. I think I better call up Sonny Stevens. He said I was not to say another word unless he's present. Now I find the sheriff standing over me while I was getting a little shut-eye."

"Have you heard from TJ Byrd?" Quinn said. "She's saying some pretty rough stuff online about you. Accusing you of stealing her money. She says what happened to her momma was your doing."

"Yeah," Chester said, still standing. "I saw it. A bunch of goddamn lies. Folks been harassing me wherever I go. Had to shut down the liquor store Facebooks. People saying I'm a liar and a killer. How's that look for my business?"

"Okay," Quinn said. "Then why'd you call me?"

"Call you?" Chester said. "I didn't call you."

Quinn reached for the phone and played back the message he'd found on the SO's voicemail. Chester slurring plenty but pronounced when he said, *"Call me back, Sheriff. Those kids are in some real trouble."*

"What kind of trouble?" Quinn said.

"Hell, I don't know," he said. "I was just talking is all. You know they're out there alone and in trouble. After what TJ did to her mother . . ."

"Let me stop you there," Quinn said. "I think you know that TJ didn't kill her mother. Neither did Ladarius McCade. You're the one who put that whole show in motion."

Chester looked as if he might throw up. He closed his eyes and then opened them, wobbling a bit on his feet, squinting as if the light might turn him to dust. He swallowed and stared back at Quinn, but he didn't answer. He didn't speak.

"Got you a nice new roof on this place," Quinn said. "I didn't notice it until I drove out today. Some real heavy-duty tin up there. Kind of job that will last a lifetime."

The coffee maker started to beep, signaling it was ready. Quinn poured Chester a hot cup, the same as he'd poured for Holly Harkins earlier that morning. This stuff smelled a hell of a lot stronger as Quinn had doubled the dose.

Chester took the coffee mug. "I think I'm gonna be sick, Sheriff."

"I heard you used the Nix family on the job?" Quinn said. "Nix & Nix Roofing and Remodeling. My deputy Reggie Caruthers said you also used them to build out the liquor store. Is that right?"

"Yeah," he said. "What's that got to do with nothin'?"

"Plenty," Quinn said. "Guess you don't check out your workers. Or just happen to be a good Christian who puts his faith in the power of forgiveness."

"They're just a couple roofers," Chester said. "I don't ask my roofers about their goddamn life history."

"Flem Nix did a ten-year stretch at Parchman for manslaughter," Quinn said. "Killed a man with a screwdriver on a job site. Poked him full of more than a dozen holes, including both his eye sockets. His son seems cut from the same cloth. Aggravated assault. Meth running. He's been a suspect in two killings over in Parsham County. He was once accused of dousing a man with kerosene and setting him on fire. They'd gotten into some kind of property dispute and the man tried to run him off his land. On the other, they couldn't make a case because they never found the body."

Chester nodded, dead-eyed and silent, while he ambled over to the kitchen counter, looking like he'd lost something, opening cabinets and rifling through drawers. "I need to call Sonny Stevens," he said. "You can't do this. You can't try and cornhole me just as easy as you please."

Quinn leaned against the kitchen doorframe. He picked up a half-burned cigar and started to light up. "You don't mind?" he said. "Do you, Chester?"

"'Course not."

"I think you set something in motion that you couldn't control,"

Quinn said. "Whatever happened is eating you alive. Sonny Stevens can complain all he wants. But that phone call you left me is enough to go to a grand jury."

"I didn't say nothing."

"You said Gina's kids were in trouble," Quinn said. "And that it was all your fault."

Quinn lied about the last part, but Chester Pratt didn't look to be in any condition to contradict anyone about anything. He stopped shuffling around on his skinny white legs and just stared at Quinn from across the kitchen counter.

"What do you want?" he said. "What are you saying to me?"

"What worried you so much that you went on a morning bender and started drunk dialing the sheriff?" Quinn said. "What happened? Why are TJ and John Wesley gonna get hurt?"

Chester wobbled on his feet. He lifted the coffee to his lips and took a good long pull. Over the rim, his eyes closed for moment and then he straightened up a little. Swallowing hard and trying to find even footing on those chicken legs.

"Those men," Chester said. "The Nixes. They're headed down to New Orleans. They're gonna get that rich girl back and might kill TJ Byrd along the way. Goddamn, that little bitch sure caused me some trouble. A whole lot of trouble. But I can't have her on my damn ledger, too."

"Did they kill Gina?"

"Oh, hell," he said. "I don't know."

"Bullshit."

"I talk too damn much."

"Who sent those boys to pick up the Bloodgood girl?" Quinn said. "Did you set that up, too? Or are you working with someone else? Talk to me, Chester. It'll make your future a lot brighter on down the road."

Chester shook his head. He pointed to the door. "I shouldn't've opened up my goddamn mouth. I need to get my head straight and then I'll come in. I need to call up Sonny. Sonny will know what to do."

"Chester," Quinn said. "You can call Sonny on our way to town. Your sorry ass is under arrest. If I were you, I'd spill everything I knew about those kids. TJ Byrd and her little brother sure as hell better make it home alive."

Lillie and Charlie Hodge were southbound and down on Interstate 49, headed to New Orleans and feeling good after they'd recovered the Bloodgood girl's phone. The hell of it was knowing that poor girl at some point had entered the cab of the late Floyd Eugene Hicks. Damn, if a one-eyed trucker didn't make you cautious, Lillie thought maybe a rig called the Purple People Eater just might. Of course, Miss Chastity Bloodgood didn't seem the look-before-you-leap type.

The Feds had already been working on tracking Chastity's phone after she disappeared from Hot Springs. But that shit took days to get sorted out. Depending on the service provider, it would take anywhere from three days to a week to ping the phone. Now they had the real thing in hand. It was locked by a passcode, of course, so Lillie figured it was another dead lead until one of the local cops tried Chastity's DOB on the damn thing and it opened. What followed was a goddamn Russian novel of bullshit between that crazy girl and a fella named Graham who lived down in New Orleans.

The messages sweet and dirty. All about love and forever mixed in with some up close and personal titty pics. Seemed like the titty pics were what put this Graham guy over the damn edge, messaging two nights ago, I HAVE TO SEE YOU OR I MIGHT DIE.

Lillie let Charlie Hodge drive the Charger that night, and he'd just gotten off at an exit in Natchitoches. They hadn't eaten all damn day and the road had graced them with a decent-looking restaurant called Fontenot's Cajun Café. Lillie had been dreaming of a shrimp po' boy ever since they crossed the state line.

Her phone buzzed just as they were headed into the café. Seeing it was Quinn Colson, she took the call. She motioned for Charlie to go on in without her. Charlie saluted her and disappeared into the restaurant.

"This better be good," Lillie said. "I haven't eaten in twenty-four hours or showered in forty-eight."

"It's good," Quinn said. "I got an ID on the men I'm pretty sure killed Gina Byrd."

"Hell," Lillie said. "I just might jump for joy. But Charlie and I just stopped in to get a bite to eat. Can I call you back?"

"There's more."

"There's always more," Lillie said. "What you got, Ranger?"

"Where are you?"

"Natchitoches Parish," Lillie said. "Headed down to the Big Easy for an all-expense vacation courtesy of the U.S. Marshals Service to pick up TJ Byrd and her little brother. Might just rescue that Chastity Bloodgood from getting it on with a dopey-sounding dude named Graham."

"You got an address?"

"What do you think?"

"I'd like to meet you down there," Quinn said. "The situation has gotten a little more complicated."

"You having the urge for a shrimp po' boy, too, or do you just miss me?"

"I don't know how and I don't know why," Quinn said. "But the suspects in Gina Byrd's killing might be down there, too. They took a job to get the Bloodgood girl back."

"Wait," Lillie said. "What the damn hell. For who?"

"For her daddy," Quinn said. "Chester Pratt and me had a real heart-to-heart tonight. He thinks these two fellas might kill TJ and her little brother if they get in the way."

"Can't a woman get a goddamn break?"

"I'll text you," Quinn said. "The men's names are Flem and Dusty Nix. You can find them easy in the system. Their records light up the NCIC like a fireworks display. Arson, manslaughter, aggravated assault. The younger one was a suspect in a big murder over in Calhoun County. But they never found the body."

"Anything else?"

"They work as roofers and both of them are so short, they couldn't make the ride cutoff at a carnival."

"Couple of midget killer roofers," Lillie said. "Well fuck me, Quinn Colson. This just brightens my damn day."

"Meet you down there."

"Sure," Lillie said. "And bring some goddamn coffee."

"Just like the old days?"

"Really?" Lillie said. "I sure as shit hope not."

TWENTY-FIVE

TJ wished she'd kept that nice Kia that Ladarius had stolen in Hot Springs instead of stripping the tags and abandoning it two miles from that loser Graham's house. When she and John Wesley had walked back to find it, the car had been towed or stolen again, leaving them with no money and stranded with those junkies, Chastity dragging her ass on getting them down to Grand Isle. At one time, Grand Isle was all Chastity could talk about, but now she wouldn't even speak to TJ, heading out to some bars with Graham and his lowlife druggie friends. All their eyes half-closed, stumbling, smelling like they never met a bar of soap or owned a razor.

She was worried they were all onto her now. One of the junkie buddies asked if she was really "that TJ Byrd" and wanted to know if she really killed that trucker and her own mother. TJ told him to go fuck himself, but could tell the reward money was heavy on his mind.

"What do you think?" TJ asked John Wesley.

"Why you asking me now?" he said. "Hell, TJ. I don't think we should've ever left home."

"Come on," TJ said, walking back along St. Charles Avenue. Purple and gold beads littered the big oak branches overhead and hung off the electric lines. The parades had already passed through, folks wandering the streets free and loose or hanging out in the front yards of mansions and apartments. She'd given John Wesley her only coat, the sleeves about six inches too long for him, while she shivered in a thin flannel shirt.

"I wish Momma wasn't gone," John Wesley said.

"Me, too," TJ said.

"Why'd folks blame you for what happened?"

"I don't know," she said. "I guess 'cause it was easier that way."

"Was it really that Chester Pratt?"

"Afraid so."

"I'd like to kick that bastard right in the nuts."

"Me, too," TJ said, grabbing his hand. They moved as a team in and out of the crowds, TJ keeping her head down, trying to come up with a new plan, a better plan, to get them out of the city and away from these broken people and all Chastity's damn bullshit.

They were close to the big park now, the neutral ground separating them from heading on across the wide avenue and back to the house. They waited for a streetcar to pass, electric lines sparking overhead. Folks crossed back and forth over the tracks, carrying coolers and folding chairs.

While they stood there, TJ decided to wander behind a wrought-iron fence and into a big lawn party with lots of folks eating and listening to music, crawfish shells crunching beneath their feet. John Wesley followed her over to a big linen-topped table where she grabbed a china plate and helped herself to some little cut-up sandwiches and some sticky jambalaya like her aunt used to make.

John Wesley caught on to the idea real fast and stacked his plate with nearly a dozen little sandwiches. They found a nearby cooler loaded down with soft drinks and she found a couple bottles of root beer for her and John Wesley. It was a break. A little time out from the craziness. TJ felt she could breathe a little easier, getting something to eat, trying to get her mind right before she'd have to face Chastity. That girl either needed to help them get gone or get them a goddamn car. She'd derailed everything since they met up in Hot Springs. Nothing but empty-ass promises. Now they were in some strange house with folks coming and going at all hours. Too many of them taking long looks at her and staring back at their phones.

Maybe she was getting paranoid now, but TJ started to notice a group of teenage girls, her age or maybe a little older, staring at her and John Wesley. She was sure she'd been busted and told John Wesley to fill up his damn pockets, as it was time to leave. He nodded, mouth full, and she grabbed his hand, the kid dropping his china plate to the ground, but moving fast to the gate. Eyes were everywhere.

One of the teenage girls walked over to her. TJ ducked down her head and pretended not to see her. "You're her," she said. "Aren't you?"

"I'm nobody," TJ said. "Sorry. We're at the wrong house."

"We won't tell anyone," she said. "I promise. I hope they get whoever killed your mother. I know it had to be that Chester Pratt. Especially after he stole all your money. Sounds like he was covering his own butt."

TJ stopped cold. John Wesley looked up at her, not sure what to do. Somewhere far off she heard the sound of a jazz band starting up and people beginning to clap along with the music. A real wild party. Good times. She could see the park on the other side of Saint Charles. They could just ignore the girls and make a run for it.

"I want to help," the girl said.

"Why would you help us?"

"Because what you did is right," she said. "Stood up. Fair is fair and all that. Love the hair, by the way."

TJ watched John Wesley dig into his blue jeans for a tiny sandwich. She shivered some more as she hugged her arms around herself.

She looked at the girl and girl grinned back at her, so much time, space, and money separating them. But the girl looked at TJ as if she was looking at something made of gold or altogether new.

"We need money," TJ said, just kind of blurting it out. "And a phone. Especially a phone. I'll pay you back. I swear on it."

The girl said her name was Anna and that this was her family's house. She was tall, with glossy, dark brown hair and perfect teeth and skin, pretty in her big puffy coat with a fur-lined hood. TJ watched as the girl wandered back to her friends, four other girls, and they all reached into their purses and pockets like they were at some kind of church revival. *Raise your hands. Praise the Lord.* They did it secret and slow, eyes darting around the party to see if anyone noticed. Anna came back and pressed a wad of cash into TJ's hand. "There you go. You're one of us."

"What about a phone?" TJ asked.

"You can have mine," she said. "But can we take a selfie first?"

"You can't post it."

"I know," she said. "I'll mail it to myself. You know. For when it's all over."

TJ felt her face heat up, reaching for John Wesley's hand, and looking back at the girl. "You mean when I'm dead?" she asked. "Shit. This ain't no goddamn reality show, Anna. I swear to you this shit is real."

"That's not what I mean," she said. "I'm sorry."

TJ nodded slow as the girl stepped up, reaching her arm around TJ's waist, pulling her close and stretching out her camera from both of them. TJ didn't smile but looked dead center of the camera lens on the phone.

"That sure is a cute coat," TJ said. "Looks warm."

TJ slid into it as she and John Wesley headed across St. Charles. Pride was long, long gone.

* * *

Dusty and Daddy parked on Calhoun, right down the street from the address Mr. Stagg had given them. There wasn't a damn thing to it, punching up the number on that telephone and riding this way and that on those crazy one-way streets till they found the old house. A basic two-story with busted, worn-out shingles saddled up against a big green park with water, and twisty old trees that grew more sideways than straight up and down like back home. Daddy took a piss in the park while Dusty kept an eye on that house. It was coming up on midnight, but all the lights were on, Dusty not seeing much but some shirtless guy with tattoos coming to the window to smoke a cigarette.

Dusty figured they'd wait till they saw either TJ Byrd or Chastity. He'd gotten a good look at both online and he had to say that TJ Byrd sure did favor her mother. Dusty remembered a lot about that woman's features as he held her by the neck and Daddy done bled her out. *Lord, how that woman could scream.*

He enjoyed doing this kind of work. Was a heck of a lot easier than putting shingles on a two-story house in the middle of winter. Or slathering tar up on top of a barn in July. This was about the same as sitting in a tree stand waiting for a big fat doe to pussyfoot right into a baited field. The only hard part was getting the girl away from the boys inside and making sure she didn't scream her damn head off. He recalled him and Daddy snatching some woman up in Memphis after she posted pics of her ex-husband's little ding-dong online. They'd done wrapped her head in duct tape but could still hear her yelling. Barely got her in the truck before some old fella wandered out in his busted bathrobe, pointing a gun and telling them to stop. They had to kill that old fucker, too. Weighted both of them down good and dropped them off an overpass into the Wolf River.

Well, shit. *Live and fucking learn.*

Daddy crawled back in the truck and slammed the door shut. "Them girls ain't in there," he said. "Only three fellas getting high and listening to the devil's music."

"We can wait."

Daddy nodded. He lit up a long-ass cigarette and settled back into the shadow, a brown Carhartt hoodie up over his baseball cap. The old man breathing loud, smacking at his teeth while he settled in.

They sat there a good hour before the first cop car rolled by, god-damn NOPD checking out that house they were watching and then finally moving on. It wasn't five minutes later that another passed, or maybe the same one, and stopped for a moment on the street, seem-ing to take note of the goings-on around the block. Everything still and so quiet that Dusty could hear the buzzing of the streetlamps in the cold.

"I don't like this shit," Dusty said. "Not one damn bit. What are they looking at?"

Daddy leaned up and squashed his cigarette in the ashtray. He grunted.

Dusty cranked the ignition, turned on the headlights, and headed back down the road. Slow and easy. "Maybe we should call Mr. Stagg," he said.

"Naw," Daddy said. "What I'd tell you? When an animal gets wind of you, it's best to leave a bit. We'll come back later when the gettin's good."

"Listen to me, TJ," Holly Harkins said. "You got to get the hell out of there now."

"What I need is a car," TJ said. "We lost the one Ladarius stole and I don't know a damn thing about stealing cars. Maybe an old one. Try that trick with a screwdriver."

TJ was walking while she talked to Holly on Anna's phone, cutting right through Audubon Park with John Wesley ahead of her, trailing through the crooked paths as if he didn't have a care in the world.

"You'll figure it out," Holly said. "You always do, TJ. But leave. Go."

"Okay, okay," she said. "That's what I'm about to do. Me and John Wesley are walking back right now. We're gonna get our damn shit and I'm gonna give Chastity one last chance."

"One last chance?" Holly said. "What are you thinking? How many chances does that girl need? From what I heard from the sheriff, she's why you had to shoot the damn one-eyed trucker dead."

"You heard about that, huh?"

"'Course I heard about it, TJ," she said. "Are you crazy? Everybody's heard about it. That's what happens when you decide to tell your story to anyone who's listening. Have you seen you got a hundred thousand folks following you?"

"More like three hundred now," TJ said, talking low in the phone while she and John Wesley turned into another wide curve of the park. "After I shot that trucker."

"You proud of that?"

"Hell no, I'm not proud of it," TJ said. "What would you do? Don't get so damn cocky, Holly Harkins. What would you do to protect yourself and your little brother? This world hasn't left me with too many options. Although I did just get me a nice coat and this phone I'm calling you on."

"You're lucky I answered," she said. "The number wasn't familiar at all."

"You knew it was me just by the ring," TJ said. "Didn't you?"

"Maybe," Holly said. "Me and you always had that. That thought connection."

TJ stopped and let John Wesley walk on ahead, the streetlamps shining in the dark along the path. The old oaks looking like something from back in the dinosaur times. There wasn't a single tree in Tibbehah County that could grow that thick without attracting greedy men with axes trying to make a quick dollar. Seemed like everything back home of any value got cut down or uprooted.

"You okay?" TJ asked.

"Sheriff Colson called again," Holly said. "He said your life's in danger."

"What did you say?"

"I said, 'No shit, Sheriff,'" Holly said. "But he said it for real this time. He said that Chastity Bloodgood's daddy hired some bad folks to come snatch her up before she'd get arrested and that you'd get killed if you stood in the way."

"Don't worry," she said. "They can have her."

"Please, TJ," Holly said. "Just quit. Just stop what you're doing. You can't run and run till there's no more road. That was just a fantasy we were telling ourselves."

TJ took a long breath. She looked to John Wesley playing on the long branch of the tree, so damn heavy and fat that it touched the ground. "Erase this number," TJ said. "When I call you again, it'll be from a new phone."

"What do I tell the sheriff?"

"Tell him you never heard from me."

Chastity and Graham got back from the parties at close to five in the morning, the sound of the brass band at that corner bar pounding in her ears, the pills and cocaine in her blood making her feel like her heart might explode. The night just couldn't move fast enough, everything jumping from place to place, thought to thought. Time to time. Maybe if she hadn't called Daddy at the dealership, she could've kept this party going on forever. If Graham could get some more cash, maybe sell his car, they could keep this up for a while. Maybe until Jazz Fest. The only thing that she needed to get rid of was TJ Byrd. That girl had been nothing but a goddamn anchor since she rescued those hicks back at the lake. TJ got what she needed and Chastity got a wild little ride. But that shit needed to end and that girl and her creepy little brother needed to go. When she got back to Graham's house, she'd make it plain they couldn't stay there anymore. Who was TJ to pass judgment on her life or on Graham's friends? She wasn't the one who was a goddamn killer.

Graham nearly rammed into the side of his house while he squealed into the short driveway, parking sideways and leaving on the headlights as he stumbled up the front steps. Chastity followed, knowing he'd want her to meet him back in the bedroom. She'd already took care of him in the nasty bathroom stall and he'd felt up under her skirt while they were at the bar, enjoying her keeping eye contact with the bartender while he reached up into her panties. That's when they'd decided it was time to go, feeling like they just might start doing it there right in front of the whole brass band going to "Little Liza Jane." Everything so hazy and wild.

She closed the front door and tiptoed around some new dude sleeping on the couch, before she nearly walked into a wall. Graham was waiting for her. His shirt already off, gripping her shoulders and pushing her down to her knees. She didn't want to go to her knees but did anyway.

Everything was spinning. Her mind racing so damn fast. "Oh, yeah," Graham said. "Come on. Go. Do it."

Then there was a bright light. Someone had hit the switch and walked into the room. Chastity tried to cover her eyes with her forearm while she looked up to see TJ standing there with her daddy's

AR-15 in her hands. The one they couldn't sell because of the inscription. VINCE BLOODGOOD. AMERICAN BY BIRTH, SOUTHERN BY THE GRACE OF GOD.

The light sent her head reeling, feeling like she might puke. She gagged, putting a fist to her mouth. Graham looked paralyzed where he stood, his jeans below his knees, and hands over his boner.

"You're better than this," TJ said.

"Why would you say that?"

"We're both better than where we ended up," TJ said. "Come on."

"I told Daddy where I am," Chastity said. "He said he's sending people for me. Don't you get it? You're just a sideshow to this party."

TJ walked over to where Graham had thrown his keys. She picked them up and stashed them into her new coat pocket. "Don't be so stupid," TJ said, pulling Chastity off her knees. "Get your shit and let's go. You're done with this creep."

Chastity looked to TJ, squinting into the light, and the halo around the girl's determined face. She nodded and damn well did as she was told.

"And Graham?" TJ asked. "You say a goddamn word about who took your car and I'll make sure you go down for statutory rape. I had me two uncles who did time down at Angola. A skinny white boy like you won't last a week. Them boys will plug every damn hole you got."

Dusty and Daddy rolled up on the house again at a little after five. Dusty up and alert after tossing back three Red Bulls and smoking a half pack of Vantage Lights. Daddy fast asleep in the passenger seat, coming to every so often and asking Momma if she'd taken the dogs out yet. What confused Dusty now was that there was a brand-new black Land Cruiser parked sideways in the house's driveway with the headlights on and the doors wide open. Dusty got the idea to get out and stretch and have a little look-see.

He didn't get about halfway to the house when he saw a girl and a little boy come around to the Land Cruiser and open up the back hatch. As the hatch lifted up, he got a good view of the girl's face and was at least eighty percent sure it was that outlaw TJ Byrd. Now where in the world was Miss Chastity? Dusty had been thinking on that name long and hard. Clean and pure, unspoiled little rich girl, down and dirty with the country folk. Ole Dusty would save her. Dusty and Daddy Nix to the fucking rescue. Fucking heroes for the ages. Maybe that ole boy in Fayetteville would let them trade in their old beater truck for a brand-new Silverado.

Dusty stood there, cigarette dangling loose in his right hand while he adjusted his nuts with the left. He turned back to the truck to see Daddy out of the cab now waving to him like a goddamn idiot. "Hey," the old man said. "Hey." Dusty waved him off, giving him hand signals so no one else could hear. *Hush, old man. Hush.*

Ten seconds later, there was Chastity Bloodgood herself coming out, acting of her own free will and toting a little pink bag. She looked about as steady on her feet as a newborn fawn. Nobody held a gun on her. Nobody had her tied up like he'd been expecting. Dusty figured him and Daddy would bust in with guns drawn, finding that poor little girl hog-tied and gagged like pictures of the women he'd seen on the internet. Instead, it looked to all the world like she and that TJ Byrd was friends. Hell, she even stopped to hug TJ's neck and pat her back.

"What the gosh-dang fuck?" Dusty said, his cigarette burning down in his fingers.

The big black Land Cruiser started up, red taillights aglow, and backed out in the empty street. Dusty stood there, looking into the windshield, the Byrd girl glancing over his face and then driving off.

Dusty hobbled on back, his right knee acting up on him again, and crawled back behind the wheel.

"You ready?" Daddy asked. "Whoo-wee."

"They're leaving."

"What you mean, 'leaving'?" he said. "It's five in the goddamn morning."

"Miss Chastity got into that truck with TJ Byrd and some little kid," Dusty said. "How the fuck should I know?"

"Come on, boy," Daddy said, pointing. So excited spit flew from his mouth. "*Go. Go.* Follow their ass, son. We ain't getting paid to sit around and scratch our damn nuts."

Dusty cranked the ignition and made a sweeping U-turn in the old truck. Daddy wide-ass awake now, nibbling on some homemade jerky he'd brought along special for the trip. He slurped at the strips of meat, spit dripping down his chin.

As they drove away, Dusty noticed two flat black cars and a silver Charger speed past in the opposite direction. He wondered where the hell they were going in such a goddamn hurry.

TWENTY-SIX

At dawn, Lillie and Charlie Hodge, along with ten more marshals, four FBI agents, and six NOPD officers, raided the house on Audubon Park only to find four unarmed junkies inside sleeping it off. Lillie, never a stranger to threats and intimidations, kind of felt sorry for the kid who owned the house. A skinny-looking frat boy named Graham, with dark circles under his eyes, greasy black hair, and forearms poked so many damn times by a needle they looked like bruised fruit.

"And you're sticking by that story?" Lillie asked, standing over Graham, who sat on his unmade bed, head in hands. "Chastity Bloodgood left New Orleans with TJ Byrd and her little brother sometime last night? But you don't know why or where they're headed?"

"That's right."

"You don't look so good, Graham," Lillie asked. "How long's it been since you shot up?"

"I don't shoot up," Graham said. "Shit, lady. I don't mess with that crap. What makes you think that?"

"Besides the marks on your arms and the fact your pupils are smaller than a mouse pecker?" Lillie asked. "Oh. I don't know. You're also about to fall asleep with almost twenty federal agents and cops tromping around your daddy's house. Either you're the chillest dude in the Big Easy or you're on the backside of the big rush. Which is it?"

"You're crazy," he said, leaning forward on the bed, shivering like he'd been locked in a deep freeze. His teeth wouldn't stop chattering. "I say no to drugs. And yes to life."

"You're a goddamn laugh riot, kid."

Charlie Hodge walked into the room and lifted up a baggie full of white powder and a box full of what the cool kids call drug paraphernalia. Lillie nodded to Charlie as he turned back to the main room with the other agents and Graham ducked his head back between his legs.

"I spoke to your father," Lillie said. "He sure is disappointed in you."

"My father is a massive dick," Graham said, lifting the shaggy bangs from his eyes, smiling in a sleepy, lazy way. "He and his buddies aren't any better. Only difference is they get high and order up strippers like they were pizzas. My dad better be careful, or I'll show my mom a video I found in his sock drawer. I have to admit. I wasn't sure my old man had it in him."

"Heartwarming," Lillie said. "Maybe after you get out of jail, y'all can go on some kind of bonding trip where you both admit your weaknesses and shortcomings. I'm sure you both can hug it out by the campfire."

"Jail?" he said. "Why would I go to jail?"

"Son of a bitch, kid," Lillie said. "You sure do take the goddamn short bus on your way to Law and Order 101. You just gave shelter to a two-time murder suspect and the girl she's accused of kidnapping. Not to mention the old-time opium den y'all got started here on the park."

"I didn't know that girl Chastity brought a murderer to my house," Graham said. "How was I supposed to recognize her?"

"You follow TJ Byrd online," Lillie said, scrolling through her phone and flashing the screen to the boy. "Or isn't this your profile?"

"I'm so damn tired," he said. "Can't we do this later? God. I'm so fucking tired."

Lillie looked about Graham's room. The dirty bedsheets, empty beer bottles and bongs, pizza boxes, T-shirts, and jeans tossed haplessly across the floor. Lillie spotted a grouping of framed photos up on a chest of drawers and plucked one out the dead center. A little boy with black hair and big sad eyes stood with his parents on a tropical island Lillie couldn't visit as a kid or afford as an adult.

"This you?"

"Sure."

"Your life doesn't look so hard," she said. "Where is that, Hawaii?"

"Costa Rica," he said. "Who said my life is hard?"

Lillie set the framed photo back down and walked back to the bed. Graham's eyes fluttered closed and she kicked at his bare feet to keep him awake. "Where are those kids headed?"

"You can't believe anything Chastity says," he said. "Did you know she told me she was eighteen?"

"I'm sure you were a true upstanding gentleman with her, anyway," Lillie said. "Right?"

"She lies," Graham said. "Like all the fucking time. I could tell you what she said. But I don't believe it. And then you'd come back here and blame it all on me."

"Oh," Lillie said. "You won't be here. You're headed to the Orleans Parish Prison. You know that great old song? Oh, how I do love Johnny Cash. *They found him down by the Ponchartrain and cuffed his ass with a big iron chain*."

Graham lifted his dark eyes to Lillie and shut them for a long moment, exhaling from his nose and swallowing. "Will you let me go if I tell you what Chastity said?"

"Nope."

"Will you let me go if you find them?"

"Nope."

"Then why would I want to help?" Graham said.

"'Cause you're fucked five ways from Sunday, Graham," Lillie said. "If I put in a good word, old Daddy Warbucks in Atlanta might loot the stripper fund for some hot shit rehab in California. You'll be up to your asshole and eyeballs in naked yoga, veggie frittatas, and circle jerks before you know it. But if you don't help and something happens to those kids, I just might hold that against you. And that wouldn't be good."

"Shit."

"That's about the tall and short of it."

"If I help, I need my shit back," he said. "Just one last time. Before you take me in."

"Your drugs?" Lillie asked. "Come on, Graham. That's between you, the locals, and Lord Jesus. *Comprende?*"

Graham nodded. He stared down at his feet, and then back up at Lillie. He looked like a rat squirming in a steel trap.

"I need help."

"Sure you do."

"I didn't touch her," Graham said. "I swear she wanted me to. But I didn't touch Chastity. She's like a little sister to me."

"Ain't that so Louisiana," Lillie said. "Where is she?"

"Her father has a fishing cabin," Graham said. "Somewhere on the Gulf. I think that's where they were going. I don't know. Maybe. They were talking about it."

Lillie nodded and left Graham to fall back into his bed while she walked out to the second-story patio to look out across Audubon

Park. The early morning joggers, walkers, and bikers bundled up to exercise on the bright clear morning. Lillie had left her jacket inside and her breath clouded before her as she started to make a few calls.

A few minutes later, someone below whistled and called out her name. Lillie looked down at the pedestrian street facing the house. Damn if it wasn't Quinn Colson. All the way from Tibbehah County.

And he'd brought four coffees in a cardboard tray. God bless him.

They made it out of New Orleans and down to Cut Off in Lafourche Parish before they needed gas. Chastity had three hundred and forty-two dollars in her purse, explaining how she'd sold most of her daddy's guns and kept a little money hidden from Graham.

"Why'd you keep the semiauto?" TJ asked.

"Sentimental, I guess," Chastity said. "It was Daddy's favorite."

TJ stayed behind while Chastity and John Wesley went into the convenience store, with Chastity promising John Wesley sausage biscuits and all the boiled shrimp he could eat once they got to Grand Isle. TJ wasn't exactly sure how it was all gonna work once they got down there, unhitching her daddy's big boat, fueling up, and navigating all the way over to Old Mexico. All she knew was that they were gone from that goddamn zombie house and those dark-eyed druggies, and that fresh air blowing through the windows in Graham's Land Cruiser felt like a little slice of heaven.

TJ got out and started pumping gas after Chastity had paid thirty dollars. She said that would be plenty to get them where they were headed. TJ hadn't slept all night, worried how they were going to get free and what they'd do if they'd been stranded in the city. At one point, she thought about leaving John Wesley in a big fancy hotel, telling him to let the folks there know he was lost and needed help. But her little brother would've never gone for that. Through this whole fucked-up road trip, that boy had never left her side. He was tough and brave as hell. And the idea of leaving him while hiding out somewhere else made her guts turn inside out.

"That's a sporty little wagon you got there," a man said. She looked up to see some short fella standing beside an old truck.

TJ nodded and turned back to the spinning numbers on the pump. Behind the store's plate-glass windows, John Wesley and Chastity flitted about bright colors of snack cakes and candies, stacks and stacks of Coca-Cola and Sprite.

"Tight little chassis, tires with fresh treads," the man said. "Whew. Sure would like to take that vehicle out for a spin, break it in and loosen up them struts."

TJ glanced over at the odd little man again. He stood in the shadows, but she still got a good view of his stocky body, black beard, and coal-black eyes. He had on a ball cap, a heavy camo hunting jacket over his blue jeans and mud boots. The man's chapped face and dirty beard made him look like some kind of creature that had crawled out from the center of the earth.

He licked at his lips before lighting a cigarette. His right foot back behind him resting on the rear tire.

"Where y'all headed?" the man said.

TJ shrugged.

"Where y'all been?"

"Everywhere," TJ said.

"Everywhere, huh," the man said, topping off his tank and tapping at the nozzle to get every last drip into his old Chevy. "Ain't that somethin'. Say, don't I know you from somewheres?"

TJ didn't answer. She hadn't finished pumping thirty dollars but hung up the nozzle anyway and got back behind the wheel, cranking the engine, and wheeling out hard and fast to the front of the convenience store. She honked the horn and Chastity and John Wesley came running out, holding armfuls of candy and Cokes. They were laughing like hell as they jumped into the Land Cruiser.

"What's so damn funny?" TJ said, spinning out onto the highway, headed south.

"We didn't pay for nothing," John Wesley said. "Chastity said I had two minutes to grab everything I wanted to eat."

"That's not us," TJ said. "That's not what we do."

"Bullshit," her little brother said. "Since when?"

TJ cut her eyes over at Chastity, who smiled and popped the sunglasses down off the top of her head. TJ looked up into the rearview mirror to see if she saw that old Chevy truck anywhere. When she didn't, she let out a slow, easy breath.

"A man back there recognized me," TJ said.

"You need some sleep," Chastity said. "You're not thinking straight."

"He looked at me like he knew me," she said. "Kept on talking about this Toyota like it was a woman."

"Men are gross."

"He had these small, crazy eyes," TJ said. "I could smell him through all the spilled oil and diesel fumes."

"So what?" Chastity said. "He stinks."

"I smelled that somewhere before."

"When?"

"When I washed Momma's bloody clothes," TJ said. "That funk was all over her."

That fine bright morning, Johnny Stagg was finished with a tour of the halfway completed Frontier Village with ole Randy Nichols and Danny Hayes from the county supervisors. Both of them good ole boys since birth; Stagg working with both their daddies while they were still in diapers. Stagg was glad to learn they knew the ways of the world while promising unlimited and unconditional support to Stagg's plan to give something back to the community. Of course, a tidy little campaign contribution would be made to both in their private accounts at Tibbehah First National.

The boys tipped their baseball caps and climbed their fat asses in the shiny new trucks provided by taxpayers. The best part about it was the truck was theirs for the taking, along with a brand-new metal barn and all the equipment they needed. Ain't a better dodge than being a Mississippi supervisor. Stagg sure hated that he couldn't run again because of slanderous lies and his current criminal record.

Stagg stood in the parking lot waving goodbye to Randy and Danny when his phone jingled in his pocket. One of his waitresses had set the ring to the tune of "(What This World Needs Is) A Few More Rednecks."

"You got Johnny Stagg," Stagg said. "Start talkin'."

"That Bloodgood girl's with TJ Byrd and her squirt brother."

"I told you not to call unless you needed something."

"You sure they headed to that fishing cabin?"

"Got it straight from the girl's daddy," Stagg said. "How many other places does that highway lead?"

"You mean south?"

Stagg didn't answer such a dumb goddamn question. He took a long beat to let that Nix boy figure it the hell out.

"Only one."

Stagg plugged his right ear with his finger, the drilling and hammering commencing again now that the official tour was over. He turned his back to the new kiddie wonderland and started to walk through the semis back toward the Rebel. He could finally hear that peckerwood Dusty Nix as he got between two tractor trailers.

"Y'all did good getting out of New Orleans," Stagg said. "God-damn marshal service raided that house this morning. Ain't nothing in there but a bunch of dopeheads. Those boys are fucked good."

"The law know where the girl's gone?"

"If they knew, them kids would already been caught," Stagg said. "Now listen, son. The whole goddamn point of this here exercise is to get that Bloodgood girl safe, lily white, and clean and back to her daddy before ending up in handcuffs. Do y'all understand?"

"Mm-hmm."

"I said, do y'all understand?" Stagg said. "I ain't got any more time for niceties and pecker pulls."

A long silence followed, so long that Stagg thought they'd been cut off before that Nix boy started to breathe heavy on the line. "Me and Daddy waiting for the right time," Nix said. "Just hope that little bitch don't give us no trouble. 'Cause Daddy sure ain't in the mood."

"Aw," Lillie said. "Isn't that sweet? You brought me and Charlie coffee. Who are the other two for?"

"I'm about a quart low this morning."

"Should've figured," Lillie said. "That's a long ride on that hurt back. You okay?"

Quinn nodded and fired up a new cigar with his lighter, spewing smoke behind him. His back and legs ached like hell. He'd only stopped once for a pit stop and some gas, rolling steady from north Mississippi on a big thermos full of coffee that gave out around Kent-wood.

"Sorry you came all this way for an empty house," Lillie said.

"Any idea where they've gone?"

"Maybe," Lillie said. "The Bloodgood girl's boyfriend is a real prize. Shooting up with his best pals with TJ Byrd and her little brother around. Talked to him right before he nodded out again. Sounds like TJ got tired of the shitshow and moved on. Says they've gone down to another family property on Grand Isle."

"You believe him?"

"I believe him as much as any junkie willing to sell me some bullshit for some time off."

"Do we know if her father has property down that way?"

"Checked on that very thing before you rolled up, Ranger," Lillie said. "I sure as shit taught you well. Ole Mr. Bloodgood seems to have a spotty memory of where he owns all his houses. But property records seem to confirm it."

"The girl's daddy wasn't sure if he owned a house on Grand Isle?"

"You know what they say about the rich."

"That they're different?"

"No," Lillie said. "That they can be lying, conniving, backstabbing bastards."

"Hadn't heard that one," Quinn said. "You ready to roll?"

"A team-up?" Lillie said. "A Ranger and U.S. Marshal?"

"Told you it'd be just like the old days," Quinn said.

Lillie took the cigar from Quinn's fingers and took a few puffs. She handed it back as he opened the tab of his second coffee. The wild, green beauty of the park opening up to him, and he wished he could return sometime with Maggie and the kids. Oaks trees starting to bud and small green flowers poking up from the grass.

"Let me talk with Charlie," Lillie said. "Maybe he can babysit these assholes in case something changes. I don't want to be on some coon-ass highway if TJ Byrd decides to blow up goddamn Mardi Gras."

"That kid's better than that," Quinn said. "She just wants to make things right."

"You keep telling me that," Lillie said. "And maybe one day I'll believe you."

TWENTY-SEVEN

Dusty and Daddy crossed that little bridge from the mainland and rolled up on the stilt house later that morning. The skies so dark and gray along the Gulf it damn well looked like night. Dusty had to elbow Daddy awake, the old truck smelling of cigarettes and gas station chicken, turning down the radio playing old-timey accordion music with some French fella wailing and carrying on about some dead woman. Even though it was colder than a Minnesota well digger's ass, he let down the window to get a feel of what was happening on that neat row of houses, not spitting distance from the beach and backed up with a canal full of docks and boat lifts. Sure was a wonder how some white folks lived.

"Wake up," Dusty said, hammering the dashboard with the flat of his hand. "Come on, old man. This ain't no fuckin' lunch break."

Daddy garbled out some nonsense and went right for a cigarette, eyes staring straight up at the odd house, built high off the ground like some kind of weird bird standing quiet and still along the street. Row after row of nothing but stilt houses running across that little island, looking cold and dark and shut up for the winter. He figured maybe he and Daddy might come back with Momma Lennie after they got paid by ole Johnny Stagg. Easiest money they'd ever earned.

"Where's that girl?" Daddy said.

"In that house, I reckon."

"You reckon?" Daddy said. "Ain't that her black car parked across the street? One we been following since New Orleans?"

"Engine still warm," Dusty said. "Just walked over and touched it."

"Anyone see you?"

Dusty shook his head, smelling the salt on that cold sea air blowing in. They could hear the waves from where they sat, Daddy blowing smoke up into the cracked windshield. *Lord have mercy.* They sure were a long way from Tibbehah County.

"I ain't never taken your momma to the beach."

"Just thinkin' on that exact thing."

"Me and her always working," Daddy said. "Paying for you and your sister to have new britches and shoes on your feet. I think Momma might like to get out some time, get her big white-ass ninnies wet and her old toes in the sand."

"Y'all deserve it," Dusty said. "You're like me. Swinging a hammer your whole life."

"Didn't have no other choice," Daddy said. "My daddy kicked me out of the house after I knocked up your momma. Hell, I tried to explain I couldn't help it. I was so goddamn horny, I would've screwed a sidewinder right in the mouth."

"Y'all were just kids."

"Momma was fourteen," he said. "She done told me that if I held my breath and she prayed real hard no harm would come of it. And we did it each and every Sunday after church let out. Right there out in the woods by the Assembly of God like a couple animals in the rut."

The flat gray clouds blanketed out the sky, turning everything around them cold as steel clear out to the Gulf of Mexico. Dusty wanted so bad just to close his eyes for a minute, the sound of the surf and the smell of the air soothing him.

"Don't kill nobody this time," Dusty said. "You hear me? No matter what happens."

"This ain't much different than me and you up on those rooftops chasing water," Daddy said. "Sometimes it's easy to see where it goes to hide, but it's another to see where it sprung a leak."

"You telling me to be patient?" Dusty asked. "Bide my time?"

"Little Goldilocks will come skipping down those stairs soon enough," Daddy said. "I can almost smell her."

Dusty kept on staring at the row houses and all those fancy boats parked up under them, something so damn foreign about it, feeling strange being so damn far away from their land. The unease of it made him feel like he wanted to reach for Daddy's book of matches and burn something hot and fast.

"Remember what we did to that son of a bitch's barn back in Parsham?"

"Ha, ha," Daddy said. "How could I forget?"

"Remember me and you in the woods, laughing our damn asses off as he come out his trailer buck-ass nekkid with nothing more than a garden hose between his legs?"

"I can still smell that horsehair and charred meat," he said. "Burned up his stock to a crisp."

Dusty turned his head out the window and spit onto the crushed shells of the road. He looked back to Daddy and nodded down to the gear shifter. "Mind if I borrow that there book of matches?"

"Help yourself, son," Daddy said, passing along the book with the cover reading SOUTHERN STAR LOUNGE. JERICHO, MS.

*   *   *

Nothing was as promised with Chastity Bloodgood. She'd led TJ and John Wesley straight down into the ass crack of Louisiana and onto the narrow sliver of Grand Isle to find a stripped-out house on stilts with no power, no furniture, not a speck of food. They were all freezing inside, sitting around the first meal of the day, a twenty-three-dollar bounty from Jo-Bob's Gas & Grill from down the road. Two shrimp po' boys they all shared along with a big Styrofoam clamshell full of dirty rice and three egg rolls with a Cajun dipping sauce. Two Diet Cokes and a Mr. Pibb for John Wesley.

They ate silently in the weak light of their dying cell phones, Chastity getting a short charge on the one she found in Graham's Land Cruiser while she waited for food at Jo-Bob's. She pecked away fast and furious, answering fans on the FreeByrd handle and finally speaking, claiming she'd touched base with folks who might help them if the boat to Mexico didn't pan out.

"Hold up," TJ said, leaving half an egg roll stuck in the Cajun sauce. "Hold up one goddamn minute. What do you mean if the boat doesn't pan out?"

"News flash," she said. "When we drove up, did you see a fucking boat parked at that dock out back? Now, Daddy may have stuck it in dry dock or something for repairs. But just in case he sold it or something, we need a plan. That's all on me. Nobody else is doing any long-range thinking."

"There's nothing here," TJ said. "Your daddy lost this place just like he lost y'all's house in Hot Springs. Why can't you just admit you're just taking us down goddamn memory lane? There's nothing here anymore. Nothing for you or me or John Wesley. And your daddy ain't no different from mine. A man who got big dreams but keeps on getting knocked on his ass. Least my daddy never quit on nothing."

"You don't know shit about my family," Chastity said. "Or my father. He's the biggest seller of Chevy trucks in all the Ozarks."

John Wesley looked from girl to girl, his mouth open while he held an unsteady fork of dirty rice.

"I know he chose some new hot piece of ass with silver dollar titties over you."

"And what about you, TJ Byrd?" she said. "You think you'd have gotten this far without me? I helped you. I made you. If it wasn't for me, you'd already be up in prison for killing your own mother."

John Wesley looked up hard with his big eyes, mouth hanging open. "That's a lie," he said. "My momma was real sick. Holly Harkins told me. TJ didn't have nothing to do with it. She died. She's up there in heaven with Jesus and Dale Earnhardt."

"Are you deaf or just a retard?" Chastity asked. "Have you been listening to anything this whole ride, kid? Why do you think your sister is out here running from the law? Holly wouldn't stand by her. Ladarius got nearly eaten up by some dogs. And I'm the only friend she's got left."

"You're not a friend," TJ said. "You're about as real as those boys sending me messages how they want to marry me."

"Ladarius got eat by some dogs?" John Wesley said. His face bloodless and blank in the soft glow of TJ and Chastity's phones.

TJ wasn't sure what to tell her brother as the phone in her hands died out and went black, the only light in the room coming from the glow up under Chastity's face. She had her head down, already scrolling through like everything was fine and nothing at all had happened between them. TJ held her words until Chastity pulled a whole po' boy up toward her and snatched up half of it.

"Give it to me," TJ said.

"Yeah, right."

"John Wesley hasn't eaten all day."

"You sure are a great mother," she said. "Taking the kid on a wild-ass robbing and killing spree."

"Better than the one you got," TJ said, knowing she may have pushed things a little too far.

Chastity threw what was left of that shrimp po' boy right at TJ, smacking her square in the face with the shredded lettuce and mayonnaise dripping onto her shirt. "Here you go!" Chastity said, screaming. "Take it. Just like you've taken or stolen everything else in your life. The world isn't all about handouts."

TJ launched herself off the floor and onto Chastity, knocking the girl onto her back, trying to pin her down by the shoulders. Chastity spit into her face and tried to roll away from her, TJ headbutting the girl just like she'd seen on *WWE SmackDown*, those Bella Twins taking care of business. But damn if that little girl wasn't tough, grabbing TJ by the waist and driving her straight into the wall, her ass ramming clear though the sheetrock.

John Wesley was yelling. "Y'all stop it!" he said. "Stop it."

TJ wiped the mess off her face and looked square at Little Miss Perfect, holding her forehead, a big old egg already beginning to form. Both of the girls were red-faced and breathing hard, and TJ did her best to listen to her little brother, promising him on the way down that they were now partners in this. *Holly is gone. Ladarius is gone.* Now it was up to them to see this to the end. "Family," she had said. "We're all we got now."

TJ told him she was sorry. John Wesley just stared at her, putting a finger to his lips and shaking his head. "Don't you hear it?" he asked. "It goes *thump, thump, thump.*"

"Damn," TJ said. "I had the music cranked up too high on the road. That's Rikki Rockett's kick-ass drums on 'Nothin' but a Good Time.' I can still hear it in my head, too."

John Wesley shook his head, a big beach towel up over his shoulders, and pointed up to the ceiling. TJ didn't say a word and listened.

He was right. Someone was on the roof.

"Not that it matters," Quinn said, riding shotgun as they sped down to Grand Isle. "But TJ Byrd had a solid reason for knocking the hell out of her mother."

"And where did you receive this bold revelation?"

"Holly Harkins," Quinn said. "She said TJ was trying to kick Gina Byrd out of their trailer and out of their lives after she kept on bringing one shitbird after another home to beat up her little brother."

"Holly said that?"

"Yep."

"Gina did have awful taste in men," Lillie said. "But I saw Gina after they got into it. TJ left her momma in some bad shape."

"Apparently all that damage wasn't done by TJ."

Lillie didn't say anything, doing seventy with her hand on the wheel, a straight shot of Louisiana highway in front of them. The gray clouds and darkness across the flatlands, a big-ass plant of some kind in the distance churning up smoke into the sky. Everything was so empty and desolate, they looked like they were on the other side of hell.

"Gina and I were friends for a long while," Lillie said. "Maybe I should've listened to the kid more."

"I've been out there," Quinn said. "TJ doesn't make it easy."

"Maybe you can talk her into joining the Army?"

"I'll do my best."

Lillie shook her head, catching a sign pass by, only twelve more miles to Grand Isle. "I was only joking, Ranger," she said. "The military isn't for everybody."

"What worked for you at that age?"

"Me?" Lillie said. "I've always had this sunny and sweet disposition. Folks used to call me Little Miss Fucking Sunshine."

"The truth is you haven't changed a bit."

"You, too, Quinn Colson," Lillie said. "I guess we all had to grow up real quick."

Dusty Nix had shimmied up onto the roof with a crowbar he'd grabbed from his toolbox, going to work on a tin sheet and lifting it up to the rafters. His pockets full of an old shirt and underwear of Daddy's soaked in gasoline to stick up under the stilts and up and under the tin. Didn't take long before the fire caught hot and fast while he held on to the satellite dish and giggled to himself.

Daddy was down on the road, smoking another cigarette on that empty street, a dozen houses looking just like the Bloodgood place, all in a pretty straight row, lightless and empty on a cool February morning. The only lights he could see were two streets down by the Gulf. Dusty figured those two girls and that little boy would come running out of that house like a family of scared rabbits.

Dusty waved down to Daddy.

Daddy waved back.

Dusty covered his mouth as he started to giggle some more, gripping that satellite pole, about to monkey down onto a window, when he saw a dark-colored Dodge Charger hauling ass up the main road and come wheeling in hard where Daddy was parked. Goddamn Daddy, deaf as a damn post, kept on waving to Dusty up on the roof until he finally turned and hobbled up toward that Dodge.

The dumb son of a bitch reached for his gun. Dusty yelled for him, but the man wouldn't listen. He never listened.

The doors jacked open and two folks got out onto the road, a woman yelling for Daddy to put down the weapon. Dusty knew he'd never forget Daddy's final words as the old man raised his pistol, yelling, "Y'all can suck my damn dick."

Guns were drawn. Shots were fired.

Daddy lay dead not fifteen feet from that Dodge Charger with its motor still running. Dusty felt all the air leave him as he gripped the drainpipe and lowered his feet down onto a railing. That's when he heard the shots fired from inside the house and saw the silver tin bucking up wild and free.

Dusty grabbed hold of that pole and pulled himself back up onto the roof. His feet slick as goose shit under him as someone started to unload a magazine full of bullets up into his ass.

Three minutes before, TJ asked Chastity: "Where's your daddy's gun?"

"Why don't you use *your* daddy's?" Chastity asked. "Since you love him so damn much."

"My daddy's gun's right here on my damn hip," she said. "But I need that big-ass gun, the one with the AMERICAN BY BIRTH, SOUTHERN BY THE GRACE OF GOD written on it, to shoot the goddamn nuts off whoever is up there setting fire to your place."

The smoke was already pouring in through the vents and down into the house. She'd told John Wesley to get low and crawl to the door after they'd smelled the smoke. They could hear the cold wind, the crackling of the fire, and footsteps above them. Soon came the squealing tires, the gunshots, the yelling.

"Where's the gun?"

Chastity disappeared and TJ pressed her body around her little brother, believing the girl was finally gone for good. But then Chastity was back and handing over that AR-15 she claimed she couldn't sell out of sentimental value.

TJ checked the magazine, jacked it back into the gun like she'd learned out at her Aunt Tabitha's land with all her hippie, lesbo friends hooting and hollering, swilling cold beer from the can.

TJ got off her knees and went to hunting where she heard that sound. She didn't need any light, moving with the creaking, finding it up close by the window where she saw a man's old boot dangling off the roof and trying to find some purchase on the porch railing.

TJ raised the gun and squeezed the trigger, hearing an *oof* and a big thud. More scrambling up above as the man's boots thudded right up over them, moving crossways over the roof. She raised the gun and shot more, the shots so loud they made her ears go numb and silent, an electric hum in the room after she stopped.

"Quit," Chastity said, yelling nearly up into her ear. "Stop it now. You're ripping apart my house."

"Little too late to worry about that," she said. "Get John Wesley and get to the back door. We're getting the hell out of here."

TJ lowered the big gun, trying to listen for anything. But it was stone-cold quiet again.

"Chastity?"

Nothing.

"Chastity?" TJ said. "Goddamn you."

Cold air rushed into the room and she looked over to find the front door wide open and hearing more yelling outside down on the street. She started to cough from the smoke spewing out from the vents.

"Chastity," she said.

When TJ turned back, she saw the man with a gun, holding his meaty little forearm up around John Wesley's throat. "Get me that Chastity Bloodgood and I won't blow your little brother's gosh-dang head off."

It was the man from the gas station back in Cut Off, blood on his filthy face and across the front of his shirt. As he walked toward her, the little man and John Wesley, both about the same height, disappeared in the smoke. TJ felt like she couldn't breathe as the ceiling started falling down around them.

"You're the sorry bastard that killed our mother."

"Better ask ole Chester Pratt about that," the man said. "We ain't nothing but hired help."

"Y'all just did it for the money?"

"When the Nix boys take on a job, we go that goddamn extra mile."

As the smoke blew past, John Wesley snatched up that man's stubby little forearm and took a big ole bite right out his flesh. The man yelled and stumbled, John Wesley scurrying back into the darkness of the house, smoke and fire coming out from damn near everywhere.

TJ called out to her little brother while her eyes watered. She could barely make out the face of the little man. He came up fast with a pistol, aiming right toward where she stood looking for where John Wesley had gone.

TJ tried to raise the big gun. But it was too late.

That short little fucker shot her twice, sending her ass reeling hard onto her back, the ceiling roiling and burning like an oven. Son of a bitch. *So this is how easy and fast it all goes?*

Lillie called in the fire as Quinn ran up to look at the dead man. He checked out the surrounding houses for a flicker of movement, looking to all the high wraparound porches, as good a place as any for someone to take a quick and easy shot. It was the old man who was dead, only eleven years older than Quinn, but looking all of eighty with his wrinkled face and white hair, black eyes staring up into damn near nothing. There would be another Nix lurking about, probably the one who'd gone up to set the fire. The smoke trailed up into the morning sky, flames showing from inside the windows.

Quinn pulled his gun, taking the stairs up to the top of the house, yelling to TJ Byrd. The front door was open with a rush of black smoke spewing out. He could feel the heat baking his face and singeing the hairs on his arms.

He rushed inside, calling out for the kids, and hearing nothing. The flames were zigzagging about, painting the walls over half the house. The entire house creaking and bending in the heat, the metal roof pinging and popping above him as he kicked in every door he could find, arm over his mouth, eyes watering and the heat searing his face and scorching off the stubble on his jaw.

When he felt the house was clear and the stilts began to rock under him, he bolted from the door and ran down the steps, finding half his shirt on fire and ripping it off his body, stomping on it good with his boots.

The cold air felt fresh and clean and he bent at the waist to try and catch his breath. He only had on a thin T-shirt now and the wind blew hard at his back.

Lillie walked down the narrow street, while loose sand skittered across the crushed-shell drive like a broken fog. Dusty Nix stood by his old Chevy not forty meters from her.

Quinn couldn't hear what was being said as he raced from the house to behind a pile of lumber and then over by a sailboat covered in a tarp and set up high on a trailer. He snuck around the side of the boat to where he could see and hear Lillie dog-cussing Dusty Nix, telling the man to lower his weapon or he'd be sprouting a new asshole in his forehead.

Nix stood close to the old Chevy truck, his dead father on the ground between him and Lillie. He pointed a military rifle right at Lillie. Lillie's headlights shone bright on the compact little man.

"Goddamn," Nix said, yelling. "Just get out the way, bitch."

Nix lifted up the AR as Lillie pulled the trigger, the man's weapon spewing and chewing up the front of Lillie's Charger, shattering the glass and knocking out one of the headlights.

"Woo-hoo," Nix said. "Come on. Get you some."

Quinn popped up around the side of the boat with his Beretta 9 and shot the man four times. He dropped hard and fast. The house fire grew with the wind, chewing up the house, flames higher now and shining down onto where both Nixes lay dead by the old truck.

"TJ and John Wesley?" Lillie asked.

Quinn shook his head, still tasting the soot in his mouth. "House was clear."

"That Dusty Nix sure had a way with words," she said. "It's killing me not to know what he was about to say next."

"He told you to get you some."

"And I was fixing to when you popped up and shot his ass," Lillie said. "Damn. Can't you let a woman have a little fun?"

Quinn was still catching his breath while Lillie walked up to the old Chevy and opened up the driver's-side door. Inside, they found a young white girl with a blonde ponytail shivering in the backseat. When Lillie placed a hand on her shoulder, she jumped as if being zapped by a live wire. Her lip was split and her face was a mess of makeup that looked to have been melted away by the fire.

"Chastity Bloodgood?" Lillie asked.

The girl nodded and Lillie offered her a hand to pull her out of the beaten old truck. As Quinn stood by, he glanced over Lillie's shoulder and down the road as a black SUV started up and sped out fast back toward the bridge.

"All that girl knows how to do is run," Chastity said.

"She can't get far," Lillie said.

"Go to it, Marshal," Quinn said. "I'll make sure everything gets sorted out here."

Lillie ran to her Charger and cranked it, the car revving to life with one headlight. She fishtailed out in the busted shells and sand following TJ Byrd. Chastity stared down at the dead men and then up at the burning house, the stilts under it creaking and groaning.

"Daddy's sure gonna be pissed."

She wore no expression at all.

They headed back up the way they'd come down, a straight shot north on Highway 1 driving back to the interstate. Only this time John Wesley was behind the wheel, the driver's seat pushed as far forward as he could, TJ laying down in the back pulling a torn piece of blanket around her leg. It hurt like a son of a bitch, but she wasn't about to stop, not with the law coming up behind them looking to put her away for two killings and now the burning mess they'd left back on Grand Isle. She just knew they'd blame her for that, too.

"Am I going too fast?" John Wesley asked.

"You're driving just right."

"Does it hurt much?"

"Don't hurt at all."

"Where we going?"

"Don't know," TJ said. "But we'll sure know it when we get there."

TJ bit down hard as she tied that cloth as tight as it would go, knowing the bone wasn't broke but she was bleeding like a stuck pig. She hadn't seen all that had gone on back at that stilt house, the dead man lying in the street and that stinky midget dragging Chastity

Bloodgood out from under the house. Lillie Virgil and Quinn Colson so focused on the burning house and the Nixes that they didn't even see her and John Wesley make their way from house to house along that canal until they could cross back behind them and get in Graham's Land Cruiser. She didn't know where they were going, but they sure as hell weren't going back to New Orleans.

The pain didn't really get to her until they got about ten miles outside town to somewhere that looked like nowhere with no buildings, no signs, no trees, nothing but big ole factories belching smoke up into the gray skies. It was then that her daddy come to her, sitting just as clear as day down by her feet, smiling across at his little girl in all that hurt, his golden mustache and mullet damn near perfect.

One more mile to go, Bug.

I'm worn out.

Your old daddy got worn out, too, and got hisself drowned hanging upside down in a crik.

Why'd you leave me? Momma wasn't cut out for this.

Like Bret Michaels sang, "every rose got its thorns."

I love you.

Love you, too, Bug. And don't you ever forget it.

TJ closed her eyes and tried to push away all that pain, thinking they'd head west now and take 90 over to Morgan City and on to Lafayette. They didn't have no one, didn't have any money, but maybe she could connect with folks to help on her phone. They had three hundred thousand TJ Byrd supporters out there; at least one or two had to live around Lafayette.

"TJ?" John Wesley said.

"Keep driving," TJ said. "You're doing fine."

"Someone's been bird-dogging our ass since Leeville."

"Is it that old beater truck?" TJ asked.

"It's a gray Dodge Charger with one headlight busted out," he said. "Damn thing looks like it's winking at me."

"Don't stop," TJ said. "Whatever you do, don't stop for nobody. Drive like hell."

If that kid hadn't been so damn stupid and would check her Insta messages, TJ might've known all Lillie wanted to do was talk. She'd written her as clear as fucking Doris Day that Tibbehah County had arrested Chester Pratt and was charging his sorry ass and the Nixes with murdering her momma. COME ON IN, TJ. IT SURE IS COLD OUT THERE. What the hell else could she do? Write that shit across the sky?

Now Lillie was following that kid Graham's Land Cruiser straight up Highway 1, TJ Byrd driving not like a teenage hellcat but like a fussy old woman out for a Sunday drive, not hitting fifty miles per hour and swerving back and forth, crossing that center line so many times she couldn't count. Lillie kept on flicking her high beams at the Land Cruiser, but it didn't seem to make a difference—TJ had no intention of quitting. Now it was just a question of where she might be headed.

Lillie called up Charlie Hodge and briefed him on the situation. Charlie noted the mile marker and her location and said he'd make sure Louisiana Highway Patrol would set up a roadblock somewhere about Lockport. The thing that concerned Lillie most was TJ trying to bust through that, too, refusing to stop and maybe getting herself and her little brother hurt in the process. Nobody wanted that. Nobody wanted to see a wrongfully accused girl lying dead in a drainage ditch as a bunch of state troopers stood by with itchy fingers.

Lillie knew she had to slow them down, let TJ know she was on her side before they got up to Lockport. Lillie mashed the gas on the Dodge to ride up alongside when she heard from under the hood what sounded like a tumble of junk in a toolbox. The red light flashed on her dash and her Charger turned off and started to slow down real quick. Lillie slapped the wheel, calling the car everything but a Christian.

She was soon stalled in the middle of a two-lane, a big ole tanker truck blowing past her before she got out and saw steam and smelled the antifreeze coming out from the engine. The Land Cruiser kept on moving north across that flat, desolate gray landscape. Not another vehicle or building around them, just acres of yellowed weeds and water. The Land Cruiser moved slow and easy as if they were on an Easter parade.

Lillie left her driver's door open and walked around to the trunk. She grabbed her scoped Winchester inside and found a solid place along the doorframe to steady her shot. She took in a deep breath and just as easy let it out, just like when she'd been on the Ole Miss Rifle Team, finding the rear tire of the Land Cruiser square in her sights. She made a quick adjustment for the wind and the distance and squeezed the trigger. *Blam.* The crack final and precise.

After the shot, the car skidded onto the shoulder and then back onto the road, the right side riding low and uneasy, the Land Cruiser finally slowing down. Tired and slap-ass worn out from these kids, Lillie walked forward down the highway, holding her rifle in her left hand and waving into TJ's rearview with her right. She tried her best to look friendly.

But damn, it was hard.

"What do I do?"

"Keep driving," TJ said. "Don't stop for nothing."

"Back tire's blown," John Wesley said. "I'm all over the place, Momma. I can't control nothing."

"What'd you call me?"

TJ gritted her teeth and pushed herself up in the backseat. When she turned around, John Wesley not driving but ten miles an hour, she saw that gray Dodge stalled and Lillie Virgil jogging up toward them waving her hand.

"Don't stop."

"Don't have no choice."

TJ looked forward through the windshield and saw a mess of flashing blue lights coming from up north. Highway patrol parking crooked and blocking the highway, men crawling out of their vehicles with guns drawn.

"I'm sorry, Momma."

"I ain't your damn momma," TJ said, leaning back into the backseat. "I'm your sister, John Wesley. That's a hell of a lot more important."

"You gonna die, too?"

TJ didn't answer. She looked down to see the blood had started flowing again from her leg, soaking through the ripped towel tied about her thigh. The engine was still running as John Wesley lowered the driver's window, TJ seeing Lillie Virgil's face up close and personal.

"End of the road, kids," Lillie said. "Let me see your hands, TJ."

"I can't," she said. "Holding down the bleeding."

Lillie Virgil looked deeper into the car before knowing she was telling the damn truth. Lillie yelled over to those folks in the highway patrol to call up an ambulance right fucking now.

"They're dead," Lillie said.

"Who?" TJ said.

"The men who killed your momma," Lillie said. "Figured y'all would want to hear that."

"What about Chester Pratt?"

"I'm no Sunday school teacher so I'll tell it to you straight," Lillie said. "That good ole boy is fucked five ways from Sunday."

TJ could only see the back of John Wesley but saw his head bow and heard him start to cry. The front door opened up and she saw big Lillie Virgil hugging her little brother, telling him everything was going to be okay. She was a friend of his momma's.

"Is that really true?" TJ asked. More men in uniforms came up and surrounded the Land Cruiser. Back door opening and cold air rushing inside. Damn, her leg hurt like a son of a bitch, that white cloth now a dark and deep red.

"Your momma and I used to run together," Lillie Virgil said. "Way back when. I'm sorry for what happened. I should've known there was a hell of a lot more going on inside that trailer."

TJ felt herself crying now, all of it breaking apart inside her and feeling like she just might damn well choke on all that pain and finality of never seeing her mother again. Maybe she'd even forgive her for the hell she put her kids through. One day.

"Momma sure used to be beautiful," TJ said. "Before everybody used her up."

TWENTY-EIGHT

By mid-March, it was finally warm enough for Quinn to put the jon boat into Choctaw Lake for a little bass fishing. Brandon had joined him, holding the tackle box and a sack full of sandwiches and healthy snacks that Maggie had made with implicit instructions not to ride by the Sonic on the way home. The water had warmed up quite a bit but was still cold down deep, Quinn knowing they'd have to do a little searching to find some bass active enough and ready to bite. They motored on over to one of his favorite spots on the lake where he knew an ancient old oak had fallen years before. He explained to Brandon where it lay and how to be careful not to snag his hook on any limbs. The boy listened, holding the fishing pole with a serious expression on his face, his eyes hidden by the Tibbehah Wildcats cap about two sizes two big.

Quinn stood and cast right into the little nook where he knew some big ones liked to hide, taking a seat again, reeling in the rubber worm nice and slow, just enough to animate it, make sure the fish thought it was alive and a tasty treat.

"John Wesley's back in school," Brandon said.

"I heard."

"He's got a new family."

"A foster family," Quinn said. "For now."

"He's got clean clothes and cleaned up some," Brandon said. "He's not as mean as he used to be. I don't know how to explain it. But he's just gotten real quiet. Kinda sad. And he ain't fighting nobody."

"You mean he's not fighting *anybody*."

"Yes, sir," he said. "That's what I mean."

"You know what happened to his mother?"

"I do."

"Be kind to the kid," Quinn said. "He could use a friend."

"Also heard his sister's in prison now, too."

Quinn shook his head, reeling in the worm to the boat, and then recasting back into the same place, right into the crook of that big arm of the oak, where the bass could find a nice place to hide.

"She's not in prison," Quinn said. "But she's in jail. There's a difference. She's got to answer for something bad that happened over in Shreveport."

"What happened?"

"A man attacked her and her friend," Quinn said. "She protected them."

"What's the crime in that?"

"I agree," Quinn said. "But sometimes it takes a while for justice to shake out. For some it never does. Lot of times it depends on who you are, what color you are, or how much money you've got."

"The Byrds don't have any money."

Quinn smiled, reeling the hook back in just as slow and deliberate, careful to tilt the end of his pole away from the tree and free from any snags. "I think that might change," Quinn said. "Some fella tried to accuse John Wesley's sister of all kinds of things and now he's the one paying for it. I think when the truth is out, the Byrds may own everything that man's got."

Brandon looked deep in thought as he faced Quinn on the opposite bench. He had cast his hook but hadn't started to reel it in. The
kid had something pressing on his mind.

"Something you want to talk about?" Quinn asked.

"Well," Brandon said. "I was wondering if after we go fishing, we
might stop off at that new place by the truck stop?"

"Are you talking about Johnny Stagg's Frontier Village?"

"Yes, sir," Brandon said. "We got coupons at school yesterday for
free tokens and free slices of pizza."

"Hate to break it to you, Brandon," Quinn said. "But nothing's free
with Johnny Stagg."

"You know him?" Brandon said. "He came to our school yesterday
to talk to kids about finding faith and family values after he'd made a
few bad mistakes. Straying from the Lord and all that."

"I bet he was wearing a cowboy hat."

"How'd you know?"

Quinn kept on reeling in the line, the shadows along the bank of
the lake stretching out to the water's edge. He could feel the sun on
his face and along his arms. Tonight, he and Maggie planned to host
a cookout at the farm with his mother, Boom, and maybe a few sur-
prise guests. His mother hadn't said it outright, but he expected his
sister Caddy, his nephew Jason, and his old friend Donnie to show up
from over in Austin. Lately, there had been some talk about Caddy
and Donnie finally getting married.

"How about we hit Sonic," Quinn said. "But skip the Frontier Village."

"You don't like that man Johnny Stagg," Brandon said. "Do you?"

"I think some folks become mean," Quinn said. "And others are
born mean."

"You think he can change?" Brandon asked. "Like John Wesley did?"

The thought of Stagg changing made Quinn smile quite a bit, reeling in the hook, and casting it back into the lake. He knew those big fat ones were hiding down there slow and deep, but they'd strike soon.

"I think Johnny Stagg won't be satisfied until he uses up everything and everybody in Tibbehah County," Quinn said. "It's just in his nature. He'll never quit. And he'll recruit other soulless people like him to join his effort."

"What're you going to do about it?"

"I'm going to put that old man back in the cage where he belongs," Quinn said. "I don't quit, either."

"Sure do appreciate you coming, Sheriff," Johnny Stagg said, standing at the ticket counter to Frontier Village on opening day. The registers were pinging with all the cash and credit cards being run, Stagg now sure that this new direction had been the way to go.

Bruce Lovemaiden shook his hand and removed his white cowboy hat that he'd worn special for the occasion. Johnny Stagg had one on, too, bought from the Western wear shop on the Jericho Square. Black with a silver concho band.

"Brought my two grandboys with me today," Lovemaiden said. Two big-headed fat kids, looking like miniature versions of the sheriff, stood up right next to him. The boys looked for all the world like twins to Johnny Stagg, except one boy was about two inches taller. They both had the same wide, doughy face and haircut with the bangs cut straight across their foreheads. Tweedle Dee and Tweedle Dumber.

"Send 'em right on in," Stagg said, reaching into his slicker for some golden tokens. "And take these. You two rascals let me know when y'all run out."

"We weren't asking for no special favors, Mr. Stagg," Lovemaiden said. "I'd be glad to pay the fifteen dollars to let 'em in."

"Not today," Stagg said with a wink, opening up the rope for them both. "Y'all go have yourself a good ole time."

The two boys jostled off over toward the line to the bouncy inflatable Haunted Gold Mine. The metal walls of the old titty bar echoed with kids' voices and laughter, jumping and playing, the tinkling of that player piano in the old-time saloon where they served up Coca-Colas and Icees. Stagg's face went soft, grinning big at the whole scene, thinking that maybe his heart really had changed after being put away. This sure was something special for the entire community.

"Well," Lovemaiden said, still holding his hat in his hand and looking around at the kiddos leaping from attraction to attraction, bounding up the stairs to the crow's nest where Fannie Hathcock used to keep her office and was now filled with video games and pinball machines. "I thought I might try my hand over at the shooting gallery."

"That one's special," Stagg said. "Used to be up at Libertyland in Memphis before it all got torn down. Bought it from a black fella who'd kept it safe in storage over up in Frayser."

Lovemaiden nodded, placed his smallish cowboy hat back on his huge head, and moved toward the entrance.

"One thing before you get down to that Ole West fun," Stagg said, touching Lovemaiden's shoulder. "I got a fella that I sure would love you to meet."

"Yes, sir," Lovemaiden said. "Who's that?"

"Someone who's gonna turn our counties into a better, stronger, God-fearing world."

Lillie Virgil drove over to Hot Springs that afternoon to visit with Ladarius McCade, who was still being held there for stealing that brand-new Kia Sorento out at Lake Hamilton. The old couple that owned the car hadn't had it two weeks and wanted Ladarius prosecuted to every inch of the law. Weeks later, and out of the hospital, he was being held at the Garland County Juvenile Detention Center. It wasn't the Peabody Hotel, but it wasn't exactly Parchman Farm, either. The guards found Lillie a nice big concrete table by the basketball courts to meet with Ladarius.

He was still on crutches as they brought him through the gated fence. He hobbled along fast, his right leg bandaged and braced, and he had to sit crossways because his knee wouldn't bend.

"Congratulations," Lillie said. "You don't look like I expected."

"And how's that?" Ladarius said, smiling. The blond cut out of his hair, shaved down tighter on the top.

"I expected you to look like shit warmed over," Lillie said. "But you appear to be half decent, kid. A little fucked up, kind of crippled, but you may just make it."

Ladarius laughed. He looked off at the basketball court and waved to a couple boys shooting hoops. It was a bright, sunny day, not a cloud in the sky. She figured she might stop off for barbecue at Mc-Clard's before riding back. She had the next four days off and Rose had already planned out their itinerary: zoo, botanic gardens, Pink Palace, and maybe a hike along the Wolf River and lunch at Las Tortugas. That kid loved some tamales.

"You taking me somewhere?" Ladarius asked.

"Nope," she said. "Just figured I'd check in. I promised your grandmomma I'd look out for you."

"Momma Della Mae won't speak to me," he said. "I tried calling her, too."

"That woman has her ways," Lillie said. "Be patient. You're gonna be just fine."

Ladarius glanced away for a moment, looking like he might get emotional. Lillie wasn't expecting that and for a hot second regretted her ride over from Memphis. She didn't plan on spending her day crying around a juvie basketball court.

"I ain't worried about me," he said. "I'm worried about TJ."

Lillie smiled and shook her head. Damn, that kid was pussy-whipped.

"What is it?"

"That man TJ shot at the truck stop was a shitbird pedophile."

"So?" he said. "Doesn't make it legal what she did."

"He tried to molest Chastity Bloodgood in the cab of his truck and was coming for TJ," she said. "TJ didn't have a choice. Did you know his truck was called the fucking Purple People Eater?"

"The word of two kids won't mean shit against a full-grown man."

"Maybe," Lillie said. "But dash cam footage doesn't lie. The whole thing was caught on video by the truck right up behind them. You can see that son of a bitch grab Chastity by the neck and come right for TJ. Sorry you don't have a phone to see it. That whole show is online now. You should've seen the crowd at TJ's last appearance before the judge. Standing room only. Everyone holding up signs. Free-Byrd T-shirts. Damn. I wish I got a piece of that action. Whoever is printing those must be making a mint."

Ladarius nodded. Lillie folded her hands in front of her, watching the boy's face, recalling the few times she'd busted him when she was with the sheriff's office. He'd always been polite and respectful, promising he'd go straight and stay away from his Uncle Dupuy. She knew that wasn't going to happen then and wasn't going to happen now. There'd be another time between them, Ladarius running from the law again, and holy hell, how Lillie didn't want that to happen. She kinda liked the kid.

She reached into her leather jacket and passed along a business card. Ladarius read it and looked up at Lillie.

"Who's this?"

"Meanest lawyer in Memphis," Lillie said.

"You know him?"

"He's a real bastard but kind of a friend."

"I can't afford this."

Lillie nodded. "I know," she said. "Give him a call on Monday. He'll get you out by the end of the day. Make sure to play up your leg hurting to the judge."

"It does hurt."

"You're doing it already," Lillie said. "I just might shed a tiny tear."

Ladarius smiled big, holding the card tight in his left hand. One of the kids from the basketball court hit an amazing shot, the other kids yelling and talking shit. She could tell Ladarius wanted to join them if his leg wasn't still so mangled.

"Why you doing this?"

"That's easy," Lillie said. "Because I said I would."

"Nothing more."

"Not a damn thing, kid."

Johnny Stagg walked out of Frontier Village, the front entrance covered with red, white, and blue balloons, one of those big inflatable dancing men rocking to and fro in the parking lot, beckoning in the family travelers off Highway 45. Outside, he spotted a middle-aged man with graying hair and sad brown eyes, standing talking to some woman and two teenage girls. All them laughing and laughing at something he'd said. The man's hand rested on one of the girl's bare arms, a real light touch.

Lovemaiden followed and stood by Stagg as the man turned to him. He was wearing a gray fleece sweater, some of those fancy jeans with nice stitching, and high-dollar ankle boots. He had leather bracelets on his wrists and kept the humbled expression of a man who liked to tell folks about his grand and great adventures with his old buddy Jesus Christ. *Oh, hell.* Stagg didn't ask any questions. But he did respect the man for all he'd done up in Memphis after his most humble beginnings down here in Tibbehah County.

"Sheriff," Stagg said. "This is Pastor Ben Quick. I know you mentioned you'd been wanting to meet him."

"Yes, sir," Lovemaiden said, sticking out his hand. "Me and my wife come to see you last Easter at your service up in Memphis. And we watched them Bible studies you got online, too. I love that one you have about generosity and love. How random acts of kindness can come on back to you like a gosh-darn boomerang. You ain't giving nothing away. It's all gonna come out to roost. Help all of us prosper."

"That's the idea, Sheriff," he said, shaking his hand. "Sure is an honor to meet you."

"I ain't no one," Lovemaiden said. "Just a humble servant."

"Aren't we all," Pastor Quick said, his face all lit up like Christmas morning, taking in the new Frontier Village, the bustling Rebel Truck Stop, and the big Tibbehah Cross planted huge and tall on the hill by Ole Man Skinner. Lord bless his crooked and wretched ole soul.

"You mind me asking what you're doing back in town?" Lovemaiden asked.

Stagg grinned so big that he could feel the wind on his teeth. He reached for a mint in his pocket and plopped it into his mouth, savoring this very moment. The grand and beautiful moment of a new era down in Tibbehah County.

"Well, sir," Quick said. "I came back to express my sincere appreciation and welcome back to the world my dear brother in Christ, Mr. Stagg. I'm proud to call him a friend and proud to see him putting his talents to work here back in my hometown."

Lovemaiden just beamed, hitching up his britches, the white cowboy hat looking like he'd just swiped it off some poor child's head. To think he was gonna be his go-to man over in Parsham County. Thank Jesus Stagg had a sensible crook like Ben Quick to partner with on everything else in north Mississippi.

"You plan on sticking around some?" Lovemaiden said.

Pastor Ben Quick smiled, his face softening, a cool light in his sad brown eyes, like a man who knew and understood all the mysteries of the universe. "Mr. Stagg and I've been discussing that for the last few years," he said. "Even before he came back home. And now, I just came into some land from the late Mr. Skinner that fronts the highway."

"You thinking of building another church?" Lovemaiden asked.

"Right across the Jericho Road on that hill by the cross," Quick said. "Not as big as Memphis, but outreach for the folks in Tibbehah and all the surrounding counties. A place for everyone."

"Heck, Pastor Quick," Lovemaiden said. "Doesn't that beat all. Just tell me where to sign up."